Winner of the City of Edmonton Book Prize
Shortlisted for the Georges Bugnet Award for Fiction
#1 *Edmonton Journal* Bestseller
An Amazon.ca Best Book of 2009

Praise for *Waiting for Columbus*

"What a wonderful, mad mongrel of a book – part mystery, part passionate romance, part postmodern historical romp. . . . [Thomas Trofimuk's] compassion, intelligence, shrewd humor, and taste in wine make for an irresistible read." – Steven Heighton, author of *Afterlands*

"The emotional impact of the novel's conclusion is devastating."
– *Vancouver Sun*

"One of those rare gems that works on a number of levels and makes ingenious use of eras shadowed by anxiety, uncertainty and tectonic, historic change – times like ours." – *Globe and Mail*

"An impressive work, masterfully blending the history of Columbus with a real-world mystery." – Macleans.ca

"Deliriously imaginative and heart-wrenching. . . . The novel probes [love and sensuality] with extraordinary sensitivity and perspicacity. . . . Utterly gripping. . . . *Waiting for Columbus* inexorably pulls readers along until its conclusion, which is fitting and devastating – and unforgettable." – *Alberta Views* magazine

WAITING FOR
COLUMBUS

THOMAS TROFIMUK

EMBLEM
McClelland & Stewart

Cloth edition published 2009
Emblem edition published 2010

Emblem is an imprint of McClelland & Stewart Ltd.
Emblem and colophon are registered trademarks of McClelland & Stewart Ltd.

Library and Archives Canada Cataloguing in Publication

Trofimuk, Thomas 1958-
Waiting for Columbus / Thomas Trofimuk.

ISBN 978-0-7710-8547-5

I. Title.

PS8589.R644W35 2010   C813'.54   C2010-901482-0

We acknowledge the financial support of the Government of Canada through the
Book Publishing Industry Development Program and that of the Government of
Ontario through the Ontario Media Development Corporation's Ontario Book
Initiative. We further acknowledge the support of the Canada Council for the Arts
and the Ontario Arts Council for our publishing program.

Typeset in Caslon by M&S, Toronto
Printed and bound in Canada

ANCIENT FOREST
FRIENDLY

This book was produced using ancient-forest friendly papers.
This book is printed on acid-free paper that is 100% ancient-forest friendly (40%
post-consumer recycled).

McClelland & Stewart Ltd.
75 Sherbourne Street
Toronto, Ontario
M5A 2P9
www.mcclelland.com

1   2   3   4   5   14   13   12   11   10

For Cindy-Lou
and
Kathleen Marie Trofimuk

Imagine a man standing on a rocky shoreline looking out to sea, pondering the question, the same question we whisper when we look up at night into a star-crazed sky – swirls of light millions of years old – everything moving away, or toward, or around: What's out there?

This man is an average guy except for this need he has when it comes to the ocean. He is a man who will go out of his way to stand on beaches and look out to sea. He will pull over to the side of a highway or a road, he will get off a train or disembark a bus and then stand at the edge of whatever ocean is there with his awe and wonder vibrating. Often, depending on how he feels, he will hum Barber's Adagio for Strings. He thinks he remembers this music was one of the pieces played at JFK's funeral. He could be wrong about this, but it is easy for him to imagine this music: a military band playing regally, painfully, marching in front of a long line of black vehicles. It is the perfect music for the funeral procession of a president, and it is the ideal music for oceans. Oceans are big enough to handle the sorrow of Barber's Adagio. Sometimes the first notes of this music are just there, in the back of his throat, waiting, ready. He begins to hum and all the following notes seem to know what they must do to make the melody.

It's raining. He's wearing a ratty dark blue baseball cap that's seen better days. It's pulled down to his eyebrows as protection from the rain. He shakes his head, marvels at the redundancy of rain while standing next to an ocean. So much water just there in the rising and falling swells, in the ebb and flow, in wave after wave – so much water and yet it rains. He smiles at the ocean.

This is a desolate, rocky place. Its rocks seem old, as if they have been written down in an ancient, forgotten language. He read somewhere there were fossil beds along this shore. He does not doubt this. He inhales deeply. Thinks: green, humid, incomprehensible.

He glances up, squints through the streaky grey sky, and drifts back to the only question that matters. He knows he is not the first to stand in wonder at the edge of an ocean. Human beings across the spectrum of time have stood at the edges of things they couldn't comprehend and drifted in the mystery of not knowing. We no longer think of oceans as frightening, mysterious, or forbidding. Not today. We have lost our deference and awe for oceans because we are no longer dependent. We fly over them, look down from 35,000 feet, maybe notice a glint of sunlight, or the way colour dances.

But this man can easily conjure up respect and even fear. He can easily muster a meditation on courage. He looks out and feels the ocean's coldness – understands the uncaring green and grey, the undulating deep heart of it. It takes courage to face the unknown with gusto. He wishes he didn't know about oceans. That way he could be certain that he has the courage. But you cannot erase your own knowledge, he thinks, so this rumination is only a game played by an idiot who fears the unknown.

Sometimes the best map will not guide you
You can't see what's round the bend
Sometimes the road leads through dark places
Sometimes the darkness is your friend

– Bruce Cockburn,
from "Pacing the Cage"

ONE

Sevilla Institute for the Mentally Ill
Sevilla, Spain

THE PASSAGE FROM FREEDOM to incarceration is never an easy one. The passage from an unacknowledged, untested sanity to a diagnosed insanity is equally problematic. The first time Nurse Consuela Emma Lopez entered his world, it was with nervousness – with the trepidation of a sparrow pecking the ground a few metres in front of a perfectly motionless cat. He was immobile on a bed in the admitting area, restrained and drugged. He'd arrived at the institute kicking and screaming.

Consuela heard the shouting, wondered who it was and what it was that had him so upset. She could have written this off as just another ugly and loud admittance in a long string of ugly and loud admittances. But the sound of someone in pain or distress always gets through to her heart. The sound of this man's voice caused her to pause, to look up from her work and ache a little. The timbre of this particular voice vibrated in her. She cared, immediately. This is not something she likes about herself. Not that there's anything wrong with caring. It's a good quality for a nurse. It's just that she wishes she were tougher, more thick-skinned.

Consuela almost tiptoes into the room – silently but not so timidly as to suggest she is uncomfortable in the admitting room. The lights have been dimmed and a curtain drawn around his bed. They've drugged him, she thinks, and they're waiting for the drugs to kick in. She peeks through a slit in the curtain. It's difficult to say how old he is but she would guess thirty-five, maybe thirty-eight, despite the greying-verging-on-white hair. He has a kind, narrow face but he's obviously been through something, some sort of trying experience, an ordeal of some kind. There are bags under his eyes, and there are scratches – some deeper than others – across his forehead. His jaw has been bandaged.

Consuela finds his chart hanging on the far wall. She flips it open and finds an exercise in ambiguity. Scant details about where he was found. The words "Strait of Gibraltar" and "Palos." No name. A notation on the sedative he'd been given – a hefty dose of Rohypnol. And a number.

Nurses talk. They tell stories at coffee. Two hours earlier a black van had arrived and out had climbed three members of the National Police Force with the new patient wedged between them. They delivered him, wrapped tightly in a strait-jacket, to the admitting area. His clothes were bloodstained, his shirt ripped. Despite the restraints, he was wild. He'd broken the nose of one of the policemen with a lurching head butt to the face. They'd said something about his name being Bolivar and that he'd been found in the Strait of Gibraltar. "In the strait?" a nurse asked. "Surely you mean near the strait?" The policeman had looked at her with dehumanizing, flat disdain, signed the papers that were thrust toward him, dropped the pen on the counter, and departed quickly. It seemed that the transport and handoff of this patient had been a trying experience for these men. They were glad to be rid of him. Consuela saw them as they were leaving and remembers thinking they were very serious, severe – if they'd had clowns in both pockets of their trousers, they wouldn't have smiled. They reminded her of her ex. The black, stiff uniforms. Those intensely earnest faces. The type of men that follow orders unquestioningly.

~ ~ ~

When Bolivar opens his eyes two days later, he is calm and seems rational. He's restrained in the bed and there is still one policeman outside in the hallway – just in case. The guard sits straight in a wooden chair to the left of the door. He checks the identification badges of everyone who enters, makes a note on his clipboard. This is Consuela's fifth time in, and the guard barely looks at her.

"*¿Qué día es éste? Por favor.*" The new patient stares at Consuela. His voice is demanding, almost commanding. It's a voice that is perhaps used to giving orders. His head is lifted and he's trying to see what it is that's keeping him down in the bed.

"*Qué?*"

"*¿Qué día es éste?* What day is it?"

"It is Sunday," Consuela says.

"Sunday? What date?" He pulls at his wrist restraints, still checking.

"Sunday, the fourth day of April."

"April? You mean August. Where am I?" He flexes against the ankle restraints.

"Sevilla."

"How did I get here? What happened to me?"

"You were brought here –" She stops. What exactly can she tell him? She's not sure.

"I was in Palos. It all went sideways. There were two girls. Are they all right? Everything went horribly wrong . . ." But his voice trails off as if he is slowly finding the answers to his own questions.

"I was in Palos. I remember broken glass. People shouting. The ships were in the harbour." He stops. He looks at her with such expectant eyes. "And?" he says. "And?"

What did this man want? *And* what? What is he looking for? What was he expecting to hear? Consuela shrugs and looks at him hopefully, looking for help.

"Why am I tied to this bed? I'm perfectly fine. My ships, though. Have they . . . have they sailed?" He's irritated. Yanks at the wrist ties.

"Ships?" She's thinking she should probably not say any more. There ought to be doctors here. The psychologists at this asylum are some of the best in the world. In the institution's lengthy history, they'd had people from all over Europe as patients – even a couple of kings and a few wayward princesses had called this place home for brief periods of time. It had been one of the first asylums in the world to actually attempt to help the mentally ill – to get at the root cause of an illness. When it first opened, so-called treatments in other parts of Europe were still muddled in the casting out of devils or burning people or drowning them as witches – remarkably final and fatal cures – while the Sevilla Institute was actually caring for the mentally ill. This place, this hospital of innocents, has been a relatively safe haven for many, many years.

"I'll get a doctor," Consuela says, turning.

"Wait."

She stops.

"Get me a phone," he snaps. "I want to make a call."

"Pardon?"

"A phone damnit. Look, I am Columbus. Christopher Columbus. I know the queen, the queen and the king. They can vouch for me. I am to lead three ships across the Western Sea. We've got a deal, damnit! Just get them on the phone."

Whoa, she thinks. Consuela can hear the earnest certainty of his voice. He believes what he's saying. "You want to fall off the edge of the Earth?" Consuela is performing her own little experiment. "You want to die?"

"You don't believe that. Nobody but a simpleton would believe that old wives' tale. Try not to underestimate my intelligence and I'll do the same for you."

"I'll let Dr. Fuentes know you're awake."

"Yes, let your doctor know that I'm hungry, and I have to piss, and I'm not crazy."

She shuts the door – the click echoes in the stone hallway. Consuela walks past the admitting desk and around the corner to Dr. Fuentes's office. She knocks on his door. Waits. Knocks again.

The door squeaks open, slowly. "Yes. What is it?" He says this with the bearing of someone who has been doing something frustrating and this intrusion is the icing on the annoyance cake. Dr. Fuentes is a tall, clean-shaven man who is a fastidious bureaucrat. He's just been appointed chief of staff at the institute. Consuela is honestly uncertain about his skills as a doctor.

He holds the door open with one hand and fumbles with his labcoat buttons with the other. The sound of a chair scraping on a tiled floor comes from inside the office.

"Patient 9214 is awake." Consuela decides she does not want to know who else is in there. Damnit! She hates stuff like this – office politics. Knowing the human contents of Dr. Fuentes's office would put her in the middle of something. There was no scraping sound, she tells herself. It was nothing. There was no scraping.

"Thank you." The doctor releases the door but catches it immediately. "Wait. Is he still sedated?" She nods. Fair enough. There was no way to know for sure if this new patient was going to explode again or if he was done.

~ ~ ~

Consuela wakes up at her usual time, thinking about this patient who wanted her to call a king and queen who've been dead for nearly five hundred years, on a telephone. She's intrigued. Regardless of his ranting, she liked the colour of his voice. It sounded like burnt sienna, and at the bottom, the colour and texture of fine sand.

She does not work today, and so she grinds the coffee beans, boils water, and makes a leisurely French press. She pushes the kitchen window open and is immediately aware of the difference in the quality of air. It never really cooled off overnight. The air conditioning in her flat is now at cross-purposes with this open window. The warm, dry air pushes up against the cool, forced air of her apartment.

She's been moving around her apartment, waiting for sunrise on the Guadalquivir. This riverside flat has been her home for six years and sunrise is one of the benefits. She loves her mornings with the fine, dusty orange colour inching its way up her walls. This apartment came with a wall of bookshelves in the living room, which Consuela had no problem filling.

She added two more stand-alone shelves in her bedroom. She pauses this morning in front of a row of her to-read books – books she's bought because of a review, a mention in another book, or a recommendation, or because the cover spoke to her. She pauses at Calvino's *Invisible Cities*. She runs her finger down the spine of *Ridley Walker*. She tilts a book called *Tropisms and the Age of Suspicion* by Nathalie Sarraute as if to slide it off the shelf – this was a recent addition, found in a bookstore in Madrid, bottom of a pile, hideously ugly cover but there was something about the title. She eventually picks Bulgakov's *The Master and Margarita*. But decides mornings are not for starting novels. She takes the Bulgakov into her bedroom and places it on the bedside table.

In the kitchen, she opens the newspaper and immediately wants a cigarette. The coffee, the newspaper, and the time spark a memory of smoking. Four years of not smoking and still the cravings come. Less frequently now, but still. Consuela performs a mental checklist of the places where she's stashed cigarettes in the past. Ridiculous because her stashes have long since been pillaged or abandoned. She knows, positively, there are no secret stashes of cigarettes in her flat. But she remembers where they used to be.

The sparrows are playing in the orange trees and palms along the river. Flirting with the dark river, thrilled at the prospect of light, as if they have the most ridiculously brief memories and sunrise is always an excited surprise. Do birds remember days? There are no clouds in this pink-tinged, predawn sky. It will likely be another blistering hot day.

It seems the front section of her newspaper is always about bombings and killings and scandals. The ramifications of bombings and killings. Accusation of scandals, and the fear of more actual bombings.

Consuela flips to the entertainment section where there are movies, some stupidly violent and even one about bombings – this makes her smile a bit – but for the most part, the news here is pleasant. In fact, it's not really news at all.

Consuela pushes the French-press plunger and pours herself a mug of coffee. She looks across the river, across the city, and wonders what it was like five hundred years ago, before the New World was discovered by Europeans, before Columbus sailed out of Palos. Why would this new patient go *there*? Why Columbus? Why not Genghis Khan or one of the Roman emperors, or, keeping with Spain, Pablo Picasso, Salvador Dali, or Ferdinand of Aragon? Christopher Columbus doesn't seem like much fun. Obsessed with the prospect of discovery.

Desperate for people to believe him. Pigheaded to the point of ignoring all those absolutely correct scholars who repeatedly told him that China was too far – that he'd never make it. Not fun.

She takes a big gulp of coffee. Ah, we don't pick our delusions, she thinks.

Consuela can't tell if she actually knows about Columbus, or if she's simply half recalling the Hollywood renditions of Columbus from the movies about him.

"God, I could use a cigarette," she says to the sun as it pushes its way onto the river, into the sky, and splashes yellow into her eyes.

~ ~ ~

Consuela wasn't at that first meeting, but she could see the change in her patient. Columbus had gone from lucid and slightly outlandish to frenzied and implausible – from conversational to incoherent. Must have been a hell of a session. Afterward, it seems he truly went mad inside a steady, over-prescribed lineup of sedatives and antipsychotics, some of which were so obscure that Consuela had to look them up. They threw everything and anything at Columbus to keep him quiet, harmless, and unagitated. Columbus refused to wear clothing. At most, when in the hallways and gardens and courtyards, he wore a robe. He just didn't care. In his room, he was naked, always. He spent days and weeks as a drooling idiot in a corner of his room, slumped over and muttering to himself. He would stare at the stone wall, rock back and forth, and mutter, "Ships to sea. Ships to sea. This is me. This is me. Ships to *sea! Me! Me! ME!*" This became his mantra – this, and his constant inquiries as to what day it was. The passage of time was important to Columbus. He was diligent about it – obsessive. Even when he was hazy from some new adjustment to his meds, he found a way to know what day it was and how long he'd been at the institute.

The orderlies dreaded going into this cell. *Room.* They dreaded going into this room. Dr. Fuentes insists his staff call the cells rooms. They're far more like cells than rooms, but the doctor is the boss. Patient 9214 was crafty and fast. Further, he hadn't weakened. At least, not physically. When they had to get in to clean or check on Columbus, Consuela would dope him up on as much Diazepam as she could safely administer. Even then, while slower, he was still dangerous. He was always good for one crazy lunge or kick. There were times, in the weeks following his arrival, when Consuela had to swallow fear as she looked at him; she had to will herself to be calm, to breathe with long, even inhalations. She remembers being scared silly.

Up until a few weeks ago, Consuela did not go into his room unless she was with an orderly. Those first few days, when he was restrained, she was fine being alone in the room. But after the restraints came off, he was unpredictably violent, as well as incoherent, with occasional bouts of lucidity and a lot of gibberish. Even now he still strikes out with a righteous violence, and his resolve to escape is emphatic. Columbus wants to go to sea. This is clear from his babble. Apparently something horrible will happen out there. Something only he can stop. There are days when Consuela wonders if she should just tell him how the real Christopher Columbus has already made the journey to the New World – that it's all been discovered. And it wasn't exactly India or Japan. It was more a dangerous wasteland filled with risk – not exactly profitable. Not much gold. Some interesting birds. A lot of land for the taking. The real Christopher Columbus has been to the New World and returned. But she thinks that telling this story would be mean. This man does no harm by believing himself to be Christopher Columbus.

For the remainder of April and all of May, Columbus is a testing ground for antipsychotic drug regimens. Near the end of May, Dr. Fuentes announces his engagement to the nurse who was very likely in his office that April day. Sergio, one of the better orderlies, dies in a climbing accident in the mountains at the beginning of June. And Consuela carries on as usual. She continues to date but finds most men uninteresting after a few hours of telling lies over dinner. Once the thin veneer of genuinely interesting wears off, Consuela escapes into drinking too much wine, which eventually leads to her saying something true – usually brutal and true. And, confronted by blunt truth, most men run screaming from the room. Second dates for Consuela are rare.

~ ~ ~

June 25 is Consuela's birthday. When she arrives at work, she looks through the barred hatch at the man who has only a number in her world, though he does have a name for himself.

Officially she refers to this man as patient 9214. Unofficially he is, of course, Christopher Columbus.

Consuela stops in front of the door to patient 855's room in D wing. Inside is the pope – at least, a patient who thinks she's the pope. Rather optimistic to think there could actually be a female pope in the first place, and of course, she is not the pope.

Regardless of the odds against there ever being a female pope, Consuela likes this one. Pope Cecelia the First. There is a regal gentleness about her. Consuela likes chatting with her, is always blessed by her, and certainly does not mind kissing her ring every time she enters or leaves the room. She's not sure if this is what happens with the real pope. Do people kiss his ring? Is kissing somebody's ring the highest form of respect?

Consuela opens the door. "Good morning, Your Holiness."

"Oh, good morning, dear. Bless you. Bless you."

The pope is wearing two housecoats and an ornate purple smoking jacket. She smiles her gap-toothed smile at Consuela. Ashen skin, sandy grey hair. She stretches out her hand and Consuela recognizes her cue.

She takes her leave of the pope and checks again on Columbus.

He's sleeping soundly. The light in the room is faint but she can see a few strands of grey hair across his pillow. Consuela pushes the viewing portal door shut and turns around. She shakes her head, partly with pity and partly with admiration at his dogged, undaunted determination. In his almost lucid moments, he has never wavered from his story.

He is Christopher Columbus, and his mission in life is to venture out onto the Western Sea, straight across the dark ocean, until he finds a route to the East Indies and China. He is going to find a new way to acquire the much-needed spices from the East. Even inside his drug-induced state, his babbling confirms this obsession.

TWO

FOR CONSUELA, MORNINGS at the Sevilla Institute for the Mentally Ill are divided by routine, peaceful and usually uneventful. She arrives early, makes coffee, and moves gently into her day. She checks on seventeen patients, makes notes on anything unusual, and then has time to herself.

Two days after her birthday, Consuela is a couple of hours into her shift when Columbus stands up and looks into the two-way mirror, behind which Consuela is slumped with her morning coffee, her legs over the arm of the chair. She'd been thinking about a man she'd slept with a few weeks back – the first in more than a year. She'd been imagining him and actually feeling quite aroused. His name was Antonio and he was certainly not a keeper. But as a physical distraction, he was exquisite. He was a generous lover, thought about her pleasure, liked to kiss. Consuela had an hour to herself every morning, in between her various duties at the hospital. This morning, she wants to meander with Antonio. Just a little reverie. Just a little drift into recent memory. The door is locked. All is well and quiet. She just needed to focus. But Columbus looks straight into the mirror – looks directly at her. "I know you're there, Consuela," he says, smiling, his eyes flashing with clarity.

She drops her coffee mug on the floor. It shatters and hot coffee splashes up her legs.

"Jesus!" Relax, she tells herself, he can't actually see you. But it's unnerving.

He clears his throat. Swallows. "It's time, Nurse Consuela, that I told you about how I got my ships. It wasn't easy, you know. I want to tell you the one true and only, emphatically accurate, and undeniably authentic story of how Christopher Columbus" – he smiles a little boy's smile, innocent and playful – "that's me, got his ships and set to sea."

She has no idea about the true identity of this man. But what if we are what we believe ourselves to be? Consuela has no doubt about his belief that he is, in fact, Christopher Columbus. That's the easy part.

~ ~ ~

Everybody knows Columbus had three ships. A couple of days after Columbus announces his intention to tell her his story, Consuela gets the twelve-ship dream, a story that is more of a delusion built into a forgery of a dream. Dr. Fuentes, who seems distracted, verging on indifferent, has directed her to listen carefully to everything Columbus says and to make notes. This is what she does.

"I had a dream," Columbus says. His back is to her. He's picking at a scab of lifted paint on the windowsill, flicking at the jagged, pale green edge. Thick woollen socks on his feet and a housecoat that is never done up constitute his only clothing. Consuela glances at this patient who is so uninterested in wearing anything but socks and a robe. She has adjusted to his oddly timed erections, which she gets to see quite often. She has become used to his body – the parts that, as a psychiatric nurse, she would not normally see. Columbus's erections have become common in her work world. She was fascinated, in the beginning, to have these semi-regular glimpses into the workings of male genitalia. It was a rare morning that Columbus did not wake up with an erection. He seemed to be unaffected by these pointed morning intrusions. He just carried on. She did not find this to be erotic. It wasn't sexual. She did not think for a second that she was the inspiration. But there was something intimate and vulnerable about his semi-nakedness – beyond the obvious. Compared to the nurses she worked with, Consuela hadn't had much experience with men, even though she had been married once, when she was seventeen. Not a sound decision on her part. She married as a way to get out into the world, away from home. And Rolf could dance like an angel. Dancing with Rolf, for Consuela, was like flying. But the man was not yet a man – completely jealous, macho stupid, controlling, and nowhere near to understanding himself. Emotionally retarded. Intellectually banal. He was a bodyguard for one of the ministers in the government. She couldn't figure out why a minister of Health and Consumption would need a bodyguard, but she never asked the question out loud. Rolf was probably a very good bodyguard. He was self-important but serious about his duties. Eventually he found a woman even less evolved than himself, and one day Consuela came home from the university, put her books on the kitchen table, and knew he was gone. She didn't even bother with the faintly hopeful "Hello" or "Anybody home?" or "Honey, I'm home." Nothing had changed physically in their apartment – Rolf took nothing with him except for his clothes and all the money from their bank account. Even though Consuela knew it was for the best, she still grieved. She vowed to live in darkness until she felt better, and used an entire roll of Rolf's duct tape on the light switches so she was forced to live up to her vow. Her illogical sadness lasted three weeks, two cases of wine, three bags of oranges, and forty candles. And at the end of her grieving, she only remembered that Rolf was a very good dancer, a good kisser, and always smelled good.

"I had a dream," Columbus says again, a little louder this time.

"Really! A dream! Fascinating!" Consuela is changing his sheets. She has no idea he is at the edge of a story.

Columbus smiles. "Your humour, this sarcasm of yours, becomes more and more appealing to me. I love it. In fact, your smart-assery is so witty I'm stunned into silence by its brilliance. How could I possibly carry on? I would rather have one of Nurse Felicia's enemas, with all its implicit unpleasantness, than go on with this conversation."

She stops with a pillowcase halfway snuggled onto his pillow, looks at him with clean eyes. She quickly finishes his bed, tucking and folding back the angles with the same care she gives her own bed. She does not want to appear eager. He does not turn around. Remains propped sideways in the window, seated on the sill. It's raining. A drizzle at best, but steady since 5 A.M. Consuela knows this because she starts work at 4:45 A.M. "Okay. Okay," she says. "Tell me about your dream."

The grey invades the room. The rain light seems almost a physical presence as he begins to speak, his words cutting through the gloom – his word pictures carving space.

~ ~ ~

"Perhaps," he says, "it begins with fourteen ships embedded in a dream of a dream, tucked away inside yet another dream . . . And at the bottom of this illusory funnel is a glorious beginning . . . Imagine Columbus arrived. Imagine him in his polished breastplate, about to step onto the beach of Japan or India after many days at sea. After all the doubting and lying and cajoling, he and his men are finally in the land of Marco Polo. They did it by sailing straight across the Western Sea. Can you imagine that?"

~ ~ ~

Columbus thinks he remembers it. Thousands of cheering people, brushed clean by unreality. Everyone smelled good. There was no reeking, fetid human stench. No rotting meat. No toilet water in the streets. No boatloads of expulsed Jews in the harbour. No inquisitors lurking in the back streets. No disease. No. This was a brilliant parting. The air was filled with flower petals. Colourful banners snapping in the breeze. The thousands were waving and shouting their good wishes. Even the king and queen were there, nodding their approval, watching with the same hopeful eyes as everyone else. Then fourteen ships put out to sea. Fourteen ships unfurled their sails and moved out of the harbour.

At some point near the beginning of their journey, after a particularly severe storm, two ships turned back. There were problems, either with the ships or with the hearts of the men who sailed them. So now, many days across the Western Sea, only twelve ships are anchored off the coast of first land. Many days? That's the best he can do! Many days! Many days could mean anything. A hundred? Two hundred? Twenty-one? Forty? What? This lack of detail in his dream vexes. He keeps turning the dream over and repeating the loss of the two ships, and the arrival of the twelve at this place, wherever that is. No matter how many times he flips it over, it always comes out as "many days across the Western Sea."

They smelled it first. At dusk a warm breeze arched over them from the west. The cool underbelly scent of plants and trees wafted out to greet them, to draw them closer. Fragrances most of the men had never experienced. The scent is green and luxuriant. And there were birds. Multicoloured birds circling their ships and landing in the masts. Birds with secrets, he remembers thinking.

Some of the men argued as to which one of them spotted land first. There was a substantial financial reward for being the one who first brought the news of land. In the end, the captain of the lead ship takes credit, takes the reward because he believed he was the first to see the hazy outline of land. Yes, yes, yes, the boy, Alphonso, called out that land was there, but nobody could see! They all looked and there was nothing – just the grey cloud, swirling mist, nothing! It was the captain who said "There" and pointed at it. The boy saw nothing!

The crewmen all knew it wasn't him. But it doesn't matter. All that matters is they have arrived after a long journey many thought would end in starvation and death. Despite the naysayers and the many meetings and persuasions and back-room deals in Spain, they have finally arrived. Their spirits are high because there are going to be rewards for taking this risk. No one is thinking about history or legacy – they are motivated by something more basic. Fame and title, and the immediate: riches. Nobody knows how much gold and silver there will be. Nobody knows if the current owners of gold and silver value it as much as these hungry men do.

Darkness falls and a thick mist eddies around the ships, but every now and then they can see the tops of trees teasing in the dim light.

In the lead ship, a ship called the *Isabella*, there is a man writing in his journal. He is writing about how many days they had been at sea. "We have been at sea for," he writes, but the pen stops and the ink blotches the paper. He tries it again. "We have been at sea for . . ."

But surely this is important, he thinks. We've been at sea for how many days? Why don't I know! How can I not know? I am the captain of this venture!

"Boy," he snaps. The captain's boy, Alphonso, approaches the desk. He has been in the corner polishing the breastplate Columbus will wear in the morning when he steps ashore in India, or Japan, or wherever this place is.

"Yes, sir," the boy says slowly.

"I have a question for you. It is a question to which you should have an answer."

"I will do my best, my captain." Alphonso is not afraid of Columbus but he is aware of his volatile temperament. The captain sounds grumpy right now so caution is warranted.

"How many days have we been at sea?"

Alphonso knows this number. Every one of the crew knows the number. It is the most important number they have. It is more important than birthdays or years of age. But because it is so important, Alphonso thinks Columbus is testing him – testing his intelligence. It's a trick question and so requires a careful answer. "We have been at sea since we left from port," he says, smiling.

Columbus sighs. "Yes, that is true. And that translates to how many days, exactly?"

"As many days as it took us to make this glorious journey," Alphonso says. Columbus frowns. Alphonso notices this shift, so he decides to lay on the God-and-country routine in order to protect himself. "This journey that was inspired by God and completed in God's name and was performed in the name of our king and queen." He's more than a little wary now. Columbus is glaring at him.

Columbus sighs more heavily. "Yes, yes, yes. God, God, and more God. King and queen. Queens and kings. But how many days, exactly? The number. *The number, Alphonso!*"

"Ten?" he says timidly.

"Do you know how to count?"

"For the most part, yes."

They both turn to look toward the door as they hear steps down the inner corridor. Someone knocks heavily. Three quick, light knocks followed by a clunk.

"Come in, Bartholomew," Columbus says.

The door creaks open and Bartholomew enters. He is smiling, beaming with joy. One would be hard-pressed to see any resemblance in these brothers. Bartholomew is wider in his face with a thick black beard, and his eyes are dark and set farther apart than Columbus's. His voice booms, where his brother's voice commands. "In the morning you will finish what you started," Bartholomew says. "Those dullards in the universities will shake their heads in wonder and awe. They will have to bow down to you, Christopher! You will be more famous than Marco Polo. In the morning we will meet with the rulers of India or of Japan, and we will let them know that Spain is open for business from across the ocean!"

He produces a bottle of wine from his robes and holds it up. "I think we deserve a drink, my brother. It's been a long, hard journey. I have been saving this."

"Alphonso," Columbus says. "Glasses." Alphonso makes his escape toward the cabinet in which glasses are kept. "Nothing is finished, my brother, until we get back to Spain and prove we've been here. By the way, Bartholomew, what is the official count on the number of days we have been at sea?"

"The official count? There is no official count. That would mean there is also an unofficial count. There is only one count and you know – Are you all right? Are you feeling ill?"

"A little weary, perhaps."

An uncomfortable silence grows between them. Columbus

dearly wants someone to tell him the number of days they've been at sea, and Bartholomew wonders about his brother's mental well-being. Alphonso – who doesn't want any more trick questions – avoids eye contact and goes back to his polishing.

Bartholomew pours the wine and raises his glass. "Well, to the new route and the man who found it."

"To those who unwaveringly believed and followed," Columbus says. "And to God who blesses us at every turn. And to the king and queen of Spain."

They down their wine. Bartholomew pours again.

"To the man who first spotted landfall after our long journey."

"To me, again," Columbus says. "It was I who pointed to land. I did the pointing. You have to point or it doesn't count."

"Wouldn't actually *seeing* land be as important?"

"And how do you signify to those around you that you have seen? You point! I pointed."

Columbus spends the rest of the evening alone in his quarters reading over his journal entries, which turn out to be a long, run-together diatribe on everything from the weather to women and the colours of clouds. They are undated, unnumbered, and hold no clues as to how long it took them to arrive.

In the morning the mist burns off quickly, and they can see they are very close to a spectacular city nestled between two mountains. What fortune to have anchored so close to a city! The dock is swarming with thousands of people. Red and silver and gold banners fly from the domes and spirals.

Columbus stands on the deck and looks across the harbour. There is a small boat in the water waiting for him. Bartholomew is on board. They are flying the Spanish flag. They also have red banners. The sun is shining. The sun is very bright. It hits the water and splashes in his eyes. He raises a hand as a shield.

On the dock, Columbus prepares to walk on a carpet of red flower petals toward his destiny. This is the moment he has been moving toward his entire life. There at the end of the square is the emperor, or the king, of this place. Red flower petals seem to fall from the sky. Columbus is presented with gold and silver, frankincense and myrrh. Then he is bowing a greeting to the emperor. "Your Majesty," he says. "It's very bright here. The sun is very bright. In fact, it's almost too bright." Yet I'm cold, he thinks. The breeze is chill. You would think with all this blasted sun that it would be warmer. It's so bright. But it's cold. I'm cold . . .

"Columbus!"

He hears a frantic voice. "Yes, Your Majesty."

"Columbus! Christopher, wake up!"

"Wake up?"

"Yes, wake up!"

Columbus sits up in the bed and looks around the room. The sun is streaming through open windows. He is naked on top of the blankets and he has goose bumps on his arms. The sun has not yet warmed the night chill out of the morning. Through the window is a view of the ocean, but Columbus can't see anything except that it is very bright. Beatriz is frowning at him from across the room. It takes a few minutes for him to see colours. Her robe is wrapped tightly around her body – a pink, protective armour. Her arms are folded across her chest.

"You were dreaming – speaking in your sleep," she says.

"Mmmmm," he grunts.

"You were dreaming about her again, weren't you?" Her words are pinpricks.

There is no right answer to a question like this from Beatriz. Columbus has been down this road many times. He could explain it was just a dream and the things that happen in dreams cannot be controlled, but he's not sure that's true. Even though he was not dreaming of any women, he's inclined to try and rationalize dreams in general. By saying our dreams cannot be controlled, however, he is also saying that he is guilty of dreaming about the woman in question. He could just deny it – speak the truth. But then she will likely not believe him.

Beatriz stands up, lets her armour fall aside. She turns her back to him and fills her glass with water. "You were crying out her name."

"I was? Why would I be calling out the name of someone I was not dreaming of? What name did I call out?"

"You said, 'Your Majesty.'"

Relief. "Yes, yes, of course, because I was dreaming the end of the journey across the Western Sea. And there was a *majesty* there to greet me – a man, a king of some kind."

"A man?" she says with a mocking edge to her voice. "You want me to believe you were dreaming of a man?"

"Yes. He was smiling and there were thousands cheering. I led twelve ships, in my dream, across the ocean, and it seems I did it with very little hardship. Bartholomew was there and –" Columbus stops. She doesn't need to know everything. She doesn't need to know he could not remember, or did not know, how long it took to sail across the ocean. She's liable to ask if he continues his report.

Beatriz is not yet smiling but her face has softened. She has not wrapped herself back up. It's okay for Columbus to see her body now. It's okay to open herself to him, a little. She moves a candelabra from a shelf to the table across the room. The candles are not lit. There's no need for candles as the room is awash with sunlight. Her robe feathers as she moves. She shows him her body in this movement. Columbus relaxes a bit. After all, this was just a dream. How can he be held accountable for his dreams? One cannot control one's dreams.

"And in this dream, you made it back in one piece?"

Columbus tenses. Breathe, he tells himself. Breathe. There are times when it is all right to lie, he thinks. In this dream he remembers having no hope of being able to return. No idea of how far. No idea of how many days. Nobody on the bloody ship knew how long it had taken them to get across the Western Sea. He thinks there are times when God, being a man and also a god, will understand that a lie is sometimes required. God will draw upon all He knows of men and women and instantly forgive certain small untruths, even infidelities.

Beatriz turns toward him, finds his face. "Columbus? You made it back, right?"

"Yes, of course," he says. "Piece of cake."

~ ~ ~

Consuela stands up. Looks at him. Flat-lines her voice. "You dreamed about Columbus having a dream?"

"Yes, I dreamed *I* was having a dream."

She sighs. "And Beatriz is . . . ?"

"Ah, yes. A delicate flower. The most amazing green eyes! She was my woman. She bore me a son."

"Your woman, not your wife?"

"What is it with women and marriage? You think all your problems will be solved and your life complete if only you can marry. Isn't that a bit delusional?"

"So you did not marry Beatriz."

"We exchanged vows. We exchanged rings."

"But you did not marry her."

"No. It's complicated."

This perks Consuela's ears. A woman and a child. This is a first. A woman, according to Dr. Fuentes, could be at the heart of his illness.

"But you loved her."

"Of course I loved her. Don't be so stupid. She was my woman."

"What happened to her?"

"Beatriz? Nothing happened to her. She's in Barcelona. She works as a barista. She doesn't have to. She has a stipend. It was arranged."

"I notice she doesn't visit very often. She doesn't visit at all."

"Ah, yes, well, that can be explained by reminding you of the unique vagaries of all women. While I love Beatriz to this day, she was not my only love. No offence to you, Nurse Consuela, but this ability to love more than one woman is one of the traits of men that is not appreciated by most women."

"You fooled around on her."

He's not sure how to answer her. He does not have the language to speak his heart about Beatriz.

"I'm not judging," Consuela says. "I'm just interested."

Columbus leans forward. Hands on his chin, elbows on his knees. He seems on the verge of saying something but then pulls back – just closes his eyes and sighs. "Look, there were days when I was daunted. I was depressed about this journey. I would wake up in the morning in a new town and yes, there were, sometimes, distractions." He sighs again. "Look, this is a brutal, ugly time. The Inquisition is running around accusing and burning people and saving us from ourselves. People are scared . . . I was scared most of the time."

THREE

AN INTERPOL *YELLOW NOTICE* flashes on his screen and Emile Germain can't recall what the hell the yellow alert means – not exactly. It's been a while. He has to look it up. Emile pulls a white binder from the shelf beside his desk and flips to the section that deals with alerts. Yellow, he recalls with the help of the binder, is to assist in locating missing persons, often minors, or to identify people who are unable to identify themselves. His computer beeps. A blue notice pops up attached to the same file. He scans down the open page to blue: to collect additional information about a person's identity, location, or illegal activities in relation to a criminal matter.

Merde! Two alerts on one man. They have no idea if he's a threat. There was no colour code for a person of interest, but Emile could read between the lines: Interpol wanted this guy found.

The man, his assignment, was declared officially suspicious and off the grid in April. Under the circumstances, it's understandable that one missing person was shunted down the priority list. The likelihood that he is dead is high. The trail had gone cold. His file was basically forgotten. The report says he had been seen by several unreliable witnesses, and then he was gone. A magic trick. A disappearing act. Spain is a vast country

– forty million people. This was just one vanished man inside a chaos of people and landscapes.

Cold trails were Emile's specialty. Hopeless cases were his forte. His ex-wife used to say it was because he could tap into the artistic side of his brain and make oblique connections.

Emile pushes his shoulders into the back of the chair and breathes deeply. The wooden chair was a gift from her. She'd found it in an antique shop with a cement Buddha head sitting on it. She was assured by the owner of the shop that the chair was well over a hundred years old and in excellent condition. She probably paid too much but she was in love, and the Buddha head had been there a long time. It had to be good karma to act as a platform for a Buddha, she said – to serve the Buddha in this way. This booga-booga side of his ex-wife was annoying as hell when they were together, but now Emile found he missed her booga-booga: the incense, the strings of tiny brass bells above the bed, soy milk in his Cheerios, the incessantly changing colours on the walls in their bedroom. She had taken most of this away when she left. Though she did leave a small silver Buddha in the bathroom. And, of course, she'd left the chair.

Emile has the luxury of working out of his home, a penthouse in the heart of the Right Bank of Paris, the market district of rue Montorgueil. It's a small flat but it's rare to find an apartment with a private terrace and a view. From the roof, he can see Montmartre and Sacré-Coeur, and the Museum of Modern Art.

He was up for a glass of water, and on his way back to bed decided to check his e-mail. He had been expecting the cases to begin arriving again and this mysterious person of interest is the first.

Somebody at headquarters in Lyon has attached a brief newspaper story about a baffled stranger in Valdepeñas, south of Madrid – a man asking for directions. Police were called but the man was not found. He'd disappeared. The thing is, he kept asking for directions to different places: Sevilla, Granada, Tarifa, Marbella, and half a dozen other towns, cities, and villages. First he'd ask for food and then directions, always to someplace new. He was very courteous, always grateful. The good people of Valdepeñas were worried about him.

Emile makes a little whistling sound. Well, that's a long shot, he thinks. But at least it's a place to start. Two years of being away, two years of therapy, and now he's thrown right back into the mix.

Emile scrolls to the top of the file. *Who the hell is this guy?*

~ ~ ~

Sometimes the map will not do. The map will never be the territory. One must get out in the field in order to understand. While Emile can make telephone calls and send e-mails and look at maps from the comfort of his flat, it's not the same as going out into the world and having a look-see. He's never found anyone by just looking at a map. He'll rent a car in Madrid, interview the people who may have seen this man, and follow any leads.

Soon he'll be working the same hours he was logging before the incident. Admittedly, he'd been one of the busier agents.

He was always trying to find someone. Even when he wasn't on the job, his thoughts drifted easily to the missing people to whom he was assigned. He'd been away from work for a long time, and now the cases had already started arriving and his bosses in Lyon would be relying on his unique talents. Yes, he was going to get busy again.

~ ~ ~

"If I leave you clues, could you find me?" his wife had asked him before it went to pieces. "I want to be one of the people you find."

Emile smiles. She does not.

Emile was baffled. What the hell did she want from me?

She'd complained that he obsessed over his work. "These people you're assigned to find – you make it so personal."

"Focus. I focus," Emile says to himself, trying to shake away the cobwebs of his past.

~ ~ ~

He takes his laptop to the roof terrace with a Thermos of coffee. He places the computer on the small wooden table and pours coffee into his mug. He turns the knob on the little propane heater. It clicks to life with a small flicker, then slowly, as Emile turns it on high, the flame glows a bright hissing orange. He finds comfort in this sound. He does not open the computer. He drifts to the suspicious man in Madrid.

Emile does not think he is dead. If he is as hot as the two

alerts suggest, this man is likely holed up somewhere licking his wounds like a big cat or a bear. He's found a cave. Maybe he's damaged in some way and he needs to stay off the grid – he's going to wait it out. Emile can relate to this – he understands this. He's had experience with holing up. He worries, though, that this guy is just an innocent who needs help. Emile has read and reread the interviews with the witnesses, looking for that snippet of information that will point in the right direction. One of these witnesses says the man he saw was Chinese, or Japanese, or Korean. Another witness swears she saw him crying, sobbing uncontrollably. Another says he was Arabic-looking, he was holding some sort of bag under his arm, and he was most certainly not weeping. He's gone over the file a dozen times. He knows everything there is to know. If there's an oblique connection to be made, he's not seeing it. There is one thing he knows about this man that was not written in the file: not one of the witnesses reacted out of fear. They all seemed to be concerned about his well-being. This man may be suspicious but he is not frightening.

Emile will begin in Madrid. Then he'll go to Valdepeñas and talk to the people who fed and gave directions to the apparently lost man. The likelihood this is the same guy is remote but it's all he's got.

Emile closes his eyes to the grey city. The hazy sky. The diffused lights. He can feel warmth from the heater on his cheeks. In two hours he'll be on the train to Madrid.

~ ~ ~

"Oh, there's land out there all right. I know there's landfall out there in the Western Sea." He's pacing Dr. Fuentes's office. Back and forth, frenetic energy barely contained.

Dr. Fuentes motions for him to come and sit. An open-handed gesture toward the offered seat, which is a low, flat-armed, dark brown leather chair directly across from the chair-and-a-half monster in which the doctor sits. Columbus sits, interlaces his fingers, and looks up at the doctor.

"What happened to you?" the doctor says. "Do you know why you're here? Do you have any idea, Bolivar?" He scribbles in his notebook.

His therapy consists of long conversations in which he uses the patient's first name, his real name. No assumed names, ever. He has never called Columbus by his assumed name.

"Bolivar?" Columbus is smiling, playing with the doctor.

"Yes. You are Bolivar."

"How can I be this Bolivar when my name is Columbus?"

Fuentes's voice becomes a silken rope. "I've told you this before, but repetition is fine. We think something happened to you and the defensive part of you has conceived this alternate persona."

"You think this Bolivar is inside me?"

"Yes, that's our theory."

"A theory?"

"Yes, we don't know for sure."

"How long have I been here? And all you have is a theory? Should I look for a new doctor? Someone more competent?"

"Three other doctors have consulted on your case, Bolivar. All we have are theories right now."

Columbus has his hands clasped tightly. Everything in him wants to punch Dr. Fuentes in the face. "And?"

"And they concur –"

"They *agree*. They don't teach you how to talk like a human being at doctor school do they?"

"They all *agree* that you have this disorder. Yes."

"Nonsense. I am only me. Have been only me since I got here, and before this I was also me. For instance, I was Christopher Columbus in the spring of seventy-eight when we came across Vikings. You see, I, Cristóbal Colón, had the most extraordinary meeting with a Norseman. He was a big man and we had an amazing conversation . . . I found out a few things about the world that are not taught in the universities . . . Things that would astound even you, Fuentes, Mr. Smarty-pants."

"The fact you seem annoyed – your anger – is an indication that there's some truth in what I'm saying."

"You'll have to try your first-year psychology tricks on somebody else, Fuentes. I'm not buying it."

"And the fact you are just now changing the subject is also indicative. I want to talk about your disorder and you change the subject to Vikings. You want to tell stories about Vikings. You're avoiding the subject by telling made-up stories."

"All stories are true, Fuentes."

~ ~ ~

Columbus is sitting on the end of his bed, rocking, looking directly out the window into a narrow gathering of palm trees.

"Fuentes is an idiot," he says to Consuela as she gathers a pile of laundry and pushes it into a cloth sack. "Are you sure he's a doctor?"

"I think he's under a lot of stress," she says. She pulls hard on the rope and ties a knot, then tosses the bag into the hallway. "I gather your session was less than satisfactory?"

"Isn't this the work of orderlies? Or nursing assistants?"

"I don't mind helping out where I can."

"Alternate persona, my ass," he mutters. "Never heard of such a thing. I do know about Vikings, though. Everyone's heard about Vikings."

~ ~ ~

Fourteen years *before* Columbus came to Palos with three ships in the harbour; fourteen years *before* he was to embark on an incredible, unprecedented, and courageous journey; fourteen years *before* all of this, he was on the open ocean near Iceland and had a chance meeting that connected the dots – sparked his obsession into a full-fledged fire.

It's a shouted conversation above howling wind and rain across the bows of two ships bobbing in the ocean off the coast of Iceland. Three men from three different lands who speak three different languages shout back and forth. The two vessels are loosely lashed together. Crew members from each craft keep a distance with their oars – pushing and giving way in order to maintain a half stability. This is a full-time fight against crashing together. Eight-foot swells don't help. These rising and falling motions, and the blustering wind, are proving to be great inconveniences to conversation. The man from Britain, called Hardy, barely translates between Columbus and the big Norseman.

"WHAT'S HE SAYING?" Columbus screams above the wind, frowning.

All three men are soaked by a wave that sprays a fanned-out sheet of icy water across both vessels.

Water dripping in rivulets from his nose, Hardy screams: "HE SAYS THERE ARE TALES ABOUT A LAND TO THE WEST."

"WEST? WHAT DOES HE MEAN WEST?" Columbus is thinking this is a joke. And then he thinks it could be the break he's been waiting for, and then he thinks it's a cruel joke, and then . . .

Hardy begins to translate but Columbus stops him. "IS HE SURE THAT HE MEANS WEST? GET HIM TO POINT TOWARD THE WEST."

Hardy begins again to translate and Columbus stops him again. "ASK HIM IF HE'D TELL US ONE OF THE TALES ABOUT THIS LAND."

Hardy finally delivers his message and the Norseman smiles before he speaks.

The Briton translates: "HE SAYS THERE'S A LAND BEYOND THE WESTERN SEA. HE SAYS THEY DO NOT GO THERE. BUT THERE ARE TALES OF SUCH A LAND. HE SAYS THEY ARE VERY OLD TALES. HE ALSO SAYS HE IS NOT GOING TO POINT."

"WELL ASK HIM HOW LONG IT TOOK THE PEOPLE OF THESE TALES TO SAIL THERE."

"HE SAYS DEMONS LIVE THERE."

"WHAT?"

"MONSTERS."

"BUT HOW LONG DID IT TAKE TO GET THERE? AND WHERE DID THESE JOURNEYS BEGIN? HOW DID THEY NAVIGATE? BY WHICH STARS?"

Hardy and the Norseman scream back and forth at each other, the Briton pointing west several times. Finally, the Norseman shakes his head.

"HE SAYS THEY ARE JUST STORIES. SAGAS. HE SAYS DEMONS LIVE —"

"BUT HOW LONG WOULD IT TAKE TO SAIL THERE?" Columbus says. "ASK HIM AGAIN. HOW FAR?"

"WHAT?" Hardy screams.

"LET'S GO INSIDE THE CABIN! LET'S GET OUT OF THIS DAMNED RAIN." Columbus points toward the door. "ASK HIM OVER." He points at the cabin and then at the Norseman and back again.

They both reach out a hand to the Norseman and pull him across. This manoeuvre is a trick of balance and timing between the rising and falling ocean, and the expanding and contracting gap between the boats. A miscalculation could be deadly.

Columbus marvels at the odd-looking craft with its dragon's head. It's the only contact they've had since leaving Britain.

"Land is all around us," the Norseman says, "to the west and to the east. My people have always known it." They are huddled in the dim light of the small lower cabin. Chickens cluck in a corner.

"What do you mean?" Columbus says. "What do you mean there is land all around?"

"In every direction. My people believe there is land in all the directions. To the north and the south, east and west."

"Do your sagas mention the distance to the west?"

"This I do not know: it's not far."

"But how far? In days?"

"Not many." The Norseman looks evenly into Columbus's eyes. He smiles again. "From Iceland, to Greenland, and then to Vineland."

"Vineland?"

"That's what the sagas call it."

"What's it like there?"

"I cannot say. I have not been there."

"What do your sagas say it is like?"

"It's nice," he says.

"Nice?"

"Beautiful. Green. And much rock."

"So the land to the west is beautiful?"

"The sagas say so, yes."

"And how far are these lands?"

"The sagas also say do not go there. There is only death there."

"What?"

"Why are you so interested in this place? Why do you ask so many questions about the sagas? How is it that you are in these waters?"

A creaking sound whines through the small cabin. Steam rises from a stove in the corner. The stench of sweat and smell of wet fur blurs the air.

"We're not so interested. Not really. Uninterested is more like it. How's your fishing been going? As for us being here, we are . . . what's the word? We are sailing out of Britain but we have made a diversion. A deviation. A digression in order to see what is there."

A voice from above shouts that the boats should move away from each other because the swells are growing.

One of the crew hands the Norseman a steaming drink. Columbus looks at him carefully. He's a big man. So big that he looks down on both Hardy and Columbus. Light brown, stringy hair. Eyes far apart and with the colour of fair weather in them – an azure colour they have not witnessed for a week.

"So you're saying your people have already been to the new lands across this sea?"

The Norseman grins. His smile is generous and kind. There is almost pity hidden in this man's face. "It's a harsh land filled with demons. Horrible rocks and twisted trees. Twenty-five ships set out and only fourteen arrived. Many of our people were killed. We will not try to make a home there again."

Columbus tries to focus. Breathe, he tells himself. Breathe and think of something to say. Go slow. "Why not go back? I mean to these new lands."

"These lands are not new. Our sagas date back five times a hundred years. There is nothing new about these lands." The Norseman stands.

The ship rolls to the port side and the sailors adjust their stance. They recognize the danger in that sudden shift and begin to move to the upper deck.

The Norseman waits for the right moment and then jumps to his ship where three of his fellow sailors stop his momentum. He disappears belowdecks. His crewmen unfasten mooring lines and the two ships begin to drift apart.

The vessels are thirty feet apart when the Norseman re-appears from below. He tosses a leather bundle across the gap and the Briton catches it.

They wave to each other. *"Watch out for the Skraelings!"* the Norseman shouts.

"What did he say? Sky rings?" Columbus looks to Hardy but Hardy only shrugs.

In the cabin, Columbus opens the bundle. Inside are three stones.

"What the hell?" he says.

"Rocks," Hardy says. "Worthless rocks."

"This I can see." Columbus spreads the leather wrapping flat on the table. Burned into the other side of this piece of leather is a very basic chart: Britain, Iceland, Greenland, and then jagged inlets and a large, triangular land mass on the other side of the ocean with the name Vinilanda Insula across it.

The sound of the ocean, water lapping the ship, creaking sounds. In the corner, chickens scratch at the wooden decking, looking for something left behind.

"Does this look like Japan to you?" Columbus looks up from the map and finds Hardy's eyes. "I think this looks like Japan."

Hardy glares at him. "How the fuck would I know? You're not going to trust a Viking are you? Are you daft, man? They're a bunch of godless, filthy buggers. You'll be sailing to your death if you give any weight to that chart. They kill and eat their own children is what I heard."

Columbus just smiles and nods. "How is it that you were able to speak his language?"

"I've always had a gift with the languages," Hardy says. "All I've got to do is hear it spoken. It doesn't take much before I start to understand."

~ ~ ~

"There were days when I could not bear humanity. Days when I was disgusted. Days when I'd seen too much death, too much cruelty, violence, and despair," he says. "All this, added to the search for funding and support for my voyage across the Western Sea, was a heavy load."

"I can't imagine," Consuela says, encouraging.

Columbus takes a bite of his ham sandwich, followed by gulping half a glass of milk. Then another bite of his sandwich. "We all need sanctuaries, Consuela – places where we can feel safe."

~ ~ ~

When Columbus needed to escape his own mind and heart, he would go to Salvos's bar, a hidden enclave two blocks off the river in Valdepeñas. Few people knew about it. It was widely rumoured to exist. One would only wind up at this bar if somebody on the inside brought you. It's an exclusive, unknown, rundown haven.

Salvos is a pig of a man. He's fat like a stuffed sausage and leers at most women, but he serves decent food and cheap drinks. He runs a couple of girls in one of the upstairs rooms. Both of these women know better than to approach Columbus, who has never taken advantage of their offers. The best thing about Salvos's bar is that it's a relatively safe place in which to speak. Salvos may be an ugly man, but he edits his clientele carefully. There are no ears from the Holy Brotherhood. No ears from the Inquisition. No clergy. It's not a perfect system, but after any given night, what was said at Salvos's place was swept up in the morning, carried across the threshold, and thrown into the Jabalón River. Also, this bar is, compared to most bars along the river, well ventilated.

"*Hola*, Columbus," Salvos says. "How many days does it take to sail to Japan?" He smiles. All his smiles are a variant of lecherous. Usually Columbus feels soiled after just looking at him. Mercifully, his service is not great, and his one waitress, Sophia, takes on most of the bar.

"Ya, good one, Salvos. It gets funnier each time. Today it's hilarious."

"What?"

"Hilarious. It's a word that means . . . really funny – mirthful."

"I know what hilarious means. Why is it hilarious today?" Salvos finishes pouring the wine. He leans toward Columbus as he passes the drink but he does not let go of the glass. They are stuck like two planets revolving around this glass of wine. "Seriously, how does it go, my friend?"

Columbus is surprised that Salvos's breath is not foul. He's not sure what this is about, this suddenly serious and concerned Salvos. So he is honest. He's got nothing to lose, especially in the safety of this temenos. "I have high hopes for Spain," he says. "But it is difficult . . . sometimes I . . . I'm daunted."

Salvos considers this, releases the glass of wine, and whispers, "*Noli nothis permittere te terere,* my friend."

This stops Columbus. He did not expect Latin from this man. This blessing from such an unlikely source moves him. It props up his hope. He nods his thanks at Salvos. Indeed, he won't let the bastards grind him down. Salvos grunts and moves to the end of the bar. Columbus watches in the mirror over the bar as the doorman opens the door the distance of two hands, enough for Salvos to see who is there. Having seen, Salvos shakes his head. The doorman closes the door and delivers the bad news to the man on the outside. Perhaps he advises the bar is full, or that it's a private party.

There are three booths at the back wall. Columbus likes the booths because he can spread out his charts and notebooks. There's breathing room, elbow room, and they've got the best light. The candelabras are not bright but they hang low over the wooden tables.

He's just about to sit down when someone bumps into him, causing him to almost spill his wine. When he turns around he's irritated. He is also instantly embroiled in a conflict of some kind. He appears to be in the middle of a standoff.

"She's a stinkin' Jew and I won't drink with Jews." The man is massive, has a tattoo of a black skull across the top of his left hand, and spits when he talks. His hair is black, thick, and greasy. His tunic is filthy. Columbus can smell him from across the room. But regardless of the man's odour and apparently foul disposition, Columbus reminds himself it's just not a smart thing to confront large men with tattoos of black skulls on their hands, no matter how right you are about any given

issue. This he has learned. Not much else, but this he knows
for certain. The tattooed man looks down on two smaller men
who stand in front of a woman. This big man has three friends
behind him – hands on hilts. The tattooed man is the biggest
of the lot, but the others are also undeniably large. The woman
has her back to the wall and has been pushed there by a table
– she can't move. She's bleeding from her lip and there's a
redness across her cheek, below her right eye. She does not
wipe the blood. She is resolute and unflinching.

"Juan?" Columbus says. "How are you, my friend?"

Juan smiles. "Couldn't be better. Just in the middle of something right now."

"I see," Columbus says. He glances over at the four big men.
He steps forward to the point where the tattooed man will
have to step back in order to draw his sword if that's the way
this is going to play out.

"What's this about?" Columbus says.

"She's a stinkin' Jew bitch." The man spits out the word
"bitch."

Columbus glances over his shoulder at Juan. "*Brevior saltare
cum deformibus viris est vita*, my friend," he says.

"Huh?" the big man says.

"He said, life is too short to dance with ugly men." Juan
also steps forward, joins Columbus in crowding the giant, who
backs up a step, then another. Juan and Columbus take two
steps forward. The big man's three friends spread out.

"Now why would you say such a thing?"

"Well, you are ugly as sin," Columbus says. "Surely you
know this."

The big man appears to have no idea how to respond to this. Looks confused. "Look, this is not your concern. It's about her. I want this fuckin' Jew out of my sight. She's a filthy whore. I will not drink with stinkin' Jews. She and her kind bring disease, they bring the Black Death."

"You could leave," Juan offers.

"You defend this Jew? Why? She is no better than disease-infested cow shit."

"It's not so much that I love Jews, but rather that I despise those who hate for no reason."

The tattooed man's hand twitches slightly – a tell. Columbus can see he is about to draw his sword. He's going to make that cross-body movement and draw his blade. This is when Columbus draws his own, an Italian-made dagesse. It's short, and he does it quickly. The blade is at the tattooed man's thick neck before his own sword is half drawn. Columbus is fascinated by the intense throbbing under the skin where the tip of his sword presses into tattoo man's neck.

"Stop," Columbus says. "Enough. I just wanted a glass of wine, not a minor war." All eyes are on Columbus.

"Who are you?" the tattooed man says through clenched teeth. He moves his eyes toward Columbus – but moves nothing else.

"I'm the guy holding a blade to your neck. I like Jews, and I'm rather fond of filthy whores. Tell your friends to get out."

"But –"

"Now. Just do it." He presses the point.

Columbus doesn't know much about swords, but any idiot could see this man's weapon was way too long to be effective in close spaces. The tattooed man nods, delicately, toward his companions and they start to pick up their coats and bags – one guy pounds his drink down first.

Salvos appears in the archway, slightly out of breath, a short thrusting sword in hand. The ring of a sword being drawn is a sound that cuts through any din. It's not something he would ever miss. "Everything okay, my friend?"

"Has this guy paid yet? And those?" Columbus motions with his chin in their general direction.

"Yes," Salvos says. He looks them over with a scowl.

"They're leaving. Those three first." The crowd parts as the men make their way to the door. Columbus looks over at the woman, who seems a bit shell-shocked. "What's your name?"

"Selena," she says. There is vulnerability in her eyes but they are also ferocious. Columbus thinks he can smell vanilla.

He turns his attention to the tattooed man. "Goodbye." The big man backs away until Salvos grabs his shoulder and roughly guides him to the door.

Columbus looks at Juan and Selena. "Join me for a drink," he says.

Up close, Columbus finds Selena to be stunningly beautiful. "Do you always draw such a crowd when you come into bars?" he says.

Selena blushes. "Not usually. Do you always show off like that, with your knowledge of Latin?" Her eyes are downcast. But then she looks up with an even, self-assured strength. "I did not wish to have sex with him. Then my face accidentally ran into his fist, twice, and then . . . well, you know the rest. Thank you, by the way, for what you did. I'm in your debt."

"It's nothing. You're probably not even a Jew are you?"

She touches the gash on her right cheekbone. It's stopped bleeding. She winces. "It was never about being a Jew or not being a Jew. He was only rejected and stupid." Selena wears a long, maroon-coloured skirt gathered above her waist, a blouse with tight sleeves, and no corset binds her bosom. This woman, Columbus finds out later, is a chambermaid. She's gorgeous – apart from her injury, her skin is smooth, flawless, and her hair is an exotic tawny mane – yet she seems to have no awareness of her beauty, which only makes her more beautiful in his eyes. This is a woman with whom he would dearly love to dance – because life is also too short to dance with ugly women.

Selena and Juan move toward Columbus's table and Selena trips, lurches forward – falls hard. Both men can hear the dull thud of her body hitting the floor.

"Fuck," she grunts. "These goddamned shoes." She pulls herself up before Columbus can even start to think about moving to help her. Her top is covered with sawdust. Sprays of undone, sandy hair cover half her face, which is bleeding again. Still, Columbus finds himself completely enchanted by her – he feels a little light-headed.

Salvos appears with a jug of wine and places it in the middle of the table.

"The good stuff," he says, smiling. He turns to leave and adds: "You drink on the house tonight."

They sit down and Juan pours wine all around. "The big one," he says, "was a soldier. Not a particularly well-trained soldier but the marking on his hand is indicative of a regiment from near here."

"You're very good with your sword, sir," Selena says.

"Please, call me Columbus. And I'm no swordsman. I'm a navigator, a sailor. I have no idea how to fight. I barely know how to hold a sword."

"But –"

"Sometimes," Columbus says, "one only needs to be quick."

~ ~ ~

"Surely you don't think all women need saving? That we're basically helpless, frail little creatures, and –" She stops, shocked at the intensity of her reaction. Her questioning mind flits to her ex-husband. Was that who Rolf was? Did Rolf save her? Or try to save her?

Columbus smiles. It's a warm gesture – even-tempered and innocent. Not condescending. "But Selena did need saving. It was not a nice bar. Sometimes it takes the threat of violence to stop a greater violence."

Consuela is immediately embarrassed. This is her patient. It's just a story. She's overreacting.

"I do not think you need saving, Consuela," he says. "But I would not hesitate if you were in trouble."

"I . . . Listen, I'm sorry. I . . . Of course, Selena needed some help. It was a good story. I'm curious, though. Exactly how many women does Columbus . . . do you get to bed in this tale?"

"Some other time," he says. "We shall have to talk about passion and love, love and passion. With some women, I shared passion; others, I loved. One mustn't confuse the two."

~ ~ ~

Later, at home, Consuela picks up her phone book and looks under *S* for Salvos, or any such derivation. But it wouldn't be in the phone book anyway. Not a bar like this. Besides, he never actually named the bar. He just named the owner, or the manager. And the bar was in Valdepeñas, she reminds herself. She pulls a bottle of wine from the refrigerator, slips the point of the corkscrew into the soft cork, and starts to twist it in. She hesitates. That was five hundred years ago anyway, she thinks, before she catches herself. Jesus, Consuela, it's a story. It's just a goddamned story.

FOUR

IT'S AROUND THIS TIME THAT Columbus finds the swimming pool. It's mid-July. The temperature in Sevilla had been rising to forty-three degrees Celsius and higher every day for nearly a week, with no relief in sight. In spite of the heat Columbus had been suffering from a cold and was told to report to the steam room. He followed directions the best he could. But instead of the steam room in the south wing, along the bottom edge of the building, Columbus found the empty shell of a swimming pool. He almost fell into it after pushing between a stack of boxes and a pile of old bed frames. Abandoned, but more or less structurally intact, it seems the pool at one time had been fed by an underground spring and a small stream. A fill pipe extended into the stream and was blocked by a rock. The stream, a combination of the spring and the original up-mountain trickle, was warm. A hot spring. Columbus was thrilled. He spent the day cleaning the pool, sweeping, and scrubbing, while Benito, one of the better orderlies, watched, read the newspaper, and watched some more. Before supper, Columbus removed the rock from the fill pipe and the water began to pour into the empty receptacle.

Three days later, Columbus starts to swim. Each morning before breakfast, he and Consuela – or on her days off, Benito – would head for the pool. He swims laps for an hour, sometimes more. It's a good steady workout. It gives him joy to move through the water. It becomes a morning ritual.

"When I am in the water, I almost forget I am not free," he says to Consuela one morning, walking back to the main building.

"What would you do if you were free?"

"Sail west across the Western Sea to India, China, Japan. Drink much wine. Go fishing."

He does not mention his family, or women. Consuela wonders why.

She has been keeping meticulous notes on Columbus and filing them with Dr. Fuentes. Columbus's sessions with Dr. Fuentes are infrequent. She wonders if the doctor is actually reading any of her reports.

Within three weeks, Columbus's body becomes leaner – his muscles, more concentrated. He seems happier. One morning, Consuela thinks she hears him humming. She can't be sure but what else could it have been? This little snippet of an almost-heard melody coming from him is not serious, or focused, or driven. It has lightness to it, and normally he is anything but light.

Columbus does not speak about the pool. Nor does Consuela. This silence is a facility of age. They are both old enough to know that in a bureaucracy, a beautiful, innocent thing like this pool can become desecrated. There would be rules and lifeguards, hours of operation, and probably forms to fill out. It's better to just remain quiet. Benito assumes someone has approved the use of the pool. Consuela does not ask for permission. The pool was there but forgotten. Columbus is just using it. Once a week, Consuela gets up early and enjoys a thirty-minute swim, a luxurious, tepid immersion, before starting her day. This is a gift. She thinks of it as a gift from Columbus. She swims naked. She and Columbus, separated by a few hours, share the same warm water. Consuela does not swim laps. She flounders, drifts around in the water – perhaps she will pull the breaststroke from a childhood memory, swim to the end of the pool and then stop. Mostly, she delights in the feel of the silky, mineral-rich water.

~ ~ ~

On the morning of the feast day of Saint Clare, after Columbus swims his laps – eighty-six laps this morning – and after she leaves him in his room, Consuela finds an envelope in her mail slot in the nurses' lounge. There are identical envelopes in every mail slot. Someone has given all the nurses tickets to the bullfights next weekend. Consuela, who has never been to a bullfight in her life, tells Columbus about the tickets and his face disappears into a memory. "Beatriz loved the bullfights," he says. "The bullfights are how we met."

~ ~ ~

It was at the El Prado Café, near the Plaza de Los Califas, in Córdoba. Columbus was a great lover of the bullfighting. Despite its inherent brutality, for him there was something beautiful about it. He was having an espresso when she walked in – stumbled in. She quite literally fell at his feet. He offered his hand, which she accepted, and then she was sitting at his table.

"Are you all right?"

"I don't know," she says. "Embarrassed. I'm embarrassed. I don't suppose there's any way that we can pretend that didn't happen?" Her hair has fallen – a black splash across her face. She attempts to pin it back into place but fails.

"You and I can pretend, of course. But I'm afraid the café is full."

"Yes, you're probably right."

"Are you okay?" he says, looking her over. "Oh, there's a little blood there, on your lip."

"I think I bit it." She touches her finger to her lip, pulls it away, and examines the blood.

"Let me get you a cloth."

"Are you a physician?"

Columbus smiles. "I'm a navigator. A stargazer. An explorer."

"Three occupations. My, I'm honoured to be sitting with such a busy man."

He's not quite sure about this, about her. She's not smiling. Is she making fun of him? Or is this a verbal thrust that he must now parry? He nods in the direction of the doorway.

"It was quite an entrance," he says. "Is it something you practice?"

Now she smiles. "It's these damned shoes," she says. "I can't get used to them. All the women at court are wearing them – it's the fashion of the day. How do they say? The rage? Yes, all the rage." She raises her foot from under her skirts, exposing her narrow calf and a black shoe with a three-inch heel.

"I see. I see. Well, anyone might have problems with such footwear." Beads of sweat form on Columbus's forehead. It promises to be a sweltering hot day but this assurance is still hidden inside the cool morning. He sweats because he loves that curve of the leg – the way the calf curves up into the knee – the ankle, her slender foot.

"Are you okay? You appear to be sweating. Have you a fever?"

"Perfectly fine. My name is . . ." What the hell is my name? Oh for pity's sake. What's my name?

"Your name is?" She tilts her head, offers her perfect, crooked smile.

"Cristóbal. Cristóbal Colón."

He invites Beatriz Enríquez de Arana to the bullfight that afternoon. Beatriz, it turns out, follows the bullfights with a passion.

She meets him outside the stadium. Columbus is carrying two botas full of wine and sandwiches. She is wearing a blue dress designed for easy movement. There is nothing frilly. But the dress rises to golden embroidery across her shoulders and around her neck. Even this is a simple elegance. They find their seats and watch the corridas as the mounted matadors fight and eventually kill their bulls.

"It seems to me," Beatriz says, "that it would be more interesting if these men got off their horses and then tried to kill the bulls. Those men, there" – she points by lifting her chin in the general direction – "the ones on the ground, with the capes, the ones coaxing the bulls into charging. What they do is interesting." She hands him the bota and he lifts it and squeezes a healthy stream of red wine into his mouth.

"This is something that has been discussed in the bullfighting papers," he says. "There is talk of outlawing the horses except for the beginning. They're suggesting an angry bull and a lone man on foot will be the new bullfighting."

"That would be wonderful, I think," Beatriz says. She lifts the bota and drinks again.

They build the desire between them for three days, rest one, and then continue. On the fifth day, a storm blows in from the coast. Storms are inevitable at this time of year. The bullfight is cancelled. Inside his borrowed villa, they lock the doors, drink icy white wine, and eat olives with feta cheese. Bruised clouds bank up at sea, then hurl themselves onto the land in waves of rain and wind. Columbus and Beatriz are pushed together in the rain. His need for reassurance is perfectly matched by her need to give it. She listens to his dream of crossing the Western Sea and does not treat it as a dream. To her this is something beautiful that will occur. It frightens her but she believes he will do whatever he wants to do. There is an absolute belief, a built-in faith. This belief arrives quickly, lands softly in her.

Columbus does not try to seduce her. This she finds very attractive. He shares his dreams. He is a man who has feelings and communicates those feelings. He becomes weak because he is unsure, and this pulls at something inside her. She talks about her life and her dreams, and he appears to listen, although she suspects he is just resting.

The wind howls all evening. They can hear the rain pounding down outside, and then they are on the bed in his room. Lightning flashes burst through cracks in the shutters. The room is sliced into shards of black and white.

They are drinking wine. They are light-headed and happy children, playing just out of the rain. Relishing the nature of the storm.

The storm blows hardest as they begin their lovemaking. It stokes the moment and amplifies the humour. The small awkwardness of first-time loving tilts the room and the bed and the floors in the dramatic storm light. There is no room for the world, no matter how big or how small. There is only the body, and the desire, and there is her unbelievable scent.

Another flash of storm jabs its way into the room.

"Like the storm has eyes," she says.

"Crying eyes," Columbus says.

They listen to the slapping of the rain on the leaves outside the window and on the stones in the street.

"Sobbing eyes," she giggles.

"Weeping eyes."

"Wailing eyes."

In this physical realm, too, they seem absolutely suited for each other. She knows his needs before he does. It feels right that she knows. When she follows her intuition there is new pleasure in her.

Columbus allows himself to be lost, perhaps the ultimate vulnerability for a navigator. He does not know where he is – in the storm and with Beatriz and in the room and in the bed. It all gets washed together. He is completely lost but it does not feel dangerous.

~ ~ ~

After, they turn on the television. Columbus has the remote and he's flipping up and down the channels, looking for a movie. He's looking for the right movie – something seriously romantic or a Western. He loves Westerns.

"It's amazing," he says, "that we have this many choices yet there seems to be nothing at all on."

"What's that, my dear?"

"It's like having an entire hold filled with fish but the fish are all rotten. The selection is nearly limitless yet it's all gone bad." He turns the picture off and places the remote on the bedside table. "They say this is progress."

"That's nice, dear," she says from the kitchen.

She brings a plate of sausages, goat cheese, and fresh bread. Under her arm is a bottle of wine. Columbus watches as she moves into the room. The dark strands across her face. The long whip of a braid down her back. Her face, curious and narrow. The delicate enclaves of dark hair under her arms. The exceptional curve of her belly down to her pubic mound. Columbus feels blessed to have this woman in his life. She places the plate and bottle on the side table, and slips into bed beside him. She frowns and cocks her head suddenly, as if she's trying to hear something. "May I ask a question?" she says.

"A question?"

"The crinkling sound. Is there something –"

"You mean the storm?"

She shakes her head.

"The lightning?"

"No," she says. "Crinkling."

Columbus shifts to his side and there is indeed a crinkling sound.

"Oh no," he says, jumping out of the bed.

He stands at the edge of the bed, apprehensive, wired. He doesn't know what to do with his hands. As if he does not own them, he holds them out like he wants to adjust something but doesn't know how or what.

"What is it, Cristóbal?" She hops out of bed and stands beside him. Beatriz is terrified of spiders and this is what's going through her mind. The size of this spider must be substantial.

"The chart! I placed a chart there. Under the blankets. I put it there to make it flat."

"Under the blankets?"

~ ~ ~

It's almost ruined. The blood in the bed and on the chart is menstrual. They use a cloth with water to try and lift some of the red stain off. Both of them get down on the floor and dab at it but it's useless. They smudge the lines. The chart, according to Columbus, was created by an old mariner named Zuane Pizzigano in the 1420s. It shows a small cluster of four islands far off in the Western Sea. Regardless of the fact that no one had ever confirmed these islands existed, Columbus was thrilled to find them situated so far out into the darkness. These islands are now tinged a reddish brown. While the chart is stained, it still has value. They hang it on a rod near the window and scamper for the bed. It's cool and humid in the room. Under the covers, they hug each other warm. There is only the sound of thunder, leagues away, and a dripping sound, and a dog barking, and the sound of the moon behind the clouds reflected in a puddle.

~ ~ ~

They had televisions, she thinks, in the fifteenth century? Consuela leans forward, quizzical. She does not want to appear confrontational, so keeps her voice uplifted. "So, Columbus was . . . you were flipping channels?"

"And there were many, many channels. But not much of it was interesting."

"You're saying there was television in the fifteenth century. Does that make sense to you, Columbus?"

"Everybody knows this, Consuela. Have you not read Zimmerman? Zimmerman references this repeatedly in his dissertation on fifteenth-century domestic commonalities. What's your point?"

He's left her nowhere to go. She has no idea who Zimmerman is. And really, what does it matter that he imports televisions into a story that is set five hundred years in the past? But if she were trusting the *tale* and not the *teller*, like the saying suggests, she'd have some serious problems, because this tale is a crazy, mish-mashed, time-crossed slip down a rabbit hole. And the teller is, of course, institutionalized.

"Was it colour or black-and-white?" she says hesitantly.

"Was what colour or black-and-white?"

"Nothing."

~ ~ ~

Consuela had slept in. She was not there for Columbus's early morning swim. She had arrived at work in a panic of apology and moved quickly into high gear. This quick coffee and check on him was her first pause.

She came onto the patio deck and saw him hopping up and down on one foot, tilting his head back and forth. Sunlight slices through the high branches of the holm in the centre of the courtyard, and the upper branches move in the breeze. The sunlight speckles the ground where Columbus continues to hop. What now? What gimmick or scheme is this? What's he up to? He stops hopping when he sees her and smiles. He is genuinely pleased to see her. Is she reading something that isn't there? "Got water in my ear. Won't come out," he says.

Consuela sets her coffee mug on the table and sits down. Columbus clears his throat, something he does whenever he's going to tell another story. Consuela isn't sure how to take these rambling tales. For her, the details of his stories are remarkable. The clarity with which he paints these word pictures is sometimes quite marvellous. She sometimes finds herself caught beyond redemption, so enthralled that she *wants* to believe him. Something denied inside her yearns to believe him.

~ ~ ~

He clears his throat again. "He, Cristóbal Colón, realizes he has always been a bit insecure with women, and at the same time he loves the fleshy union. He adores this woman, Beatriz. He loves her. But he does not marry her. Columbus will not make the promises of marriage. Not when there is a chance that he may in fact sail across the Western Sea. It would be unfair to her. While he is a brilliant navigator, sailing is dangerous. And there is much fleshy union to be made."

"Fleshy union?"

"Yes, the lovemaking."

"Are you aware that you are talking about yourself in the third person again?"

"Am I?"

"It's as if you are standing outside yourself, observing. Why do you do that?"

"I don't know. It just comes out of me. It's easier to pretend I am a character inside a story."

"So, Columbus . . . you, are a lover."

"Of women, and the bullfights."

"And Beatriz was all right with the other women in your life?"

"Beatriz had the most wonderful scent." Columbus closes his eyes inside a memory.

"She smelled?"

"Yes. Down there."

Consuela looks down quickly. And then up at him again. "What do you mean, she smelled?"

"It was spicy and sweet. Cinnamon and rain. Completely distinctive. I have never experienced anything like it. It was heavenly. It must have been associated with her diet. It was extraordinary."

Nurse Consuela hasn't blushed since . . . well, she can't recall the last time she blushed.

FIVE

On the morning of the liturgical feast of Saint Pammachius, Columbus is in a lawn chair, overlooking the garden. He's wearing his standard, institute-issue maroon robe and grey socks. He looks like any number of other patients wandering around in the courtyards and gardens surrounding the institute. He's speaking to Consuela over his left shoulder. "I have to tell you, people used to roll up on the beach on a regular basis – well, chewed-up bodies anyway. When I lived in Palos we'd find them all the time – stinking and rotten. Even the foulest of birds or animals wouldn't touch them."

"I'm sorry?" She really was not in the mood for a story. She was unfocused – half watching the ducks in a pond, half keeping an eye on him. She'd rather be curled up in bed reading.

"Dead people. On the beach. The result of shipwrecks."

Consuela feels out of sorts. She couldn't sleep – flipped from side to side throughout the night. She had been searching the Internet until 1 A.M., looking for information on Christopher Columbus, staggering through the maze of information. She wanted to know if there really was a Beatriz. And she found Beatriz in the fifteenth century – a woman Columbus never married. This got her wondering about a *doppelgänger* Beatriz in the twenty-first century. If there is one, why doesn't she visit? Wouldn't she be worried? Wouldn't she file a missing person report at some point? And why doesn't Columbus talk about his kids?

Wouldn't a father wonder where his children were? Then it was 3:30 A.M. – time to get up, get ready for work. The bread was mouldy but the bagels in the fridge were fine. She sliced and toasted a bagel and ate it with Nocilla. Her tea was excellent, but she was alone. She woke up alone, made breakfast alone, showered alone, and ate alone.

"Why are you here, Columbus?" she says slowly, carefully. Apart from telling ridiculous stories about Vikings with maps and bloody charts, she thinks.

"I beg your pardon?" Columbus looks back over his shoulder at her.

"Why are you here? You show up here looking like you've had a bath in blood and claiming you're Christopher Columbus. Now I'm not saying you're not. But do me a favour. Look at your hands."

Columbus looks down into his palms.

"No, the other way. Good. What do you see?"

He wants to say *hands* but he has the good sense to know she's after something else. "A ring," he says. "A silver or white-gold band with a rope design."

"And what finger is it on?"

"On my ring finger. It's a symbol of commitment." As if he's almost surprised.

"And you are committed to . . . ?"

"Beatriz. Columbus is – I am, committed to Beatriz."

"You're telling me that's not a wedding ring? Goddamnit! Who are *you* married to? You! Who's your wife?"

Clearly he does not know what to say. He looks at her, lost.
Genuinely bewildered. She recognizes this and feels forced to
retreat – to honour his reality.

"I don't believe you're crazy," she says. "Why are you here?"

"Because you suggested a stroll in the garden and I asked if
it might be too hot today, and you said, no, it's comfortable,
and I said . . ."

Consuela sighs. Enough, she thinks. I can't take this today.
"I'm going to have an orderly take you back," she says.

"What are you going to do?"

"I'm going to feed the ducks. Read a book. Maybe take my
shoes off and walk on the grass. Anything but put up with this
bullshit. I'm just not in the mood."

He sits up and turns around in the chair – looks over his
shoulder at her. Silence presses in on them.

A squirrel chatters in a tree behind Consuela. The wind
brushes through the high branches. Something splashes in the
pond.

"I'm lucky to be here."

"Lucky how?" she says. She'll be damned if she's going to let
him off the hook.

"Lucky to be alive."

"That's not what I asked."

"But it's the truest thing I know, since we're navigating
around bullshit today."

"You're lucky to be alive?" She raises an eyebrow, gives him
a look that says: Oh for Christ's sake, get on with it then.

~ ~ ~

Usually they're dead. They wash onto the shore in the darkness, bloated and stinking and ugly. Half naked and chewed up. Unidentifiable.

Usually they're long-gone dead. But this man rolls up on the beach near Palos, in the south of Spain, after a vicious storm pounds the coast for five days, and he's only half dead. His ship is either destroyed by the storm or pushed out to sea. This sailor somehow managed to tie himself to a plank. He drifted onto the beach still attached to his makeshift life preserver.

Once the man is discovered, the people of the town rush to the beach and carry him to the monastery. They had to cut the ropes in order to extract the man from the board. Believing the man would not live, Father Paulo's church seems the logical choice. They pass him through the arched doorway into the hands of the monks who live there. Father Paulo knows several languages. The sailor, they find out later, has limited Portuguese, good Italian and English, passable French, and excellent Spanish. Father Paulo chooses Spanish as the language in which they will conduct their discussions of navigation and the ocean. He chooses English to talk about the everyday nonsense of eating and cooking and going to the bathroom. He chooses French to speak of women and love. He chooses Portuguese to speak of poetry. For the first three or four days, the sailor says very little – he moans and sometimes talks in his sleep. It is Father Paulo who sets the parameters of language and subject matter. He is quick, loves to hear his own voice, and is seriously opinionated. He asks many questions but barely breathes before answering these questions himself, and he is definitely verbose. If he has a captive audience – and with the sailor this was certainly the case – Father Paulo carries both sides of the conversation. The sailor is too weak to do much more than eat the thin broths, sleep, and listen to the ranting of this Franciscan father.

"It is perhaps an odd notion but it is my experience, from the days before I was a monk of course, that women like to pursue as much as they like to be pursued. To have them chase you, you must show yourself to be charming and then retreat. This takes understanding and creativity. Make a study of women. Learn what makes a man attractive. It is not just the eye. There is more to attractiveness than being pleasant to the eye. There is great pleasure in the chase, my friend – no matter who is doing the chasing. Take it from me, the journey is everything. Once you arrive, one must devise new goals, new challenges." He leans back in his chair, the wood creaks under his shifting weight. He closes his eyes. "I remember the curves of a woman in Paris, her skin, her green eyes. And she had the most peculiar but pleasant scent. Oranges and cinnamon. The smell of rain and dirt. Moist earth. Don't get me wrong, my friend. Just a hint of this scent and you would need more. Desire would blossom in you as it did in me. Ah, she would have been the one who kept me from God had she not already been married. Her name was Maria, and she was not only beautiful but she was intelligent." Father Paulo opens his eyes. "I wonder if you are intelligent."

He assumes I can't hear or understand him, the sailor is thinking.

Father Paulo nurses this man back to health. It's a slow process as he passes through fever after fever. It takes two weeks for him to speak his first words. The monk has been sitting quietly waiting for him to wake up. When the sailor opens his eyes he sees the balding pillar of a man sitting against a white stone wall, his eyes closed in a meditation. The father has a warm, open face.

He's asleep, the sailor thinks. It is the first peace I've had since I got here. This man never shuts up. He is the most opinionated, pigheaded, domineering, and often-very-wrong man I've ever encountered. He never stops talking. Thank God and all the heavens he's asleep.

"I am not asleep, my friend," says the monk. "I was meditating – something I learned from a friend, a Chinese monk who came through here a few years back. It's a completely conscious, focused prayer."

He reads my mind, the man thinks. He smiles cautiously. "Thank you," he says, finally.

"I was worried about you, my friend," Father Paulo says. "You are very welcome. You're going to be all right."

"No, thank you for stopping your talking."

The monk tightens the rope that secures his robe, clears his throat. "What are you called by?"

"Cristóbal. I am Cristóbal, a navigator. I was a navigator."

"Where were you sailing to?"

"To Portugal, and then Spain with the *Barto* out of Venice. From Britain and the North Sea." He pauses. "You said I was the only survivor? Nobody else came ashore? Nothing else? No other wreckage?"

"A few planks, and you attached to one of them. That's it, I'm afraid."

"I am grateful."

"Listen, do you know the sextant, my friend?"

"Yes, I understand the sextant. I understand how it works."

"And you understand the stars?"

He's testing me, Columbus thinks. He wants to test the limits of my knowledge. The sextant is new. Dead reckoning and a compass is the standard for navigation. "I have guided ships by the stars. But I do not understand the stars."

This stops Father Paulo.

"You guide your ship by the stars yet you do not understand the stars? Is this a riddle? Are you any good as a navigator?"

Columbus laughs. "I do not understand the *beauty* of the stars. It is simply that. I do not understand their beauty."

The monk smiles. This is something he can sink his teeth into. There is a built-in dichotomy in this man who plays with language and apparently loves the stars. He arrives on the beach tied neatly to a plank and barely survives this ordeal. Nothing else comes ashore. He knows the sextant and knows about navigating by the stars. In his delirium he called out at least three different names – all women. So perhaps he is also a lover.

"I should let you know, I was not the navigator of the ship that went down – I was a passenger only."

"It was a hell of a storm. Yours was not the only ship lost."

"How long have I been – ?"

"Two weeks. You were brought here two weeks ago. I will bring you more soup."

~ ~ ~

"You're trying to tell me that you washed up on shore the sole survivor of a shipwreck?"

"Not the most auspicious of beginnings, I admit. But it could have happened."

Consuela is thinking she should have fed the ducks in the pond – sent him back to his room and enjoyed the peace of this courtyard.

"And where is Father Paulo now? I've noticed he does not visit."

"I'm not sure he knows I'm here. And that was many years ago," he says. "Father Paulo could have passed away by now."

~ ~ ~

Consuela goes out with a group of nurses from work. They meet at the Cerveceria Giralda, which is a former Islamic bathhouse. With its vaulted ceilings, marble floors, and beautiful *azulejos*, the place screams Arabian Nights . . . romantic and whimsical. The restaurant has incredible tapas. They sit outside, under the orange trees, with a fine view of the cathedral. Much of the conversation centres on Dr. Fuentes. He's not focused, forgetful. His head is not in his work. So they sit around and drink pitchers of *tinto con limón* – red wine with lemonade – and speculate on what could be the matter. His marriage is floundering, somebody suggests. He never talks about his wife. Once married, Gloria Fuentes stopped nursing. She stayed at home. She lunched with other women who did not work. She did not stay in touch with her former workmates. The nurses pool all they know of the doctor's personal life, and it is a very shallow basin of information.

Consuela doesn't want to talk about Columbus, but he is one of the most interesting patients in the hospital. Interesting in a good way. He's not a self-abuser or an obsessive masturbator. Well, he is almost naked most of the time but this is a minor sin.

"And he's hot," one of the night-shift nurses, Sarah, says. "It's a shame he's delusional because –" She stops, blushes, and picks up her glass. "I should drink more wine and shut up."

"He tells stories," Consuela says. "He told a story about an orange."

Tammy looks at her like she's lost her mind.

"No, really," Consuela says. "It was a story about how someone might have figured out the Earth was round. But you have to imagine it's five hundred years ago and we don't know anything about North America. Columbus is standing on a beach. He holds up an orange, then sticks his finger behind it and slowly begins to lower his finger, following the curve of the orange. He's trying to explain the curvature of the Earth – he's trying to show it to Beatriz."

Consuela studies Tammy's face. She's giving longing looks to her drink, which is nearly empty.

"Columbus's mistress. Beatriz is his concubine. His lover. Columbus keeps saying, 'Do you see? Do you see?' But she doesn't see. She needs time to think. She's feeling stupid about not getting it. Later on, they're walking on the beach. The gulls are lifting and descending in the air currents above the water. The clouds are a stretched-out afterthought. The waves are of little consequence. A small fishing boat is sailing out of the cove. It moves slowly and Columbus stops to watch. Can you see him? He puts his journal on the sand and stands there in the bright sun, hands in trouser pockets, squinting out into the ocean.

"Beatriz walks a few paces ahead, notices Columbus has stopped, and then turns around. She sees Columbus is absorbed in thought and so she sits on the beach and joins her own gaze to his. The boat moves out of the sheltered water toward the open sea. Its mast begins to sink.

"And then Beatriz is jumping up and down, shouting, 'It's the orange! It's the orange!' She runs over to Columbus, who is beaming with pride. He reaches into his pocket and pulls out the orange – tosses it to her and says, 'I knew you'd figure it out. You just needed a little time. You just proved the Earth is round.' Columbus laughs, but then adds: 'Do you have any idea how big it is?'"

"So he still believes he's Christopher Columbus?" Sarah says. "Is he giving history lessons?"

"No, it seems to be personal. It's his story – Columbus's story. I looked it up. The real Columbus had no idea of how big the Earth was. If he had known, he'd never have tried to sail to Japan. A while back, my Columbus told a story about arriving – washing up on shore somewhere near Palos. The thing is, nobody knows how Columbus got to Spain. We just don't know how he arrived. He could have been in a ship-wreck and washed ashore. He could have been on the run from Portugal. They don't know for sure."

She's been trying not to sound too enthusiastic about these stories but fears her excitement is seeping out.

"What does Fuentes think the stories mean?"

"I don't think he has time to care. I'm honestly not sure he reads my reports."

"What do you think, Connie?" Tammy reaches over and fills Consuela's glass.

"Well, for one thing, he knows a lot about Christopher Columbus. It's not just incoherent muttering. Somewhere in there is a man who has knowledge about the fifteenth century."

"But he believes he's Columbus?"

"Yes. As far as he's concerned, he's being prevented from sailing across the Western Sea to China, or Japan."

"It's romantic in a sort of twisted way."

"I think something may have happened to him," Consuela says. "Something that is very likely not romantic at all."

~ ~ ~

He wishes this ballpoint pen was a fountain pen. Even a pencil would be more elegant than this plastic throwaway thing. But he's lucky to have it. He'd signed it out earlier and then turned it back in after two hours, without having written a word. He'd sat at the writing desk in good light and watched the bees work the lemon blossoms on the tree just outside the window. In the afternoon, Columbus tries again.

(i)

He has this image of a sleeping woman, her still form on a bed, lying on her side. The sheets are a mess of grey around her. A thick, regal-purple quilt is scrambled at the end of the bed. Her hip is thrust up, exposed – the line of her body is a sculpted, curvaceous desert landscape, supple and long. There is nothing hard about this body – it holds no tension.

Three candles on the dresser across the room, two of which are still lit, make a pale yellow light. Dark wooden venetian blinds are pulled down but allow slivers of light to section the darkness. A bottle of champagne is upside down in a silver bucket on the bedside table. Books are piled on this table and also fill a narrow shelf that runs the length of the headboard. Piles of sideways books at either end hold the upright books in place. There's a painting of a narrow, long-necked nude woman on the wall beside the bed. This picture is enclosed by a thick, dark frame. This is not a hotel room.

The scent of vanilla hovers in the room. Her face is not visible, but it's easy to imagine this woman is satiated, happy. He wishes this for her. He cannot say why.

The picture-taker is standing in the hallway looking into the room. Did this person take this picture on their way back with another bottle of champagne? Pause in the doorway, see her body on the bed, think: Jesus, she's beautiful. Wonder: Where's my camera? Place the bottle of champagne on the floor. Get the camera, frame the picture, take the picture.

He wonders if she will hear the shutter, lean up in the bed and say, "Hey . . . what?" And perhaps the picture-taker captures her question as well. But there is no hint to suggest that she sat up into the room. Nor are there any hints to suggest pictures prior to or after this one. There will *be a perfect circle of condensation on the hardwood when he lifts the sweating champagne bottle off the floor.*

This is a vulnerable position, he thinks. To expose one's back and buttocks like this speaks about trust and faith, and comfort. She trusts the picture-taker. Perhaps this speaks of love. Does love follow trust, faith, and this level of comfort? Are these dependent on each other?

He thinks he ought to know this horizontal woman. There is some nuance he cannot put his finger on that resonates with familiarity. But what? He looks closer. If only this mental image would move. If only she would sit up and turn toward the picture-taker and smile. Then his heart would break with a yearning tenderness. But at least he would know.

SIX

SITTING UP IN ONE OF THE CHEAP seats on the night train from Paris to Madrid would have been a painful experience, but Emile had a new company credit card, so he booked a berth on the Elipsos hotel train. He slept for most of the trip – let the clicking of the tracks soothe away all the rough edges. In Madrid, Emile reinterviewed two of the witnesses. A student at the Universidad Complutense de Madrid remembers yelling at a man on the stairs. "He was going the wrong way," she said. "His eyes were steely, hard. He ignored me. I just remember his eyes and that he was going the wrong way." Another witness, a lawyer, said he was pushed by a man carrying a bag under his arm – a leather bag. "This man, he said nothing – just pushed his way through the crowd – he seemed desperate, agitated." The confounding thing is that these witnesses each seem to have a different idea of what this man looked like. Emile was intrigued. Either these people who claim to have seen the guy each saw somebody different, or this man was some sort of chameleon.

~ ~ ~

He's driving south from Madrid. The day before, the woman at the rental-car agency at first did not believe Emile's new credit card was real. This woman, who teased with her smile, was flummoxed by the black card and embarrassed when her boss took over. He saw the card and began fawning – upgrading, double-checking the readiness of the car, offering a free map, offering to get coffee, and waiving fees. Emile was grateful for the muffled silence of the car when he finally drove away. This credit card, he decided, was a pain in the ass.

There are many roads that lead south from Madrid. If this mystery man, this person of intense interest, went south, he had his pick. South was a guess, based on the flimsy newspaper story about a man in Valdepeñas. And if south was a guess, well, Valdepeñas was a leap of faith. Emile didn't have much to go on. He had the usual checks in place, and a junior agent in Lyon was monitoring newspapers for anything about a lone, disoriented, or suspicious man – anything out of the ordinary.

It's a bit of a drive to Valdepeñas. Perhaps it was this man of interest wandering around town asking for directions, Emile thinks. He could certainly have found a ride. This is Emile's only clue right now. He thinks back to the rental-car woman, the one who'd questioned his credit card. This was the sort of woman he would have felt comfortable asking out. There was nothing severe about her. In fact, there was a natural playfulness, which was shunted aside when the sycophant manager stepped in. He'd have enjoyed looking across the table into those eyes and seeing that smile. Emile presses the button on the door panel and the window opens. He lets the car-rental woman slip out the window into the hot day.

Emile enjoys being on the road, driving long distances and thinking. For him, it's a good place for those bits of subconscious – the renegades – to float to the surface. It's a good place to figure things out. One sits still behind the wheel, motionless, while at the same time engaged in movement. The Paris shooting is suddenly there demanding attention, but Emile pushes Paris away – he elbows aside the reason he's been off work. He has been turned inward long enough. His wounds are only scars now. He'd rather think about the rental-car woman and her teasing smile.

~ ~ ~

In Valdepeñas, Emile decides to check bars and cafés near the train station and around main thoroughfares. He asks his questions in four bars and two cafés the day he arrives. This morning, he had an espresso in the restaurant in his hotel and made inquiries. Just before noon, he visits his fifth Valdepeñas bar. He sits down at the bar and asks the same questions regarding any strangers making an impression or acting oddly.

"Ya, there was a guy here a few months back. I couldn't place his accent. He was not from around here. Went after a group of our regulars with a pool cue."

Emile sits up straight. He nods his encouragement at the bartender who had put down a copy of *Don Quixote* when Emile came in. If that's not a sign from God that this is some sort of idealistic, absurd adventure, Emile thinks, I don't know what is.

"He pulled it out of the rack on the wall and snapped it on the table," the bartender says. "Held it like a goddamned sword. Pushed Pablo up against the wall, made him apologize."

"What had this Pablo done?"

"He was a little rough with his wife. Verbally. Not physical or anything. Pablo is a mean drunk, that's all."

"And?"

"The guy looked crazy – like he might actually push the pool cue through Pablo's neck. Pablo apologized."

"What did this swordsman look like?"

"Scraggly. Greasy hair. Dirty clothes. Definitely not from around here. He was fairly tall. Obviously he was crazy. I had to toss him. He was very polite about it. Understood completely."

"Did he say anything else? Anything to indicate where he was going? Anything? Even the most insignificant bit of conversation."

"Look, I told him that what he'd done was something a lot of us in the bar had wished we'd done ages ago. Pablo is a big fucking mean bastard of a drunk but his father employs most of the men who drink here." He picks up a cloth from inside the sink and begins to wipe down the bar, adrift in this automatic action. "Why are you looking for this guy?"

I wish I knew for sure, Emile thinks. "He's missing," he says, thinking, well, it could be true – this man might be missing. "I'm just trying to get him back home," he adds.

The bartender weighs this. It seems to Emile that he is being protective. He's protecting a man he barely knows, a man he'd tossed out of his bar, a man who had attacked – or at least threatened – one of his customers.

"Let me see your identification again," he says.

Emile hands him his badge. The bartender looks it over carefully and hands it back.

"He asked me which way it was to Morocco. When I told him to go south, he looked confused. I told him to head for Córdoba. I had to point. He had no idea about directions. Clueless. I think he was going to try and hitchhike."

~ ~ ~

Emile is more confounded now than he was when he first read the alerts. As the details of this man's journey pile up, clarity is not forthcoming. The newspaper story about the mysterious stranger in Valdepeñas who asked for directions to almost every city and town on a map of Spain could be his man. But one of the witnesses in Valdepeñas said the man spoke Russian, or at least had a Russian accent. Another witness, who provided a nice meal and a bottle of wine for the stranger, said the man was short, no more than 170 centimetres. And now add this man in the bar and a bartender who is protective of a patron who threatened to kill a favoured customer.

Emile gets out of bed. He finds the bottle of cask-strength Laphroaig on the desk across the room. He pulls the cork out and pours a hefty portion. In the quasi-darkness, Emile fumbles with the minibar key and locates a bottle of spring water in the back. He spills a couple of spoonfuls of the water into his glass and takes a sip of the smoky whisky.

Somewhere in this hotel, there is a whirlpool and steam room. He'd love to soak for a while but there is always the risk of running into a stranger who wants to talk. Emile does not feel like talking. Nor does he feel like being friendly. He tries to open the window but it sticks. He has to lean into it to get it to open. The air is surprisingly cool. He looks up into grey and remembers when he was a child, stepping out in front of the house and looking up into the sky at stars. He remembers the blackness of the sky and what seemed like layers of stars behind swirling layers – and some parts of that night sky seemed alive with movement, a blurred gossamer net of starlight.

The clouds over Valdepeñas are socked in, thick and grey. The stars are up there somewhere, Emile thinks, and perhaps the moon as well, but tonight these heavenly bodies are not for me. A dog barks in the distance. A car drives by on the street below. A light comes on in a fifth-floor window in the building across the road. He leans on the iron balustrade and fights the impulse to fall back into the loop of the accident. It was an accident. Not his fault. It was not him who started shooting in Paris.

~ ~ ~

Emile is driving south, away from Valdepeñas. The swordsman in the bar was given directions to Córdoba so that's where Emile will attempt to pick up the trail. He can't seem to get the radio to work, and he has no discs in his bag. There's music inside his laptop but no way to get that music to play on the car's stereo system. He'd kill for anything by Keith Jarrett right now. The first few notes of *The Köln Concert* or any of the solo piano recordings. Funny how his musical cravings go. Last month he absolutely had to hear Heinrich Schiff's Bach cello suites. He found a CD of the recording but it was the vinyl he wanted. So he drove an hour out of Paris and found himself, at three in the morning, in his father's garage going through boxes of vinyl records. He's driving inside a muffled silence. The hum of the tires on the road and the sound of the air conditioning become white noise. Emile considers turning on the GPS system to see if there's a friendly voice to keep him company. A female voice would be lovely.

~ ~ ~

They are sitting in the common room. There's a haze across the city today, making everything appear softer. Consuela likes this diffusion. They're alone in the room, which is rare – there are 480 patients at this institution, give or take about a dozen due to the constant stream of discharges and admittances. It's a sunny, warm day, and many of the patients are in the court-yard or wandering through the lemon orchard. A wall of windows allows light to splash across conglomerations of chairs and couches, clustered around tables. There is a sturdy wire mesh covering the windows, but most who spend their days here do not notice this. After the first week they become just windows, not barred windows.

"How long did you stay with Father Paulo?"

"We had a couple of months of discussions. He proved to be a most fascinating man. He was no normal monk."

Consuela sits up – presses her back into the chair. "Well, the question I have is about understanding beauty. Did you find an answer? Can you define beauty, Mr. Columbus?"

"Not without poetry or art."

"So you're defining beauty with beauty?"

"Beauty is nothing without the *language* of beauty."

This stops her. When he says things like this she leans heavily to the port side – the side of her that believes he's more sane than not. For most of the time he's been at the institute she has been starboard, but he was also heavily drugged for much of that time. She carries the weight of this. It was convenient for him to be sedated for this time. It made her life, everybody's life at the institute, easier. "So we need words –"

"Not just words . . . language."

He leans forward, reaches slowly across the table, and takes her hand. Her first impulse is to pull away. This is her patient. But she leaves her hand in his – she's curious. Where's he going with this?

"I want to breathe the piquant fragrances of a mature woman – to rest my head atop her thighs and breathe her in, make her scent such an essential part of my being that I will never be able to forget. So living without her would be like living without lungs, heart, legs, arms. And I want to write words for her, capture my frailest feelings and the smallest details of loving, find the words that resonate with life, love, sex, desire. And I want to write the words: I cannot hear your voice, not now, because your voice is my desire, a knife that cuts both ways . . ."

Consuela looks into his eyes. Are they grey? Or is that blue?

There's certainly a hint of green, but as for the rest, she's not sure. Columbus seems to be on the verge of tears. His eyes do not waver from hers. She is suddenly, irrevocably connected to his sadness. It takes her breath away.

She pulls her hand out of his. Breaks eye contact. She tries to shake him off. This is far too close. She thinks for a moment that Columbus is talking about her. But that can't be. She takes a deep breath. Beauty. We were talking about the idea of beauty. "Um, what about a combination of qualities that make something pleasing to the eye," she says, "or ear, or touch? Does that not define beauty?"

He smiles, seemingly unaffected by her pulling away. "What about metaphor? Or, here, let me define beauty for you . . . It was 1485, March, and she was most decidedly beautiful. But it was a sad beauty."

"Who?"

"Cassandra. Aren't you listening?"

~ ~ ~

"It's like this," she says, and then Cassandra drops the towel – she's picked a white towel. Her first impulse was to choose one of the burgundy towels – red is lust and desire – but for her, white is the perfect colour for seduction. It does not speak directly of innocence, but it's there. Uncharted territory. Virginal ground. "I have feelings for you, Mr. Columbus. Very strong feelings. Feelings so strong that if I let them out you would perhaps be frightened."

"Nothing much scares me," he says. Columbus is staying in a borrowed villa – he's travelling, trying to muster up some interest and, of course, money.

I love you with all my heart, Columbus, she thinks. "I have never felt like this," she says.

"What?"

"This connection."

"Connection?"

She sighs and looks into his eyes. Could this man be so incredibly dense that he cannot see my love, my need?

Cassandra loved him the second she saw him in the bar. He'd come in to ask for directions and wound up sitting down for a drink. He was trying to find an apartment that was, as it turned out, just around the corner. He'd been invited to a dinner party. The bartender free-poured the Scottish beverage, the Uisge Beatha, into a small, squat glass. She knew instantly she wanted him. She'd heard him introduce himself to the bartender: Christopher Columbus – the man who wanted to sail beyond what is known. Sitting in a darkened booth, she dabbed perfume under her armpits and then approached the bar. It's crowded at the bar and she trips on a foot, or the leg of a stool, or her own feet, and falls to the floor. "Goddamnit," she says, pulling herself up. "It's these fucking shoes. I can't get used to them."

"Are you all right?" Columbus says. "I think you might need a cloth. Your chin is bleeding. I think you've cut yourself." There is a gash along her jawline, close to her chin. The bartender passes Columbus a cloth, which he holds to her face.

"This is not what I'd envisioned. I just wanted to meet you, introduce myself. I'm so embarrassed."

"Oh, don't be. I see falling women all the time."

The first thing that struck her was that Columbus had almost white hair, yet he was not so old. He hunched a bit, like he carried a great weight across his shoulders. She loved him instantly when he spoke. That dark-blue voice could have convinced her to do anything. Just the intonations of his voice charmed her.

~ ~ ~

Columbus looks at her. There's some sort of Celtic symbol tattooed on her thigh. One of the lines of this tattooed design has come loose and wrapped itself around her entire thigh. "Connected?" he says. We just met, he's thinking.

"Yes, there seems to be something, um, old, between us."

"What?"

He sees her as a dream, an entire tapestry – a woman with an aura in the dim light of the room. Her eyes are dark green and continually searching. They look for signs in other humans like a good navigator reads the sea. But tonight they project determined lust. Her eyes *want*.

He'd taken her to the dinner party, where he held court on all things oceanic – kept the other well-heeled guests enthralled – and at the end of the night collected support in the form of three hefty cheques. The dreams he wove of faraway lands. The romance of sailing into uncharted territory.

The lure of gold and silver and spices at the end of the day. He performed and Cassandra bought it all, without question.

When the towel slips and she is as beautiful as he thought she would be, he lives that moment. Breathes deeply. Recognizes vanilla scent. Can smell something spicy above the vanilla. He tries to hold this image of her: the full curve of the bottom of her breast, and the way the light touches her face; the loose strands of her hair at her shoulder, and the shadow between her legs – he wants all of this fixed in his memory. A phone rings somewhere in the villa, in another room. She offers to drag the loud thing down the hall so he can do something with it – stop the ringing sound. "No," he says, "don't worry about it. If it's the queen, I can always call her back tomorrow." "How will you know?" "She'll leave a message," he says. Cassandra wants to ask how the queen will leave a message but she feels she's exposed enough of her ignorance. If Cassandra loved him before, this dismissal of a queen on her behalf caused a rising up of love in her that was not measurable. This was it. This was the man of her dreams.

The phone has prolonged the juxtaposition of skin against the stone texture of the wall for a few seconds longer. Columbus quietly blesses whoever it is that called. This is the conclusion they've been slipping toward.

They are both old enough to highly value restraint. They luxuriate in not touching, the almost-nibble, the withheld kiss, the pulled-back caress. They almost surrender to loving for three blissful hours. Tempt from room to room. Slowly unfurl feelings meant to capture the other. Taunt each other. When they finally give in to desire it is the result of consuming three bottles of thick wine. The wine, and the question. The unspoken question. Do we surrender to this? The question itself is something to love – it becomes a tangible thing. The sound of the leaves rustling beyond the courtyard. The unexpected moon barely above the horizon, big and golden and damaged.

She stands up, naked except for her black pumps. They entwine each other in a dream state of drunkenness and lust. White silk floats above them. Flickering candlelight against a rough stone wall. Mozart's *Requiem* plays from the stereo. They smooth and caress and become gentle with each other. They . . .

"What did you just call me?" Cassandra asks carefully. Columbus stops. Her voice is a cold wire that cuts the room.

"I . . . I was remembering something."

"I think you called me Selena."

"Why would I call you Selena, when clearly your name is, and always shall be, the beautiful combination of consonants and vowels that make the name Cassandra?"

"You've confused me with someone else! Goddamnit, Columbus, at the very least you could get my name right."

Columbus remembers what Juan said about sticky situations with women. When you feel backed into a corner, always tell the truth enthusiastically and they'll likely not believe you.

"I saw Selena two days ago."

"And did you share this with her?"

He pulls away from her in the bed. Seeks her face in the darkness. Breaks from the dream.

"Several times. She is an incredible lover. Such enthusiasm and she's so young. Touching her was like touching a flower that begins to bloom in spring rain."

Cassandra peers at him. Reckons him. She weighs what she knows is true and what she wishes were true. She thinks she can see what he's doing.

"Several times?" she says.

"Many, many times."

"Well then this shouldn't be a problem." She leans toward him and kisses hard. Her loving pushes into recklessness, becomes violent. She is determined to make him pay. She's not certain he slept with this Selena, but she will punish him for calling out Selena's name while he was with her. And now? Now he will never go back to Selena, of course. Columbus is hers. Hers in love. She rakes her fingernails down his back, digging into his skin, bites and sucks at his neck, marks her property.

~ ~ ~

"So this Cassandra is the one you . . . but then how does Selena fit into all of this?" Consuela sips at her coffee. It's too hot, so her sip is more a peck at the surface. She's confused. "Is Cassandra the one you cheated on Beatriz with?"

"I never married Beatriz. I should have. But I did not."

"And that's an excuse for cheating on her?" Columbus takes a gulp of his coffee, which has been cooled by copious amounts of cream and four big spoonfuls of sugar. He looks evenly at her face.

"And what about Mozart?"

"Mozart? I don't know."

"Because his music was playing in your story."

Columbus shrugs. "What difference does it make? I don't remember saying it. Don't know anything about it. This is a story about obsession and discovery, discovery and obsession."

"And a lot of making the fleshy union, I've noticed."

Columbus shrugs again. "I'm frail. I get lonely. I love women. I love all women."

"I see," she says.

"And I love wine. There is nothing like a good bottle of wine."

"I see."

"And being at sea. I love being on the ocean."

She nods.

"And I love the Moorish influence on the architecture in this place. Oh, and I love fishing."

"Moorish influence?"

"Like you didn't know. It's everywhere. The horseshoe-shaped arches, the courtyards – how many are there? four? five? – and the ornate ceilings, and the repetition of geometric and nature-based designs."

Why do you know this, Columbus? she thinks.

~ ~ ~

Columbus finds a table in a corner of the cafeteria, as far away as possible from the chaos of the institute – the crazies with vocal agendas, the wall knockers, the head bangers, the nonstop talkers – the TV constantly droning, never loud enough for anyone, and other rooms with banal, calming music that Columbus finds infuriating. He places his pen at an angle on the notebook, corner to corner. He looks up and across the room to an arched doorway that leads to another room with an arched doorway, and eventually to a small courtyard with a fountain. This fountain is broken. The plumbing is mostly gone and it is a big job to fix it. It offers only a sad dribble of water. Columbus looks down at the pen and paper, then watches with fascination as his hand moves to pick up the pen and begins to write.

(ii)

But he does know about Mozart. He remembers listening to music in a dark room and the name Mozart is connected to this music. There was someone else in the room. He thinks he remembers feeling safe, loved. The sound of the oboe and of French horns building to a powerful chorus, but all within the scope of sadness – the low male voices first, then the female voices joining. A lone female voice extends into the melody. He leans back into a soft couch. The music washes over, through him. Is that a woman over there at the desk in the window, across the room, writing in a journal? Maybe she is writing with a fountain pen because it is what she has always done. The ink is sepia-coloured. Perhaps later on, during the same piece of music, she will push the cap onto her pen, join him on the couch, and lean into his shoulder – float with him for a few minutes.

But who is this memory woman? Is this someone he loves? What does he feel? Why does nothing ever move in these images? No names come. Nothing moves.

He can see the side of her face as she writes but can muster no name for this face, no relationship. The music has a name but not this woman stranded at her desk, suspended in time inside his memory. He knows this beautiful music is Mozart.

There are framed certificates above the desk. Someone in this house has earned degrees from universities. Someone volunteers. There's a certificate of appreciation. He cannot see the names on these certificates. Her chair is leather. It looks comfortable but not so comfortable that it would lull its occupant to sleep.

It's snowing. Snow floats by the window, is caught – made to stand still in the window frame. He remembers feeling something about this snow. Sorrow? It is natural for men and women to sit still occasionally, to ponder, consider, or reflect. But snow, snow in the air has falling as its sole purpose. Movement! This snow needs to move and it's not. This snapshot has stopped the snow.

He's grasping. He knows he's grasping. He'd like to think he's not alone in the world – that somewhere, somebody misses him. He'd like to believe that he's loved, that he loved. But nothing in this picture suggests this. This is just a woman sitting at a desk in what appears to be a study, with snow falling past the window. The music is Mozart, big and sad. That's all the evidence he's got.

There is no verisimilitude about his relationship to any of this. It just is. He can see the books, the degrees on the wall, and the woman writing in her journal. He can see her leather chair and the snow. She may be writing with a fountain pen that has sepia ink. Perhaps he only wants her to come and snuggle with him on the couch. He cannot distinguish what is real from what he desires to be real.

SEVEN

THEY ARE WALKING IN THE lemon orchard on the day of the feast of Saint Cornelius and Saint Cyprian. Clouds are pillowed above the city, as if they were pushed up against an invisible wall. Walking among these yellow globes is a cheerful thing – an antidote to the grey oppression of the clouds.

Consuela plucks a lemon, buffs the dust from its skin, and bites into it. She is prepared, does not make a face in reaction to the sourness. The juice runs down her chin, and she wipes her face with her sleeve.

"Why did you do that?"

"Because I've never done it before," Consuela says.

"And?"

"It was a good lemon. It was a delicious lemon."

They walk in silence for a few minutes. Then Columbus clears his throat.

"I'm not the only one who knew," he says. "In fact, there were many who knew."

Consuela laughs. "You're going to have to brief me a bit better for these conversations where you start halfway through and I'm expected to know what you're talking about."

"Look, all I'm saying is that you could go into a bar, and if it was the right bar and you were a good listener, you found out things about the world. I was in Jaén. I just wanted a glass of wine. In the booth behind me, there was a man named Manuel, who sold Bibles. Apparently he was buying them from a guy who was producing them by the hundreds.

"He called them Gutenberg Bibles. A couple of sailors came in and sat with him. I listened. After much wine, they mentioned they had been driven far out into the Western Sea by a storm. This is something that happens all the time. The important thing is, nothing happened. As far as they could tell, there was just more and more ocean. But while they were out there in the unknown, they saw gulls. It took them twenty-one days to sail home."

"So they saw birds."

"Yes, they saw the kind of birds that indicate land is nearby. They were twenty-one days out. Then one of the sailors said the most extraordinary thing. I almost choked on my wine. This sailor started to talk about a small, dark-skinned corpse in a narrow boat made from a single tree, adrift in the ocean. The other sailor tells him to shut up about it."

Consuela purses her lips.

Columbus looks at her with furrowed brows and such sincerity that she almost feels like giggling.

"What's out there, Consuela? If that's not a clear indication that these men were close to Marco Polo's Japan, then I don't know what is."

~ ~ ~

Apparently somebody other than Dr. Fuentes's wife has been scraping chairs across his office floor in the last few months.

And because the current Mrs. Fuentes started off scraping chairs, she knew when and where to look. She discovers that what she'd suspected was true, and Dr. Fuentes has his back against the wall. Consuela doesn't care. But one hears things. So Dr. Fuentes is distracted, off balance. Perhaps even a little unfocused. His wife is threatening divorce and promising to take the house, the Jaguar, and a holiday home on the coast that's been in the Fuentes family for three hundred years. It appears he's lost interest in, among other things, the Columbus case.

Consuela looks in on Columbus when she arrives for her shift. He's sleeping. His room is more or less unchanged from the day he arrived. There are no pictures of family. No packages of letters. It's austere. He lives like a monk, an ascetic. He has made requests for writing paper and wine – each week he asks for wine from a particular vineyard just outside of La Rábida. Of course, the wine is denied. The writing paper is fine, but not a pen. Pens are not allowed because they are potential thrusting weapons. If he wants to write, he has to go to the common room and sign out a pen.

~ ~ ~

At breakfast, Columbus is quieter than normal. Pope Cecelia is louder than usual. She stands at the doorway to the dining room. Holds out one skinny, shaky arm. "I want to remind you of God's word," she commands. "Remember the Lord your God. You shall have no other gods before Him. You shall not make for yourself any image and nor shall you bow down to them or worship them. You shall not make wrongful

use of the name of the Lord. Remember the Sabbath day –"
She stops.

Mercedes, a short, forty-year-old blonde who is always
hitting on the women in the institute and washes her hands
every ten minutes, stops and listens. "Could happen," she says,
nodding enthusiastically. "Could happen."

Cecelia is lost. She's looking around the room like she recognizes nothing. Consuela's compassion rises up and she
moves to her side.

"I can't remember when the Sabbath is. Which day? How
can I be pope if I can't remember the Sabbath? How can I keep
it holy when I don't know . . ." Tears squeak from her eyes,
flow down her wrinkled cheeks.

"You remember the Sabbath is Sunday, Your Holiness.
I know you do. Six days of work, and then the seventh, Sunday,
you rest."

"Keep the Sabbath holy – Sunday's a holy day, that's right.
The Sabbath is Sunday. And you must honour your mother
and your father," she says. "Thou shalt not murder, nor
commit adultery. Nor steal –"

"Nothing wrong with stealing," Mercedes says. "I steal all
the time."

"Nor shall you bear false witness, or covet your neighbour's
wife, or ox, or donkey –" She stops, looks at Consuela with an
expression that is almost an offer to add something. "And that's
it, then. You may eat!" She makes the sign of the cross in the
air in front of her.

Almost everybody is eating already. They're so used to
these pre-meal holy rants, most don't even hear them anymore.

Consuela fills her coffee mug and sits beside Columbus. "Good morning," she says quietly, evenly.

He ignores her, shovels more scrambled eggs into his mouth, slurps at his orange juice.

"Good morning, my ass," he mumbles.

Elena, a tall blond woman with slender fingers, who does not speak, is sitting across from Columbus. She smiles. Columbus has never seen, or heard, Elena speak a single word. Nothing in all his time at the institute. He heard from one of the orderlies that there is no physical reason for her muteness. She just stopped speaking. There are days when he can relate.

"Did you just call me an ass?" Consuela asks.

Elena smiles again. She places her mug of coffee carefully on the table.

"What in particular is good about this morning? Perhaps it's good for you because you get to leave. This is your job. You come, you go. This" – he looks around the dining hall and gestures, points with open hands – "this, is my life. No leaving. You get to go out into the world and have a glass of wine, make love, sleep until noon if you want. I am not free. I am completely surrounded by crazy people." He looks across the table at Elena. "I don't think you're crazy, by the way." Elena nods.

"It is not a good morning, Nurse Consuela. It won't be a good morning until I am waking up with a beautiful woman. A woman with curves like waves. A woman whom I love. A woman who will drink wine with me and drift inside a dream about the other side of the ocean. So fuck off with your cheery greetings."

Consuela stands up. The thing is, she was trying not to be too cheery. She is aware that this is an institution.

"Sit," he says. "I'm grumpy. I'm sorry."

Consuela sits down but she's bristling, hesitant.

"There was a morning – in my memory – when I was very happy."

"Oh really. What was her name?" She takes a sip of coffee.

He looks at her with a pitying, downward glance. "I was with my son."

Well, she thinks, at least my feet are getting clean from sticking them in my mouth so often this morning.

~ ~ ~

Morning does not come quickly when one is looking for it. It becomes a lugubrious, lumbering animal that moves only when it wishes. Yet mornings are inevitable. This one had sifted in through thick clouds on a blanket of fear. Columbus only hopes that they have successfully crossed the border from Portugal into Spain. He and his son, Diego, have been alternating between walking and running all night, and now they arrive inside a thick fog.

We must be safe now, Columbus is thinking. We must be across the border. We should stop at an inn and ask just to make sure. If I were at sea, I would know exactly where I was. If I could have seen the stars last night, I would have been able to tell when we crossed over.

"Why are we leaving, Papa? Did we do something wrong?" Diego is six years old. He has been quiet most of the night and now, as he begins to get hungry, he also begins to hunger for information.

"No, I said some things to the king and the king didn't like what I said. That's all. That's why we're leaving."

A long pause. The boy is tired, has been travelling at a severe adult pace along the dusty roads all night. It's finally morning. Travelling at night is dangerous – insanity, some would say. Wild animals and desperate, vicious people lurked at the edges of highways at night. These two had had little choice but they'd been lucky. They'd met no one, heard a rustling in the bushes twice but that was all.

"What did you say to the king, Papa?"

"Some things about taking chances. Some things about taking risks if you ever want to achieve greatness. Some things about guts. And I guess the king took the things I said to heart."

"Who were those men with swords?"

"They were some of the king's friends."

"Did they want to hurt us?"

"They were angry. They wanted a map created by a man named Toscanelli."

"Did they find it?"

"Actually, they did not find the map they sought. They did find a map, but not the one they were seeking. They couldn't tell the difference."

"What was so great about the map?"

"Well, Toscanelli felt we could get to the Indies by sailing west to an island called Antilla, and then beyond to the Indies and Japan. He figured Antilla was a halfway point toward the Indies. Well, he put Antilla on a map, and a little bit more."

"I'm tired, Papa."

They come over a rise in the road and see the lights of a small village. A few shops, a stable, and farther down the street, an inn. As they approach the town, Columbus can see several young men leaning against the front wall of the first shop, talking.

"Look, Diego, someone here can tell us where we are. Someone can tell us if we are yet in Spain."

Father and son walk inside – side-glance at the leaning boys.

"Hello," a woman says. "How are you today?" She stands behind the counter smiling at them benignly. She has long brown hair pulled back into a ponytail that reaches down the middle of her back to just above her buttocks.

Columbus bows to her. "My lady," he says, "we have just come from Portuguese territory and I was wondering if in fact we had crossed over into Spain."

"Huh?"

He then tries the same question in Spanish with the same result. He attempts the question in English, then French, then Portuguese again. She seems to be permanently confused, addled beyond hope.

"Is this Spain?"

"Spain?"

"Yes, I need to know if this is Spain."

"Spain is a good country, yes?" She smiles kindly.

How can this woman not be aware of where she is?

Columbus places his hand on the hilt of his sword. Grips it firmly. Visualizes this woman's discombobulated head rolling on the clean floor, dumb smile fully intact. But then realizes she may be muddled in her mind. This may not be her fault. But then why was she in this position of responsibility?

"Come, Diego, we're going."

Diego has picked up a chocolate bar.

"Put that down. It's bad for you."

"But, Papa –"

"I said no."

The boys outside are gone, which makes Columbus twitchy. Where are they? He and Diego move swiftly through what Columbus hopes is the village of Palos. They try to stay in the light, avoid the back alleys. They do not encounter another soul. This, too, worries Columbus. Finally they walk slowly up a long hill to what Columbus hopes is the Franciscan monastery at La Rábida. There is no sign. There were no signs. Nothing that indicated a location. Columbus is beginning to think he's in a bad dream. Apart from the fact that it looks like every monastery he's ever seen – stone walls around an enclosed inner courtyard, the thick wooden door – he's nowhere near certain this actually is a monastery. He is tired beyond tired, paranoid, and scared. He knocks on the door, then turns around to see if anybody has followed. He knocks again. He's not thinking straight – and the boy cannot be expected to go any farther. Either they are in Spain and safe, or he will beg sanctuary at this monastery.

Father Antonio de Marchena opens the door. By necessity, this is a slow and hesitant movement. The father has a friendly, welcoming face. He is not an old man but is accustomed to being around older men, and so his body language is mismatched to his age: he moves a bit slower than he needs to and squints when he doesn't really need to squint. His physical health is fine, and his eyes are perfect. One could not say the father is fat, but he is certainly well fed, and there is, of course, a vineyard attached to the monastery.

~ ~ ~

"You what?" Father Antonio says, smiling.

They have been sampling the wine, an amber-coloured white with an earthy, nutty flavour, served slightly chilled with cheese and bread on the side. The monks have been producing the Condado Pálido wine for as long as the oldest of them remembers.

"In retrospect, it was not wise. But I was angry. And it was only the truth."

"I hope if you ever get a chance to pitch your idea to Ferdinand, that you apply a little more tact."

Diego is sleeping, and while Columbus was tempted to sleep as well, there was something in him that would not stop. He was too wound up. Columbus was relieved to learn that they were, in fact, in Spain.

"King John does not joke around. If he sent men after you, you'd do well to align yourself with a different king or queen. What did you say?"

"He's an imbecile. I told him he was an imbecile. Sometimes these things just come out, especially when I am faced with an enormous stupidity."

"Kings and queens are rarely wise – they're certainly not born with any special degree of intelligence. Decisions are thrust upon them, and if they have good advisers, they sometimes make good choices. But it is even more difficult to rule if your main concern is hanging on to an empire to rule. The people tend to get lost along the way."

"Three months! They had enough information to make a decision in a week, a few days. But they took three months! What in hell were they doing all that time? I offered them a direct route to the kingdom of the khan. A direct route to Marco Polo's Asia."

"They were waiting for news of the African route to the East Indies."

"Yes, I know. Many have attempted –"

"You don't know, do you?"

"Know what?"

"Dias is back. He found a way around the southern point of Africa."

"Dias made it?" Columbus's face goes white. He hears the fire in the corner. He knows a fire like this ought to take the chill from the room, but he is cold to the bone. The light from the fire flickers in the wine. Dias found a new route to the Indies and made it back. Dias made it.

Father Antonio waits until the stone of this news has had time to sink to the bottom of whatever water exists inside Columbus. He does not mind the silence – respects the enormity of such news to a navigator, especially to one who wishes to cross an uncharted ocean.

Columbus begins to embrace all the doubts that have been lurking in the shadows of his hope.

"There is no question about this?"

"None."

"I was plan B, then. Never seriously considered." Columbus drifts into the realization he'd only been humoured for the past months.

"It seems that way."

"Have you more of this wine?"

Father Antonio pours – fills his glass.

"Getting stupid with wine will not make Dias go away. Nor will it buttress your belief in the western route. Nor will it get you an audience with the Catholic kings. And it will only temporarily make you feel better."

"I am told it is very difficult to meet with the king and queen. It may be years before I can plead my case. So I'll take feeling better temporarily. Tonight, *temporary* is plenty."

"And tomorrow morning?"

"I am only here, right now. Tomorrow morning is not important. I am alive and my son is safe. This wine is excellent."

"Then let me offer a small lecture, just in case you decide to press ahead with your scheme. Ferdinand and Isabella need money. They're spread thin with the war against the Moors in Granada, and problems with infrastructure, and pressure to get rid of the Jews. Even Portugal is sabre rattling, poking around for a fight. So money is the key. If you can promise money, with only a small amount to fund your venture up front, you'll get your ships."

"I definitely need more wine."

"I know that nothing I say will cure what ails you. But proving the Portuguese wrong, making the western route a reality – bringing home gold and riches – this will gall King

John more than anything else you could do. But you are right. This sort of talk is for tomorrow. Sailing off the edge of the world is a morning conversation." He smiles and the missing teeth on the upper left side of his mouth become obvious.

Columbus sighs. "Tonight, my fine little monk, I do not wish to be cheered, or hopeful, or happy. I am disheartened and this is not a crime. I am without hope – also not a crime. And thanks to you, I am safe. I only wish to be lost in this wine, warmed by this fire . . . and then sleep. Tomorrow, tomorrow will take care of itself."

"Okay, okay, wallow in self-pity tonight, but take this little bit of information to bed with you Mr. Columbus." The monk stands up, tosses another hunk of wood onto the fire. "I can get you an audience with the queen. Next week." Father Antonio gently pulls the door shut behind him. Just before the door clicks, he adds: "Close your mouth Mr. Columbus, or the flies will get in. Sleep well."

~ ~ ~

In the morning, Diego has already eaten breakfast and is playing in the courtyard with an orange cat when Columbus lifts his sorry head from the pillow.

"Coffee," he says in the dining hall. He feels sick to his stomach – does not know for sure if the coffee will stay down but he's willing to try. It's more for the comfort, the normalcy of drinking coffee in the morning. He hopes the routine will dispel the pain in his head. He takes his mug, sits in the shade of an enormous oak, and watches Diego.

Father Antonio sits down behind him. "This came for you this morning," he says, handing Columbus an envelope. "It's scented."

Columbus sniffs at the envelope. Sickeningly sweet and pungent. He places it beside him on the ground and closes his eyes. "Just kill me," Columbus says.

Father Antonio hands him a mug. "Drink this. All of it."

"What?"

"Just do it. It's a sort of whisky mixed with cream and sugar. You won't exactly be out of pain, but you won't care."

Columbus drinks the thick liquid and almost immediately no longer feels nauseated. Eventually he rips open the envelope. It's a rhyming birthday card but it's not his birthday. It won't be his birthday for months. It's signed, "Love, Cassandra."

"Good news I hope," the father says.

"Birthday greetings but it's not my birthday."

"So good wishes but at the wrong time."

"How long have I been here?"

"You and Diego arrived last night. You were well-met." The father smiles, pours more of the creamy liquid into Columbus's mug.

"How is it that I got mail when just last night I could not have told you where I was?"

~ ~ ~

Consuela wakes up with a start and in a sweat. She was dreaming about fishing. She and Columbus were fishing somewhere in the mountains. There were several bottles of wine cooling in the stream. The air was fresh and exquisite. She remembers breathing deeply and drawing great pleasure from the scents of pine, the forest bottom, the water, and the alpine flowers, which seemed to be everywhere she looked.

He said he loved fishing – how many days ago was that? But the subject of fishing has never come up again. At the time, she'd thought, well, sure, you go to sea and there are fish in the ocean. Good that you like fishing. Better that you like eating fish. But this fishing in her dream, in a stream with a long pole and a snaky line, is something quite different than she imagined.

"It's like throwing," Columbus had said in her dream. He was wearing hip waders, a khaki shirt, and a duckbill hat, and smiling. His hair looked healthy – was pulled back into that ridiculous ponytail he likes. His eyes were penetrating, alive. He was beaming.

She was naked. Completely naked, standing in the cold water up to her crotch, her feet grounded in the sand beneath the stones. But her nakedness seemed ordinary. He barely looked at her. It was as if she was always naked. She did not feel the cold. The water sporadically splashed her hips and belly. Eventually she got the hang of it, managed to cast the line along the surface of the water to where she wanted it to go, and caught several fish. In the dream, Consuela enjoyed standing in the water with the mountain peaks in the distance, fingers of white down the slopes, the pines enclosing the stream, the sun on her skin, the sunlight splicing, glancing off the water and sparkling in her eyes.

Then they were eating the fish out of a frying pan, over a

fire. The fish were fried in butter – he throws crushed pepper and salt on top. He moves the fish around the pan with a stick. She and Columbus eat the fish and drink the wine. It's white wine in the stream. Three bottles of a sturdy pinot grigio. They drink from the bottle. The wine bursts with flavour – pear and hints of apple. It is so cold it hurts her teeth. She does not dress herself. It was not an option. Nor does Columbus notice she is without clothing. It does not seem to matter.

When Consuela wakes up, it's her nakedness in his eyes that is distressing. At the bottom of her discomfort is the realization that in this dream of fishing in the mountains with Columbus, she was happy. This happiness, despite her vulnerability. She can't remember the last time she felt so happy.

~ ~ ~

Columbus is lying face down on the massage table. His snoring thunders like an ugly rasping storm as Tammy massages his back and upper shoulders. She's been working on him for half an hour. He's been asleep for ten minutes. He moaned with pleasure for the first twenty.

Somewhere down the hall of D wing a telephone is ringing. There is no machine attached to this phone and it's not forwarded to reception, so it rings for a good long time. Each ring has a cutting edge to it. This is no twitter. There are sharp-toned bells in this phone. Finally the caller gives up.

~ ~ ~

"It's for you," Beatriz says. "It's a woman." She swishes quickly from the room and Columbus calls after her.

"What's for me?"

"That thing there," she says, her voice a cold echo down the stone hallway. "There's a voice in it asking for you. You should pick it up and speak to it."

He picks it up and brings it close to his mouth.

Hesitantly. "Hello?"

"Columbus, it's me."

He looks around the room. Stone walls, simple wooden furniture, a tapestry, and four candles on a simple table.

"Hello?" he says.

"It's Isabella, Chris."

He thinks he should stand, or bow, or something. Realizes he's already standing and does not really know what he would bow to. Finally he takes off his hat.

"Your Majesty," he says.

"Look, just listen. I have to meet you. The deal is going to fall through."

"What?" He cannot hear the specific words she speaks. He only hears the loveliness of her voice. An excitement overwhelms him. Her voice is a hymn. I must be dreaming, he thinks. This cannot be real. The queen is in Barcelona. Either I am dreaming or I am mad.

"Chris," she screams. "Do you hear me? The deal is going down in flames. Las Palos has the king's ear and he says you can't make it. The king is listening. You have to get your skinny little ass to court and fight for your ships."

"I think I am having a dream," he says. "But it's the middle of the morning. I am awake, yet –"

"No, it's me, Isabella. Do you hear me? Las Palos says the world is bigger than you say it is. He says you're way off in your calculations. You have to tell the king what you told me. You have to show him the things you showed me. I've set up an appointment for you –"

"You are in my dream. I can hear you but I cannot see you. You sound far away but still wonderful. I can see your face only if I close my eyes."

"You stupid ass, get your head out of the clouds."

"Yes, Your Majesty, my queen. I will get my head out of the clouds."

Then faintly: "Scribe! We're going to have to write him. This isn't going to work. Our Columbus is apparently incoherent. Get me a courier for this letter. Hurry up!"

Columbus hears muffled voices, then the queen again, crystal clear.

"What? No. A courier, not a courtier."

Columbus puts the thing down and wanders out into the garden. A most interesting experience, he thinks. I am hearing the queen's voice in my head. Perhaps I have gone mad. Perhaps tonight I will bark at the moon, renounce my faith in God, and be burned painfully and efficiently by the bloody Inquisition.

~ ~ ~

Beatriz comes to get him in the map room. He is there with his bottle of wine every afternoon, studying the charts. Sometimes he is quiet and solemn. Other times he rages in the small room, paces frantically.

"They're stuck in their minds! They still think Jerusalem is the centre of the world. And regardless of the facts, they do not budge. They do not perform geography. They create statements of Christian dogma. Their *orbis terrarum*, their *mappae mundi* are more philosophical statements than maps. The Church knows nothing about mapmaking!"

Beatriz approaches from behind and starts to massage his shoulders. She begins to take the tension from him with strong, loving hands. Then quietly, he says, "If Jesus had lived in the Canary Islands I would have already been across the Western Sea to the Indies and back again. Stupid ignorant bastards."

"You will go to petition the king and queen again?" she says. She can feel the tightness creep into the muscles in his upper back.

"Las Palos is going to be trouble. He knows as well as I do that the distance is much farther than my calculations show. But he does not know how far exactly, just that it is farther."

"What will you do?"

"Well, if I let it be known the true distance is far greater than what I have said in public already, I won't be able to man a rowboat, let alone three or four ships. I need at least three caravels."

"You cannot lie, Cristóbal."

"I don't know how I can't lie. Las Palos and his band of *bastardos* have the king's ear. What can I do? The truth is not known exactly."

"What can you do?"

"I might have to have Las Palos killed," he says in a whisper, barely speaking the words. A subconscious undertow of fear nags at him. "There are men . . ."

She stops her massage. Columbus reaches across his chest to her hand on his shoulder.

"Just a morbid thought. It will not ever come to that."

"What will you really do?"

"He is a small-minded bumbler. He has no art. There is no adventure and no conviction in him. He is dry, dead with his calculations. He may as well be dead."

"But you say he is right?"

"Of course he is right! He may be dead inside but he is utterly brilliant!"

"So you truly do not know how far –"

"I have no idea." Columbus drinks from the goblet. "While this is an unfortunate truth, it is also true that Las Palos does not know either, exactly."

"And you will go to the university court and fight him?"

"I will have to be louder, bolder, and inspire with words of gold and spices and riches. I'll have to promise things to this poor cash-starved monarchy. I will have to use my wit." He sighs heavily. "Mostly, I will have to be louder and bolder."

"And at the same time as you try to impress the royals, will you anger those of the Inquisition?"

"This nags at me every day. I will have to hope that the idea of profit rules even those of the Inquisition. And after all, I will be discovering whatever there is to discover in the name of God, and king, and queen. God first, of course."

Beatriz stands in front of a large chart that hangs from a rod, near the wall. Her eyes are drawn to the blank area in the western zone. She thinks about the blankness of it. She remembers swimming beyond land's sight, getting to the place where there was only water and how lonely it felt, and the small, gnawing fear in her stomach. She cannot imagine only seeing the water in the four directions, and for weeks at a time. She cannot imagine the faith it would take. *I am going to lose him to the unknown*, she thinks. *I've already lost him. He sees nothing but the blankness there. It pulls him.*

She touches the unknown area on the chart with three fingers, and then presses the palm of her hand there. Closes her eyes, wishes to feel something, imprint safety, imprint her love there.

"What is it that you feel?"

"Fear," she says quickly and without thinking. She turns to look at him. Green eyes flashing. "And I feel a small amount of excitement."

"Excitement?" he says.

"The unknown."

"But they say there is nothing there. They say there is only the uncrossable Western Sea. They insist that we know the entire world already, that there is nothing new to discover."

"There are the stories you speak of," she says.

"Stories that should never be repeated."

"I know, my love, but what about the dark-skinned man in the treeboat? And the Norseman?"

"Also not to be repeated," he says.

"I know, my love." She walks to the window, places her hands gently on the sill, and looks out. It is hot and bright, clean-smelling. The sun is directly above. A tiny breeze moves from the sea to the land. There is a becalmed, midnight quiet in the courtyard. The sound of the sea is there but it does not remain in the conscious. It circles to the back and lurks with heartbeats, birdsong, and the wind in the leaves.

She pulls herself up into the open window frame and stands on the ledge.

Columbus leans back in his chair and watches. He smiles, takes a gulp of wine, nods to himself. He does not feel the urge to save her. She does not need saving. She certainly does not need warning. He finds this very interesting.

Beatriz begins to remove her clothing. Her dress, shoes, stockings, and undergarments all fall from the window. They drop the forty feet to the ground until she is naked. The warm flesh tones of her body contrast the harsh brightness of the day. The cool stone ledge is a luxury to her bare feet.

Columbus is bewitched. He begins to feel the strong warmth of love welling up inside him. What a woman to love. You have my complete attention, he thinks. I am watching you with all my heart.

~ ~ ~

Do you see me? she's thinking. Do you see me standing on the edge of this world? I am your mistress, not your wife, and you should know it does not matter. But because I am your mistress, *I* am on the edge of your world. Do you see me standing on the edge of this life? Do you see me standing on the edge of what is accepted? I wish to be with you. Am I with you now? Am I?

She does not turn around.

"What if I was to jump?" she whispers.

"Perhaps, you would be dead." He is standing directly behind her.

"And what you propose to do is so different?"

"Yes," he says. "There is no edge of the world, there is only distance."

"But there is the unknown."

Columbus laughs.

She lifts her foot and there is a faint sweaty impression on the stone. She places her foot back inside the imprint.

"Each next moment is the unknown," he says. "A moment ago I would not have dreamed you here on the ledge, without clothing, beautiful."

Beatriz almost turns to face him but stops halfway. "Will you remember that for your defence against Las Palos?"

"Yes, I will remember it."

"Good," she says.

She turns around. Columbus lifts her off the ledge, moves her to the table, places her on top of the layers of charts. He begins to kiss her and she begins to whimper. It is the hot, dead space in the day. They bathe in the sweet scent of the sun. Their loving is slow and gentle and hazy. The only roughness is the near-empty bottle of wine that falls to the floor and breaks. And the charts. Beatriz perspires and there are areas of sweat where her body presses. The contour of her body is imprinted. The sweat lines from her buttocks carve a crease across the unknown area.

~ ~ ~

They are curled on the table, side by side, two cats in late afternoon sun.

"When will you go to the university?"

"Tomorrow."

"You will propose your journey to the scholars?"

"Yes, to the close-minded dead people," Columbus says, smiling.

"But you will be careful? And treat them with the respect they require?"

"Yes. But it is hopeless. I know what they will find."

"Don't say that."

"They have already decided but I must do this anyway. Perhaps I will sway a few in the process."

"But if it is truly hopeless, why do you do it?"

"For the queen."

"Oh," Beatriz says, a coolness to her voice.

"The queen is the only hope I have. If she likes the idea and can see I have tried to obtain permission for the journey her way, perhaps she will overrule or just ignore the university. If I can convince her in the end, there is hope. Even then, it depends on the king and queen getting rid of the bloody Moors."

"It seems such a long journey just to begin another long journey."

"Yes, it does. But there is much profit to be made in this adventure."

"Profit?" Beatriz says. "Surely profit is not the true reason you wish to sail across the sea."

"Nothing is done for the simple love of doing. Nothing worthy anyway. There must be a profit of some kind or nothing would get done."

"I do not wish to live in that world." She moves like a sleek feline to the wall where a sword hangs and pulls it from its sheath. She thrusts it at him and kneels down. "Take this sword and plunge it into my heart. Take it!"

He takes the sword and places it on the floor.

"Can't you see that profit and commerce make the world run? We have often spoken about the Church and its love of money and power. I will not get my ships if I do not promise a profit. Gold, silver, and spices."

"This is a world I despise." She picks up the blade and pushes it into his hands. He throws it across the room and it clangs loudly against the stone wall.

"All right, Beatriz," he says. "All right. Mostly I wonder what is there. I have a mad wonder in me. Is that what you wish to hear?"

"You're not just saying this to please me?"

"No. I have to know what's out there." Columbus sighs, walks across the room to a window, looks down into the courtyard. A cat stretches, then sits in a shady spot, licks its paw. There are no clouds in sight. Just sunlight and perfect blue from the horizon all the way into the heavens. "Sometimes I get so caught up in the money, and ships, and crewmen, and supplies I will need that I begin to lose sight of the reason." He turns around. "It's simple, Beatriz. I have always wanted to find out what's out there in the unknown."

"Now I wish to live again," she says, smiling.

"But still, I will have to beg the bankers and the scholars and the kings for the ships to satisfy this wonder."

"Can't you convince them that you are right?"

He smiles. "It is difficult when one does not know if one *is* right."

"I am certain that you are right," she says.

"You shouldn't be."

"Yes, I should."

"In the end, it comes down to one woman," Columbus says. "I have to convince one woman that I might be right."

"One other woman."

He sighs and sits down heavily on a chair against the wall. "I must convince a queen. All of this game playing and risk is to persuade one damned woman. It's not going to be the steadfast scholars, or the bankers, or the shipbuilders, or really anybody in Spain, except for that one woman. Her and her aristocratic friends."

"The queen," Beatriz says.

"Yes, the queen," he says. "Remember, Beatriz, nothing truly inspired or beneficial to mankind has ever been accomplished by asking for an agreement from the masses. It's the elite. It's the elitists who drive society forward."

"To the queen then." Beatriz raises her glass.

"Yes," Columbus says. "To Isabella."

~ ~ ~

Two days later, just before he leaves for the university, Columbus makes one of his most important discoveries. He finds a crease in the chart – the one upon which he and Beatriz made love. He makes an important decision. He takes a huge leap of faith. Columbus decides the crease is the route to the Indies. He decides he will follow the map of his love for Beatriz. From the crease in the far western unknown area where he hopes to find the Indies, he draws a line back toward the known world, across the Western Sea, to find his starting point: the Canary Islands.

EIGHT

EMILE PLACES THE TV remote on the bedside table. He's been in Córdoba for two days – poking around, looking for something, anything that might be a clue to the whereabouts of his mysterious man. It's 5 A.M. He crawls into the shower to try and shake off his dream, which was more a lucid memory. Perhaps the dream is a bit more violent than the memory. There's more broken glass. More screaming. More shame.

It was six months after the shooting and he was slated to return to duty. Emile shows up at the Lyon office. Everyone is smiling and happy to see him back at work. He's ushered into a meeting before he can get settled. In the boardroom, there's a man wearing a bad tie and a cheap suit talking about the importance of something called an augmented business planning process and managing risk. There's a three-day seminar on risk management this man highly recommends. He somehow segues into the vision and values of their organization. When he fires up his PowerPoint presentation, with whirling text and fading screens and headings that outline the levels of bureaucratic functioning of Interpol's role in the overall security scheme for the European Union, Emile starts to lose control. At first it's just a twitch. He's holding tightly to a company coffee mug and the twitch jerks his hand – creates a splash that almost escapes the mug. He wants to run from the room before anything bad happens. He knows something bad will happen if this man continues his earnest presentation. Emile starts to actually see hazy silos of information, silos of processes, silos of small-brained bureaucrats like this man, and none of these silos communicate in person – they all e-mail each other, copy subordinates and sub-subordinates, obscure information; rewrite memos dozens of times, make simple memos into academic dissertations so laden with cover-your-own-ass modifiers that they become meaningless. Emile breaks into a cold sweat. His breathing becomes shallow and quick. He worries that he's going to say something stupid. But he can't move. At least not right away. Emile remembers thinking: It can't last much longer. It's got to be over soon. But it doesn't end. The presentation goes on for another fifty minutes, with no end in sight. Finally Emile has had enough. The dull man asks if there are any questions. Emile stands up. "What is the relevance of any of this?" he says. He draws his gun and fires two shots at the projector, which is suspended from the boardroom ceiling. The projector falls and shatters the glass table, which collapses on top of the people who have taken cover under it. Emile remembers holstering his gun and going home. They let him go home. They admit his return to work was premature. His bosses insist on more therapy. He was apparently suffering from something called post-traumatic stress disorder. Nothing to be ashamed of, they said. Happens to the best of us.

In his dream about shooting the projector, there are glass windows all around – nothing made of glass ever makes it through his dream intact. In one version of the dream, the presenter gets shot. Just shot, not killed. His therapist had a field day with that particular wrinkle.

~ ~ ~

He's been to most of the bars and cafés around the main roads that skirt the edge of Córdoba. He's tried to stay away from the A-4, but he now finds himself in a small nook of a bar called El Gatito, just off the Autovia del Sur – the highway that runs mostly uninterrupted from Madrid to Cádiz.

Emile sticks his nose into the opening of the glass, inhales the peaty, sweet aroma of the whisky, then looks up to meet Carmen's eyes.

"I have no doubt in my mind, addled as it is by this brilliant whisky, that God is a human invention. We invented God, and now he's got to go. It's time we grew up."

"I have no doubt in my mind that you are too much with the Scottish beverage," she says.

The day he'd arrived in Córdoba, Emile had done a circuit of bars and cafés closest to the train station, asking his open-ended questions, gently prodding. "He probably has better Spanish than I do," Emile would say, a line that always got them smiling, and added an immediate layer of trust. Emile used this self-deprecatory statement about his ability to speak Spanish when, actually, his Spanish is very good. As is his English. His Italian? Not so good. Spanish was a cradle language for Emile. His mother was Spanish; his father, French.

There was a nanny for a few years, a woman who spoke English – loved American films. His limited Italian can be credited to a long-ago lover.

~ ~ ~

Emile had started to doubt this approach. Four days in Córdoba and nothing. He would be hard pressed to say what it was exactly that caused him to strike up a conversation with an elderly man feeding the birds in the park just off Avenida de Cervantes. It was just after noon. He'd been on his way to visit Carmen at El Gatito. Maybe it was a hunch. It was more likely dumb luck. Perhaps it was the fact that this park was only a stone's throw from the train station. Regardless of the motivation, the conversation paid off. The old man, who was wearing baggy grey flannel trousers, a pressed white shirt, and a black sports jacket, had seen a man wandering the street with a stick stuck into his belt like a sword. "It was a couple of months ago, maybe a little less than two months. He was talking to himself. Fighting demons, you know? He was dirty. Dirty hair and clothing. I thought he might be on something or drunk. But he was just strange."

"What did he say, exactly?"

"Nonsense. Half sentences about sailing. Something about navigation. But there was something warm about him. He didn't seem dangerous."

The old man tosses a handful of crumbs onto the ground and immediately the pigeons are there at his feet. "This man said the North Star was not always true. He kept repeating this. He said he wanted me to remember that the North Star was not always true."

"What do you think that means?" Emile says.

The old man looks overtop of his glasses at Emile. "He's crazy. That's what it means. He's crazy, but nice. I gave him directions to Jaén. I told him about my brother-in-law's place in Castro del Rio. It's on the way to Jaén. My brother-in-law rents a few rooms out. I don't like my brother-in-law too much."

"The North Star is not true?"

"Yes, he said it just like that. Though his inflections were odd; he sounded like he came from the north. I felt sorry for him. I gave him a few euros."

In the morning, Emile will follow the trail east. If this is my man, he's certainly not travelling in a straight line toward Morocco. But this feels right. Emile can feel it in his gut.

~ ~ ~

Emile takes a gulp of his whisky. "I'm drunk only on your beauty," he says to Carmen. He stops. Finds her eyes again. "Tired lines like that do you a disservice, Carmen. I apologize. Perhaps I am too much with the Scottish beverage."

Truth be told, Emile is worried about his liver. He thinks he drinks too much and is concerned his liver is not able to keep up with its detoxification function. He worries but he does not curb his drinking. He'll wake up in the middle of the night and know for certain he has cirrhosis because of his drinking, or that he's dying of hepatitis because he drank something bad somewhere in his travels.

His ex-wife used to lean over and check the time, and then try to calm him down. She'd go through all the symptoms she could remember, some of which he had. He gets headaches sometimes. He gets fatigued occasionally.

"Calm down, Em. Breathe. We all get headaches," she'd say. "We all get tired. Come to bed before one or two in the morning and you won't be so tired."

He still stays up too late. He still gets the headaches occasionally. And he is still worried that his liver is ruined. He will not allow his drinking to interfere with his work, but there are times when he is not certain where the line between work and life is drawn – and he drinks in this grey area.

It's the kindness in Carmen's face that has kept him coming back to this café for the past two days. There seems to be a built-in compassion – an acceptance of anything he might have to say. Her eyes are hazel. Her eyes seem to listen – as if they can follow the words in the air. Emile shakes his head, watches her pour beer at the end of the bar. Her hair is cropped blond, thick, and seemingly ruled only by its brevity. She has a grey sweater under her white apron. The sweater is unravelling a bit at the back, along the bottom. It must be a favourite sweater, he thinks. He has no idea what the landscape under that sweater might look like and this is part of Carmen's beauty. The sweater makes a mystery. Or in the heat of noon, a baggy T-shirt makes a mystery. Yesterday he'd heard a table of customers comment on how crowded her balcony is, referring to Carmen's breasts. But he does not really care how crowded it is there. And Emile does not know if, in fact, she is kind. Any appearance of kindness is untested. She has been a good listener, though, and there is kindness in this.

If only I had a euro for every proposition, proclamation of beauty, or pass, Carmen thinks. But this guy has a damaged charm she finds interesting. And he's tall. He's taller than she is, which makes him rare and attractive in her eyes. She's six feet. He must be six two. It's not much but she will not be with a man shorter than herself. This is one of her rules. He is not wearing a wedding ring, but for Carmen it would not matter if he was. In fact, he would be more attractive if he was. She does not acknowledge it, but she is attracted to unavailable men. There is safety in this condition. He has never mentioned a woman. On his first night at the bar he spoke about love. The next day he asked pointedly what it was women wanted, to which Carmen had no answer. Half the time she has no idea why she moves toward a particular man. In her thirty-five years, she's not kept anyone around for longer than ten months.

She does know a little about her likes and dislikes. For instance, Carmen does not care about hair. Men who attempt to cover it up, disguise it, or solve it she finds annoying. Men who lose their hair with grace – this, she finds very sexy. Emile is such a man. He's thinning but seems not to care. His hair at the front is wistful. He wears glasses that seem a throwback to the thirties or forties, gold-coloured wire-rimmed glasses that hook around his ears. She recalls seeing them sitting on a pile of papers, him rubbing his eyes. She remembers thinking the guy must work hard. She has no idea what he does. She knows he is looking for someone. She thought she saw a gun behind his hip on the left but dismissed this as her imagination – it was probably a cell phone.

"We're alone," Emile says. He sighs. "We look up into the sky at night, and we feel terribly alone. This is the reason we invented God. At least, it's the reason our gods are still around. In the beginning, I'm sure we were trying to explain the weather, or why volcanoes erupted, or why hunting expeditions failed. But now? Now religion only holds us back. If we are to evolve as a species, religion must be punted to the wayside. It explains nothing – is based in nothing but fear and loneliness."

"But what about faith?" she says. "What about ritual and holiness?" She deftly removes his glass and slides a clean one into place – then half fills the new glass with whisky.

"We do not need religion to have rituals. We can be holy about all the things that place us in a state of awe or wonder. Things like beauty. Art. Poetry. Music. A child's laughter. Love. These are the things we should find holy. This is where holiness lives."

"And faith?"

"We should have faith in each other."

"Not always an easy thing."

"Well, I have faith in your kindness, in your compassion, in the way you listen with your eyes."

"Faith?"

"Yes, though I have never witnessed an overt act of kindness or compassion, I have faith that you possess these qualities, based on nothing but my observations of you."

"Sometimes faith is misplaced, misguided, wrong – is it not?"

"Oh, now you're turning me on."

Oh my. There's the line, she thinks. It's dangerous because she's fascinated, amused, and enjoying herself. They have danced toward the line, and now it's there, in plain view – easy enough to cross. She's very interested in pushing across this line with Emile, but she hesitates. He must recognize this because he pulls back from it. He stands up, places too much money on the bar, and gathers his bag.

"Until next time, Carmen. I will continue to hold my faith in you. Tomorrow I must continue my search." And then he's on the street; Emile, thick with whisky, part of the human landscape of Córdoba at night. Tomorrow I will be a bit closer to finding this man who inspires loyalty in strangers, Emile thinks. Tomorrow we will unravel a bit more of this puzzle.

"*Buenas noches,* Emile," Carmen whispers to the empty room.

~ ~ ~

Emile wakes up with a dull ache in the back of his head. He does not question what it was that caused this stunning ache but, rather, vows to not let it happen again. He searches his bag for the pain medication. What was it that Hemingway used to call it? The medicine. He looks for the medicine. He finds the small plastic bottle and pops two pills in his mouth, grabs a bottle of water from the minibar, and gulps them down. In the Hemingway book, the pills were dropped and rolled under the bed, and a cat helped find them. Emile can't remember the name of the book and chalks up this lapse to the hangover. He downs two espressos in the café on the ground floor of his hotel, and is on the road to Castro del Rio in under an hour. He stops for gas, and in addition to the gas he buys two CDs: Miles Davis's *Kind of Blue*, a remastered, slowed-down version, and a CD of five tangos performed by Astor Piazzolla and the Kronos Quartet. He gets into the car and slips Miles into the CD player. The first strains of "So What" come alive in the car as he pulls away from Córdoba.

"Islands in the Stream," he says to the windshield after half an hour of driving. "It's in the book called *Islands in the Stream.*"

~ ~ ~

Consuela feigns sickness, takes three days off. She needs to shake her dream away, find her footing before she faces Columbus again. On her first day, she reads in bed until noon, drinks a bottle of Cava with a bowl of strawberries, and sleeps. She walks to a restaurant for dinner, meets her sister, Faith, who is a psychologist. She's married to a really decent man named Rob, has two amazing girls, and lives in an upscale neighbourhood in Córdoba. She has a thriving practice and is in Sevilla for a convention of clinical psychologists.

"I think I'm in love." Consuela blurts it out even before Faith sits down and then doubts herself immediately. Why in God's name would I start down this road when I know very well what's at the end? Shut up, shut up, shut up, she tells herself. Change the subject. Talk about the goddamned weather.

Faith pushes her sunglasses up into her hair, which is chestnut-coloured and pulled neatly back behind her ears. Perfect silver earrings the size of pesos in each ear. Her face is narrow, kind, open. She's wearing a grey silk blouse with too many buttons and a black, ankle-length skirt, slit on one side to the knee. There's roundness at her belly, a small roll – in fact, if Faith was not as tall as she is, she might qualify as plump. But she is tall. She does not appear to be overweight. The net result is softness. There are no hard edges to Faith. The only thing that is not soft is her walk. Faith has no sway – there's nothing fluid in her stride. She walks with a stiffness that screams she's all business – very serious.

"I don't think I can remember you being this excited about a man," she says. "Is it serious?"

"Oh, it's nothing. I got a raise."

"What do you mean it's nothing? I've never seen you this bubbly. Tell me."

"I'd rather talk about you, Sis. How are the girls? What's new with Rob? I haven't seen you for too long."

Faith persists. "Is it serious?"

"Of course, it's serious," Consuela says, finally giving in, and feeling every bit the younger sister.

"As serious as Rolf?"

Consuela looks at her sister's concerned face. She tries to keep her own face neutral. She fights the impulse to throw her drink at her sister.

"Actually," Consuela says, "I'm getting back together with Rolf." She smiles hopefully, as if she hopes Faith will join her in her joy regardless of any past history. And she waits. Watches.

Faith's face tightens. Rolf and she did not see eye to eye on politics and fought often. Ugly fights about Spain's immigration policies, about the conflict in Iraq, and about the rampant corruption in government.

Rolf wanted tighter borders, thought Spain ought to be more involved in the Middle East, and believed the government was innocent as the day is long. It didn't take much to get them going. Faith breathes long and exhales even longer, like she's meditating, trying to regain her calm. She leans back in her chair – places a foot on the seat, drapes her wrist over her knee – strikes an at-ease pose. Probably hoping her mind will follow, Consuela thinks.

"I . . ." Faith starts. She clears her throat of whatever words are stuck there. "I'm happy for you –"

"Oh relax. It's not Rolf. He's remarried and living in the south of France. Didn't I tell you?"

"It's . . . it's not Rolf? Why would you lie about something like this? I'm happy if you're happy. You know that, Con."

"Why do you always bring me down like that? Why did you have to bring up Rolf? I mean, I was feeling good, and you remind me of a failure . . . rub it in my face. Let the damned past be, Faith." Consuela blinks away her tears, looks across the square at a small fountain with a horse sculpture at its centre. Children splashing in the water. Sparrows flirting in the thickness of dark green above the café patio.

"I'm sorry, Connie. I only want you to be happy. I don't mean to bring you down."

"I know you don't do it on purpose."

"It's one of my many faults. I know how far from perfect I am. I am a deeply flawed –"

"Stop it, Faith. You're trying to manipulate me into feeling sorry for you. I'm not going to feel sorry for you. I love you. Can't we just enjoy each other's company?"

Faith gulps down her glass of wine. The waiter is there almost instantly to fill their glasses.

"So who is this man?"

"He's a chart maker, a stargazer, a navigator, and an amazing storyteller. He is possibly the most romantic man I have ever met. He's been to Iceland!"

"Iceland?"

"Yes."

"Does he make a living?"

"Not right now. He's on a hiatus. But he does and will again."

"Where did you meet?"

"And he's very good-looking."

Then Consuela is quiet. She's not stupid. She knows this is going to be classified as a failure in Faith's lexicon of Connie failures. She's not sure why she's trying to explain Columbus to Faith. The fact he's a patient is bad enough. The fact he believes himself to be Christopher Columbus will be several steps beyond bad.

"And where did you meet this man?"

Too late to stop now. "I met him at work," she whispers.

Faith's eyes widen. "My God! You've fallen for one of your patients! You have to dump him. Immediately! Please tell me you haven't fucked him yet."

"It's not that kind of love –"

"We're going to have to get you a lawyer. What were you thinking, Sis?" Faith is in full "save Consuela" mode.

Consuela sits silently as her sister rants. Of course she's right. Falling in love with a patient is ethically, morally, and professionally wrong. The only place it makes sense is in love.

"Does anybody else know about this?"

"I wasn't thinking," Consuela says flatly, "I was feeling. I was really feeling."

"You have to stop treating this patient. What ward is he in?"

A nice way of asking how crazy he is, or what form of crazy is manifesting in him.

"Doesn't matter," Consuela says. "Doesn't matter."

NINE

"THE BODY IS AN OCEAN. An ocean of delight. Making love with a woman is always a voyage of discovery, is it not?" Columbus looks up from the chessboard, laughs. "What a foolish thing to say to a beautiful woman. Forgive me, please." He has a towel around his neck as he always does after his morning swim. His hair is still wet and pulled back into a ponytail.

It is the day of the feast of Saint Hilarion. They are sitting at a table in one of the upper-courtyard patios. Consuela is winning. Columbus has never even come close to winning a game against her or, as far as she knows, anyone else. Regardless, he seems to enjoy their games. He approaches each match with pleasure – seems fascinated by the journey. He studies her moves as much as his own. Each game is different. He has never repeated an opening, and his responses to her opening moves are always interesting – ultimately stupid but interesting.

"Oh it's not so foolish," Consuela says. "I have thought long and hard about making love with a woman. Curious, you know? Surely you've considered another man? While on those long, lonely voyages? All alone in your cabin, late at night – you've never thought about being with a man?"

"The Bible says it is forbidden for a man to lie down with another man. It says you should not lie with a man, as with woman: it is an abomination. It's written in Leviticus."

"So you have thought about it – considered it but dismissed it? Because of some vague mention in the Bible?"

"No, I never considered it in the first place, and then I recognized that the word of God backed up my inclination to not consider it."

"Ridiculous. Check."

"It's a sin. Where?"

"Don't be silly. Here. My queen."

"But the Bible –"

"Doesn't the Bible also say eating shellfish is a greater abomination? In Deuteronomy, I think it mentions shellfish –"

"Okay . . . okay . . . but –"

"But you love our crab dinners. That's checkmate, by the way."

"Yes, I see." He studies the board as if he's memorizing it. Eventually he looks up. "Where was I? Oh, yes . . . the body is an ocean of delight. Making love with a woman . . . discovering her secrets, the unknown."

~ ~ ~

"It's like this," he says.

He massages her breast, focusing his attention on the nipple. When she arches her back in their lovemaking, her breasts disappear. They flatten out and only her nipples protrude.

"When we are at sea, we are this nipple on your body." His lips brush her nipple and she shivers.

"And this?" Beatriz says, taking his hand, and sliding it downward, across her belly and into the hair of her pubic mound.

"That is what we dream of."

"Then why do you leave?"

"So that we have something beautiful to dream."

"And if you stayed? What would you dream?"

"The ocean and what is beyond."

"There is nothing beyond," she says.

Columbus smiles in his eyes. "Only the edge of the world," he says, "and perdition."

"Why is it that you wish to rush toward death?"

"Death is the ultimate journey, is it not?"

"But you already know what will happen after death," she says.

"Yes, of course. I know what I have been told. I know what the priests say."

"And you know that you will sail off the edge if you go too far west."

"Don't be ridiculous," he says. "Nobody, including you, believes the Earth is flat."

"Shhhh, there are ears everywhere. And besides there are some who still believe the Earth is flat."

"I can't speak the truth in my own home?"

"Better to speak the myth. The ears of the bloody Inquisition are everywhere."

"You are right, of course. The Earth is flatter than a pita bread and there is always the danger of falling off the edge into a great nothingness."

She smiles. "Then you will stay here with me?"

"Yes, of course . . . for tonight."

Her skin holds fading blue-sky tones that enter through the window next to the bed. Each second there is more shadow in the room. He thinks about the sun and where it sinks now into the unknown. The sun disappears into the blank paper beyond the Canary Islands. On all the maps of the world there is only the blank paper for certain. There are theories and dreams and speculations but only emptiness for sure. Well, there was the one chart, which showed some tiny specks far across the sea, but only one chart among so many.

We do not know what is there. But if I sail far enough, I will be there. And if I sail far enough I will get to where I am. That is the way it is with spheres. And whatever is in between will be discovered. All I have to do is survive the obstacles of starvation, thirst, and storms – and hopelessness. It would be easier to sail across the ocean if I had ships. The ships will come, though. The king and queen cannot afford to pass up an opportunity like this.

He looks at her darkening body. I am sailing off this body, which I know well. I am moving beyond that blank paper, at the edge of the world, beyond the rain. That is where I exist.

"Where are you going?"

He turns at the door, looks back at Beatriz on the bed, sitting up, the sheets pooled around her. He'd like to memorize this picture. This image of Beatriz in bed, asking him with her silky voice where he's going. *Where are you going?* she says. And the big answer is: *I have no idea, except west.* But he'd love to memorize this image of Beatriz in bed, doing a great favour to the light of the room. "To get another bottle of wine," he says.

~ ~ ~

In the morning Columbus is sitting in his favourite wooden chair, dressed in the housecoat the boys gave him last Christmas. As the sun rises, he pulls out another cigar. He slices the end along the blade of his sword. He lights it with three small puffs, two more small puffs. Then a slight roll so the end is evenly lit. He leans back into his chair and looks out to sea. He observes the wisps of pink cloud stranded at the horizon. Red sky in the morning, sailor's warning, he thinks. Red sky at night, sailor's delight; red sky at morning, sailor's warning. He knows the nursery rhyme but has no idea how or when he learned it. He takes another puff of his cigar.

Before coming down to the veranda, he'd picked up his razor in the bathroom and looked in the mirror. The colour of his hair still sometimes surprises him because he does not feel old enough to have white hair. Despite his seemingly endless struggles to get his ships, he does not feel as old as he looks. True, there are days when he is so tired he teeters at the edge of giving up.

Sometimes he does not understand what Beatriz sees in him – what any woman sees in him.

"What is that awful stench?" Beatriz has come up from behind him but now backs away. She's wearing a corset, nothing else. "Has something died? Have you an illness?"

"It's a cigar. A Montecristo number 4." He smiles, but there is fatigue in his eyes – something resigned. "There's a box of them in the big room, on the table. I honestly do not know how they got there. I must have had them in my bag. But I've brought some down here with me. Do you want one?"

Beatriz leans forward suspiciously. Watches him suck on the brown thing that burns and smells like death.

"Why? Why do you do this?"

"Well, after I smoke, I feel I am not quite walking on the Earth. I am, but I am not. I feel strangely at peace. Calm yet focused. When I awoke this morning I found I had this knowledge. I knew how to smoke them. I've had two already."

"What do you mean you had the knowledge? Is this some sort of sorcery? Have you been taken by demons?"

"Beatriz. It is merely the knowing of something that cannot be explained. Perhaps I dreamed of this knowledge long ago and now I recall a dream."

"But where did they come from? Shall I pray for you, Cristóbal?"

"I'm afraid praying wouldn't do any good."

"You mean there are demons in you?"

"Demons! I mean it is merely something that cannot be explained."

"But –"

"Look, you have given birth."

"Yes."

"How did you know what to do?"

"I . . . I just knew," she says.

"And when the baby arrives, what is the first thing it does?"

"It cries."

"Yes, and then?"

"Then it seeks its mother's breast."

"And how does the baby know to do this? How does it know there is nourishment there? How could it possibly know?"

"I –"

"It is unexplainable is it not?"

"I suppose," she says quietly. "But this is different. You're forty years old! You are not a baby!"

"True, but this does not make me immune to mystery."

~ ~ ~

"Only idiots and the very superstitious believe the world is flat. The curve of the Earth is easily proved. I could explain such things to a child, a cat, or a dog. It's determining the actual size that is a problem. And it will always be speculation until someone sails out there and actually has a look-see."

Dr. Fuentes leans forward, places his elbows on his knees, and cups his chin in his hands. "So what happened? How come you're here and not at sea? Doesn't that tell you something?"

"I am not here of my own accord, Doctor. And anyway, why would you want to jump to the end of a story?"

"You have a story?"

"Everybody has a story, Fuentes."

"You're telling a story right now?"

"You're not reading Nurse Consuela's reports are you?"

Dr. Fuentes pauses. Makes a few notes in his notebook. "What if I told you I believed the world was flat?" he says without looking up.

"You would confirm my theory about your lack of intelligence. I believe hundreds would concur."

"I think we're done for today."

"Why don't you read me what you've been writing in that little notebook of yours? It must be very insightful and important."

Dr. Fuentes slaps his notebook shut. Slips his pen into his shirt pocket. Smiles a cool, professional smile in Columbus's general direction.

"You don't want to share your shopping list? Maybe you're writing a novel. Were you composing a poem? A ghazal perhaps?"

"A ghazal?"

"Yes, an ancient Persian style of poetry. Five, or more, two-line stanzas. Each stanza is a complete thought and unrelated to its neighbouring stanzas except by a thin emotional thread. Surely you've heard the term before?"

"Sounds fascinating."

"Except that you are the type of person who demands neatness and logic and a chronological order. You could never write a ghazal except by accident. It was wrong of me to accuse you of writing a ghazal. You're much too stupid for that. Limericks are more your style."

"We're done here." Dr. Fuentes stands up. "Have a good day, Bolivar."

"Yes, that's perfect. Dismiss me with a phony wish, a platitude, and an incorrect moniker. Well done, Fuentes. You must have a lot of friends."

"We'll try again next week."

Columbus ignores him. Focuses on his cuticles. Observes his fingernails. Lets the doctor stand for a long minute. Then he stands up. "I can let myself out," he says. "Thanks for a lovely chat."

~ ~ ~

The dayroom is crowded. It's been raining for days. The whole institute has a gloomy and claustrophobic feel. Tempers are short. There have been five fights in the last two days, which is unusual. These fights were serious enough for the nurses to call the orderlies to break them up. Pope Cecelia is in isolation for smashing a plate on an orderly's head. Yesterday Dr. Fuentes slipped and fell, broke his tailbone, is going to be off work for a month, maybe more. He's managed to reconcile with his wife. A miracle of sorts.

Columbus stays away from these confrontations. He lurks at the edge of things. Consuela finds him in the games room, watching a chess match between Mercedes and Arturo. Mercedes washes her hands after every move on the chessboard. As a result, they are red, chapped, and sore-looking. Mercifully, Arturo needs a lot of time to contemplate his moves. Arturo thinks and thinks and ponders, and eventually Mercedes complains. He moves, she moves, and then she gets up and goes off to wash her hands. Arturo damaged his head in a fall. Before he fell, he was a brilliant lawyer – a prosecutor with a reputation for being a pit bull. There are still glimpses of brilliance but these are veiled behind a plodding, lethargic man.

Consuela moves quietly, comes up behind Columbus. "It's a slow form of insanity," he says, without looking up.

She's impressed. But she wonders. Did he see her reflection in a window?

"I can smell you," he says.

Arturo looks up from the game. Smiles. Consuela blushes. She clears her throat. "Are they any good?"

"Arturo is better than you. But he has much practising to do before he will give me a game. He would do well to study the Greco Counter Gambit."

Consuela thinks hard about this. Greco Counter Gambit? She has never lost a game with Columbus. What the hell is he talking about? This doesn't make any sense. Is this a clue to another life? Did she just get a glimpse?

"Though I doubt Mercedes is smart enough to know it, she has been playing the Italian Quiet Game: E4, E5, then Nf3, Nc6, and finally Bc4, Bc5. You see how white prevents black from advancing in the centre?"

"Gambit?"

"Yes, a risky attacking style of opening. It avoids the calculated buildup of classic games."

Columbus looks up at Consuela's confused face.

"A gambit is an opening in which something is sacrificed, usually a single pawn, in order to achieve some sort of advantage. Gambits are not normally successful in the highest-ranked games. By the way, thank you for taking such good care of me," he says, "and goodbye."

"You're welcome. I –" She stops. "What do you mean goodbye?"

"You never know. I could die in my sleep. A tree could fall on me. I could choke on my dinner." He half smiles.

"You're not planning anything stupid, are you?"

"Define stupid."

"Suicide is stupid."

"Suicide is a sin." Columbus seems appalled at the suggestion.

Consuela takes a deep breath. She looks him over through squinted eyes. "Then you're going to try and escape again, which for you is only mildly stupid."

Arturo stands up. "I have to . . . please excuse me."

"I'll watch the board. Not to worry."

"What are you planning?" Consuela is hissing.

Mercedes arrives back at the table, looks over the board, and makes her move. She gets up and disappears again down the hallway toward the washrooms. She passes Arturo in the entranceway.

Columbus smiles as Arturo sits down. "Six moves, Arturo. It's over in six moves. Your knight, yes. You've got her. If she makes the right moves, it's checkmate in six. If she's careless, it may take fewer, but the result will be the same."

"I see I'm going to have to do some practising," Consuela says.

"Aren't all our games practice games?"

~ ~ ~

Later that day, she walks along the edge of the pool. He's swimming, a seemingly effortless sidestroke through the water almost silently. The evolution of his initially rather noisy swimming to this almost-silent-in-the-water stroke has been a slow but steady journey. It's not something he was trying to achieve but something he noticed happening as he tried to make his movements more efficient. She is reading out loud from a small book of ghazals. Reading a stanza, then walking a few steps, reading another – keeping up with him as he swims and listens. She reads, walks, reads, walks. After a while it is difficult to determine if she is matching his pace, or he, hers.

"Into the mirror of my cup the reflection of your glorious face fell. And from the gentle laughter of love, into a drunken state of longing I fell."

She walks a few steps, and then: *"Struck with wonder by the beauty of the picture that within my cup I beheld. The picture of this world of illusion from the reflection of my mind fell."*

He pulls himself out of the pool after just under an hour, sits on the rough stone edge, and looks up at her. "Why did you choose this particular style of poetry?"

"You don't like these? These are in translation. They were written by a poet named –"

"Hafiz. I know who wrote the poems. That's not what I asked."

The edge to his voice, the clipped tone, takes her off guard. She cannot, will not say that this book of poems is one of her favourites – that it is a book her father gave to her mother. This book is one of her few treasures. These poems move through her as an old lover would; they know where to touch, and when, and sometimes they surprise. "I found the book in a used-book shop," she says. "Ghazals are Persian. They –"

"I know what a ghazal is. Why did you choose Hafiz?"

"I don't know. I thought you might enjoy it. They're odd poems. At first glance, they don't make sense."

"These are poems of longing! Of love. Of illicit, impossible love."

"You seem agitated." Oh God, that's jargon, she thinks. It's stupid and lazy of me. He's angry. He's really angry. But this may be a weak spot in Columbus's defences, a way in. She can't remember him this angry, this quickly. The question is why. Why is he so angry about some poetry by a dead Persian poet named Hafiz?

He is angry, he realizes. To hear this poetry reminds him, in a new way, that he is trapped in this place. The truth of this poetry, the power, is too much.

He swallows. Breathes. "No, no, I enjoyed your reading of Hafiz."

"I just thought they were beautiful. That's why I picked this book. Perhaps I should have chosen something else . . . a novel –"

"Hafiz was a good choice." He stops in the narrow hallway that leads up to ground level from the pool. I never did find the steam room, he thinks. He motions with his hand that she should go first through the doorway. As she passes, he whispers, "You ought to hear them in Persian."

~ ~ ~

Columbus looks around the cafeteria but this is not what he sees. He is no longer at the institute. His pen begins to move on a new page in his notebook.

(iii)

This picture could be in any café in any city in the world. There's a thirty-something brunette sitting in front of a chessboard across from an empty chair, and he begins to imagine a story for her. She's been studying the board, her narrow chin in her hand, her head leaned slightly to the side. The grey, even light in this café softens the contours of her face. It gives a kind, tender feel to this place. But she's not interested in the facets of light. She's looking at the chessboard. Perhaps she's waiting for an opponent to come back from the washroom. Perhaps she's just interested in the final positioning of an abandoned game – divining the stories of kings and queens, knights and soldiers. This is a woman who wears scarves, winter, spring, and fall – and quite often in the summer. She is a woman who appears to take great care when it comes to her shoes. They are always high-heeled, and they consistently straddle the line between elegant and fashionable. This is the same woman who wears amazing leather boots that hug her calves with such perfect clarity – boots that persuade her legs to become beautiful and curvaceous.

He knows this woman but does not recognize her.

These imagined stories always start with questions and more questions, which eventually lead to suppositions.

Abstractions. Oblique theories. Why does she come to this café alone on a Saturday morning? Does she have a family at home? Is this negotiated alone time? There is an "awayness" about her that speaks of an older place of origin. Was she born in a small town in France? Or Nebraska? A village in Ireland? To be able to say you are from the Basque region of Spain would be very romantic. Perhaps her name is Mary Francis and she was born in Trois-Rivières, halfway between Montreal and Quebec City, in Canada. Maybe her name is Mary and she comes from Hope, British Columbia. Of course, there's no way to know anything about her origins because nothing ever moves in these images.

It's easy to imagine she has no immediate family, not here anyway. Her narrative is there in her eyes, which flash with a hazel rawness and lust for life. Maybe she loved someone she was not supposed to love, and this chasm, this crack in her life, is her best story. Does she choose to be alone now? Is she alone? Does she tell her story? Does she whisper this narrative to a lover in a burgundy bedroom at 3 A.M.?

If this picture could move, there might be a younger woman sitting across from the first woman now. When she arrives, the first woman stands; they hug and kiss each other's cheeks. This kissing of cheeks is not obligatory; it is a loving ritual between them. The young woman has short but careless blond hair and wears the tortoiseshell, thick-rimmed glasses that represent the trend of the day. She is tapping her foot with nervous energy. She wears runners with red laces.

There are more questions now, about the first woman, who today is wearing a chestnut-coloured scarf . . . and additional questions about this new blond woman with reckless hair. This "away" woman and the younger woman seem genuinely pleased, comfortable in each other's company. It is as if they are mother and daughter. But they cannot be related by blood. The colour of their eyes, the line of their jaws, their hair – all these things speak to the lack of blood between them. These women are not playing chess. They are only talking and having coffee.

He would bet that they are more than friends. But all of this is a fabrication – everything but the clear and vivid picture of the first woman sitting silently, motionless, in front of a chessboard across from an empty chair. Everything else is a lie.

TEN

At 3:30 a.m., COLUMBUS and two others break a window and manage to bash out a section of wire mesh with a chair. Five security guards arrive moments later, before any of them have jumped into the courtyard, and the guards quietly take them back to their rooms. In the morning, Consuela and all the other staff are asked to produce their keys. The three somehow got out of their rooms without breaking anything. All keys are accounted for. So how did they get out? Dr. Balderas, the acting director, is put in charge of the investigation. Security is tightened on the three would-be escapees. Meds are upped. Rooms are searched. Nothing is found. A thong is found in Columbus's room – tucked in the bottom of a drawer. Consuela has no idea how Columbus would have wound up with a pair of women's underwear. She tells the orderly to just put them back where he found them. Three weeks pass before Consuela is able to have a chat with Columbus. For two weeks, he's an isolated, drooling idiot – doped up on sertraline and kept away from the other patients. It takes another week for the drugs to clear his system.

She finds him in the upper courtyard, sitting in the sun, his eyes closed, an orderly thirty feet away, leaning against the main building, watching. Another orderly is sitting in one of the three stairways reading. She's not sure if he's taking a break or if they're that worried about Columbus. She looks at her patient. He's got sunglasses propped on his face – not exactly square but they do offer a scratched, half protection. The institute offers all its patients utilitarian sunglasses – signs them out to whoever wants a pair. Insists they be returned intact.

"How are you?"

He flips open his robe, reveals a steady erection. "First one in weeks."

Nothing surprises her anymore when it comes to Columbus. "Side effect from the drugs?"

"One can only hope," he says.

"You must be pleased."

"It scares me. These drugs scare me. I spent months that felt like years out of my mind and . . . now, two weeks stuck in a hellish nightmare in which I am at sea, and tempted by Satan. And I don't do well." He stops, looks up into the sky, moves his hand along the stubble at his jawline. Swallows hard. "I don't know if I was dreaming or hallucinating."

She can't see his eyes. Consuela was not expecting this vulnerability. She drags a chair over, makes a shushing sound in the morning, makes two long lines in the gravel, sits down, and looks at his unshaven face.

~ ~ ~

"Columbus is at sea. I am at sea. I am on the deck of a ship, which I command. And we are adrift in a thick mist. The mist hangs, it persists, clings to us and we are becalmed. We do not see anything but the paleness, the heat is oppressive and every time the young man walks by I am bothered. It is not a feeling I expected."

~ ~ ~

The crewman is named Bertrand, a skinny young man. This is impossible, yet there it is again. Just thinking about him causes a reaction. There must be something wrong with me, Columbus thinks.

It has been two full days of this becalmed, thick fog, and each night Bertrand and Columbus meet at the starboard bow and talk about what to do. Tonight, Columbus cannot believe his ears.

"If you take me to your cabin," Bertrand whispers, "I will tell you how to get out of here."

"What?"

"Bed me," he says, "and I will save you and your ships."

"I do not lie down with men, and anyway, from what will you save us?"

"This fog, this becalmed death, this sitting dead in the water while food and water run down, this calm that numbs all hope, this –"

"Enough. I admit we are in a little trouble. But we are only twenty-six days out. How do I know you have the power to save us from this?"

"You will have to act on your faith, your intuition, trust."

Columbus turns away from the young man. With both hands firmly grasping the railing, he looks into the thick black night. "No," he says, "I will not."

At noon of the next day there is only a white, even light all around them. Sunlight is brightly diffused. They cannot tell where the sun is, exactly.

Crewmen begin to grumble out loud. Columbus stays in his cabin all day. He studies the charts and drinks. At sunset he walks the deck speaking to his crew. He tells them not to worry. "I have seen worse off the coast of Britain. There will be wind tomorrow," he says. "This won't last." The men are silent in the face of his buoyancy.

That night, Bertrand continues his pursuit. "You are famous for your faith in the unbelievable, Columbus. Is my offer too much of a push for that faith?"

They are near Columbus's cabin, sometime after midnight. The watch has just changed. It is another dead, black night.

"I have faith in things that have small slivers caught up in reality."

"If you bed me," Bertrand says, "not only will I get you out of this fog but I will find the land you seek."

"What?"

"I know exactly where the land is."

"How could you? Nobody has ever been there before."

"Has nobody ever been there before?"

Columbus peers into the shadow where Bertrand's face is hidden. This boy could not possibly know how to find land, he thinks. He is bluffing. It is a bluff I would dearly love to call. How I would like to bed him if only he were a woman. Even with his scarred face and whispered voice, there is something irresistible. If only he were female. I have never had such feelings of lust, passion.

"Are we going to your cabin, Columbus?" Bertrand says.

God don't let me say yes. I want to say yes, but I can't. I yearn to say yes and take this young man to bed and see what happens with the weather and landfall.

"No, not for all the riches that Marco Polo spoke of," Columbus says.

The next morning there is blue sky above the ship. Fresh air descends and there is muffled cheering from the decks of the other ships. Columbus is woken up by the cheers and celebratory shouting on his own ship. But as he rushes out on deck the cheers turn to cries of anguish and outrage as the blue sky is eradicated by a fog even thicker than before.

"It must be breaking up," Columbus says. "You there. Climb up the rigging and see if the ceiling has lifted. Keep a watch up top and let me know if there's any change." A sailor drops a coil of rope and begins to climb up through the fog. When those on deck lose sight of him, they know the fog is not breaking up. Columbus turns and silently retreats to his cabin.

~ ~ ~

Consuela leans forward and tries not to smile. "This story, in which you found a man to be beautiful, horrifies you?"

"I am never attracted to one of my crew in a sexual way. How can this be, when I have had such affairs with Beatriz and Selena, and so many others? And then this young man comes along and I am suddenly attracted? How can this be?"

"You've had a rough few weeks. Relax."

"Oh, it doesn't end there."

"There's more?"

"Yes, there's more."

~ ~ ~

The four captains meet at noon on Columbus's ship. Talavera, Varela, and Pinzon all take the wine Columbus offers them, make their perfunctory offering to Jesus and God and the king and queen, and then drink in silence. Varela and Pinzon both choose to sit at the head of the table, Talavera doesn't care, and Columbus invites them to gather at one end.

"Things go well on my ship," Talavera says. "The men are happy in their work and do not concern themselves with the weather." After a few minutes, he adds: "Admittedly, the weather is odd, but nothing to fear. Everything is fine."

He's grown a full moustache and beard since they left port. Varela and Pinzon have three or four days of beard growth. Columbus himself has not shaved for six days. All have dark shadows under their eyes and their clothing is unkempt. Varela and Pinzon nod their heads. In reality, they are just barely able to keep their crews from turning on them. The only thing that saves them all is the utter hopelessness of the situation regardless of who is in command.

"There is no fear on my ship," Varela says. "We will wait it out. I've been in much worse situations off the coast of Africa."

"Everything is fine on my ship as well. We are eager to move on to the new discoveries," Pinzon says, holding his glass out for more wine. He's a small weasel-like man with a long nose and throaty voice.

"I have never witnessed the calm seas such as these," Talavera says.

"It is very interesting."

"This fog is thick as shit," Varela says.

"Very thick," Pinzon says.

"But everything is fine," Talavera says. He stands up and walks to the door. "I must empty myself at the rear of your ship, Admiral Columbus."

"Nothing to worry about."

"Could you pour just a little more wine?"

"God and his son Jesus Christ will make the winds blow soon," Varela says.

"God will not abandon us," Pinzon says.

"The grace of God and all his mercy will end this . . . interesting calmness."

"All the saints and His Holiness the Pope have blessed this voyage."

Talavera comes back in, sits down heavily, and looks at Varela and Pinzon. *"Mentiras,"* he says.

Pinzon and Varela stand up. Both men place their hands on the hilts of their swords. Columbus leans back and smiles.

"I include myself in that statement," Talavera says. "Sit down, please. I wish to clear the air of the smell of *mierda*. There has been a great deal of shit spoken since we sat down." The two captains sit. "I apologize to you, Don Columbus, and to you, my esteemed fellow captains. But we are in trouble and we have been speaking as if this was not the case."

Columbus pours another round. The four men drink quietly for a while.

"We could link up the ships by rope and then row." Varela looks around at the tired eyes of the other captains. He knows how ridiculous this suggestion is. Row toward what, and in what direction, and to what end? On the first day of fog this suggestion would be laughable, but after four days it does not sound so silly. Working at something is better than sitting still in the water.

"Morale might rise a bit if we rowed in a direction, even a few hours a day," Talavera says. "One thing is certain, we must leave this cabin in agreement and with a plan, or it will be the last meeting we four have."

"Rowing might work," Pinzon says, holding his glass out again.

Columbus sits back in his chair and rubs his face. Washes a hand through his hair. His hair is black in his dream, not the white it has been since he was twenty years old.

Varela frowns, picks up the bottle, and empties it into Pinzon's glass. "If we row, we must appear to be certain of the direction. We must behave as if we know exactly where we are going."

"Columbus, you lead this expedition. What do you say?" Talavera leans forward and looks down the table at Columbus who is half hidden in shadow.

"I say we get more wine." He twists in his chair and pulls open the door. "Bertrand! More wine," he says loudly. Bertrand leans into the cabin and Columbus whispers into his ear.

"I really don't think we can drink our way out of this situation," Talavera says.

Columbus shoots back. "I would not suggest this. I do have

a plan, though." He whispers something else to Bertrand and then turns around.

The three captains sit up, shift in their seats.

"You will hear my plan when Bertrand returns."

The gentle sound of lapping ocean is disturbed by a knock at the door. Bertrand places three bottles of wine on the table. He leaves for a moment and then returns with two enamel washbasins filled with water, soap, razors, clean towels, and a bundle of clothing.

"I hope you're not suggesting we kill ourselves here in your cabin." Talavera smiles. "Because while it seems hopeless, weather is a woman who changes her mind often."

"Gentlemen," Columbus says, "the first thing we are all going to do is clean up."

"Clean up?" Talavera says. "Do you mean to insult us?"

"He does insult us." Varela half stands, bumps his head on a hanging lamp. "Shit! This is insulting."

"Sit down, Varela," Columbus says. "This is no insult. Hear me out."

Varela sits. The lamp swings back and hits him on the head again. It cuts his forehead in the shape of a small crescent moon. Varela pulls his hand away from his head with blood on his fingers. He shrugs and goes to pour wine into his glass, but the bottle is not yet opened. He is indifferent to the blood dripping from his forehead.

Talavera takes the bottle from him, opens it, and pours wine for everybody. "Very well, Columbus, why is this insult not an insult?"

"What do you usually feel when you shave in the morning?"

The three captains look at one another.

"Well, what do you feel? Varela? Pinzon?" Columbus looks around the table.

"For the past few days we have not been shaving," says Varela. "We get up now and feel dread."

"Yes, dread."

Talavera leans back in his chair. "Do you mean normally, Columbus?"

"Yes, if you were back in Spain, with your woman in bed and the children eating breakfast with their nanny, and then got up to shave."

Talavera smiles and the two teeth he is missing at the left and front of his mouth take nothing away from the joy of his comprehension. "I feel good. Happy."

"Do you feel hope?"

"Yes, usually I feel hopeful about the day."

"My plan is to present the image of absolute hope. Even though we men do not say it, I believe it is impossible to shave in the morning without some hope. If we captains look and behave like we have hope, it will calm the men."

Silence. They sit thinking about what he has just said.

"There are also fresh clothes here. From now on, we shall all shave in the morning, and I order each man in the fleet to do the same. Today we will look like we have hope. I will shave with you."

"And tomorrow?" Talavera says.

"Tomorrow, we will shave again. And we will row."

"In what direction?"

"Whatever direction your ship is facing, Talavera. That is the direction of our rowing."

"That's absurd," Pinzon says. "We can't see the sun nor can we see the stars nor the moon, and we are to row? We are going to row –"

"You're right, Pinzon," Columbus says. "We'll row in the direction *your* ship faces in the morning."

Pinzon closes his mouth.

"And we'll call our technique for finding directions in fog the Pinzon Manoeuvre, after Señor Pinzon, my friend and eternally optimistic captain. And yes, Pinzon, this is another random choice."

Columbus slides one of the basins down the table. "Repeat after me," he says, "the Pinzon Manoeuvre. A new system for finding direction. The Pinzon Manoeuvre."

The four men perform their shaving, talking quietly about how long each day they will row and speculating on how the crew will react to the odd order about shaving. But for some reason, Columbus cannot shave himself, or does not shave himself. Bertrand enters quietly and begins to shave Columbus. Columbus has an erection that bumps the underside of the table. He acts as if everything is fine but he is wild with lust for this ugly young man. And when the captains are finished, they dress in fresh clothing, call smiles to their faces, and go back to their own ships. Columbus does not get up to see to the departure of the captains. He dismisses Bertrand and sits in agonized misery.

So everybody shaves. The crew grumbles but they shave, and they do feel a bit better regardless of the oppressive sky and fog and calmness of the sea. They row for two hours in the direction Pinzon's ship is facing. The following day, they perform the same routine. And the following day it is the same thing. And the next day, the grumbling begins and shaving does not feel quite as hopeful anymore. The crews begin to gather in small groups, which fall silent when a captain draws near. There are direct questions about the Pinzon Manoeuvre. And at midnight, the hooded Bertrand comes to Columbus for the final time.

"You're dead in the water, Columbus."

Columbus nods into the empty darkness. "I am hard-pressed to remember blue sky."

"I will get you out of this if you bed me."

"How?"

"Faith, Columbus, have faith."

"How is it that you have this supposed power to save us?"

"Faith, Cristóbal, my friend."

"You are the devil!" He crosses himself and backs away.

"Oh don't be such a child. You know better than that. Satan is back running the Inquisition. Running Rome. Selling passage to heaven and pocketing the money."

"Who are you?"

"Someone who can save you. Someone who can get you wind and sky. Who can find your new land. Who can do all these things if you simply take me to bed."

"No. I can't."

"How badly do you want to find the new land, Don Cristóbal?

Why don't you give in to your gut and your heart, and your desire, and forget your brain?"

Columbus turns away, looks out at the nothingness. "Certainly, yes, somehow I am attracted to you in a different way than friendship. Different than comradeship. It is a strange thing that I cannot understand. It is an evil thing."

"Why do you say evil? Does it feel evil? Is not an urge an urge?"

"It goes against God's will."

"Didn't Jesus say we should love one another?"

"Not like this."

"Bed me, Columbus."

"There are those on board who would report this to the Inquisition."

"Not if we're alone behind a locked door." Bertrand takes Columbus's hand and leads him slowly to his cabin.

~ ~ ~

"That's not such a bad dream," Consuela says. "A tad embarrassing I suppose, but it's just a story, yes?" Consuela smiles.

Columbus sighs heavily. "I am a navigator, a pretty good navigator . . . and in this nightmare, I am useless. How is this a good story?"

"Does it matter how you get there?"

"Yes, of course it does. Do you not know me by now? The journey is everything! The way one does something is everything."

"By the way, your last escapade through the window, your journey toward freedom, your attempted escape – how in the hell did you get out of your room?"

"Can't say."

"Can't or won't?"

"The end result is the same."

"But the journey is the thing. The beauty is in the way a thing is done."

"That, Nurse Consuela, is a beautiful thought."

"But you're still not going to tell me, are you?"

"Nope."

"What were you thinking, anyway? You know how tight security is around here."

"There's nothing for me here. I'm not sick. I'm not delusional. I'm Columbus. I'm happy being Columbus."

"I don't think you're sick. But as long as you insist you are Columbus, I'm afraid they're not going to entertain the idea of letting you out." This is the first time she can remember that Consuela puts herself on Columbus's side and "them" on the other. It's a small shift but she notices it.

"How can I not be Columbus when he is exactly who I am?"

"I don't have an answer to that question. Someone smarter than I am once said we are what we do. I can't tell if you are doing what Columbus would do."

"Take a look over there at those two muscle-bound idiots." Columbus waves and smiles. The orderly who was reading, continues to read; the other one smiles and waves back. "I can't do what Columbus should be doing. If your axiom is true then

I'm spending time in a mental institute, most of the time doped up on pharmaceuticals. What I do is put up with being treated as if I am insane. What does that make me?"

"It's not like you don't try to get out. This was your third failed attempt in what – six months? It's no wonder they have two orderlies watching you. Listen, seriously, just between the two of us, how did you get out of your room?"

"No. I may need it. And those orderlies have nothing to do with my escape attempts."

"Attempting to escape is futile. There's too much security."

"It would only be futile if escape was the goal."

"You're telling me that escaping was not the goal?"

"This sun feels good on my face," he says.

"Yes, yes, it's a nice day Mr. Columbus." She closes her eyes and focuses on the warmth on her face.

Consuela drifts into silence. If escape was not the goal, then what? And what about their chess games? Is he losing on purpose? She'd not considered this. Is he *playing* her?

She opens her eyes and looks at him. He's got a wild, half-undone look about him that she has always found attractive. It is as if some part of his psyche does not care about how he appears to the world. There are more important things than appearances. The result is style. Consuela has been trying to maintain a professional demeanour toward Columbus – ever since her luncheon with Faith. But her imagination skips a beat when it comes to Columbus, her fantasies; her longing grows each time she rubs up against him. She'd like to do some serious physical rubbing up against this hopeless cause.

She'd like to do a lot of things. She wonders if he knows how she feels.

"One can only truly learn from failure," Columbus says. "The valuable lessons come from failures, not from a continual stream of successes."

~ ~ ~

"There are three candles in her room," he says at breakfast the next morning. It is the morning of the day of the feast of Saint Bertilla. "Always three," he adds. "Not two. Not four or five. Why would she choose three?"

"Who?" Consuela is tired. It had been a late night, and her air conditioning was not working. While temperatures were hitting only the mid-twenties in the day, her apartment was uncomfortably hot. Sleep came late. She's grumpy – holds her third cup of coffee protectively.

"Selena."

Oh good Christ. Another story about a lover. Another woman. Another tall tale of lovemaking. When was the last time she made love?

"If you had a choice, how many candles would you choose?" he says.

"I wouldn't, Columbus. I'd turn on the light. You've noticed the light switch in your room, haven't you? And its clever relationship to the light in your ceiling?"

He ignores her. "If you were choosing to light your bedroom with candlelight, how many would you choose?"

Consuela sighs. "Fifty. I don't know."

"Selena always had three. There was only giving and tenderness that first time with Selena, and it set the pattern for all the rest."

~ ~ ~

"End of the hall, on the left," she'd said. Columbus enters her room hesitantly, pushes the door shut with his back. He is moderately thick with wine.

Selena is naked as she moves gracefully across the dusky room – through the shuddering candlelight – hands him a glass of wine, and disappears into the bathroom. There are no bubbles in the tub. The water is steaming hot and clear. Three more candles in a high windowsill dance the light and shadow through the water and across the walls.

"What's that scent?" he says. "It's nice."

"Lavender."

Columbus sits on the toilet seat and looks at Selena. Blond strands scattered across half her face, which she does not bother to push aside. He notices the scar along the top of her cheekbone, traces the pale line of it with his finger.

"The bar?" he says.

"Yes."

Everything is softened by the candlelight. She makes a harbour of her legs – at one end, her feet, and at the other, the sandy-brown triangle of her pubis. Her arms ride the edges of the tub. "Do you have any idea how beautiful you are?"

She looks directly at him – finds his eyes. "Tell me," she says, serious and intense.

He had not expected her to want him to clarify his question. It is one thing to be romantic, to say romantic things, but quite another to be called to account for what you say. He thought the question explained itself. Her response knocks him slightly off balance. "I'll be right back," he says. When he reappears, Columbus moves the candelabra to a chair beside the tub, drops his clothing, and slips in behind her, so she is between his legs. Her hair smells like vanilla.

"You, my dear woman, are like these poems of love, and desire, and longing, and wine. These are the poems of Hafiz. They dare to speak to unspeakable beauty or desire." And so he begins to read her Hafiz's ghazals, his voice softly filling the small bathroom. Selena sips her wine and listens. Sometimes she is lost in the words; other times, the words lose her. When she leans out of the tub to retrieve the wine bottle, Columbus stops reading. She fills her glass, leans back, and takes a sip.

"Proceed," she says, and he does.

Eventually they are tired. The wine is gone. The hot water has worked its magic. They make love by spooning. She draws his hand around her body to the soft nest between her breasts and he kisses the back of her neck. Then the wine and the country air, the hot bath, the cool sheets, and the down quilt work together to lull them to sleep.

ELEVEN

COLUMBUS IS PLAYING WITH his thumbs. He's sitting on the patio in a chair experimenting – attempting an illusion in which it seems that he is pulling his thumb apart. He twists his head sideways, tries to see the trick from the viewpoint of where his audience might see it. Consuela finds him before the end of her shift. "You have to see this," he says. "It's a parlour trick. Something my dad used to do."

"The senior Columbus?"

"He used to scare us kids. Watch," he says. He grasps his thumb in his fist and then appears to pull it in two.

"Impressive."

"Was that sarcasm?"

"What do you think?"

"I think a parlour trick as stupid as this can be a useful metaphor."

"Metaphor?"

"Yes. The girl is a gazelle when she runs, instead of, she runs like a gazelle."

"I know what a metaphor is. Why are you telling me –"

"Because failure is never easy," he says.

~ ~ ~

These failures, in particular, sit ugly in Columbus's stomach. He walks away from his second audience at the commission's chamber at the university knowing that even if he'd told them all he knew they still would have said no. Columbus knew it was a tough sell. He never expected them to jump up and down with excitement, shouting their approval at the prospect of his adventure. His goal was not to win his ships, not right away. It was to move some of them from a hard position to a more moderate one. This is the failure Columbus has a difficult time swallowing; he's not sure he moved anyone.

If he'd told them about Iceland and the Norseman, and what those sailors said they saw twenty-one days out into the ocean, they might have considered his journey. That might have moved a few. The problem was withholding what needed to be withheld while revealing the right amount. Reveal the one wrong thing and he could become just another dead heretic, a potential *special* guest of the Inquisition. It seemed that offending behaviour could come and go out of fashion with this holy tribunal.

One week, converting to Christianity was fine; the next, it wasn't good enough. One week, the official map of the known world was sacrosanct, not to be tinkered with, Church doctrine. The next week, new ideas about the unknown world were entertained. It was difficult to stand on this shifting sand dune.

~ ~ ~

The first commission said his idea had merit. It was a bold scheme. A new sea route to the Indies and Japan, and especially one forged by Spain, was a grand idea. Going all the way around Africa was a long and expensive and dangerous journey. And it had only been done once, allegedly. But it wasn't possible to sail across the Western Sea without dying of starvation or thirst. The second commission agreed with the first, in its own unique way. The bottom line: the world was too big, the ocean too wide, the ships too small to carry enough provisions.

"With respect, Your Honour," Columbus says, "you have no clear evidence the world is that big."

"Nor do you have any evidence that it's any smaller. We do have science. Our country's best minds." Las Palos stands up. He's a narrow man, with a large, humped nose and a full head of black hair that falls to his shoulders. "All these men" – he motions with his hand to a group of men sitting in the back row – "all these men, say you are wrong, that the Earth is vast. That the Western Sea cannot be crossed successfully. That you will only kill yourself and those who are foolish enough to sail with you."

"I bow to these learned men. They have resources and knowledge of which I can only dream. But I have a question."

"I think we're done, Mr. Columbus."

"Just one small question?"

Las Palos turns toward the back row. Raises his eyebrows. "All right, but our minds are settled."

"For the best minds of our time – because your intelligence is so dazzling – exactly how big is the Earth?"

Four men lean their heads together into a huddle. One man does not move but, rather, looks bemused.

After five minutes, Las Palos is obviously agitated. After ten minutes, he stands. "It is not our position to prove the size of the Earth, Mr. Columbus. It is, however, required that you prove your case to us. And we have doubts." Las Palos pauses. A large man at the end of the back row clears his throat. Las Palos stops, turns toward the man, and nods. The man stands. He looks down at the papers in his hands. Then looks directly at Columbus. "Well, we do not know exactly how vast the planet is, but we believe it is larger than your, ah . . . estimate."

"I want to suggest that one sure way to find out exactly how big the Earth is, is to sail out there and have a look. Somebody has to go out there and witness the ocean. Make notes on distance. Sometimes theories, fascinating as they may be, need to be proven. I am willing to –"

"Your price is too high," Las Palos says. "You will have our official answer in a few days but I can almost guarantee the outcome. I can only speak for myself, but what you are proposing is, well, quite impossible."

"With respect, how will you know for sure? Will you let Portugal discover new routes? Britain? France?"

"Enough."

"Will we beg foreign powers for the charts? Is that what you envision for Spain? Is that your grand plan?"

"Enough!"

~ ~ ~

Newspaper stories of this audience, Columbus's second, report that as Columbus was leaving the commission chamber he turned and challenged anyone in the room to stand an egg on its end, on a marble tabletop.

"A thousand silver pesos to anybody who can do this thing," he said. "Just take an egg and stand it on its end. It's a simple thing."

Eggs were sent for and four men attempted to make the egg stand on its end. Then two more tried to no avail. Columbus watched dispassionately. Las Palos had already disappeared into the back sanctums of the university.

"Impossible," the men of the commission finally declared. "An egg can't be balanced on one end – not on a flat surface. Utterly impossible!"

When Columbus took the egg, smashed one end – not hard enough to make it run – and stood it on the table, only Luis de Santángel, the queen's treasurer, could be heard laughing hysterically in a sea of stunned silence.

Columbus had made an ally.

~ ~ ~

"Oh, my dear boy," Cecelia says. "You are smiling, but there is sorrow in you as wide and deep as an ocean."

"Well, I am here, in this so-called hospital of innocents, against my will," Columbus says as he sits down. "Why would I be happy? How could I be happy?"

"No, no, no. It's much bigger than that, Mr. Columbus." She pats his hand. "This is loss, and guilt, and too much to bear."

"Well, I'm afraid you have me at a loss. I don't know what to say."

"In time you'll know," she says. "There's no rush. In the meantime, we can chat." Cecelia hands him a cup of tea. "It's green tea. It's good for you."

Columbus thinks about politely declining. He doesn't drink tea. But with Cecelia it seems as if he should. Steam rises from the cup in minuscule swirls. Its scent is so singular – simple. He sips the tea and, surprisingly, finds it to his liking. This is not a complex flavour.

They are at a table in the dayroom – near the windows – Cecelia in her robes on one side, and Columbus, wearing only a pair of socks and an open housecoat, on the other. This is the first time they've communicated beyond casual nods in passing. Columbus has a few more sips of the green tea and is about to comment – to supply mindless dialogue – something about how he is pleasantly surprised at the taste of this tea. But he doesn't. He turns inward against his impulse to fill the void of silence with his self-manufactured nonsense.

When the bird hits the window it shocks them. A loud, muffled bang, they turn, see nothing, both know immediately it was a bird.

"A sparrow?" Cecelia says. "Oh my dear God."

"We need to see – maybe we can do something."

"The doors are locked. We can't get out." She's distraught. Her hand shakes as she points at the locked door.

"This is a rescue mission – a special circumstance." Columbus stands. One of the new orderlies, a pimply-faced young man named Sylvester, follows him to the door. Columbus tries it and indeed it is locked. He yanks on it again, testing the veracity of the lock. He yanks on it again, harder this time.

"The courtyard is closed for the day," the orderly says, stepping between Columbus and the door.

"Open it. A bird has hit the window – might be hurt, suffering." Columbus looks around the room. They're alone. A minor miracle in this institute. The fact it's bingo night could account for the scarcity of inmates.

"The hours are there." Sylvester points to a small square of white paper mounted on the wall. "The courtyard is closed. It's late. I'm sure this bird is fine."

Columbus leans in close. The orderly places his hand on his walkie-talkie, puffs up his chest, draws sternness to his face.

Columbus whispers, "By the time you get even remotely close to calling for help, I could do great damage to you, my friend. Now just open the door."

Sylvester looks hard at Columbus, weighing his words, measuring height, weight, physical condition. He hesitates. Columbus lurches forward and head-butts the orderly – a hard, ugly thumping sound. Sylvester goes down. There are far too many keys on his ring for a quick exit, so Columbus hands the key ring to Cecelia and starts to look around for something he can use to force the door open. Something that could be used as a makeshift pry bar. Many of the candidates are screwed to the floor. Cecelia chooses a key with assuredness. "This one," she says and Columbus turns around. "Is he hurt?" she adds, pointing at Sylvester.

"He'll have a lump." Columbus pushes the key into the lock and turns it. The door opens smoothly and quietly. Son of a bitch, he thinks.

Outside they find the bird, indeed a sparrow. Its neck is broken. Its body still warm. They bury the bird quickly, carefully, under a rosebush and Columbus defers to Her Holiness the Pope for a prayer. Cecelia turns to Columbus with tears in her eyes, at a loss. The only thing he can think of is the first verse from the hymn "Silent Night." He recites it with apologies to the bird but it seems wholly appropriate. It seems correct that this bird should have these words. "Silent night," he begins, "holy night . . ." He and the pope stand in the garden above the small mound, with a growing indigo sky above. "Sleep in heavenly peace," Columbus says. "Sleep in heavenly peace."

They go back inside and Sylvester is still out cold on the floor. They reattach the keys to the orderly's belt. Columbus hustles into the adjoining lounge and brings back a pillow, which he slides under Sylvester's head. Columbus and the pope look at each other. Cecelia is smiling, a vulnerable, grateful, and astounded smile.

"Thank you," she says.

"You're the pope. You ought to be able to attend to sparrows whenever they fall. It was an honour and my pleasure."

"Good night, my dear."

"Sleep well, Your Holiness."

~ ~ ~

The next morning, Columbus looks at Consuela with a glint in his eye. He watches her as she approaches his table at breakfast with more interest than usual. He studies her gait.

"Columbus persists," he says. "He'll do almost anything to get his ships."

"Good morning to you, too," she says.

"You look quite beautiful today . . . I mean you always look good, but I noticed that today –"

"Thank you, Mr. Columbus. I get it." She takes a deep breath. "So what *would* you do to get your ships?"

~ ~ ~

As usual, Columbus kneels before the queen. She keeps him kneeling for all of their audiences while she either sits or swishes around the room. She likes to watch him from behind. To leave him there faced away from her voice. That way, anyone who entered unexpectedly would see nothing was going on. And truthfully, nothing was happening between them, at least on a physical level.

She also liked to sit in front of him, on the throne, her legs pulled up and apart. Her feet flat on the seat of the chair. A pose that without her flowing dresses would not have been appropriate. She did it to tease. She did it to titillate. She did it to move him off course from his obsession. To see if she could shake him.

Isabella sits before him. Considers how she should begin. She is not calm. This audience, which has been arranged by her treasurer, Luis de Santángel, is an inconvenience to her. But she likes this Columbus, more than she would like to admit. He wished to serve the king and queen and would risk his life to do it. He wished to bring glory to Spain. And he was persistent, bloody dogged, about it.

"The commission at the university has come to a decision," she says.

"They have no imaginations, no desire to explore. They are dead men with pencils," Columbus says. "I already know what they –"

"Now hear me well, Columbus. I will personally look at your plan once we take back Granada from these shit-assed godless Moors."

"My queen, you are wise. You are intelligent. You are powerful and –"

"Oh cut the crap, Columbus. I have sycophants galore. Just open that door and walk down the hallway and I'll show you a hundred completely useless sycophants. Be patient, Columbus. We will take Granada, and soon. And then, we will see about your ships."

"But –"

"Patience. Patience, Columbus."

"You'll need money after the Granada victory. I can bring the royal treasury riches from the Indies and Marco Polo's Japan."

"That's a promise we will remember, Cristóbal."

"Could you not spare just three ships, most revered servant of God? Even two ships would –"

"Look, Cristóbal, I like you. Your enthusiasm is undeniable. You have great charm and you are unequivocally brilliant. But I have to tell you – and I hope you can hear this through the haze of your single-minded passion – get the fuck off my back about these ships."

"But my queen, I –"

"I've had a snootful of you and the new route to the Indies and Japan. I have an entire city filled with Moors that I've promised to extricate. I've got a Holy Inquisition that's running amok – I have no idea what they're going to attack next. I started the damned thing, and frankly, they scare the crap out of me. I've got Jews spread across my lands who don't seem too pleased about leaving and aren't very enthused about converting. I've got God's emissaries from Rome saying converting isn't going far enough anyway. And I have a treasury that does not runneth over. I have –"

"If I am successful, when I am successful, I will fill the treasury with riches."

"And to top it off, my tits hurt. They ache. For some reason, I have to cram them into these tight dresses. Gowns, gowns, and more gowns, and they're all tight little torture suits."

"My queen, I hear you. I only wish to please God, and to bring honour to Your Majesties."

"How the hell could you know what it's like to wear these damned clothes?"

"I . . . I cannot imagine it, my queen."

She rises from the throne and shushes by Columbus so she is behind him. Columbus smells her odour and its edgy sexuality stops him.

It's a hot, muggy day to begin with and now this! His head feels light. The smell of this woman, this queen, shakes him.

She walks through an archway at the back of the room. Columbus can hear a door opening and closing. The queen comes back into the room and walks over to him.

"A couple of my girls are coming in here to get you dressed. Then we can talk some more."

"But I am dressed –"

"Trust me, Columbus."

In a couple of minutes, two of the queen's servants enter the room with a blue gown and a corset. The girls shrug, stifle giggles, and go to work on Columbus.

"But this is a dress," he says. The girls ignore him.

"And you're going to cram your body into it. So you really understand what I go through to look like this."

"But –"

"Just do it for your ships."

Isabella walks across the room and disappears through the doorway.

When the queen comes back, Columbus is on his knees in the blue dress, the corset tight across his chest and midsection.

"That's better," she says.

"I can barely . . . breathe."

"Fantastic isn't it? Welcome to my world, Columbus. Those two girls are my most trusted – they'll not say anything about this – but there are rumours about you and me. The tabloids say there must be something going on because your scheme is being entertained by the queen. Just rumours, but pile rumour on top of rumour on top of innuendo and I could be in trouble. My husband chases whatever bitch in heat he damned well pleases, but I? I must remain faithful."

"But it's not true what they say." Columbus feels dizzy, can't get a full breath.

"The truth has little to do with what the tabloids write. They print whatever they want."

"But you're the queen! Can't you just, you know, cause them to disappear?"

"And make myself look guilty?"

"But –"

"You do understand that I have to remain true to the king? That there are spies everywhere? And that there are serious consequences to any infidelity on my part?"

"May I rise, Your Majesty?"

"No, you may most certainly not rise. Stay where you are."

Columbus can't feel his lower legs but he remains facing the empty throne.

"My queen, God Almighty would never allow –"

"God Almighty probably started a few of these rumours. Do you catch my drift, Cristóbal? God Almighty can see into my heart. He can read my thoughts and most secret desires. Do you hear me, Cristóbal?"

Three days later, an envelope arrives by courier, catches up to Columbus in Córdoba. He opens it and finds a pair of black panties. There is no accompanying note. No letter. Nothing to indicate whose panties these might be. Columbus is bemused. He looks around the room – even though he knows he's alone, he wants to make sure before he lifts the panties to his face and inhales deeply.

~ ~ ~

Consuela pulls back from Columbus and looks him over. She feels a twinge in her groin. Her head is spinning.

"That was mildly erotic," she says.

"Not meant to be. It was a lesson in understanding. You've been hanging around with doctors too much. Sometimes a thing is just what it is. A lesson is a lesson."

"Still, it was erotic."

"You want erotic? The pungent, spicy smell of a woman – that's erotic," he says. "All the scents. Feet, underarms, groins. Everything."

"Yes, I know. I know you enjoy the olfactory." Consuela is no longer shocked by his sporadic, frank admissions.

Across the room, workmen have finally arrived to fix the broken window, which has been boarded up for two weeks. They hover outside the window, ladders on either side. Place the glass carefully into the frame. Consuela and Columbus sit in the dim light and watch the workmen.

~ ~ ~

He sits up in bed. It's not a spasmodic or jerky movement. He is simply, suddenly wide awake. He leans over and throws up into the wastebasket. He slides off the bed onto his knees and continues to vomit. When he is spent, Columbus presses the side of his face into the coolness of the floor and weeps. He pulls his sheet from the bed, curls into a fetal ball, and hopes for sleep without dreams, without nightmares, without armless dolls.

This is the third time in a week he has had this dream. Each time his reaction is more violent. It shakes his body. Impacts physically.

In the morning, he seeks out Pope Cecelia, finds her in the dayroom watching the birds in the oak tree outside the south window. She's wearing just one robe today, looks almost normal. Beside her on the table are a blue tin cup and a wooden spatula. Columbus looks at the cup and the spatula, decides not to ask, sits down, kisses her ring, and begins to unfold the details of his dream.

"Why would a doll speak?" Cecelia says. "Why would you have that expectation? Dolls don't speak. They don't talk."

"I don't know. I just know these dolls can talk – they can speak but they don't."

"And they're armless?"

"All of them."

"How many dolls are there in this dream –"

"Nightmare. Hundreds. There are hundreds of silent dolls."

"And what do you do in this dream – nightmare?"

"I try to wake them up. I have the knowledge that they can speak, but they won't speak."

She draws her body away from the direction of the tree and the sparrows and the window, toward him. "What do you think it means?" She rotates the tin cup on the table, so the handle is facing her, then takes a sip of tea.

"Old woman, I don't have a clue. All I know is I am horrified. Last night I was sick. I woke up and I was physically sick. I don't know what to do. I can't stay awake for the rest of my life."

He observes her face. It's kind. Wrinkled and weathered, but lacking the stray hairs that accompany so many older women's faces. Her skin is pale and apart from the wrinkles, smooth. Her eyes are faded pale blue, as if they became tired of their own colour, or simply faded with age.

"Oh my dear boy," she says. She reaches out and touches his hand. "It's all right to not know. Perhaps you're not ready to know. Dreams are never obvious. They are never what they seem. You're just not ready."

TWELVE

EMILE'S ASSISTANT IN LYON calls with two peculiar news-paper stories. A man in Cádiz tried to pay for his meal with some stones wrapped in a piece of leather. The police were called but the man disappeared before they arrived. Emile dismisses this story. The story that catches his ear is buried inside a longer feature on panhandling – the embedded tale is about a man in a café in Jaén who insisted on calling a woman Isabella, even though her name was Lucia. He would not stop talking about the colour of the ocean. The funny thing is, she bought him a train ticket to Marbella. That's what he said he needed. She said he was the most enchanting man she'd ever met.

Emile drives right by Castro del Rio, the land of wine and olive oil.

"Can you get me her phone number? Get me this woman's phone number." He flips the phone shut.

~ ~ ~

Emile finds Lucia Vargas's house in Jaén. He'd called from the road and convinced her to meet with him. He turns onto Calle de Santiago and looks for a place to park. There are cars lining both sides of the street and he can't see an opening. A brown

BMW signals to pull out half a block up and Emile signals his intention to move into this spot. He's not sure why he bothers signalling – there are no other cars driving on this street. As he's waiting for the careful BMW, he glances across the road. On the boulevard, there are two men playing a game of boules, and four men sitting at a small table smoking cigars. The men are sitting in wooden chairs and each has a glass of something in front of him. One of the men is leaning forward, elbows on his knees, head down and tilted – as if he is listening intently. Emile is pulled toward this scene. He'd like to go over there and sit down, smoke a cigar and share a drink, and listen to their conversation. In his snapshot of this scene he gets the feeling these men are grounded, completely comfortable with who they are and what they're doing. He thinks he remembers having this comfort in his own skin a long time ago. Perhaps these men smoke cigars and have a drink each day at this time. It is a pleasurable constant. Emile would love to be part of this picture. He backs into the parking space, then watches as a waiter from the café across the street brings over another round of pastis or wine – something in a bottle.

~ ~ ~

Lucia is tall and blond. Her front teeth have a pronounced gap. Her smile, Emile notices immediately, is self-conscious. She smiled as he introduced himself, but then turned her face slightly sideways. She and Emile stand on the front step of her house, on the outskirts of Jaén. She's wearing a black, wraparound sweater that reaches mid-thigh. The sound of children playing comes from inside.

"He called you Isabella, this man?"

"Yes, I told my sister, she's a reporter at the newspaper. He was looking for enough money for a train ticket. He insisted on calling me Isabella. I don't mind ... My mother was named Isabella."

"Were you afraid?"

"Is he dangerous?"

"No, not as far as I know."

"I didn't think so. He was charming, not at all frightening. He talked about his ships. He has three ships, docked somewhere down south, I think."

This stops Emile. Three ships? The guy owns three ships and has no money? Three ships and he's scrounging his way through southern Spain? And why would he be going to Morocco? He makes a mental note to get his assistant to check on any active cells in Morocco. But if he was really involved in a terrorist cell, he would not have mentioned Morocco. That can't be where he's headed. There's something else going on.

Lucia continues. "He looked at me the way my husband looked at me for the first six months after we were married."

"Then what happened?"

"Well, my husband stopped looking at me that way. We're still married but it's different now. I miss that look."

Emile smiles. He wonders if Lucia still looks at her husband the same way she did before they were married. "I'm sorry about your husband," he says, "but I meant the man who called you Isabella."

"Yes, of course you did. I'm sorry. He said he needed to get to Marbella, on the coast. But he had no money. He said he would arrange to pay me back but I don't really care about that."

"Where was it that this conversation took place?"

Lucia points down the street. "The café on the corner. The Velema."

"By the men playing boules and smoking cigars?"

"Yes," she smiles. "The neighbourhood elders. They were there that day. They're in the park almost every day."

"Mom. Mary won't share the crayons." It's a girl's voice from inside.

Lucia pokes her head back into the house. "Solve the problem, Felipa. You're a smart girl. Find the middle ground."

Lucia turns to Emile. "I am neither stupid nor naïve, Mr. Germain. He seemed a bit desperate, sad, lost. He said he needed to get to Marbella. I was able to help."

"Emile, please. Call me Emile. I hope I haven't insinuated that you were stupid. I do not think you're stupid. Not in the least. I'm just trying to find this man."

"I love my sister, but this newspaper story. I think it painted me as a bit of a kook."

"From what I've seen and heard, this was only an act of kindness."

Lucia blushes and smiles her awkward, turned-aside smile.

"Now, is there anything else – anything that we haven't covered, or that wasn't in the newspaper story – that you can remember about your conversation? No matter how small or seemingly insignificant."

"I can't think of anything, Mr., um, Emile." She reaches behind her and places her hand on the doorknob.

He hands her his card. "If you remember anything, my cell phone number is on the bottom."

Emile is on the street, his car keys in hand, standing at his car door, when Lucia bounds down the step. "Hey, Mr. Germain! Emile! He did say something before he left. At the train station. I thought he was just being funny. I hadn't thought of it until now." Lucia wraps her sweater back around, then places both hands on the railing of the iron gate. The sweater unravels again, revealing a white camisole and panties. She does not bother to cover up. "He kissed my hand and said, 'Thank you, Your Majesty.' Is that important?"

~ ~ ~

Dr. Balderas, hoping to impress the institute's board of directors, takes an active interest in Columbus's case, and more. He schedules twice-weekly sessions with Columbus and insists on a lucid patient, drops all medication. Columbus goes through withdrawal. Elsewhere in the institute, the acting director releases a bevy of patients back into the general public, saving money and lessening workloads.

He's a short man. Balding with grace. A kind and concerned face that immediately puts Columbus on edge. It's a forgiving face that makes Columbus want to open up and talk honestly. He seems to genuinely care about his patients. Dr. Balderas has a soft voice – there are no downward inflections, and there is no condescension. It's a voice that says: I'm not your doctor; we're just a couple of guys having a chat about things.

"Hello, Bolivar. My name is –"

"I know who you are, Dr. Balderas. My name is Columbus. Christopher Columbus." Columbus is not sure why, but this doctor frightens him a little. His attitude, a sort of let's-get-down-to-business aplomb, for some reason is troubling.

"Okay, Mr. Columbus. I've taken over your case from Dr. Fuentes. I've read over his notes." He pauses. "I have some preliminary questions. Will you answer some questions for me? I'd like to get more familiar with your case."

"Sure, why not. Fire away." This guy seems about 3,000 per cent more competent than Fuentes, Columbus thinks. Again, an illogical, prickling fear rises in Columbus. A small part of him wants to run out of the office.

Dr. Balderas flips through some pages and picks up a pencil. "Okay, these are some fairly standard questions. The first question is about memory. Do you ever have memories come back to you all of a sudden, in a flood or like flashbacks?"

"That's a definite yes." Columbus tries to smile. "All the time."

"Are there large parts of your childhood after age five that you can't remember?"

"I don't actually remember any of my childhood. Can't recall a damned thing."

"Okay. What about your handwriting? Have you ever noticed that your handwriting changes drastically or sometimes you don't recognize it?"

"They don't let us have pens here, Doc. We have to sign them out. Which is ironic. Thing is, my handwriting is pretty consistent. Haven't noticed any changes. It's sloppy. So sometimes I don't recognize what I've written."

"You've been writing?"

"I mean generally."

"Generally, as in, since you got here? I'd be interested in looking at some of your writing, Mr. Columbus."

"There is no writing." Columbus tries to keep his voice even, unaffected, but he can hear the edge in it. Thinks: Damnit, he's going to want to see my snapshots, my pictures with no meaning, the word pictures where nothing moves.

Dr. Balderas backs off. "Any time you'd like to share your writing, my door is open. I have just a couple more questions. Do you ever have long periods when you feel unreal, as if in a dream, or as if you're really not there?"

Christ, that's my life, he thinks. I feel like I'm going to wake up one morning and I'll be at sea, on my way – and this nuthouse, a very vivid and very bad dream. "No," Columbus says. "I'm fairly grounded in reality. That is, when I'm not medicated. Then things are hazy, unreal."

"Ah, yes, I should have added, drugs or alcohol don't count."

"Do you have any booze in here? Because I could use a drink about now."

"What do you drink?"

"Wine. The Scottish beverage. More wine."

The doctor smiles. "I love wine. It would be nice to get out of here so you could have a drink whenever you want, wouldn't it?"

Be careful, Columbus tells himself. He's dangling the carrot. Trying to get you to expose your queen. "Is that a possibility?"

"Anything is possible, Mr. Columbus." Dr. Balderas pushes on. "What about voices? Do you hear voices talking to you or talking inside your head?"

"You mean my conscience?"

"No, I mean real voices. Different voices."

"There's nobody in here but me. This is what I've been saying all along."

"Okay, almost done. Do you ever feel like there's another person or a group of people inside you?"

Columbus thinks about this. Sometimes he feels like there's a whole life, most of which he's unaware of, inside him. A life he can't touch. There have been days, and weeks, when he wondered, doubted, lost faith in himself. "No," Columbus says.

"Is there another person or more than one person inside you who has a name?"

"I said no."

Dr. Balderas looks hard at his patient. Okay. Enough, he thinks.

Stay with me. Stay with me.

"I understand you play chess, Mr. Columbus."

"Not very well. I enjoy the game, though. Mostly I like to watch."

Dr. José Balderas has played chess all his life. He is good enough to have played in a few minor tournaments. He went to Las Palmas in 1996, watched Kasparov take the championship – studied Kasparov's match against Karpov for months afterward. He'd missed his son's birthday while in Las Palmas.

Dr. Balderas flips his palm open in the direction of the chessboard set up between two armchairs in the corner of his office. It's been a long time since he's had real competition. It's doubtful, but perhaps Columbus can actually play.

It's a plain sandalwood board with comfortable black and white marble pieces. The doctor opens and a couple of moves later, Columbus sacrifices one of his pawns in the centre of the board. In another fourteen moves the game is over.

Dr. Balderas studies the board for several minutes and then, astounded, tips over his king.

"The Budapest Gambit? At least a variation on it."

"Something I've been working on."

"I was not expecting a gambit." Dr. Balderas is stunned. This loss takes him completely off guard. "Shall we play again?"

"I'm all out of tricks, Doctor. Perhaps another day."

Columbus leaves the doctor at the chessboard, going over his moves, making notes on what happened. It's the first time he's lost a match in five years. After an hour, Dr. Balderas is certain of only one thing: it wasn't a simple gambit. There were brilliant complexities at work, and Columbus's skill as a chess player was certainly not a one-time trick.

~ ~ ~

Consuela fills her mug with coffee from the steel silo in the cafeteria.

She walks with Columbus through an archway. "Columbus has charmed his way into the pants or skirts of every woman he's met so far. Why not Isabella?"

"Because it's forbidden," he says and then stops walking, turns, and looks at her. "It's not that he doesn't want to. But he needs something from her, too. He needs her to be queen, not lover."

They take their coffee outside.

"Is that the only thing stopping him from –"

"If they become lovers, everything changes. Maybe she doesn't want him to traipse off across the Western Sea. And if they get caught, I can't imagine."

~ ~ ~

"It's like this," Isabella says. "To begin this, with even a single passionate, deep, lusty hot kiss, is death – very unpleasant death." She stops walking. But at the same time, I want him. How do I hold him without holding him? And is this fair? She walks the streets of Sevilla, cloaked in dark robes, a hood pulled across her face, talking – muttering – to herself. Her guards are on the perimeter, moving tree to tree, building to building, street corner to street corner, like a pack of constant wolves.

She tries again, imagining him standing in front of her. "Okay, it's like this." She pauses at the edge of an orange grove. Inhales the rich nascent blossom scent. Looks at the hazy moon, stuck in the branches of trees. "This would be a death sentence for us both. It is dangerous to even think about this joining – perhaps more dangerous than setting sail into an unknown ocean." This is ridiculous. She would have to be completely alone with Columbus to have this conversation, and that will not happen – not if she wants to live. There will be no trysts. No surrender to lust. She moves toward Gabriel, her chief of staff and head of security. He is, for Isabella, so profoundly nondescript that he is the perfect bodyguard. She smiles. Even among these trees, he blends in.

"We will visit Mr. Columbus," she says to Gabriel, "and we will discuss his proposed voyage. Set up a meeting."

"Is that the best course? Will this not instill hope for a hopeless proposal?" Gabriel has been her constant companion, bodyguard, and unfettered confidant for more than ten years. These are the kinds of questions she expects from him. But today she's just irritated. Gabriel has shoulder-length hair that has always been, in all of Isabella's memory, in a neat ponytail. It makes him look more severe than he really is.

"Just set up the meeting. I can handle Mr. Columbus and his obsession with sailing away in the name of Spain. Make it for tomorrow."

~ ~ ~

Noon the next day, they are seated in a small chamber inside the Catedral de Santa María de la Sede. Candelabras surround them. A blurry haze of coloured light in a high stained-glass window. The light in the room flickers, bends, and sways across the walls.

"Tell me again about your proposed voyage, Mr. Columbus. We need convincing before we consent to this idea."

"I am not sure I understand your question, Your Majesty."

"I mean, tell me what's it like at sea? We want to understand the attraction – the motivation."

Isabella is elevated; her chair on a small platform, a long red curtain puddles the floor behind her. Columbus sits in a lower chair directly in front of her. He looks tired, dishevelled, Isabella thinks. His shoulders are more rounded, if that's even possible. She makes a mental note to tell Gabriel to give Columbus enough money to buy some new clothes. "Convince me."

"At sea, the ocean is an undulating, constantly changing force. Our ships, at full sail, penetrate the ocean, move through the waves with a rhythmic, plunging energy. And yet we are but a tickle on the skin, a brush of a finger along the lower back . . . of the ocean."

Breathe, Isabella, she tells herself. Breathe.

"And it must be something," she says, "to stand beneath the masts as they thrust into the sky. The power of your ship's mast must be something to behold."

Columbus has no idea how to respond to this, so he bows his head. When he looks up, he can see Isabella's face is flushed.

"It is hot today, Your Majesty. I appreciate you seeing me."

"Do you ever worry about being swallowed?"

"Pardon me, Your Majesty?"

"Swallowed. Your ships, mast and all – swallowed by the ocean, being sucked down into the water, being lost. Swallowed until the very tip of your mast sinks into the ocean?"

"I . . . I try not to think of such things." He thinks about kissing her, about spending entire lifetimes in the nape of her neck, the arch of her back, the edges of her armpits, a single nipple. He thinks about her lips, an eternity of kisses, about being consumed by her, about making love until the word lovemaking folds in on itself a hundred thousand times.

"You must love the ocean," Isabella says.

Columbus looks into her eyes and they capture him again. How can eyes be such a deep blue? Something in him begins to rip. "More than the ocean knows," he says.

"And you want to sail this particular ocean, why?" Her voice is stern, commanding.

"This ocean is a mystery, challenging and tempting – shrouded in questions. From what I have seen, it is more beautiful than any other ocean I could imagine. It becomes more beautiful because it is withheld – forbidden and untouched."

"Can you imagine what it would be like, Mr. Columbus? I mean, to sail this particular ocean."

"Oh yes, I can imagine this ocean. Is it your wish, Your Majesty, that I sail this ocean?"

"Were it that simple," she whispers. She stands – moves toward him, brushes by his chair, her gown touching his clothing, slipping across his exposed forearm. The smell, her smell, lingers.

"We're done for today, Mr. Columbus. I'll let you know."

When he turns around, she's gone. The room is empty. Gabriel meets him in the outer chamber and gives him the address of a tailor. "It's been arranged," he says. "Get some new clothes."

Outside, Columbus is dizzy in the midday heat. He cannot determine if this light-headedness is from the heat or the conversation, which had its own intensity. He cannot find his car. In fact, there are so many cars in the parking lot that after an hour of searching, he stops for lunch. Columbus cannot help but pitch the Western Sea expedition to his waitress. His steak is, of course, heavily spiced. "What would we do without spice," he says to the hesitantly interested waitress who is too old for pigtails but regardless wears her hair this way. "But it's not so easy to get your hands on spice. It's a difficult journey to the East. Dangerous and inconsistent. A new, secure route would be a blessing would it not?"

"Ya, I guess," she says.

"Straight across the ocean and back with mountains of gold and spice."

"Okay."

Even though she seemed uninterested, Columbus finds this woman's phone number on the back of the bill.

~ ~ ~

He locates his car almost immediately. It is, in fact, in front of the restaurant. He removes the parking ticket from the wind-shield and throws it in the back seat with the others. He's off through the streets of Sevilla, and soon he's in the country-side. He's staying in a borrowed villa on the outskirts of town, which according to his sense of direction is just around the corner. He sees a sign for Almensilla, passes it, and is soon on a dirt road completely surrounded by olive trees. He doesn't remember this particular road but his villa has to be around here somewhere. He has no idea where Almensilla is but enjoys the name, says it out loud several times as he continues to push generally southward.

Several hours later, after many left turns and too many right turns, after thinking that he was finally travelling north toward

Sevilla and his bed, Columbus decides that the city must be just over the next rise. At the apex of the current stretch of road, he pulls over and gets out. The blue-grey ocean stretches along the horizon. Cracked yellow clouds. The sun will be setting soon. He pops the trunk open, pries the lid off the wooden case, and withdraws a bottle of wine. He walks to the front of his car and leans on the hood, looks wistfully across the lowlands and out to sea. Definitely not Sevilla, he thinks, pulling the cork out of the bottle, but beautiful nonetheless.

~ ~ ~

Consuela sits on her small balcony, overlooking the sluggish Rio Guadalquivir. A pot of mint tea is sitting on the table, steeping. The birds are so loud that she is beginning to find them annoying. They chatter at four in the morning and don't stop. Back and forth making nests and mating, eating, and singing – always with the songs! She'd love two minutes of silence. Faith called an hour ago. When Consuela hung up she wanted a drink, but there was nothing in the house.

Mint tea will have to do for now. She's not sure if Faith is convinced about Columbus – though, for the past hour she called him Bolivar, not Columbus. This name shift felt like a betrayal to her.

"It's strictly professional, Sis. Nothing happened. It was all me. I know it's wrong. Trust me. Nothing happened, and nothing is going to happen."

"But you sounded so in love. You can't have anything to do with this man."

"I've moved away from that ward."

"You're in a position of power. It's not only ethically wrong; it's legally wrong. You could go to prison."

"I can't imagine what the Inquisition would do."

"The what?"

"A board of inquiry, you know?"

It goes like this for an hour. They circle the issue, plow through it. Poke it, dismiss it, and circle around again. Until, finally, Consuela has had enough.

"I have to go," she says. "I've got a date tonight." A beautiful fabrication that ends things neatly.

"A date?"

"Yes, I may be old, but I'm not dead, Faith."

"Anybody I know?"

"God, let me get through the first date before you disapprove, okay?"

Silence hangs between them, thick and awkward.

"Look, his name is Bart," Consuela says finally. "He's an accountant."

"I'm just curious, Con. Nothing more."

Faith pauses. She wants to ask more questions but refrains. Her voice is pinched when she finally says, "Have fun. Talk to you soon. Love you, Connie."

Consuela pours the tea but it's tepid. She decides to go out for a drink. She'd love to find a bar that offered the discriminating protection Salvos's place gave to Columbus. But he was telling a story. It was just a story. Places like that don't really exist.

~ ~ ~

"You are suffering from something we big-brained doctors call a dissociative break. These things can manifest when some sort of painful event or loss occurs, and the patient doesn't want to face the pain. I know this sounds like a bunch of bullshit jargon meant to impress, not communicate. The plain version goes something like this: you're avoiding something and it's our job to try and find out what that is. When this dissociation is extreme, and in your case, I believe it is, the emergence of alter personalities can occur. Do you understand what I've just said?"

"Yes, I'm not going to sleep with a beautiful woman tonight. Nor am I going to drink three bottles of wine. Nor am I going to sleep in a bed with soft, 600-thread-count Egyptian cotton sheets. And I won't have room service to call for coffee and croissants in the morning."

Dr. Balderas smiles. He's amused, not pitying. "What I'm seeing in you – and this is based on my reading of Consuela's notes and my observations – is that you're exhibiting a dissociative fugue, or a dissociative identity disorder. Sometimes, when a patient is faced with an overwhelming traumatic situation and there's no physical escape, the patient will resort to *going away* in his or her head. You persist in your belief that you are, in fact, *the* Christopher Columbus. And we've got to start trying to find a way to unravel this story you're telling. At the bottom of your story is the thing that happened – the thing you're avoiding."

Dr. Balderas gets up and walks over to a cabinet behind Columbus, produces a key from his vest pocket, and opens the cabinet door. He pours two hefty glasses of red wine, hands one to Columbus, who is reclined on a black leather Barcelona daybed. Columbus is stunned. He has to sit up to accept the wine. Dr. Balderas locks his office door.

"Is this legal?"

"I'm the boss. And anyway, I don't believe you're dangerous. We wine lovers have to stick together." The doctor raises his glass. "To getting well," he says.

"To getting out," Columbus says.

They drink in silence. Dr. Balderas pours more wine.

"I'm wondering if you'll answer a question for me."

"Well, I'm the one on the couch. I rather like this new wine therapy you've devised. Fire away."

"I need you to really think about this before you answer. Okay?"

Columbus nods.

"Do you remember anything? I mean the smallest fragment of a fragment of half an imperfect memory – anything? Any minor detail."

Columbus closes his eyes. He'd love to answer yes. He tries to stop thinking. Listens. Is there anybody in there screaming to get out? Hello? Hello? But no, he is who he is. Then the face comes. There is a man's face. A bald man. His voice is soft-spoken. He's looking down at Columbus – asking if he's all right.

"Nothing," he says. "I only have these Columbus memories."

"What about places? Do you remember the Catedral de Santa María de la Sede in Sevilla? Can you close your eyes and see the orange trees in the courtyard, the stained glass? When were you there last?"

Columbus smiles. "You've been reading. That's a step beyond your predecessor." He takes a sip of his wine. "And if I lied and said yes, I do remember another life, would I –"

"That would only be a beginning step."

"Well, what if you're wrong? And what if I'm perfectly happy being who I am?"

"There is a danger that you are avoiding this event in your past with such fervour that, yes, you could never come out. That's a real danger. It would mean that you'd never get out of here."

Dr. Balderas looks evenly at Columbus. There is no panic, no hint of apprehension at the prospect of never getting out.

"In my notes," Dr. Balderas says, "I saw that you believe, and Dr. Fuentes's notes confirm this, that something horrible is going to happen – a disaster is looming, something you are powerless to stop."

"That's right."

"Do you still feel this way?"

His voice gets very small. "Yes. Something too horrible to even think about."

Dr. Balderas leans forward, elbows on his desk, one hand cupping his chin. "What if it already happened?" he says.

"What do you mean? I'm worried about the future."

"What if the something awful already happened and you're running away, not moving toward?"

"I was going to sea. Three ships in the harbour at Palos. Then I woke up here. I had my ships, supplies, a crew. Everything was ready."

"You were brought here and the only name on file is Bolivar. You have no idea how you came to be here?"

"Yes. No. Ask Nurse Consuela. She was there when I arrived."

"I'll look into it."

"Thank you. And thank you for the wine, too. It has been quite a while . . ." Columbus's legs feel wobbly when he goes to stand up; he's a little unsteady but also determined not to show it.

~ ~ ~

The next morning, he stops swimming, stands up, and slow-motion walks over to the edge of the pool – looks up at Consuela. She's been reading *Huckleberry Finn*. She puts the book down.

"Balderas is the real deal," he says. "I have a feeling he's going to solve this, and that's a bit frightening."

"Why would that be frightening?"

"If he's right, there's something horrifying at the end of this. Anyway, I get the feeling Balderas is the tipping point."

"Tipping point?"

"When you've been pushing on something and it starts to move, and you realize you couldn't stop it if you wanted." He smiles and nods to himself. "But there is a moment just before this realization when everything is completely calm."

~ ~ ~

Columbus is sitting up in bed as Nurse Tammy slathers shaving cream onto his face, making small foamy circles with her fingertips. Consuela is perched on the windowsill, watching – her head tilted, bemused. Columbus's eyes are closed. He's wearing a black cotton beret pulled to one side. Where he found this beret is a mystery. He seems to have a talent for getting people to do things for him, for convincing people to give him things. Nurse Tammy is meticulous and quick with her shaving. This efficacy pleases Columbus.

"Thank you," he says. He brushes his hand along his jawline and smiles. "This reminds me of a time when I was staying with Juan at a villa near Montoro. It was midday and we were shaving. It was not nearly as pleasant as this shave, but we had only cold water."

Nurse Tammy folds the razor into the towel, nods at Consuela, and leaves the room.

~ ~ ~

Behind the stable, Juan and Columbus stand at a table beneath a generous, spreading elm. Swallows chirp and make their clicking sounds in the upper branches. The sprinklers flicker to life in the lower vineyard and begin to make their rhythmic sputtering-water sound. The sunlight is filtered green through the canopy of leaves.

A pitcher of gin and tonic sits on the table between them. Behind and away from the stable, an arching passageway leads to the courtyard. One of the queen's friends owns this villa, an eccentric woman who is a bit of a patron of the arts, and in Columbus's case, a patron of hopeless causes. Selena is in the kitchen glancing sporadically, worriedly, through a small, square window at the two men. She can hear only bits and pieces of their conversation. Somewhere inside the main house, somebody is playing one of Bach's unaccompanied cello suites. It sounds to Columbus like the third suite, the one in C major. It's happier to the ear than the others. They finish shaving and sit down.

"This came for you yesterday," Juan says. He slides a brown envelope across the table and leans back to watch.

Columbus places his drink on the table, picks up the envelope, brings it to his nose, and sniffs. He sighs heavily, rips open one end, and peeks inside. Another birthday card with his actual birthday two months past. He does not have to look in order to know it's signed, "Love, Cassandra," or "Lovingly, Cassandra," or some other adoring salutation. How does she find me? he thinks.

"A woman?"

"A mistake," Columbus says.

"A persistent mistake, it seems."

"Her birthday greetings come randomly, or so it seems. Never on my actual birthday."

"Some say nothing is ever random. Everything is dependent on prior events."

Columbus thinks about this. He wonders about the events that caused his obsession. He thinks about the possible events that might be put into motion from his crossing the Western Sea. "Could you please randomly fill my glass?"

"That would certainly be dependent on your asking me to make it so."

"Just make it so now, and then be pleasantly unpredictable."

Juan fills his glass and smiles. "Some women," he says, "refuse to be gotten rid of."

They sit in the shade and share two slow pitchers of gin and tonic. At some point in their conversation, the Inquisition is mentioned. This is something neither of them is comfortable speaking about. There are regions of Spain where one not only has to be Catholic but must be the right kind of Catholic. But this villa is a safe haven.

"Look," Juan says, "this darkness is something human beings cannot escape. It is our nature. We wallow in it. And at the same time, it seems almost sanctioned by the Church. Abel and Cain. Cain slew Abel. And ever since Adam's son killed his brother, mankind has been killing and slaughtering and mutilating. Adam and Eve march out of the garden and their prodigy start the killing."

Columbus leans back in his chair. He's grappling with his faith today. He looked into the mirror as he was performing his morning ablutions and saw a godless man. It wasn't a frightening image, but he recognized the godlessness in himself. On days like this, he fumbles his faith. Drops it, picks it up, and drops it again. His faith is a slippery trout and he is squeezing too tightly. If God is the river, he thinks, in which my faith swims, this morning, I prefer to turn my back on that water. I'll take the trees and the mountains and all the grey clouds, instead.

He looks down at a small, black, lightning strike of a cat. It appears and disappears so suddenly.

"And let me tell you," Juan continues, "I have seen much of this world and hope to see a lot more. I do not mind that people are different – that they believe different things. I don't care. Jews, Muslims, Vikings, Marco Polo's Buddhists, witches, or pagans – I don't care. Muslims love their children the same as Christians and Jews."

Columbus pets the cat, which has hopped into his lap, kneaded, and curled up. "Once we start believing in things," he says, "we're at war against those who don't believe in the same things."

"But this religion seems to hate people, even the people it's supposed to serve. Next they'll be making us grow beards because Moses had a beard, and Jesus and God had beards, and then sending groups of Inquisition cowards to make sure our beards are the right length. Punishable by death, of course."

Columbus smiles. This is exactly the kind of conversation that could get them in trouble. But Juan is not done yet.

"Should we not be free to choose our path to God, or to choose no path at all? When you have to use violence, intimidation, and fear to impose your religion, you will never succeed. It should be called the *imposition*, not the Inquisition."

"What would you suggest? To hold no beliefs?"

"Is that even possible?"

"I don't know but I would like to try."

Juan unconsciously nods his head.

"Well, to not believing, then," Columbus says, raising and tilting his glass slightly toward Juan.

"To uncluttered minds and hearts," Juan says, taking a drink.

Columbus knows this way of viewing the world is not popular with the Inquisition. His fear is that one night he'll drink too much, speak his mind, and the wrong people will be at the table. He thinks about his sons and Beatriz. He worries about their safety.

What if the Inquisition turns on him? What if he's suddenly found to be a Jew, or his desire to sail the Western Sea is considered heretical? He is not a Jew, and he simply wants to see what's out there, but what if? Or what if his ideas about the physical world, its size and scope, conflict with the prevailing wind out of Rome? What if he's tortured into confessing something idiotic?

Columbus has a well-stocked cupboard of fear.

This morning, he opened his door and the news on the street was that thirty Jews had been killed in a small town in Italy – burned to death by a mob. And four women drowned, allegedly witches, after being tortured into a confession. Sign of the times. Brutal, senseless, filled with fear and ultimately stupid.

"It would be my wish to sail toward whatever is out there with an open mind and heart," Columbus says.

"Ah yes, your voyage." Juan fills their glasses and looks hard at Columbus. "Look, I've read the reports. May I be truthful?"

"As a baby's behind."

How is a baby's bottom truthful? Juan wonders. Doesn't matter. "You don't stand a chance of pulling this off. Unless you know a lot more than you're saying, you'd have to be an idiot to go to sea and expect to reach the Indies, or China, except in a foundering ship filled with dead men. Not to mention the fact you'll be adrift in a rowboat – set there by your mutinous, starving crew."

Columbus looks across the table at Juan and smiles, then nods his head. Here is a worthy challenge. If he can convince this man, he can convince anybody.

"You can't carry enough water, or food, for this voyage," Juan adds. "Maybe on a ship five times bigger, but first, you would have to build such a ship, hmm?"

"Faith against doubt. Hope against hopelessness."

"That's not a very convincing argument. I mean, if that's it, it's no wonder you've not lined up any ships."

"Juan, you could be right. Those at the commission are probably right. Most of my calculations grossly underestimated the size of the Earth. But if this is true, then could you tell me, please, how big the Earth is?"

"Well, I don't know. The commission did not know. How the fuck would I know? But I'm not proposing to sail halfway around the damned thing." Juan leans back and lights up a beedi. The heady scent spreads like incense in the dead air.

"The thing is, nobody knows for sure. This voyage to the Indies will not be executed with the use of intelligence, mathematics, or maps. It will be made by understanding what goes through the mind and heart of a man standing alone on a beach looking out to sea."

"Look, have you actually read any of the reports? While nobody is sure, they are fairly certain it is an immense distance to India and Japan across the Western Sea. The guys that made these reports are not dull. These are the best minds of our time. This is not based in superstition. It has to do with the curve of the Earth. This is science. And please don't tell me the planet could be shaped like a pear."

"Here's what I know, Juan. There's something out there. I do not know if it is Japan or the Indies. But I do know there is something out there and it is entirely reachable by sea."

"A new land?"

"That is possible. An island, or a group of islands, between here and Japan. A group of outer islands before Japan. I don't know."

"How is it that you know this?"

"I had a conversation with a Norseman."

"A what?"

"A Norseman, off the coast of Britain. He spoke of writings that mention a land out west that his people have seen. And I overheard a couple of sailors talking about finding a small man in a death boat twenty-one days west of the Canary Islands." Columbus does not mention that the Norseman said his people had been there. Nor does he bring up the fact the Norseman said there were demons there.

"A Viking? Don't they do horrible things to their children?"

"Have you ever seen a Viking do something horrible to a child? Jesus, where do these rumours come from?"

"You talked to a Norseman and you overheard a conversation. Well, that changes everything. A couple of rumours about land being there *really* sways me to your side. I'm sold. You're not an idiot after all."

"Juan, I want to tell you something that will not sway you in the least." Columbus takes a drink. "I am no longer trying to convince you. I simply wish to tell someone what I am feeling. You are not my family but I trust you by your actions." Columbus clears his throat, pours more gin and tonic into a sweating glass, and takes a huge swig. "Do you believe in fate?"

"No. I believe we make our own lives."

"Fine. It doesn't matter. What does matter is I can feel a shift. The weight is shifting toward this journey of mine, and I don't know if I could stop it if I tried. It's almost as if I am irrelevant. It's like this huge rock I've been pushing against has started to fall over. And now, it is not so easy to stop. It's going to fall. And when it finally hits the ground, anything that happens to be in the way of the rock will be squashed."

"You're right about it not being much of an argument."

"Regardless. I want you to watch. Because it's going to happen. And when it does, I'm going to need someone, a clear thinker, to observe and record with cold eyes – eyes that question. For that reason, for your steady dubious nature, I'd like you on the voyage."

"You what?"

"I want you to come."

"You want me to die with you when we run out of water and food and hope? I'm honoured, touched."

"That's not going to happen." Columbus speaks slowly. His voice becomes throaty, seems to slip down an octave.

Juan looks at him hard – sees the steady belief Columbus has in his own words written in his narrow, stern face. He concedes this belief. Columbus, at the very least, believes he will succeed.

"Don't answer right away."

Juan was not expecting an invitation. "I won't take your

invitation lightly, my friend. Now let me tell you about Selena, who is crazy about you, by the way."

"Is she really?" Columbus says.

Both men turn at the sound of pots clanging onto a stone floor somewhere inside the main house.

(iv)

She's running toward the picture-taker. This girl, who is four years old but looks to be six. People are always mistaking her for a six-year-old. This early burst of height is something she gets from her mother. I have no names, no understanding of relationships – just this half knowing.

This tall, four-year-old girl is running toward the picture-taker. This picture captures her, one foot off the ground, in mid-stride. There is glee in her smile and in her eyes. She is loved. She knows she is loved. Her arms are outstretched – she is coming for a hug. I have no memory of this girl. This little girl does not register as a part of my life. She has no name. There is no relationship.

This picture is within mountains. There are mountains heaved up and grey in the background. Mountains tall enough to have snow in the upper reaches. In the foreground is a silky green lake. There are flowers on the ground, along the path where this girl is running, and deciduous trees and shrubs.

She has sun-bleached blond hair that hangs to her shoulders. In this picture her hair is flying behind and to the left. Her face is focused, eyes directly on the photographer, and she is happy. He can see this girl is happy. Perhaps she likes the colour pink. Her shirt is pink and she is wearing pink leggings. A jean skirt with beads around the waist. Her boots are utilitarian, useful, brown leather. A yellow teddy bear is just visible, sitting upright in the tall grass behind her. Behind the yellow bear is a circle of stones enclosing four pine cones, a hawk's feather, a clump of lichens, and pine bark. This girl has worked quietly all morning, gathering the elements of this circle. It has a name. She builds these organic circles everywhere. They're called something. I can't remember what they're called.

I can imagine the low rumble of a train across the lake. The train moving large along the lip, at the edge of the water – going somewhere.

THIRTEEN

FAITH INVITES CONSUELA to Córdoba for the weekend, and Consuela hesitantly says yes. Faith is her only sister. She's blood. Even though Consuela tends to walk away from inter-actions with her sister hurt and slightly bruised, Faith means well. Faith is on her team and that's enough. Their parents are in Switzerland, in Neuchâtel, which is a bit of a commute. Consuela talks to her dad every Saturday morning. She used to take her first coffee and a cigarette and the phone; now, though, it's just coffee and conversation. Last Saturday, he'd once again proclaimed that his nose was still in fine form – that he and his nose were still in demand across France. He'd even had a call from a winery in the Okanagan region of Canada that was producing award-winning pinots.

Consuela books passage and arrives in Córdoba by nine o'clock. Rob picks her up and seems genuinely pleased to see her. Consuela is always taken aback by his looks. He seems more psychologist-like than Faith, with his round wire-rimmed glasses and neat grey beard. Combine his appearance with soft, welcoming eyes, and Rob is definitely someone with whom Consuela could see herself talking. But he's a city planner, not a shrink. Maybe she could still talk with him. Don't need a degree to have a conversation.

But Rob and Consuela only chitchat as they zigzag through the labyrinth of side streets and alleyways. When Consuela walks through the doorway, Faith hands her a drink.

"We're having a few people over for a late dinner. Do you want to change?"

"Hi to you, too. Sure, I'd love to get out of these clothes." Consuela is always impressed by Faith's composed appearance. It was warm and humid today, but she seems cool and un-affected. Consuela is dripping, feels oppressed by the humidity.

"Rob, can you take Connie's things to the guest room?"

The house is a sprawling, one-level six-bedroom home with servants' quarters out back. A central courtyard can be seen, and entered, from every room. A full-time gardener works solely on this inner-garden sanctuary.

In her room, Consuela unfastens her bra. She thinks about corsets. Can you even buy a corset these days? She changes into a fresh dress and picks flat but stylish shoes. She splashes water on her face, washes her armpits, dabs on an adequate amount of perfume, and heads down to the living room. Rob hands her another drink. Two other couples and one man, an architect named Marc, have already arrived and are chatting, with drinks in hand, in the living room.

Consuela downs her drink. It's a goddamned set-up. That's just perfect. Faith is playing matchmaker. And Consuela, the pathetic, spinster nurse. The unwanted, unloved sister. She immediately wants another drink, begins to peer around the room for a source.

Rob notices her thirsty look, hands her a glass of champagne. Faith scowls at him, then half smiles. The other two couples both have links to psychiatry. The wives stay at home with the kids; the men play with the minds of their patients.

"Oh, Connie could have been a doctor," Faith says, as part of her introduction. "She had better marks than me. Better study habits, too."

"Well, it's never too late to pick up a degree," Rob says, possibly trying to diffuse any perceived criticism.

"That's right. You have to want it, though," Marc adds. It doesn't come off as advice. It's a flat statement of fact, like he's been there, done that.

"Did you know that Marc is the one who designed our house?" Faith picks up the champagne bottle and goes around the circle, fills glasses, skips Consuela's.

"I didn't design the outer deck," Marc says. "Which is perfect, by the way."

Faith smiles her thanks. "It's a nice night. Shall we take in the view?" Faith poses the question but they all understand it's a gentle request. On the way out, Rob hands Consuela another glass of champagne.

"Thanks," she says.

"I had no idea she was going to do this."

"It's all right."

Marc meets them in the hallway. Rob brushes by toward the deck, which overlooks Córdoba, the Great Mosque in the distance, glowing soft orange.

"I hope you'll forgive me pushing my way into this dinner party. I wanted to meet you."

"You don't know me."

"I've seen pictures. Heard lots about you."

"One syllable," Consuela says, shaking her head. "I don't date men with names that have only one syllable. My ex-husband, one syllable. Not good." She's feeling the champagne. It seems the hallway is tilted slightly. Now it's straight, oh, now it's tilted.

"My name is Marcello," he says. "I just wanted to meet you. I just came out of . . . I'm not sure I want to date anybody. Not sure about dating. This is just a dinner party, yes? If I have three syllables do I qualify for a simple conversation?"

"Oh shit, I'm sorry. Yes. This is just dinner. My sister . . . I'm an idiot. I'm sorry."

"It was my idea. You're beautiful, by the way. Even more so when you're apologetic."

Just when you think you have it figured out, just when you're sure of yourself, that's when the rug gets pulled. She feels humbled and little.

Consuela has to admit, he's pretty good at this. Her walls are down and he's standing in the front hallway. But now there are a lot of doors, and most are locked. Yes, yes, he's a deep-voiced, lovely man. Shoulder-length dark hair and a kind face. He obviously likes her, but Consuela skims across the surface of him and thinks about Columbus. The magician, the spinner of tall tales, the enchanter.

Somewhere below is a horse-drawn carriage moving under the canopy of trees. Consuela can hear the steady rhythm of horse hooves hitting the street – a hollow sound that carries.

They sit down to dinner at a long table, staggered with candelabras, fine china, gleaming silverware. An obscenely massive bouquet of white lilies and gerberas is at mid-table.

They all sit west of the flowers, Faith at the head of the table, Rob beside her. Marcello is seated across from Consuela; Donna and Alf Rubinski across from Mary and Gordon Money.

I'm in hell, Consuela is thinking. This is a decent man. He's bright and not an ass-wipe like my ex, but this is all irrelevant. She compares every man to Columbus – and they do not fare well. She's head over heels in love with a man who's locked in a mental asylum and who thinks he's Christopher Columbus. She can't shake him. She can't stop thinking about him. His stories reverberate long after he's done. His eyes and his voice haunt her on the days she is off work.

I'm screwed, she thinks. I can't speak or act like I'm in love. Not here. Faith will go berserk. I have to pretend availability. Is this love? Is it love I feel for Columbus? My God, what's the test for love? A long line of clichés come to mind, things like inability to sleep, to eat, and to focus. Anxiety attacks. Obsession. Fixations. Lust. Desire. Oh, she's got desire all right.

"I don't understand a thing about love," Consuela says.

Everyone at the table stops – forks and knives and wine glasses halted. All eyes are on her.

Fuck, did I just say that out loud? she thinks. Consuela looks around the table at the stopped people.

"This is the reason we have poetry, and art, and dance," Marcello says. "The artists help us to understand this mystery, yes?"

"Could you be any more fucking romantic?"

"You don't like the romance?"

"No, I like the romance just fine." Faith is staring at her – no glaring – waiting for her to dismiss Marcello because she's already in love. Faith is waiting to pounce on her because she's in love with a patient, because she lied about dumping the patient.

Consuela turns to Marcello. She can't see through all his earnestness, his attempt to save her, his effrontery of charm.

She lowers her voice, leans toward him. "I'm just not as grounded as I . . . I'm just not open to romance right now."

"It's not a test," Marcello says. "It's a conversation at dinner."

"I know. I know it's not a test. It's just, I feel I owe you an explanation."

"You owe me nothing. I expect nothing. More wine?" He holds the bottle above her glass, smiles encouragement, and she nods.

Freedom, she thinks. Freedom is so seductive. Take everything off the table. Take agendas, perceived or true, off the table. Take away desire, lust, attraction, even friendship. Strip all that away. Disallow it. Make it just a conversation between two human beings. What's left is a potent and dangerous form of seduction. Some part of Consuela wants to know why. Why is there no desire? Why is there no offer of something more?

The people around the table continue talking, eating, drinking. Faith continues to watch with hawk eyes.

"You said something about just coming out of a relationship?"

"Yes, it was beautiful but only for a very short period of time." He smiles – more a grimace and a smile together, actually. "Sometimes it is like that, yes? We have been broken apart for a year and three months now."

But regardless of his charm, and this spacious seduction, Marcello begins to rub her the wrong way. He's too charming.

Too agreeable. Too willing to forgive and understand. There is something unbelievable about him. Consuela would love it if he'd look at her with those puppy-dog eyes of his and tell her that she's an idiot or that she drinks too much or that she has a potty mouth.

"What happened?"

"She left *me*," he says with clear emphasis on the "me" that says: it's unthinkable that anybody would choose to leave somebody as wonderful as him, and also, he does not want to talk about this.

"Oh, I'm sorry."

"Ah, it's a painful thing." Marcello's eyes fill with tears. He looks away.

Oh for fuck's sake, Consuela thinks. It's been over a year.

"I'm sorry," she says. "It must have been a very difficult breakup."

~ ~ ~

Before dessert is served, Consuela is in the bathroom. She's just pulled up her dress, pulled down her panties, and is sitting on the toilet when someone knocks on the door. Maybe they'll go away if I ignore them, she thinks. The knock comes again, a little louder this time. "Just a minute," Consuela says. "I'll just be a minute."

"Connie, it's me. Let me in."

It's too far to reach the door, so Consuela half walks, her dress around her waist, panties at her knees, to the door and lets Faith in. She sits back down on the toilet. "I'm not done yet, Sis."

Faith is leaning forward toward the mirror, looking at her hair, running a dampened fingertip under her eyes to erase the smudged eyeliner. She lights four more candles on another candelabra – squints at the side of her face. "Isn't he a dream?" She does not look at Consuela.

"Who?" Of course, she knows who but wants to irritate her sister.

"Marc," she says. "Marcello. And I happen to know he's available."

"Yes, we had that conversation."

"And?" She pulls her shoulders up, and one at a time, sniffs her underarms. Reaches for the powder and puffs both her armpits.

"And he's charming and very agreeable."

"I knew it. I knew you two would hit it off."

"I never said –"

"Oh, you don't have to. I can tell."

Consuela wipes. Her smell – a sweet, strong, sexual scent – takes her to Columbus.

~ ~ ~

"Would you risk your deepest dream on a game? You have dreams, don't you, Consuela?"

"Yes, of course I have dreams. I want to be a mother some-day, though I'm in no panic about this. I'd like to get married again, more carefully this time. And I want to see Tibet."

They are sitting on a bench, in a long hallway of arches. Columbus has his back against the stone wall. The day is stranded inside a pewter sky, but it's warm, and not yet raining. They face a small courtyard with a tiled fountain in its centre. An eight-point-star-shaped fountain with only a trickle of water. The tiles are in disrepair but it is easy to imagine that they were beautiful once. There must be ten shades of blue in that bottom row, Consuela thinks.

"So if I said to you that I will guarantee a healthy baby and a loving husband but only if you can roll a seven or an eleven on these dice, would you?"

"Maybe."

"What if I said this was your only chance? Make the roll and it happens – but anything other than a seven or an eleven and it's over. You won't have a baby. You won't marry. You won't visit Tibet. Ever."

"Those are not good odds," she says. "I'd have to be pretty desperate."

~ ~ ~

They clomp into the fortress courtyard. The coolness of the enclosure hits like a wave as they ride from the pounding, exposed heat, into the stone fortress. The temperature difference under the entranceway arches is palpable and welcome. They dismount the horses, toss their reins, and storm up through the stone corridors to the poolroom. Royal hangers-on, courtiers, petitioners, lobbyists appear and bow and lurk in the shadows. They seem to spring up like colourful weeds who wish they were flowers. An infestation of seedy colour wherever the king and queen travel. Ferdinand opens the door and motions for them to use it. Nine men bow and mumble "As you wish" and other agreements as they leave. When they are alone, Ferdinand turns to the door and screams, "Sycophant pigs! Flattering parasites! *¡Manájate!*"

Columbus stifles a laugh. Places his hand across his mouth to hide his grin. Tries to pull his face down into an even expression.

"Oh, laugh, Mr. Columbus. It's funny, is it not?"

"Yes, Your Majesty. It is funny."

The king walks toward one of the windows and looks into the courtyard. Two chambermaids stand in the enclave talking. He stands watching them for some time. Silence lulls the room. Columbus wonders what it is the king is looking at. He seems fixated.

"What is it that they require?" Ferdinand says, turning around and picking up a stick. He cracks the small formation of coloured balls by poking a white ball at his end with the stick. The balls scatter across the smooth surface and he stands back amazed. He's thrilled every time by this small explosion of colour.

"Well, I am merely your humble servant, but I think they want to be close to power, close to greatness, close to God." Columbus sinks the six ball into the far corner and draws the white ball back so it lines up with the seven. "They hope your greatness will rub off on them." He drops the seven and leaves himself set up for the three ball, a table-length, along-the-cushion shot. "It is well understood, if you have the ear of the king, even for a short time, you have power," he says. He puts too much English on the three and it ricochets to mid-table.

"Are you speaking of our courtiers? The army of bastard sycophants who surround and annoy me?"

"Was that not the question, Your Majesty?"

"No, but regardless, your answer was an insightful one. I was referring to those enigmatic creatures who haunt me – women. What is it they require from us? That was my question, and I suspect you will have no easy answer to this. What is it that women want from us, Mr. Columbus?"

The king lines up the eleven ball and cracks the white ball with just enough bottom to send it flying off the table and through a window. They hear it clacking across the courtyard. The king picks a new white ball from a golden bowl on the window ledge and hands it to Columbus.

Columbus wonders if he should try to lose. He is playing the king, after all. It wouldn't do to severely beat the king at a game he loves. He places the ball on the table and then proceeds to clear the table, knocking the eight ball into the side on a double bank to win.

"Thank you for the game, Your Majesty. I was lucky to win."

"No. You played well. You deserved to win. Another game?"

The king smiles as he places the coloured balls into a tight formation. Columbus is disarmed. He feels closer than ever to winning the king's favour for his proposition. Here he is, a lowly navigator, not even Spanish, playing pool with the king. Riding beautiful horses with the king through the streets of Córdoba. He is inside the highest inner circle. He is dizzy with how close he stands to the power. He must certainly let the king win the next game. All the games that follow, in fact, he should lose as skilfully and subtly as possible.

"Women," the king says as he hands the stick to Columbus, "confuse and confound me. Yet they are ridiculous, necessary mysteries." He picks a white ball from the bowl and heaves it through the open window. They hear three clicks and a splash.

Columbus breaks the formation on the table. "There is a problem with the queen?" Three solid-coloured balls disappear. His next shot should be the two ball, a solid, in the far right corner. But he picks a striped ball and lines it up.

"You wouldn't purposely try to lose because I am the king would you, Mr. Columbus?"

"In all honesty, Your Majesty, I should like very much to ask a question."

"In all honesty, proceed."

"Should I try to lose, Your Majesty? Would that be a good idea?"

"Well, you're a wise and intelligent man, Mr. Columbus." He leans back against a pillar. Smiles. "We had a very enjoyable day together, didn't we?"

"It was a glorious day." Columbus stands up straight and looks at the king. A gangly, slouching young man with deep-blue eyes. If he were not the king, Columbus would not trust him. Come to think of it, just because he is a king was no reason to trust him. Deceitful, cruel, and vicious were words frequently attributed to this king, and even the queen. Too much leisure time, Columbus thinks. But this king has been nothing but honest, forthright, and kind to him.

Do I lose, or do I play the game the best I can? Do my ships teeter in the balance on this decision? How important is it to me that I win?

Columbus walks around the table. Observes the obvious two-ball shot, then sees a three-ball combination that would drop the four ball. A difficult combination shot. The formation of the three balls appeals to Columbus. He thinks about the similar star formation; three stars slashed across the sky like a belt. He chooses this shot. He chooses to try and win, regardless of any consequences. Decides he must be Christopher Columbus whether it hurts his dream or not. He bets on this king's honour and drops the four ball gently and exactly.

"An excellent shot," Ferdinand says and claps Columbus on the shoulder.

Columbus wins seven more games. The king doesn't even come close to winning a game. He misses shots completely, shoots the wrong colour, and sinks the eight ball twice. They stop and Ferdinand calls for wine.

They do not feel the direct heat of the day inside the stone building, but the air is blistering and still. Long streams of sunlight from high, narrow fenestrations slash through hanging dust in the room. The king walks the entire long room away from the pool table to an elevated throne, pulls his robes aside, and sits. Three servants bring wine to the king and then deliver a goblet to Columbus. The wine is red and slightly chilled.

"Leave," the king says to the servants, who bow out the door and shut it behind them.

"Have you had sufficient time to ponder my riddle, Mr. Columbus?" The king must speak loudly in order to ensure that Columbus hears him at the far end of the room.

"The problem with women in general or the queen specifically, Your Majesty?"

"Come down here, Mr. Columbus. So we can talk."

Columbus walks toward the throne. Stands before the elevated king and is reminded of his place. He bows his head.

"I am sorry, Your Majesty. I have no answers to the riddle of women." He thinks of the simple connection he has with Selena, the more complex but enjoyable time he spends with Beatriz. And then he thinks about the queen. His relationship with the queen has become impossibly complex and dangerous. It would be prudent to ignore any feelings or thoughts he held for Isabella. Isabella was the queen. She was the queen. This man's wife.

Ferdinand's face transforms into something awful. As if painful memories have suddenly risen to the surface of churning water. Hopeless despair. He covers his face with his hands. "Women, Mr. Columbus, women. There are times, in the middle of the night, in complete darkness, when they weep. I cannot understand why they weep and yet I am held at fault for their weeping. They cannot, or will not, say exactly what my fault is, yet at these times they wish to be held by me and told that everything is well and good. But I do not believe this to be true. So they wish me to form lies in order to comfort them and when I say to them, in order to be truthful and clear, 'You wish for me to lie to you?' they weep with more water from their eyes than I have ever seen. And these tears, also, are my doing. Does this make sense to you?"

"Are you speaking of the queen, Your Majesty?"

"The queen? No. The queen does not weep. She has never wept. She is the strongest woman I know. The queen and I have no connubial battle. We have no troubles. She chases the

Jews from our lands. She chases the Moors from our lands. She and her bloody Inquisition chase heretics from our lands. She chases people we simply don't like from our lands. And I? I chase women. A simple and elegant arrangement, don't you think, Mr. Columbus?"

Columbus does not answer.

"What troubles you, sir? Are you pondering your ships or do you, too, contemplate the quandary of women? Or are you ill?"

"Acquiring the ships is often on my mind, Your Majesty."

"And what does the queen say?"

"She says wait until the fall of Granada."

"Well, that's what you should do then. When we walk the courtyards of the Alhambra, you'll have your ships. And while we wait for the queen to reclaim Granada, we shall play much pool and do much riding. For you are also a mystery, Mr. Columbus. You wish to sail off into the unknown. Possibly to your death. To introduce Christianity to Japan and the Indies. To bring honour and wealth to Spain. This wealth part is the portion of your proposal that most interests the queen and me. We believe you are either very brave or very stupid – or absolutely crazy. But regardless of all these things, you are inspired. Yes. Mostly, I think, you are inspired. Come, let's play more pool." He grabs the wine bottle and his glass in one hand, and Columbus's sleeve in the other. Pulls the baffled navigator the length of the room.

"I tell you what, Mr. Columbus. Since you are a good friend of Spain, I will make you a proposition." He gathers the balls from the pockets around the table. "I'll play you one game for your ships."

Columbus turns toward the king, shocked by the realization that this may be it. He's shocked by the whimsical, careless nature of this offer. "What?"

"I'll play you for your ships. Win the next game and three caravels are yours. Provisions included. You'll have to find men dumb enough to follow you."

Columbus is stunned. For ten years he had been incubating the dream, cajoling the doubters, fighting his own doubts. For ten years he had been envisioning a world that was smaller than commonly held beliefs. A world that could be traversed with a journey by sea to the west. The university commission did not believe it could be done. But they did not know all he knew. The Lord Himself could speak before the commission and they would not believe. "Look fellows," the Lord would say, "I think perhaps there is a chance some of your calculations are off. I ought to know. From where I sit I can pretty well see, well, everything." But if He did not have the proper upbringing or education, the commission would deny, deny, deny. They make decisions based on the applicant's social standing or nobility, and not on truth. Bureaucratic bastards. And now, here, before Columbus the king offers to fulfill his dream, not based in a belief of that vision but, rather, on a game of angles. It was too much.

"I am sorry, sire, but I cannot."

"Why, Mr. Columbus, have you lost your faith for this adventure?"

"No, Your Majesty. I . . . I need someone to believe in me enough to take a chance. It would not be moral to leave it to a game of angles and colourful balls."

"Same thing, isn't it?"

"I'm a navigator, not a pool player."

"Do you not believe in this dream of yours enough to take a chance?"

"You ask too much, sire."

"Perhaps you do, too."

Columbus sits beside a small statue of the Virgin Mary. He feels sick to his stomach. Crosses his arms. Closes his eyes. Drinks slowly from his goblet. Am I willing to risk all on a game? Is it a risk? The king plays badly. The king is not good with these angles. Perhaps if I am asking others to take a risk on me, I should be willing to take a risk also.

The king walks to a window, his hands clasped behind his back, and observes the courtyard.

"Fine," Columbus says. "One game for the ships."

"Well spoken, Mr. Columbus."

Columbus breaks but no balls go down. It's the only chance he gets. Ferdinand clears the table in a stellar display of deceitfulness. With each ball the king sinks, Columbus's spirits sag a little bit more. At the end of it, he cannot face the king.

"Well done, Your Majesty," Columbus says. "I'm ruined."

Ferdinand smiles kindly. Turns a compassionate face to the navigator.

"No," he says, "you are not ruined. Neither is your idea of sailing west. If you had won, I would have personally seen to your ships, somehow. But the queen always has the final say in matters of the sea. In fact, she has the final say in matters of war, roads, religion. Almost everything."

"There's still a chance then?"

"Oh, Mr. Columbus, you've only proven your desire, your commitment, and your determination. These things, I will communicate to the queen."

Columbus bows his head, then very quietly says, "Thank you. Thank you." And then he looks up at the king who is eyeing the pool table. "But you do not want me to explain to you why I know this journey is possible?"

"Yes, yes, yes . . . I'm sure you have your reasons."

"This new route could be very lucrative for Spain –"

"Yes, yes . . . money is good."

"And of course I will carry God and Christianity to Japan and India –"

"Well, that's fine. That's a fine thing to do. I'm sure they'll be thrilled to hear that their own system of beliefs, whatever it may be, is . . . well . . . wrong."

"And I will claim whatever land I might discover for Spain."

"Hmmm . . . expansion is good, I suppose . . . Yes. Very good. Quite convincing. Yes."

"And I will –"

"Columbus! Enough! I tell you what I'm going to do. I'm going to buy a few thousand shares of Columbus Sails West Incorporated . . . see where it takes me."

"Thank you, Your Majesty."

Ferdinand touches Columbus's shoulder and the navigator looks up into the king's dark eyes. "Another game, my friend?" the king says.

"I'm sorry, Your Majesty. I have lost the stomach for pool today. I think I have to lie down."

"Tomorrow then, Columbus. I'll send up one of my special

chambermaids. She'll make sure you have a good sleep." He turns, draws open double doors, finds a small crowd of courtiers in the hallway. "Tomorrow, Mr. Columbus!" he shouts. "Out of the way you bloodsucking sycophants!" And they mutter after him down the hallway.

~ ~ ~

Emile, to his surprise, has managed to keep a few friends in the company. He calls one of his Spanish contacts when he arrives in Marbella and finds out that there is a concierge who will work for Interpol – for a price. "He's very reliable," the agent says. "I helped him with a family matter a few years ago." Emile finds the hotel and checks in. It's too much money, but it's the hotel where his contact works. His room faces the Mediterranean. The balcony looks out over the tops of palm trees. From the hotel lounge a walkway leads onto the beach. It's clear and windy – a good steady breeze coming from the east. Emile finds the concierge and convinces him to ask around about a confused man. Emile emphasizes the fact this man will likely appear baffled – he might not know who he is or where he's going.

"I think he thinks he's Christopher Columbus," Emile says. "A theory. This is only a theory," he adds. He'd not spoken these words out loud before, but all the pieces added up to this simple statement. The three ships down south. Isabella. Your Majesty. The concierge gives him an eyebrow-raised, skeptical stare. Emile makes his face go hard, stone cold, and flat. The concierge sighs and nods. Of course, there was much that did not add up. Morocco didn't make sense for a man who might think he's Christopher Columbus. And this man's sense of direction seems to be absent. One would think that Columbus would always know where he was. Ah, it's just a theory, Emile reminds himself.

~ ~ ~

For three days, Emile bides his time. He walks around his room naked – wearing a towel occasionally – and semi-drunk, quite drunk occasionally.

He watches television and orders room service. He curses the stupidity of television, turns it off, and drifts into the minefield of memories involving his ex-wife. Conversations about his work that turned into three-day blowouts about how obsessed he was, how he was never home, how he was distracted by his work when he was home. But she would have loved this room, this view, being in a fine hotel on the ocean. He's finding it more difficult to recall why they actually fell apart. There had to be more to it than his obsessions. But there wasn't really a defining moment. He'd been tracking someone in Berlin, and when he came home hardly anything remained in the apartment. It was an equitable splitting up of belongings. She'd been fair. Emile didn't bring a lot of material possessions into their life. She'd taken what had been hers, and not much was left at the end of that process. He sits up in bed, pours another whisky, and turns the television back on.

~ ~ ~

At 3:30 A.M. on the third night, Emile can't sleep, can't watch the television anymore, and doesn't want to drink anything. He heads for the roof of the hotel to get some air, to breathe, to move his legs. There's a jazz club on the top floor. He gets off the elevator and walks down the hallway, barefoot and wearing the hotel housecoat over his trousers, looking for a stairwell to the roof. He can hear the sound of someone tuning a piano coming from inside the club. Emile walks past the door, which is slightly ajar, and is halfway down the hall before he stops – acknowledges the pull of the piano. He hasn't played since before the Paris incident. He hasn't felt the desire to play.

Inside the doorway it takes a while for his eyes to adjust. Through the windows the sparkling lights of Marbella arc along the shore of the Mediterranean. One thin spotlight shines directly onto a piano sitting on a small stage against the far wall. The man at the piano has a full grey beard and a no-nonsense face. His focus is on tuning the piano. He looks up at Emile quickly, then back to his job. He says nothing. Emile stands in the entranceway, awkward but also drawn to the pure sound of the piano. The single notes ring out – they hang in the room. Emile thinks of a raven, or a hawk, suspended in an air current, wings motionless except for a small flutter. A minute later, the grey-bearded man is packing up his gear. He looks toward Emile.

"Still there?"

"I –"

"Come and play then. It's what you need, yes? I will have a nightcap – a little Courvoisier. It is my custom. And I will listen." The man has a thick Slavic accent. Emile's not sure that he wants an audience tonight. It seems his feet are nailed to the wooden floor.

"It's what you need," the man says again. "I'll pour some drinks in the back." He does not move like an old person. There is a lithe vitality in his walk.

Emile sits at the piano. It's a Steinway, a good choice for a jazz piano. He read somewhere that Keith Jarrett plays a Steinway. Emile plays a single note, a middle D, and lets it ring out in the dark room. Then he begins to unravel all he was taught as a child. He purposely forgets how chords work. He un-remembers scales, theories, and circles of fifths. He plays notes and combinations of notes that make no sense – he embraces dissonance, and yet there is an ephemeral order. Emile draws on feelings and colours. If he stumbles upon a musical cliché, he will repeat it, warp it, ruin it to the point where it becomes original and new. He remembers scents. Rain. Patchouli. Sandalwood. Cedar. Leather. He plays weather. He plays the stars in the village of his youth in France. The colour of ocean at dusk – the indigo sky meeting the water evenly. The way dried grasses touch the wind. He plays the memory of his wife's long legs and slender toes. He plays a scant memory of her voice speaking his name – whispering his name over and over inside an absence of periwinkle. And then he comes to what happened in Paris and he plays this, too. He plays its pain, its sadness, its loss and remorse. He begins to play the damaged parts of himself. Half an hour later, he is improvising inside a sixteen-bar blues riff he didn't know he knew. The grey-bearded man is sitting at a table in the middle of the club sipping his cognac and reading a newspaper by candlelight. Emile notices there is a snifter of cognac sitting on the bench beside him. He stops playing, turns around on the bench, and looks out into the club. "Thank you," he whispers.

The man pulls the newspaper down, away from his face. "It's nothing to pour two drinks when I am already pouring one," he says.

"No, not the cognac –"

"I know what you meant."

Emile reaches for the snifter and sips. It's lukewarm. How long have I been playing? he thinks.

"I'm here every night. Come when you like and play. Or not. Just come for Courvoisier if you prefer."

"I'm . . . I don't play well enough to do this piano justice."

"It is not always about technique – but it's *always* about heart. What more can we do? Your playing is suggestive of Monk's style. I saw him once. It was amazing the way he would get up in the middle of a song and do that little dance of his, around in a circle beside the piano. Completely absorbed in the music."

Emile finishes his cognac and begins to put his hand into his pocket. He wants to pay for the drink, at least.

"Stop. I own this place," the man says, his voice flattened out and matter-of-fact. "I can buy drink for whomever I please. Besides, you gave me this beautifully broken music of yours."

The next day, he goes down to the beach at two in the afternoon, when most sane people are out of the sun. He swims two hundred strokes exactly, straight out into the gulf, then turns around and swims back to shore. He does not remember consciously choosing the number two hundred. It just seemed like the right number.

~ ~ ~

On the morning of the fifth day, he opens the door. "Oh, hello," he says. "I desperately need coffee." The concierge is a short, efficient man with a very smooth complexion and he smells like cigarettes. He flips open his cell phone, says something very quickly, ending with Emile's room number.

"I have some news," the concierge says, and then pauses.

He takes Emile's money without blinking. "I believe your missing man was in a bar near here, a few months back," he says. "A place called the Pom-Pom. It's a gay bar, you know? Several of the patrons of this bar showed interest in your man – if you know what I mean. But it seems he only wanted to talk."

"Are you sure it was him?"

"We are quite certain. I don't think he belonged there, though, if you catch my meaning. He kept looking around – said he was worried about the Inquisition. The patrons of this bar thought he meant the police."

"Do you know where he went? Did he say anything about where he was going?"

"Apart from his nervousness, he did not appear to be confused. He did say he was a sailor and that he would be going to sea. Eventually, he went home with someone."

"Do you have a name?"

"Nobody in this bar has a name."

The concierge opens the door and Emile hands him a couple more folded bills. Emile's mind is racing. What was this guy doing in a gay bar? Did he actually get picked up?

~ ~ ~

Emile is back in Paris for a few days to catch up on paperwork, to put a few of his simpler cases to bed, to recharge. He puts his book down on the bed. The apartment misses his wife. He misses her. It's been two years, and he still carries the hole created by her absense. In the kitchen, he pours boiling water over a tea bag in a mug. I'm alone, Emile thinks.

Get used to it. So is my strange man of great interest. He's somewhere in Spain.

Emile crawls into bed – places his tea next to his laptop on the bedside table. He knows exactly what he would say to this man. He would tell him that no matter how far he runs, or how much he drinks, or how badly he wants a new beginning, his life is always with him. There is no separation from your own shadow. Emile sniffs, smiles. This is the culmination of his wisdom after two years of therapy.

He imagines this man living alone somewhere in the mountains, perhaps in the Basque region, on the French side, in a small village where he works as a labourer. He disappears into the mountains on weekends – comes back with fish. He is known in the town only as the *arrantzale* – the fisherman. He will be exhausted from his day, barely able to eat his soup. He will stagger home to his apartment above a wine store, walk through the doorway, and flick on the light. Maybe he will look down at his own shadow, which is sprawled into the hallway, sigh heavily, and reach for the *ardo* before he closes the door. He will down half the bottle in his first attack. Some of the wine will drip down his chin and he will not care. He wants sleep. He wants dreamless ironclad sleep and then back-breaking labour in the morning. And then more wine, and more dead sleep.

Emile sits up in bed. He has a sudden shadow-memory, an image of his ex-wife beside him in the bed. Like when a cat dies and you think you see the cat moving from room to room, or sitting at the door waiting to be let out in the morning. The ghost cat exists only as a hazy after-burn in your retina. But, of course, she is not there. She's in Guadeloupe with her sister. She's out of his life. Has taken her leave. Moved on. This half memory is enough to shock him fully awake. It's eerily quiet, a muffled lull – the street sounds pulled back. Even Paris can be becalmed. Emile listens. The clock in the kitchen has the loudest tick he's ever heard. Water is running somewhere in the building.

He wishes the man well. He hopes he is able to successfully escape any horrors that chase him in the night. If he is alive. *If.* He's been off the grid for a long time.

~ ~ ~

Consuela searches the words *Hafiz, Columbus, fifteenth century, Persian, chess, professor,* and *teacher. Hafiz* because of his knowl-edge of the poet, his poems, and his comment about reading them in Persian. *Columbus* and *fifteenth century* for the obvious reasons. *Chess* because she suspects he's very, very good – much better than he pretends. And, finally, *teacher* and *professor* because he lectures – he seems like a teacher. It's a guess, but a guess is all she has. On the thirty-fourth page of her search she finds an oblique reference to Mehmet Nusret, the birth name of Turkish humorist and author Aziz Nesin, who died in 1995. He had apparently championed free speech, especially when it came to the right to openly criticize Islam.

On a whim, she adds this name to a new search, with the words *April* and *March*. He came to the institute in April, but nobody knows where he was before that. These are more calculated suppositions. Consuela is sitting at her computer with a glass of chardonnay on the desk beside the screen. After almost two hours, her search is still fruitless. She forgoes the glass and drinks out of the bottle.

~ ~ ~

Columbus times his journal entries so Consuela is not working when he writes. This morning he finds a corner of the upper deck, far from the small, broken fountain that only trickles water, fills with leaves and rainwater. He can imagine what it would have been like, where the water would have flowed – the mist, the spray – what it would have felt like to have the luxury of that mist on a hot day.

(v)

Row after row of desks. These desks are tiered. They rise up and away from the centre of this picture. The lights are slightly dimmed. There are people – they are probably students. They're all looking at a focal point at the front of this room. Many of the students are typing into their laptop computers. Most of them have laptops. Many of these students are smiling. A few are laughing. As if the person teaching the class has just said something funny. There is no way to determine what kind of class this is. Most of the students are female.

He pans the front row for clues. All women in the front row. On the far right a young woman is looking down. She's holding a cell phone in her lap – slightly under her laptop, which sits on the little desk – probably texting someone. Or reading a text message.

Analogue to digital. That's what's happening in this classroom. A human being – the analogue bit – will offer up information and the students will smash it to bits and bytes, ones and zeros. They will do this 350 unique ways. And they will do it almost instantly.

There is a woman in this frozen moment who is not translating the lecturer's words into digital. She sits mid-row, about four tiers up. She is looking into the centre of the picture. If the lecturer is the one holding an imagined camera, she's looking directly into his, or her, eyes. She has shoulder-length red hair. She's wearing a navy blue blouse. Her head is tilted into her hand, her thumb rides her jawline, and two fingers rest on her cheek. Her other hand rests in her lap. Her eyes penetrate. Even in this stopped-time image where nothing moves, her eyes cut through any pretense.

A brunette-haired woman in the front row is taking notes the old-fashioned way, with a pen and paper. Is it that she can't afford a swanky Macintosh computer? When he surveys the room, the vast majority of little lights in the centre of the backs of the screens are apples. Or is it something more romantic with this woman? Perhaps she's found this method of note taking is the most efficient way for her to learn. Something in him is drawn to this woman who either purposely, or by economic circumstances, rejects the prevalent technology.

In the second tier, a man with dark-rimmed eyeglasses is focused on his computer screen. He could be playing a game or writing a book. He seems far away. Even in this snapshot, there is distance, a disconnection between him and the lecturer.

In the aisle desk, three rows up, a blond-haired woman is crying. Why didn't he see her before now? He probably went past her ten times in his mind. Her mascara is running down her cheeks. Nobody around her seems to know she is crying. She is not afraid to let the lecturer see her tears. She does not wipe them away because those around her would begin to catch on. Now that he has found her, he can sense her sorrow. The physicality of her pain is so apparent in her eyes, and mouth, and shoulders. Her eyes fluctuate from a fierce don't-you-dare-pity-me to a resigned grief. Her mouth is frozen in a sad, even line. Her shoulders are wilted, careless. Her posture is not beneficial to breathing. Her breathing stays high in her chest, never goes deep. These are silent tears. Is she experienced in crying silently? Why?

How does this picture fit into his life? He can't recognize anybody. No names come when he goes over this image. He thinks maybe he's at the middle of it. He's the teacher, or the lecturer, but what does he know that he could teach?

FOURTEEN

THE TABLE IS LONG AND NARROW, and made of oak planks. Luis de Santángel sits not at its head but, rather, stranded in the middle, surrounded by councillors. Santángel's black hair is pulled back neatly behind his ears. His hands are manicured. His clothing is plain. Nothing ornate, though he could easily afford it. His overall appearance is friendly and open but also down to business. He sits with his back to the window. He's partially silhouetted against the morning sky, which is cloudless and holds the promise of a hot day. Columbus sits directly across from Santángel. At his right hand is his lone companion, his friend, Father Antonio.

Eighteen to two, Columbus thinks. They must believe this meeting is important. Either they believe wholeheartedly in my journey or they are covering all possibilities.

"Drinks?" Santángel says. "Mr. Columbus?"

"No, thank you," Columbus says, speaking for both himself and Father Antonio.

The men surrounding the queen's treasurer are all laden with paper. Some have binders; others, piles of paper clipped together. All have cell phones either hanging from their belts or sitting on the table. Santángel opens a small black file folder that sits neatly on the table in front of him, its edges square to the table's edge. He flips the first page over and leans back in his chair. All side conversations stop.

"Very well, then," Santángel says. "I first want to congratulate Mr. Columbus on the successful financing of his impending voyage across the Western Sea to Japan and India. This is quite an accomplishment." Santángel leads the small herd of lawyers and councillors in polite applause. He clears his throat and begins again. "The purpose of this meeting is to determine the compensation Mr. Columbus will receive, if any, from the profits and proceeds of this expedition. We are here today to determine any remuneration for Mr. Columbus and his crews. I expect our negotiations to be somewhat complex but hopefully not too lengthy. Now, as a starting point, I've prepared a base-offer sheet." He turns toward the far end of the table where a diminutive, bald man with dark-rimmed glasses is fidgeting with a brown briefcase. One of the latches is stuck. "John? Could you hand out the sheet? I believe there are enough copies for everybody to have one."

"I'm . . . I'm having a problem with this latch. Just a minute."

"As I was saying, Mr. Columbus, this negotiation, while complex in nature . . ."

This guy loves the sound of his own voice, Columbus thinks. I'd love a cup of coffee. Better, an espresso. I bet they'd get me one if I asked.

"John? How are we doing?"

"I've almost got it." John's got a knife wedged in the lock, and he's prying it back and forth.

"Perhaps," says Santángel, "we should take a break until we can solve the briefcase problem." He smiles, more a twinge.

"A question Señor Santángel," Columbus says softly.

"Yes, Mr. Columbus."

"I'd love an espresso."

"Emilio," Santángel snaps. "An espresso for Mr. Columbus." One of the crowd of lawyers stands and moves toward the door. "And I'll have one, too."

Now the other lawyers start offering orders.

"I'd like a café solo."

"I'll have a double espresso with a wedge of lemon."

"Do you have decaf?"

"Could I get a latte, extra hot?"

"I'll have a café con leche."

"I got it." It's John with the briefcase. "It's open. I got the briefcase open." He's smiling and holding his left hand, which is bleeding. "I need a bandage." John sits down. A woman in a grey dress pulls her briefcase onto the table, snaps it open, and produces a bandage, which she passes down the table toward John, who looks pale, exhausted.

"I have kids," the grey woman says.

Columbus looks at his fingernails, gazes out the window. He actually doesn't give a rat's ass about what's going on around him. He knows the outcome of this meeting already. Getting to that outcome is a series of formalities. He's a sailor now. He's no longer interested in negotiating anything but oceans.

The deal is done, he thinks. I've got my ships. Just when I thought it was truly hopeless, funding for three ships and provisions and a crew appears. Why? Doesn't matter. I'm going. I'm off to make a brand new route. There is no question that there is something out there. Look at these idiots with their cell phones and mounds of paper. Look how they jump when I ask for espresso. They've bought the dream. They want, desperately, what I've put on the table.

Santángel's base offer is passed around. Everyone has a copy. A cream-coloured cover with a few attached pages sits unopened in front of Columbus. Father Antonio's copy also sits on the table exactly where it was placed.

The coffee arrives. Cups are handed around. Columbus is served first, his espresso, in a blue demitasse, is placed in front of him. He silently acknowledges the excellent *crema* but other than this, ignores the coffee.

"So if we can begin again. Can I get everyone to sit? Now, as I was saying, we are here today to . . ."

Columbus pulls out a briefcase, lays it flat on the table, covering Santángel's offer as if it is insignificant. Santángel stops talking. Columbus clicks open each catch and removes a single sheet of paper. He passes it to Santángel. "Here are my requirements. Father Antonio will hear any comments, but this list of demands is firm and final. There will be no negotiation. I'm going fishing for a few days."

Columbus stands and nods to the gaggle of gape-mouthed lawyers. Then bows deeply toward a tapestry at the far end of the room. "Your Majesty," he says softly. Father Antonio remains seated as Columbus walks across the room and pushes open the far doors. He stops in the archway. "My associate, Father Antonio, will take you up on that drink now," Columbus says. The doors groan shut and he's gone.

~ ~ ~

Two hours later, they are alone in the room. The councillors have been dismissed and Father Antonio has been escorted back to his monastery. The father followed Columbus's instructions to the letter. He listened. Engaged in no negotiations. Then listened some more.

"Admiral of all the Seas. Is he insane? This is impossible! I mean, Your Majesty, I like him but these demands are outrageous!" Santángel speaks toward the tapestry. "And he wants a percentage of all the profits from any route he finds. And he wants –"

"Give it to him," Isabella says as she steps around the edge of the screen. She'd like to use her fingernails to claw the goddamned dress she's wearing off her body. She can barely get a full breath from morning to sunset. She swishes over to the window and looks out across the dusty landscape. Would she still be able to see him? Fishing? Who goes fishing at a time like this? Isabella giggles. Of course, Columbus would go fishing at a time like this. He loves fishing.

"But he wants –"

"Give it to him."

"Forgive me, my queen, but this is too much."

"Just give him what he wants. We'll figure out how to make good on the promise once he returns, if he returns." If . . . yes . . . there is a possibility he will not make it back. Anything can happen at sea. And if he returns, we will keep our distance from him. We will not visit or encourage him in any way.

Santángel smiles. "A dangerous game."

"My game."

"But –"

"Enough! Go. Arrange to give him everything he requires. Go!"

~ ~ ~

When Columbus looked at the tapestry and bowed, Isabella had to cover her mouth with her hand. She gasped and then wept quietly. Her yearning surprised her. She felt overwhelmed by it – caught off guard. She thought she might faint. She stood with wobbly knees and tears flowing, and watched him walk out of the meeting.

I want him, Isabella thought. But to want him is to court death, tempt fate. So he must go. I must give my heart respite. Put Columbus, and myself, out of danger.

But it would be nice to see him, perhaps one more time before he sails. Just one more time. Nothing will happen. I just want to see him. To have a simple conversation. Nothing more.

~ ~ ~

"I'm done," she says. "I can't listen to any more stories. I need a break." Her voice is a frayed rope. Her fingers intertwined and squeezed white. Dr. Balderas walks across his office, two glasses in his hands – the ice tinkling. "Drink this," he says. He sits in a low, leather armchair across from her, places his drink on the arm, elbows on his knees, and leans forward. He recognizes fatigue – has seen it in himself, in his wife, when they were dealing with their teenagers. The dark circles under her eyes, a slumped weariness to her posture. There is no doubt in his mind that Consuela is exhausted.

"I can't make you do this. You've already gone above and beyond your duty here. I know you're tired." Dr. Balderas takes a drink. Wonders how he'd react to his own pitch.

If you only knew what I'm feeling, she thinks. You'd yank this patient out of my care in a second. All I have to do is tell you, and no more stories. No more Columbus. Just say the words, Consuela. *I'm in love with Columbus.* Go on, say it.

Consuela teeters. The right thing to do is to walk away from Columbus. This is her opportunity.

"Look, whatever happened to him, these stories seem to be moving toward where we've been hoping he'd go. He wants to finish his story. I think it's important that he finishes it."

"Can't he tell you, or some other nurse?"

"I've tried to get him to go there, but I really think it has to be you."

"Why me? What if it doesn't end?" Her voice is filled with a desperate frailty.

"The very first report I read from you, about Columbus's stories, you said Columbus said he was going to tell you the story of how he, Christopher Columbus, got his ships – the true story."

"Yes, I remember."

"And, when he arrived, he asked you about the ships – ships in a harbour – and what happened?"

"You read my reports." She makes a small, impressed smile.

"Carefully – some more than once."

"Well, that's certainly more than your predecessor."

"Look, he's not taking you to sea. I believe it will end when he gets his ships . . . but you've been there from the start. He started it with you. He believes he has to end it with you."

"But –"

"Just let him finish it."

~ ~ ~

On Saturday, Columbus asks her if she likes to hike. He has no idea Dr. Balderas has planned a little trip to the beach for Monday. Columbus doesn't know that the doctor has already made his list of safe patients and is visiting with his mother who is in a seniors' home in Córdoba.

"Do you backpack?" Columbus says, and Consuela is not sure what to make of the question.

"Backpack?" she says. "You mean carry your tent, bedding, and food into the wilderness?"

"That's it," he says. "Away from it all. No distractions. No work. No meetings. Nothing but nature and working the legs. The mountains are best because of the elevations. You get the vistas. Vistas are the payoff."

"Why are you asking me this?"

He smiles, clears his throat. "Because . . ."

~ ~ ~

Because they left Beatriz and the boys in the village. Columbus and Juan have come to the mountain regions between Spain and France to fish for trout. They move up through pine forests, looking for the tiny hut where they will spend the night. Columbus leads, even though Juan has been there many times before. The deer trail they were following has disappeared, and Columbus stops at the edge of a cliff with a mountain vista. He removes his cap and drinks from the large, leather water sack. The view is of blue mountain ranges against mountain ranges, fading rows of peaks against darkening indigo sky.

"We'll have to make a fire and stay here tonight," Juan says. "It's three leagues to the hut and getting too dark."

"By my calculations, it should be just over there." Columbus points into the forest with no hesitation.

"Actually, it's there, at the base of that mountain." He points across the valley in front of them.

"Are you sure, Juan?"

"Yes, Cristóbal, my friend, I have been there many times."

"Someone has made an incorrect calculation then?"

Juan looks at Columbus. A pathetic man, standing there with cap in hand, tousled white hair. The past ten years of intense dreaming have come with a price, Juan thinks, and Columbus has paid with part of his sanity. Nurturing a dream requires a great deal of energy, and this is a big dream. He might be losing his mind. But Juan knows what Columbus has gone through. The trials and arguments at the university. His dealings with the king and queen. The years of waiting. The years of not knowing. The years of doubt massing up like storm clouds.

"A wrong turn," Juan says.

"I do not make wrong turns," Columbus snaps.

"A faulty map then."

"An error in the map? Yes, this is a possibility."

"Yes," Juan says, "but look. Look where you've brought us. I have never seen such a view."

Columbus turns and smiles. This is true, he thinks. I have discovered a new view. It is my destiny. And it is my destiny to claim the entirety of this magnificent view in the name of God and Their Glorious Majesties King Ferdinand and Queen Isabella. For Spain.

Then he says out loud: "I claim all this land, all the trees, the animals, the birds and fish and gold and gems and peoples in the name of God and Their Glorious Majesties King Ferdinand and Queen Isabella." He kneels and crosses himself. "And for my beautiful Beatriz, who very much wanted to come fishing but stayed in the village. And of course, for both my sons, Diego and Fernando, may they be safe and grow into decent and brave men."

"Cristóbal, my friend. I do not think the king and queen of France would appreciate you claiming part of their country for Spain, no matter how perfect a view it is that you've discovered." Juan can see that this spot is a well-used campsite. There is a firepit surrounded by stones beside a large boulder. Somehow, Columbus does not see this.

"Is it not my destiny to discover?"

"Ah, but this land is already discovered. Beyond these cliffs is France."

"But this view?"

"A view is a view," Juan says. "This is a magnificent view but it is –" He stops. He does not want to deflate this man who stands before him. That is not the role of a friend, he thinks. Is he loopy or is he pulling my limb? Surely he knows we are on the border between Spain and France. Ahh, it doesn't matter. It does not matter if Columbus wishes to claim this small section of France.

"We should make a fire before it is too late. We do not want to wander these cliffs looking for wood in the dark." Juan kicks at the ground in order to begin to create a firepit. He does it away from the established pit. He snaps off the first dry bough he finds, tucks it under his arm, and continues to search.

When there are sparks twisting into the sky and a steady heat coming from the fire, Juan turns and looks at Columbus. He has been standing with his back to the forest, seeming to watch the light in the western sky move toward indigo.

"Columbus," Juan says, "I've got the fire going. Come and sit down."

"It's going to happen," Columbus whispers.

"What?" Juan says, poking at the fire, making adjustments.

"The journey across the Western Sea. It's going to happen."

"I have always known it. And listen, I have some news. My meeting with the Rubensteins went very well. They're in."

"That is good news. Any idea how much?"

"Enough for one ship, fully outfitted. But there is a condition."

"A condition?"

"They want transport to the Canaries."

"For how many?"

"Twenty. Maybe more."

Columbus leans in and pokes the fire with a short stick. Sparks lift into darkness.

"I have been thinking about this journey all day. There is too much to gain and too little risk for this *not* to happen. I play the role of the little risk . . ." He stops, pauses, and then shouts: "Nothing but the sea." The echo from across the valley is strong and spooky. It hangs in a circle above their camp. The echo drains into the night and Columbus makes the silence wait before he shouts again: "NO THING." And it comes back as "O-ING, O-ING, O-ing, ing, ing." Columbus turns his back to the vastness of the valley. He sits down next to Juan and observes the fire. Looks up at Juan. Nods his head.

"Sure, why not. Let's transport the Jews."

"I'll let them know when we get back."

"Good," he says. "Now, tell me about your life, Juan."

"But have you heard from the queen? Is there word?"

"No, no, not about me. Not about ocean journeys. You. I want to hear about you."

"There are no events in my life when it is compared to yours. I do not meet with kings and queens and noblemen. I do not speak with physicians and philosophers, and I do not read the latest charts."

"Just people," Columbus says, smiling. "Just things."

Juan talks about his painting. He speaks about the mixtures of colours, the brushes, the textures of the walls. Then there are the canvas paintings, the portraits and crude landscapes.

"The problem with the portraits is the skin. To mix the correct skin tone is half the battle," he says. "And then I often wish to paint not what I see but what it is I feel."

"Is it not the job of the artist to paint what he sees?" Columbus says.

"Yes. But there is the artist's feeling in each accurate portrait no matter how true to life."

"And you wish to take it further?"

"I simply wish to paint what I feel first, and what is truly there comes second."

"And what would someone think when they see such a work?"

"Only what they feel is interesting."

The fire draws them in. The heat massages and makes them drowsy. It soothes something deeper than they know. And so they are quiet for a while.

"Keep painting only what you feel, Juan," Columbus says. "I'd like to see what you come up with. Perhaps you will be famous one day."

"Columbus, my friend, no one will remember me. It's you who will be remembered."

"I have been thinking that this thing I wish to do will happen regardless of whether I want it to or not. I think perhaps some events in history are simply meant to happen. The right time, the right thinking, the right weather, the right person . . . all these things add up, and then all it takes is one small seemingly unconnected event, and then there is no stopping."

"What are you talking about?"

"I'm saying I play only a minor role in this."

"But how can you say –"

"The ball is rolling. It would take a great effort to stop it now."

"But it's been all your work, your dream, your idea."

"But it's no longer my destiny. It's the destiny of Spain, and of human beings."

"But you want it to happen, right?"

~ ~ ~

In the morning, they look out from under their blankets into a thick, white light. A vast whiteout encloses the campsite.

"Columbus?" Juan says. "It's a whiteout. We should try and climb up and out of it."

They stand up and immediately lose sight of each other. Columbus takes a few steps toward where he last saw a fading Juan. Juan gathers up his blanket and, dizzy in all the whiteness, staggers a few paces. He feels the shrubs scratching his legs before he sees them.

Columbus faces the forest, thinking it's the mountain valley. He is suddenly struck with a thought about the view. There is no proof my view ever existed, he thinks. There is only memory. Is it my memory or my faith that tells me this mountain valley existed? He turns again to try and fix where Juan is but cannot see anything. "Juan?"

"Here."

The voice is behind Columbus, perhaps. He's not sure.

"Have you moved from the spot where you slept?" It's Juan's voice again. Columbus looks down toward his feet and can barely see them.

"I don't know," he says. "I can barely see the ground."

"Well, don't move. The cliff is not far. And –"

"Juan? Juan?"

"I'm here. I think you're in front of me. Say something."

"This is stupid. I'm going to move up this ridge," Columbus says.

"Which direction is up? Where is the cliff?"

Columbus looks around at the white haze. "These are good questions," he says. "So we wait then."

"Yes. I think that would be wise."

Columbus begins to feel tightness in his chest. He wants to run for the light and open air. A hopeless desire for blue sky grows in him. His eyes squint into the blankness for a direction. Then the scream pushes up from his gut to his brain. It explodes into his feet. *Run!* it says. *Run! Get the hell out of this whiteness!* Columbus begins to run in the direction he's facing.

"Don't move!" Juan screams. But Columbus runs smack into him and knocks him over the edge of the cliff.

~ ~ ~

Before he sits up, Columbus sees blue sky, feels a cool mountain breeze on his face, and hears a faint "Help, help, Columbus."

He pokes his head over the edge of the cliff and sees Juan dangling by his sword belt from the root of a tree. "Juan?"

"Cristóbal, lower some of that rope, quickly. What have you been doing up there all morning?"

"What happened?"

"Just lower the rope and pull me up. Please."

When they are seated on the cliff's edge, passing a bota of wine between them, Columbus looks at Juan and smiles.

"How did you fall off the cliff?"

Juan takes a good gulp of wine. Winces. Touches his head delicately. Looks at his friend.

"I guess I panicked and took a wrong step." One more little incident like this and I could be dead, Juan thinks. This is the man who wants to drag all of humanity to their destiny across uncharted water? Who wants to create a new passage to India, and the lands of Marco Polo? This is the man who still has to convince men to follow him on his journey, a queen and a king to trust him? I should begin praying now and not quit until the day I die and still there would not be enough prayer.

A true friend, Columbus is thinking. Juan has lied kindly twice already to spare my feelings. This is a man worthy of much love. Here is the greater man of the two of us.

"I think perhaps it was I who panicked and knocked you over," he says.

"No, Cristóbal, it was –"

"Juan, you did no such thing. Let's eat."

Behind them, the distance of ten men, the sound of a rock falling.

The skittering sound of it down a steep slope.

"Did you hear that, Juan?"

Juan pulls slowly on the hilt of his sword. Draws it out and stands up. "Yes."

"There's my problem," Columbus says, not noticing Juan has drawn his sword. "That rock back there is my greatest problem."

"A rock, Cristóbal?"

"My biggest worry."

"A rock –"

"That rock is the one true challenge of this entire adventure."

Juan keeps his eyes and ears focused on the direction of the rock sound. "Perhaps we should eat something. I have some dried meat." He twists and rustles in his pack behind him.

"You think I am crazy sometimes."

Juan wants to scream, *Yes!* Yes, you are many, many times crazy. You are beyond crazy tenfold. Goofy, insane, ridiculous, a fool with no equal! But he remembers the dream of simply wanting to set sail and find out what's there, regardless of the dangers. He can well understand this. He knows this desire.

"You have great pressures and hardships," Juan says.

"All my pressures and any hardships are made small by my friends, by Beatriz and you, and Isabella and . . ." He encloses the end of his thought inside himself.

Columbus drinks from the skin. Passes it to Juan, who also drinks.

"Oh, getting the ships and men and supplies and finally embarking is challenge enough. Convincing ninety men that it's perfectly safe to sail out past the point of no return, and then to sail beyond the point of going back safely. This is also a challenge.

"We will discover what there is to discover. This I am sure of. But to simply discover is not a discovery. Like the rock back there. It falls whether there is anybody to notice it or not." He looks hard at Juan's face. "We must make it back and shout the discovery to anyone who can hear. We must bring back news of the falling rock. We must prove the falling rock exists. Then, and only then, is our discovery complete."

"Our discovery?"

"You are coming along, are you not?"

"I have no ocean skills. No experience. I don't know."

"Bring your paints and record what you see. Better, record what you feel."

FIFTEEN

DR. BALDERAS HAS DECIDED that a day-trip to the ocean might be just the thing for about a dozen of his patients – the safe ones.

It's about sixty miles to Punta Umbria and its nearest beach, Playa La Mata Negra. Dr. Balderas remembers these beaches from his youth. His parents used to go to this particular beach every summer for two weeks, at least in the years when they weren't fighting. He remembers the golden sand, crystal-clear water, and a particular silky quality to the air. How could this not be therapeutic?

On Friday afternoon, he sits down at his favourite café with a double espresso and makes a list. He's been through the files. Pope Cecelia and Arturo make the list. Cecelia has been experiencing spells of lucidity in which she remembers her life, her name, her family. Arturo, well, he's just slow. Not a bad thing on a sandy, ocean beach. Columbus makes the list despite his escape attempts. Dr. Balderas is impressed with the effort he's been seeing from Columbus. In his opinion, Columbus wants to get better, wants to get to the bottom of his delusion. That perceived honest effort goes a long way with Dr. Balderas. Mercedes is not on the list. The beach is a dirty place. And there's nowhere for her to wash her hands. He chuckles to himself when he thinks about Mercedes. The audacity of a kleptomaniac with a hand-washing compulsion is too much. On Monday morning he gets his nurses to gather a group of thirteen peaceful patients, five orderlies, and three nurses, including Consuela, and by mid-morning they're headed to the beach.

The temperature is a very comfortable twenty-two degrees Celsius when they arrive. Not a cloud in the sky. The orderlies set up four large umbrellas, and the nurses spread blankets. Pope Cecelia demands a chair so she is higher than everyone else. An orderly finds a beach chair and places it in the shade. She's wearing her usual three robes. Columbus is wearing an institute-assigned maroon robe, and he immediately goes down to the edge of the water and walks into the skittering surf. The water is warm but also refreshing. It jumps and spits at the bottom of his robe, tickles his calves. He goes into the water up to his knees, looks out to sea, breathes. Observes the waves. Breathes some more. He loves the smell of the ocean. The sounds. The shushing waves meeting land. The awkward gull calls. For a few minutes, he is happy standing up to his knees in the ocean, the gulls hovering carefully above the offshore waves. At the same time, he realizes there are two orderlies, one up the beach and one down the beach, watching him. There is no need to turn around and look. He feels them. He can smell them.

Alberto, a patient who as far as Columbus can see is perfectly normal except that he is openly homosexual, throws a red ball the size of a large orange toward Columbus. Shouts, "Heads up, Columbus!"

He turns and snatches the ball out of the air, an almost automatic gesture, then throws it back to Alberto. Columbus walks back to the umbrella encampment and sits down. He begins to wait.

Elena comes over and sits beside him. Regardless of the fact that she does not speak, he has enjoyed having her around. She has a good energy. It costs him nothing to be with her – she's not a taker of energy.

"What do you see out there, Columbus?" Elena says. A creaky half whisper interwoven with the sound of the waves feathering the shore. Columbus wants to turn toward her. He wants to ask her what she means. He wants to be sure he just heard her say something. But all these options would ruin it – erode the magic of Elena speaking. He decides to trust himself. Of course she spoke.

"Freedom," he says softly.

"If I can help, let me know," she says, even more withdrawn than before.

Columbus turns toward her. Finds her face, her eyes. Her eyes are hazel. She pushes a few strands of hair away from her face – in behind her ear.

"Thank you, Elena."

"It's what wounds you that you love," she says.

"I don't know my wounds," he says.

"You will," she says.

Two of the orderlies begin to set up folding tables for a midday meal. Columbus gets up and offers his assistance, which they accept. At least this way they know exactly where he is.

After lunch, he and Alberto go for a stroll along the beach. Columbus nods to Benito, who looks more weighed down than usual, seems more resigned to the fact that life is hard. Benito says nothing but follows, leaving them plenty of room.

"You really are crazy if you think you can do this," Alberto says.

"Perhaps. But will you help me?"

"Of course. It is a small thing you ask. I hope you make it."

They walk a bit more. Alberto stops to pick up a starfish and throws it back into the ocean. They both watch as it is swallowed by the incoming waves. "What exactly are you in here for, Alberto?" Columbus says.

"I like men."

"That's it?"

"That fact alone, which I do not deny, makes me crazy. I am insane because I am not physically attracted to women. There are a few other things, small problems with coping. I don't handle stress well."

"How long have you been in here?"

He closes his eyes. And then softly: "A year and a half."

It's a simple plan. Around two o'clock, Alberto kneels at Pope Cecelia's side and whispers that Elena has been spreading a rumour about her. "She's been saying that you're the anti-Christ," he says. Cecelia glares at Elena and Elena nods – confirms the alleged rumour. Cecelia goes completely ballistic. She splinters. She stands and, with strength one would not normally attribute to a woman of her age, she tosses her beach chair at the nearest food table, which collapses – spills the small loaves of bread, meat, cheese, and bottles of water into the sand. Condiments splatter across most of the patients. The collapsed table bangs into the other table and it teeters. Pope Cecelia lunges at Elena, attempts to grab her neck, wants to choke the lie out of this sinner. Elena holds out one of her long arms and keeps Cecelia at bay until the orderlies can stop her. James, who has narrow, scary eyes, has mustard spilled across his shirt and pants. He caws like a crow – raspy squawks. These caws come sporadically, surprising not only those around him but also James. He has no control whatsoever. He caws now as he attempts to get at the pope. He accidentally steps on Howard, who's mostly deaf and had been sleeping on his back throughout the ruckus. Howard comes to, sits up, in a foul mood – wants to know why James has stepped on his arm.

"Fuck you, you satanic bitch! You white devil!" Cecelia shrieks, trying to displace the anger, which seems to be aimed at her.

"Why did you step on me, you bastard?"

"Look at my shirt! Look at my shirt! Look at my trousers!"

"It's her! She's the anti-Christ! She's the anti-Christ!"

"Calm down everybody. Calm down." Dr. Balderas is holding a jar of mustard.

"I was sleeping! I was dreaming a beautiful fucking dream! Does anybody care that my dream was disturbed? I'll never get that dream back!"

"Oh piss off, you minor twit."

Nurse Tammy looks around the demented circle and tries to comprehend how something like this could happen so quickly. She looks like she's about to lose control – like this is too much for her. Dr. Balderas hands her the jar of mustard, which she holds as if it's the Holy Grail.

"This will *never, never, never, never* come out! You owe me for a new shirt. You must replace this shirt. This is silk!"

"I think my arm is broken!"

"I was dreaming! I was stepped on!"

Consuela's holding the edge of one of the tables with one knee and a hand, trying to keep the remainder of the food and bottles from spilling onto the beach. "Cecelia!" she shouts. "Cecelia, Your Holiness, it's all right. Everything is all right. Calm down. Calm down. We've called in the Vatican Guard." Balderas is fiddling with the crumpled table legs trying to get them to behave.

"Clam down. Clam down," James says. "Cawk, Cawk! Cawk!"

Elena watches Columbus edge away from the cacophony. He looks back over his shoulder at her. Elena smiles encouragement. He nods his thanks. Consuela watches him, too. Columbus moves very slowly, almost gracefully, toward the water, drops his robe, and then, naked, slips into the ocean. He's a hundred feet out before she's free of the table. He's only a dot by the time everything has calmed down. She's torn. Doesn't know what to do. Doesn't want to lose him. Wants him to be free. Wants him to live. Wonders if he knows how to find her. Did they ever talk about where she lives? What if he dies out there? Where in the hell does he think he's going anyway? Something freezes inside her. Does Columbus believe he can swim to India? Is that what he's doing?

"I can get that out." Everybody looks at Sonia, a black-haired woman in her mid-twenties. Everybody knows her story. She was raped – can't stand to be touched by anybody. She looks at Consuela. "What? I can. I can get that stain out. You look funny. What's the matter with you?"

"What do you mean, I look funny?" Consuela feels her face start to burn. Is she that transparent?

"You look like you've seen a ghost."

"Nonsense."

Sonia turns to James. "Give me that shirt. I'll get that stain out." He caws a couple of times but doesn't move. "Give me your fucking shirt, I said. Now! Don't touch me but give me your shirt!" James backs up but takes his shirt off and hands it to her, carefully dangling it in front of her.

"Thank you."

Out of the corner of her eye, Consuela can see one of the orderlies – is it Benito? – doing a head count. This is something they do every half-hour on field trips. It's the institute's standing policy. Here it comes, she thinks.

"I count only twelve."

"Do it again," Dr. Balderas says. "Find out who's missing."

"Could that be," Consuela says meekly to Dr. Balderas, pointing out to sea at a small black dot, "someone?"

"It's Columbus," Benito says.

"Well, there goes one of our innocents," Consuela says.

"Fuck." Dr. Balderas walks slowly toward the water. "How did no one see . . . Oh, forget it. He probably arranged that little fracas back there." He sighs heavily. "We're going to have to get him back. Ideas? Anyone?" The three of them stand at water's edge, turn to one another with blank faces, and then they watch the small black dot get smaller and smaller.

~ ~ ~

There is nothing she can do. They've alerted the authorities. They've called the coast guard. They round up the remaining patients and head back to the institute. On the road, Consuela looks over at Benito, who is driving. He is alert and focused on the road. She leans her head against the window, feels the road's vibration. She closes her eyes and drifts back to Columbus's last story. Was there a clue in that story? It'll be dark soon and he's out there in the strait. Was he trying to tell her about this with his last story?

~ ~ ~

Columbus and Beatriz and the boys, and Juan, have come to a small villa at Santa Isabel, near the Portuguese border. Columbus is sitting with Juan. "Look," he says, "I'm sitting alone by the sea and crying. I do not know if I have been successful or not. I do not know if I have made my journey to the Indies or to Japan. In my dream, I do not know. I am alone on the beach, by the ocean, and I am crying."

"Do you have this dream often?" Juan sips his coffee.

Columbus squints at the mid-morning horizon. His eyes do not waver from this line.

Columbus does not look at Juan. He watches Diego and

Fernando, who are playing on the beach. They're safe. He and Juan have been sitting at the table since breakfast. Beatriz has just returned from a week in Huelva. She was with her sister, who gave birth to a baby girl, whom they have named Mary. The boys have let Beatriz sleep in. Travel is always an ordeal.

Juan thinks Columbus has the look of someone who has not slept. Heavy darkness under his eyes. He is a man who is driven. Eaten by something on the inside. Or better, the Western Sea draws him, pulls at him. It is as if there is something unseen across the sea pulling him constantly. Even his shoulders are not even – one is higher than the other.

Juan watches Diego down on the beach. The boy is playing a game with the waves as they touch Spain. He lets the waves chase him inland, and then runs hard after them as they wash back out to sea. Fernando is making a castle in the sand.

"Diego is a big boy," Juan says.

"He just turned twelve."

"He's a good size for his age. They both look healthy, happy." Juan watches Columbus's face. There is such a genuine pleasure in his face as he watches his boys. His eyes become soft with love.

"Fernando turns five next week. He'll be five . . . he already reads better than his brother." Columbus drifts. The sound of the ocean becomes obvious. He is adrift once again in the dream remnant that has travelled with him into consciousness.

"What is making you so sad in your dream?" Juan says.

Columbus's vision is fixed on the horizon, yet there appears to be no focus.

"Christopher?"

"Hmmm."

"What is making you so sad in your dream?"

"My life. Life. I don't know." He opens his mouth to continue, decides against it, and then brings his eyes to wash over Juan. "It is as if life has a thickness, and in order just to live I must continually push my way through it. It is like water only thicker. Is it so for you, Juan?"

"No, life has no thickness for me."

"For me, to stand still is to die. I must push forward in a direction or I will die. I do not know why."

They are quiet. There is only the sound of the sea. Tears form and stream from Columbus's eyes. He seems not to notice. He continues his watch on the horizon.

"It is not the sadness of lost love, or of a single death, or of a dozen deaths," Columbus says. "This is the sadness of something inevitably horrible. Something that has to happen but is too awful to think about." He picks up his glass, looks at it, and carefully places it back down on the table. "I did this thing. In my dream, I did this horrible thing."

"What did you do?"

"I ruined something," he says. "It is the feeling I have."

"What do you see in your dream?"

"That." He points. "The sun. I see the sun rise on the Western Sea."

"So you are on one of the Canary Islands, looking east?"

"No, it does not feel so. Not the Canaries."

"Well then, you are in the Azores."

"No, the land behind me is different."

"You are not in Britain?"

"No, it is hot, Juan. It is hot and very green in the place of my dream. There are palm trees."

"We have run out of places that we know of where you could sit on a beach and watch the sun rise over the Western Sea."

"Have we?" Columbus says flatly.

"Are you certain of the direction you face?"

"I have told you. I face the east," says Columbus, "to see the sun rise over the sea."

"Not a lake?"

"It is an ocean." His voice is deep and blunt.

Juan smiles. Picks up his glass. "There's only one place you could be," he says.

~ ~ ~

In the afternoon, Juan goes into town to pick up supplies. Beatriz and Columbus come back onto the patio and sit in the shade offered by half a dozen palm trees. The boys are colouring at the table. Columbus has downed three Heinekens in about half an hour. Beatriz is sipping her wine. The breeze off the ocean is kind and warm.

"There are days," Columbus says, "when I am tired of the constant pushing, constant struggling. I know I am away too much, Beatriz. I know."

"Why do you do it?" She is not judging.

"Navigating. Sailing. This is all I know. What else would I do?"

"Your boys need you. I need you. We believe in you. You can do anything."

"Sailing is in my bones. My blood is home when I am at sea."

"This is for you, Papa," Fernando says. He hands his father a picture of a thin blue line between two clumps of green. In the middle of the blue line, there is a ship with enormous sails and a small stick man standing on the deck. Columbus does not need to ask what the picture represents. He knows. He picks the boy up and draws him to his chest. Hugs him. Kisses his cheek.

"Thank you, Fernando," he whispers. "It's beautiful."

"Here, Papa," Diego says, pushing his drawing across the table. "So you will find your way home after you are in China."

"Thank you, Diego. I will use it." He looks at the drawing, which is a simple representation of his hopes. He hopes it's going to be as simple as this map makes it appear. China isn't too far. The ocean isn't so vast. "This is an excellent map," he adds, and Diego beams.

"It's not a map, Papa. Maps are for land. This is a chart. Charts are for oceans."

Columbus is impressed. "I'm glad you know that."

Columbus leans forward in his chair, elbows on his knees and chin in his hands. He sneaks his fingers up to rub his eyes. "I'm doing this for all of you," he says. The boys stop colouring. Beatriz nods slowly.

"I'm going to cut a deal with the king and queen that will make it so we never have to worry about money. It's for all of us. I want you to understand that I love you. I would do anything for you. But I must do this."

Beatriz blinks away tears, reaches her hand across the table and takes his. Fernando comes to his father and crawls into his lap, tries to get his little arms around Columbus's chest for a hug. Diego looks up, nods his approval and his understanding toward his father.

The day seems to hold its breath for ten seconds.

Columbus stands. "Who's up for a swim?"

The boys are ecstatic. They both jump up. Diego's chair crashes to the patio floor.

"I'll watch from here," Beatriz says. "There are fresh towels just inside."

"We don't need towels, do we boys? We're men and men don't need towels."

"Ya," Fernando says. "We'll use sand."

"Love ya, Mom," Diego says, and he grabs a stack of towels from a storage compartment under the bench seat.

The boys are running past the palm trees and down the beach. Columbus is standing, watching them, his hand on Beatriz's shoulder. She is looking up at him, her hand in his. It's like he's on a ship, looking out at the sea, she thinks. He moves her hand up to his mouth and kisses it gently. Then he is off, running full tilt after his boys, toward the ocean.

~ ~ ~

There is nothing but breathing, the ocean, and staying afloat. There is nothing but water, and breathing, and moving slowly away from Spain. There is nothing but the ocean, the lift and fall of the water, inhalation and exhalation, and the sky. Columbus begins to turn inside out. He feels suspended between the rising and falling water, and the vast sky. He is adrift between Spain and the north coast of Africa.

What the hell are you doing, exactly? Do you know? You can't swim the entire ocean. Surely you know this. Of course you do; you're not crazy. It's just that this plan formed quickly and you only got to the escape part. The after-the-escape bits of your plan were for the most part unformed. But sometimes opportunities need to be acted upon – plan or no plan. It's not a problem to stay afloat. You're a strong swimmer. Sunset is an hour away. Perhaps you could swim a bit, drift a bit, alternate until dark, then get your bearings and find your way back to land by the stars. This is a good plan. The only sensible plan. But still, you keep pulling at the water. Pulling yourself farther and farther from land.

You keep swimming. Perhaps some small part of you recognizes that the action of swimming is life. That small part of you wants to live. What if it clouds over and you can't see the stars? Remember Tristan, adrift in a rudderless boat, adrift with only faith to guide his boat? But Tristan had a wound. Tristan was a hero, trying to save his people from being afflicted by his wound. He had a wound. You have no wound.

You continue to swim. Slow and steady strokes. You're in no hurry. Darkness is coming. Starlight is coming. There are no clouds. Your ring feels like it could slip off. You try to remember to bend that finger. Beatriz would kill you if you lost the ring. You can lose your freedom, lose your mind, but not the ring. Not this ring. This ring binds you to Beatriz. You imagine the ring falling through water. So much water. So deep and dark. Does a ring fall in water? Or does it just sink? Oh for Christ's sake, there is no falling once you are in water; everything that's not buoyant, sinks.

Tristan had a wound. You're not wounded. You're no hero. You're no Tristan.

You continue to pull at the water, to kick at the water. As darkness falls, you begin to remember names. A storm petrel appears in the water, seemingly out of nowhere. It startles you. You accidentally take a mouthful of ocean – the salt water causes you to gag and choke. The bird circles, stays close by. Hovers in the water a few feet away. You remember these dark birds are signs of bad things to come. Petrels are often found hiding in the lee of ships during storms. They're warnings of approaching storms. Is there a storm coming?

The sky remains clear. Stars start to push through the membrane of night. Something big brushes your leg. Fear rises up from the depths of the ocean under you. A shark? A whale? Just a fish? You are suddenly and profoundly aware of your vulnerability. You can feel yourself starting to panic. You are a dangling morsel for anything big and hungry. Quick, shallow breaths. Your heartbeat racing. You try to slow your breathing – force yourself to calm down. You've no choice but to accept where you are, and to accept this vulnerability. You're in desperate need of a distraction. The stars – focus on the stars. There's nothing you can do about this blackness but the stars are a different matter. "Hercules, Virgo, Leo, Libra," you say out loud. "Ursa Major, Ursa Minor, Cancer, Draco."

You're treading water now. Not swimming very much. Just floating. Moving with the current. A few sidestrokes, then treading water. Moving as little as possible to stay afloat. You remember a story your grandmother told you. About the constellations. Once upon a time, a long time ago, it began.

Somewhere in the Basque region, two thieves robbed a man of two of his oxen. The man was angry about this and sent his servant, his maid, and his dog out to chase the thieves. Not much time had passed before the impatient man also went out to look. As punishment for his impatience, everyone in the story, including the man, is taken up into the sky. The first two stars in the cup of the dipper are the oxen, the other two stars are the two thieves; the handle of the dipper comprises the servant, the maid, and the master, who is the final star. The dog is the faint star, Alcor.

"Where is Alcor?" Can you remember your grandmother's face, her name? All you can recall is the scent of cloves.

How could you forget your grandmother's name? But you know a woman named Rashmi. A Hindu name. A name that means "ray of sunlight." And you know the name Nusret. Nusret means "dangerous bear."

Why would you know the meanings of these names?

You're looking up at a panoply of stars. You're adrift in the ocean. Adrift with no boat. Nothing between you and the colour black. But is black a colour or is it merely the absence of light? You had a black crayon when you were little. It was with other coloured crayons. Therefore, black must be a colour. Who is Nusret? Panoply is a funny word. Where did you find that word? One of your daughters? Do you have daughters? Not sons? And what about your wife? Look at the orgasm of stars. Can you find a star to guide you home, Columbus?

"Who said that?" These words are swallowed by the ocean.

Do you seriously think fish can talk? Maybe that petrel you saw earlier? But the bird is gone now. You're adrift in your own head. And this blackness is impossible. This is like falling. Flying. The only sounds you have are your own breathing and the sound of your own body in water. Each small movement marked by its own unique sound.

Save your strength. You're going to have to save yourself tonight. You'll have to start to move in the right direction. You know how to navigate by the stars. Right? You're on the doorstep to the Mediterranean. Your latitude is going to be about the same wherever you are. You know the Atlantic flows into the Mediterranean and at some point, if you manage to stay afloat, stay awake, not get eaten by something, you're going to flow through the Strait of Gibraltar. Dead reckoning yourself is not possible. You have no compass. If you stop, if you stay right here, the current will carry you into the Mediterranean. Perhaps. You could stop swimming. Stay here. Drift. Stay right here.

Stay here, you said. Wait here. I'll catch the guy. You shouted this over your shoulder, you did not even say goodbye. How could you? You were running after a thief. The guy snatched Rashmi's bag. Rashmi's bag. Her journal. Her beautiful poems. A journal filled with her poems. Money and passports, too, but her poems. Her poems about the rain, and the trees, and her children. Who were you talking to? Who did you want to wait? Catch what guy?

Rashmi. Rashmi and the girls. They're waiting there on the platform.

What was that? Something touched your leg again.

You had to get Rashmi's bag back. Those poems. You could only think about the loss of those poems. Rashmi was no good with a fountain pen, but she insisted on always using one. There were blobs of ink throughout her journal, but even these, somehow, she made beautiful. *I have to slow down with these pens,* she said. *I am not so tempted to edit before I write. I must give myself permission to write badly. It is a messy joy.*

Do you remember her eyes? Of course you do. They were blue. The colour of the Mediterranean at 11 A.M. in mid-July. And her smile? The way the lines formed at the edge of her mouth when she smiled – more pronounced on the left than the right. And the freckles on her cheeks and the tops of her shoulders?

Chloe had her mother's smile. Jane smiled with her eyes the best. They looked frightened when you ran off after Rashmi's bag. It's not as if you were being the hero. You loved Rashmi's poems. That's all. You loved her poems. You couldn't know the future. Nobody can know the future.

Dark now. The stars brilliant and too many above you. You keep pulling at the current, which pulls you left. Is that east? Is that current pulling you toward the Mediterranean? You swim ahead and slightly right because there is land in front of you as well as behind. Morocco? Are you thinking about Morocco? Yes, the north coast of Africa. That would be a feat wouldn't it? Rashmi was wearing black pumps. Ridiculous for travel. But she would not wear anything else with her dress. You loved her feet. Not a fetish or anything. She had narrow, long feet. You remember trying to buy her hiking boots. Store after store. You eventually had to go online and order custom-made boots from Germany. They asked for the periphery of her feet, traced on two sheets of paper, which you faxed to Germany. The boots arrived a month later, a perfect fit. You could not bring yourself to throw the tracings away. Felt foolish about it. You hid Rashmi's feet in a book about Michelangelo. There was an elongated elegance in these simple outlines of her feet, an odd perfection.

You must be hallucinating a wife and a family. And the smiles of these women – Rashmi and the girls. The train station and the man's back running through the crowd. Glimpses of his back woven into the throng on the sidewalk. And you, catching up slowly. Gaining ground on the bag with no thought of what you'll do if you do catch him. First, catch the bugger. That's all you can think. Catch the bugger. You were indignant, angry.

Chloe is eleven. She's taller than her sister even though she is two years younger. She has an incredible memory – near photographic. She can read a book and know its contents. She leaves her shoes right in the middle of the back entrance, any entranceway, and you're always tripping over them. Chloe plays the cello.

Jane can't remember her phone number half the time but God she can dance. She's an artistically precocious thirteen-year-old. You remember asking her, when she was four, to dance a baby sparrow. Dance the sparrow, you said. What she did – her small birdlike movements ending with folded wings – moved you to tears. She goes to an art school in . . . you're not sure where . . . in the city in which you live. Inside this hallucination. Ah, parents always believe their children are talented beyond belief. When others who have no vested interest come and draw your attention to your child's talent, then perhaps it is something.

You don't know what to do about your ring – the one on your ring finger – why don't you call it a wedding ring? Because you never married Beatriz. The ring almost came off again. You're afraid to take it off and try it on a different finger, in case you drop it. There is no drop. There is only sinking. You roll over onto your back, face up to the heavens.

Your arms are numb. You're having a hard time feeling your fingers. They tingle. You have to keep working. Keep moving so you warm up. Roll over, you idiot. Start swimming again. Swim or die. You're hypothermic. You count to one hundred. Rest for fifty. Swim another hundred. A steady sidestroke brings your arms back into focus. They hurt. At least you can feel them again. You continue to pull yourself through the water toward morning.

It was March, you were at El Pozo del Tío Raimundo station. Not yet the ides of March. They were waiting for you. Two blocks away, the guy looked over his shoulder again, saw you gaining on him, and dropped Rashmi's bag. Completely out of breath, you picked up the bag and heard the storm. Was that thunder? But the sky is completely clear. There's blue sky from horizon to horizon.

Their faces begin to fade. Rashmi's face, Chloe's face, Jane's face – her bangs need trimming – become unfocused, withdrawn. Who are these people inside your reverie? Perhaps you are wounded. Maybe you and old Tristan have something in common. You walked back to the train station and found them, didn't you? You came around that last corner and found them. Emergency crews had not yet arrived. There were no ambulances. Not yet. It was eerily quiet. Oh, there were sounds, it was just that it was quieter than one would expect.

Close your eyes. It makes no difference whether they are open or closed. The stars are not changing tonight. You're not guiding yourself anywhere by starlight. This plan of finding your bearings by the stars was a bit thin on detail. As it turns out, it was just stupid. In the morning, if you don't drift off into hypothermia, or sleep, or both, you'll know the directions because the sun rises in the north. The sun rises in the north? That's not right. You know this. You know where the sun rises. The sun rises in the east, sets in the south. Chloe stands on the left, then Jane and then Rashmi. Or was Rashmi in the middle? Rashmi looks a little shell-shocked. Somebody lifted her bag – grabbed it off her arm and bolted. The girls aren't exactly sure what happened yet. The sun is low and behind them. It's early. *Stay here. I'll be right back,* you shout over your shoulder. You do not kiss them. You do not hug them. You're going to get Rashmi's bag back. Her poems inside the black notebook. Friends, who really did not understand her, had given her a pink notebook with substandard paper. Rashmi had tried to use it but the paper did not work well with her fountain pen. She went back to her Paris notebooks, which arrived three at a time every few months from France – simple, sturdy booklets, with Swedish paper.

Moonrise. Stars pull back. Give the moon room. Perhaps when you are dying, you are able to hallucinate the truth. You wish Rashmi was your wife, and Chloe and Jane your daughters. What a beautiful dream you're having. You'd better keep swimming. Keep moving. There is Chloe playing her cello at Christmas. She's playing "Silent Night." Rashmi is humming along beside you. She can't carry a tune, but she always tries. The acoustics in this room are phenomenal. A small echo adds body to the sound – forgives any imperfections. There's a tree in the corner, a fir that brushes the ceiling. And there is Rashmi smiling. Her smile shatters you. The way she looks at you can only be described as loving. There is nothing else in that look, just that she loves you. Chloe and Jane are fussing with the tree, hanging the last of the ornaments. They're dressed up. Chloe in a burgundy velvet gown that dips to her knees. She's not wearing jeans, which is a minor miracle. Jane is wearing a simple black dress far too old for her age. You don't want them to grow up too fast. She looks to be eighteen. Your own tears surprise you. You're not sure what they're attached to. You know for sure that tears are a completely useless addition to the ocean. Just keep going. A few more strokes and then you can rest for a while. Let the melody to "Silent Night" find you again. See Chloe's dark hair – pulled back into a ponytail, a utilitarian gesture. Her hair has always been beautiful but she doesn't care. Her lack of caring translates into a cool panache. Her friends follow her lead when it comes to dressing, and again, she doesn't care or notice. It's a hell of a thing to have daughters. You are surrounded by these women. You wish this was your reality, this beautiful dream. You could love these young women and Rashmi. Perhaps you already love these women. What's the test for love? Is there a litmus test? Go back to the girls standing in front of the tree. They're putting the last of the ornaments on, hanging them on their preferred branches. The light patterns on the wall are a lush combination of shadow and colour. Do you remember snow? Was there snow this Christmas? Turn around and look out the window. Why can't you turn around? You're afraid if you turn away from your girls, they'll be gone when you turn back. You want to keep them in sight. You're going to stay right there inside that moment. You will not run away. You will not turn away. Stay here. Wait here. You are well past tired. You want to sleep. Something pokes you in the ribs – a softness that intrudes but does not seem threatening. You hear the clicking laughter of a dolphin, several dolphins. What is a group of dolphins? A herd? A flock? A pack? The dolphins want me to be awake, you think. That's funny. If I stay awake, I can stay afloat. If I can stay afloat, perhaps I will live. What does it matter? Falling through water is not so bad.

~ ~ ~

You're not sure if your arms are moving. You don't know if your ring is still on your finger. You have no idea. You haven't had any feeling in your fingers for quite a while. You're breathing. That's good. You know you're breathing. Each breath is a raspy hiss. Somebody is telling you to be quiet. Shhhh, they whisper. Shhhhhh. And you want to be quiet. You want to be quiet more than anything. Shhhh. You hear waves. The sound of waves arriving somewhere. You can't feel . . . anything. A group of dolphins is a pod. *All is calm, all is bright. All is calm, all is bright.*

~ ~ ~

She doesn't know whether to read it or not. It feels like an invasion of privacy. This journal was not meant for her. He'd have told her about it. It was tucked under his pillow. The orderly who changed his bedding brought it to her. Consuela flips through the journal quickly, not landing on anything specific. This isn't reading, she thinks, it's looking. There are more than a dozen entries. She decides she has to read this journal, and if they find Columbus, she will slip this booklet back where it was found. She wants in, goddamnit. She deserves to be included. She flips the journal open at random and begins to read.

(vi)

The girl is stopped in midair, on her way to landing in the pool. The water sparkles beneath her feet. The sky is brilliant blue – dazzling, unadulterated. Scant seconds before this frozen image, there would have been the sound of slapping feet on the wet pool deck. She has such a joyous expression on her face. She is thrilled to be jumping into this water. This girl wears her hair in pigtails. Even though there is joy on her face, something in her eyes says she's not 100 per cent sure about hitting the water. This apprehension is not enough to make her pause. She smiles and trusts it'll be all right, and jumps anyway.

This picture, obviously captured by someone standing in the pool, also catches an older, taller girl, standing on the pool deck waiting. She stands on the pale green tile beside a wooden deck chair. The girl is wearing a one-piece pink swimsuit and she entertains no uneasiness. She will jump a bit higher and will land farther out into the water than her sister. Towels piled on the chair back. Perhaps she was supposed to be jumping along with the jumping girl, but no, she wants all the picture-taker's attention. She waits to say, Hey, look at me. Slap, slap, slap, slap, and she will be airborne above the water, landing gleefully with a splash, hoping the lifeguard doesn't bust her for running on the deck. Hoping whoever is there watching, sees her jump. There are a few other people reclined in deck chairs along the pool's edge. He can tell by the way they lounge, they are very relaxed, and it is very likely a hot day. He knows these girls. He knows their hearts. He knows them at a level beyond knowing. But he cannot say their names. No matter how much he wants the scene to move beyond frozen, it will not budge. One girl hangs in mid-flight, her face happy and innocent, and the other girl waits on the deck – waits for her turn to show how well she can jump and how big a splash she can make. The sun is hot. The sky is clear. But there is no splash landing. No laughing-giggling-coming-up-for-air. No screaming: Let's do it again! Let's do it again! Nothing moves.

SIXTEEN

THEY FIND HIM ON THE north coast of Morocco. He washes
up on a beach near the village of Tétouan. The ocean deposits
him on the sand and the waves push him up and roll him over
a couple of times before leaving him alone. Alerts had been
sent to all the hotels and resorts along the coast. A group of
children finds him. One of the children, a girl named Aabida,
points into the ocean and shouts: *"Dolpheen! Dolpheen!"*

"Eskoot, Aabida," a boy says. *"Shut up."*

Columbus hears seagulls. Can't open his eyes. Thinks
perhaps those voices are angels speaking the language of
angels. He's in heaven. The air is warm. The light is bright.
Angels with the voices of children.

~ ~ ~

There is a strange sort of sacredness, a holiness reserved for
the presumed crazy. Columbus is not just another Spanish
national on Moroccan soil. He's a pitiful crazy person in
trouble. His country becomes irrelevant except this is where he
must be returned. Columbus is unconscious but stable when
the medics arrive. He is transported to Ceuta, the Spanish
enclave on the northeastern tip of Morocco, and then by boat
to Algeciras. He is back in Sevilla the next day.

Two days later he opens his eyes and sees he is back at the institute in Sevilla. He sees Tammy first. She smiles at him and he starts to scream. He's horrified. He lived through the Strait of Gibraltar, through the memory of his dreamed daughters and his perhaps wife, for what? To arrive back where he started? To go through so much and not move? Tammy takes it personally, goes on stress leave, doesn't come back for a week. Columbus is restrained and eventually sedated. The Alprazolam takes him halfway back to his pleasant adrift-at-sea dream. He recalls the hazy faces of his dreamed family. Rashmi, Chloe, and Jane. He drifts back to this life with three women, life with his three girls.

Dr. Balderas told Consuela to go home on the morning of the third day. She'd been reading Malory's version of the King Arthur story to Columbus. In the hallway, she sighed and paused, recognized how tired she was, and went home.

Dr. Balderas, who has been reviewing Columbus's chart, glances over the lip of the clipboard at his patient. "Good morning. How do you feel?"

Columbus could give a flying fuck. He just wants to drift in the almost memory of what is, perhaps, his life.

"Do you know who you are?"

"Yesh," Columbus says. His mouth is not responding. It won't form words quickly enough. Won't follow his thoughts.

"Can you tell me who you are?"

Columbus sighs. You ought to know, he thinks. "Yehhh," he says finally, inside an exhalation.

"What's your name?" He leans in closer. He's hoping Columbus will say something other than Columbus.

"King Ah-thur." Columbus closes his eyes, exhausted. Slowly, he turns the side of his face into the pillow.

Dr. Balderas is confounded. He has no idea Consuela was reading Columbus the Malory. He has no idea what to think, except that his patient is still delusional and that Alprazolam is an effective sedative. Columbus is certainly sedated.

~ ~ ~

"What happened?" She glares at Dr. Balderas. His forehead is sunburned.

He takes his reading glasses off and places them quickly on top of the papers on his desk. "He came to and was extremely agitated. He would not stop screaming. He was hysterical."

"So he's pumped full of drugs again?"

"We had no other option."

"He was already restrained. Did he say anything? Anything at all?"

"Nothing but screaming. I have no idea what he went through out there in the strait. It's a minor miracle he survived. And I am accountable. I'm responsible for this. It's not going to be pretty when I get in that room with the board. They're going to want to talk to you, too."

"It's not your fault. He duped all of us."

"It was my idea to go to the beach."

"It was a good idea."

~ ~ ~

Consuela spends as much time with Columbus as she can. She reads to him for an hour each morning, and then pushes him in a wheelchair down to the pool. Each day for a week, and then two, and then three.

Pope Cecelia dies in the second week of his withdrawal into silence. Consuela finds her in the morning, a peaceful smile on her face, eyes closed, hair like a mane – almost like it's been brushed and arranged on the pillow. After the first gentle nudge, Consuela knew. She decides to sit for a while before letting others know. She needs to do something to make grace around this passing. So she sits quietly with the pope. I can give you an hour, Cecelia, she thinks. There will be no white smoke over the Sistine Chapel when a new pope is chosen. There will be no new pope to replace Cecelia. There will be just one less patient.

Cecelia's family claims her body and belongings. The duty of gathering Cecelia's life, at least her asylum life, into three cardboard boxes falls to Consuela. She is surprised to find a Hafiz ghazal in Columbus's handwriting on a piece of paper with well-worn fold lines. She knew they'd talked occasionally, but this implies an intimacy beyond casual conversation. Good for you, Cecelia.

~ ~ ~

Consuela begins to struggle with her hope around Columbus. She had hoped the sound of her voice would draw him back, or the hollow sound of the pool room would spark a connection to the present. But he does not speak. Even when they back off on his medication, he remains silent . . . eats without looking at his food, stares straight ahead. He's turned inward. He eats and goes to the bathroom and sleeps, but it seems his life is elsewhere.

Maybe this is his way of finally escaping, Consuela thinks. She misses his voice, his stories.

She has started to take Columbus down to the pool for half an hour before her shift each day, and lets him sit there while she swims. She sets up a couple of candles at either end of the pool, slips out of her clothes, and swims her lengths in the luxurious cool water.

This morning, on the day of the feast of Saint Sylvester, Columbus's eyes follow her in the water – watching her swim.

"You have an exquisite body," he says.

Consuela swims to the edge and looks him over. She'd almost given up on him coming back. But he's staring at her, eyes sparkling, almost laughing. "Welcome back," she says. "Where have you been? I've missed you." Consuela pulls herself from the pool. Tries not to act like she feels, which is self-conscious of her body, embarrassed, fat.

"I don't know. I was swimming. I remember being on a beach. I remember seeing Tammy, but after that . . . I don't know. How did I get back here?"

"Some children found you, washed up on a beach."

"Spain?"

"Morocco." Consuela wraps herself in a towel.

"Shit."

"Yes, quite the little journey you went on. They say dolphins saved you. They say the dolphins waited just offshore until you were found." She smiles. She only has one towel and needs to dry her hair. It's a big towel, but it is only one. She turns around. He can look at my butt, she thinks. As she puts on her bra – fastening it in the front, twisting the clasp to the back, and then finding the armholes – it feels too tight. She pulls on her uniform and is keenly aware of the way this uniform constricts. It seems too tight around her armpits. She wonders if she's gaining weight.

"But you don't believe that."

"I'm just happy you lived. You almost didn't." She quickly towel-dries her hair and turns around.

"I'm surprised, actually. I don't remember the end. I think I dreamed about dolphins. I dreamed a lot of things. Some not so nice things. Some very pleasant." He tries to stand but his legs are wobbly. "How long have I been . . ."

"Out of it? Six weeks. Just over six weeks."

Columbus sits back down. "Six weeks," he says, stunned.

"I know, by the way," she says.

"You know what?"

"That my body is exquisite." She walks by, the towel under her arm, and the edge of it brushes Columbus's arm. That touch shivers through him.

~ ~ ~

Dr. Balderas is pacing back and forth in his office. Dr. Fuentes was sacked three weeks ago, just after the hearing in which Dr. Balderas was cleared of any wrongdoing in Columbus's escape incident. According to the board, Balderas had taken all the necessary precautions. It was an unfortunate incident but the patient was safely back in care. Dr. Balderas was not happy about the result. Sure, Columbus was back at the institute and had lived through the ordeal, but he was turned inward, silent – almost comatose.

So the news that Columbus is cognizant and speaking makes him giddy. Consuela brings the news to him and together they trundle down to the dayroom and sit with Columbus for a few minutes.

Columbus is staring out the window, his expression not changing, head slightly to the side, drooling.

"Mr. Columbus?" Dr. Balderas moves around in front of him, into his view. "Can you hear me?" He looks over at Consuela, whose heart is pounding. She's terrified. Maybe the pool conversation was an anomaly and he's slipped back inside. Disappeared. Did she imagine him commenting on her body?

"It doesn't look like there's been any change," Dr. Balderas says. This makes him sad. Perhaps this nurse, who's spent so much time with this patient, was only hoping he'd come around. He reaches into his shirt pocket and pulls out a flashlight. Checks Columbus's pupils, looking for even constriction in both eyes when the light is only in one eye. Everything appears to be normal. Just as he's about to stand upright Columbus shouts: "Boo!" Dr. Balderas drops the flashlight in shock. Steps back gasping. Columbus catches the flashlight, snatches it midair.

Consuela jumps, too. "Son of a bitch, Columbus!"

"I was just mucking with you guys. I'm fine, really."

"I don't think I am," Dr. Balderas says. He exhales and looks hard at Columbus. "If you ever do that again I'll prescribe cold-water therapy with Nurse Sidona. And I'll insist that she use the brush."

"It was a joke, Balderas. Lighten up."

"That's Dr. Balderas and it was not funny, Columbus. Not fucking funny."

~ ~ ~

In Cádiz, Emile goes right to the harbour and looks for the office of the coast guard. He finds out that the Spanish coast guard picked a man out of the water just offshore about one month after his person of interest disappeared. This man was in bad shape – hypothermic, dehydrated, and exhausted. When he came to, he wouldn't stop talking about sailing the Western Sea and how he was the one true and only Christopher Columbus. He had no identification. There were profound questions about where he'd come from. He could have come from Morocco or from a boat offshore. They knew what they should have done with him. There were protocols when someone with no papers, no passport, no identification whatsoever, was found floating in the Strait of Gibraltar. Those protocols, in a world gone mad with fear, were not pleasant if you were on the receiving end. One of the men who helped fish this man out of the water suggested the obvious: "We should take him to the hospital – he needs a doctor."

For some reason, these men hesitated. They listened to this man. "My ships are in Palos," he said. "I have no time for hospitals. My ships are in the harbour in Palos."

"He's out of his head."

"Why don't we take him to Palos? Take him to the Franciscan monastery at La Rábida. I know Father Bolivar. The monks will know what to do with him. Maybe they know him."

"Maybe he's an actor or something. Part of some historical play about Columbus."

One of his co-workers chipped in. "But what was he doing in the strait?"

"Maybe he got drunk at a party."

"Hell of a party. He looks like shit."

The men looked at one another and knew this was something they would never speak of. This didn't happen. There was no man who believed he was Christopher Columbus floating half dead in the strait. This information was only pried out of one of these men with a hefty bribe. The Interpol badge by itself wasn't enough.

Emile leaves the coast-guard office in Cádiz, his wallet a little slimmer. He checks out of his hotel, and heads for Palos. Palos, as a destination for this man, makes sense, but Emile thought he would wind up there on his own. Emile has no idea what this man might have been doing swimming in the Strait of Gibraltar.

~ ~ ~

They are sitting on wooden benches in a simple antechamber with stone walls. Emile had waited almost an hour. Then a monk brought in steaming tea. Father Michael was a few minutes behind the tea.

"I apologize for the wait."

No reason is forthcoming – just the apology. Emile describes what he knows of the stranger and Father Michael nods.

"He slept for almost two days when he arrived," Father Michael says. "Father Bolivar nursed him, took care of him. He didn't speak for a week."

"Would it be okay if I talked to Father Bolivar?" Emile is trying hard to contain his excitement.

"Unfortunately, Father Bolivar is in the north, on a silent retreat. He cannot be reached."

"Can I ask what happened to this man?"

"He was with us three weeks."

"And then?"

"And then Father Bolivar called in a favour with a chief of police in Sevilla. It was obvious this man needed more than what we could provide." Father Michael sighs, shakes his head. "He became violent. In the end, he could not be controlled. Father Bolivar is not a young man. The police came and took him to an institute in Sevilla. They were discreet about where this man had been."

"Can you provide me with a telephone number for the institution in Sevilla?"

"I have it here. I've taken the liberty of getting my assistant to look up the name of the director for you. It's a Dr. Fuentes you'll want to speak with." The father hands Emile a piece of paper and stands up. "You must understand that he was quite violent and became more so when he found out we were sending him to Sevilla. I think he felt betrayed by Father Bolivar."

"Thank you, Father. I . . . I am curious about one thing."

"He believes he's Christopher Columbus. It's no game. He's slipped out of this reality and there was no bringing him back. We tried, but . . ."

~ ~ ~

Emile is dialing the institute in Sevilla even before he gets to his car. He asks for the doctor and is told the director will be right with him.

"Hello, this is Dr. Balderas."

"Oh, I was looking for a Dr. Fuentes."

"Yes, Dr. Fuentes is no longer here. Can I help you with something?"

"Well," Emile says, "I like people who get to the point, so here goes. I'm an investigator with Interpol. My name is Emile Germain. I'm wondering if you've got a guy there who believes he's Christopher Columbus?"

"You're either a psychic or we're about to have a long conversation," Dr. Balderas says.

"Can I take that as a yes?"

"Yes, but we also have a Pablo Picasso, a Tom Cruise, and a Don Quixote. We used to have a pope."

"But you have a Columbus," Emile says.

"We have a Christopher Columbus, yes – a man we've not been able to identify."

"He's got to be my man." Emile is amazed. He had almost convinced himself that his man would have been at the institution and then released, and the game would carry on. But it seems the chase is over. How long has he been on his trail?

Months. It's been months. He's had other cases in the interim, but this man kept rising to the surface. He kept pulling Emile back to Spain.

His impulse is to call her with this news. For the three years they were together, whenever Emile successfully solved a case – the subject was found alive – he and his wife would do the recovery dance: they would have a drink together, sometimes hundreds of kilometres apart, and they would toast over the phone. Or if they were physically together, they would go out for dinner, and at some point in the evening, they would dance – in a restaurant or café, beside the car with the radio turned up and door open, or at home in the kitchen. Emile's first thought when he hung up the phone was: *recovery dance*. But it's doubtful she would want to hear his voice.

SEVENTEEN

He finishes his morning swim and rolls himself onto the edge of the pool. It is the morning of the feast of Saint Agnes. "Shakespeare's undiscovered country," Columbus says, "is something I know about. It is a concept I understand. Nobody has been dead and come back to tell us what it's like to be dead. *Undiscovered* is an appropriate designation. All we have is speculation, rumour, hope, and, of course, what the Church tells us. The Church is so certain." He slips back into the water, ducks his body under the surface, comes up sleek and dripping. "I am not so certain, but in a sense, given the prevailing superstitions and old wives' tales at the time, I was about to tempt death with my proposed journey. But just discovering new lands is nothing. You have to come back and prove it, loudly." He looks over at Consuela, who is leaning forward in her chair. Looks at her sideways – cocks his head. "You look lost," he says.

"Well, given that Shakespeare was born nearly sixty years after Columbus died, I'm curious about how you know about his work."

Columbus shrugs. "I'm not dead, as you can see. But this is a minor detail of time. What does it matter? The story, Consuela. The story is the thing!"

"It would help the credibility of this story."

"Credibility? You want credibility?"

"Yes. If you keep getting things wrong, how am I to come along?"

"Well, it was some gigantic-brained scientist or philosopher who said, or postulated, that time was fluid – forward, backward, past and future: all the same thing. Not my idea."

Consuela thinks about the complete disregard for time and the bevy of anachronistic artifacts in Columbus's stories. She thinks about the possibility that he won't come out of this – that he'll stay locked in this cage as Columbus. It frightens her. Because if he stays there, as Columbus, in that world of kings and queens and inquisitors, she won't know what to do with her feelings. And if he comes out and they manage to unravel the mystery? She doesn't want to think about that, either.

"Forget it, Columbus. Doesn't matter."

"Trust the tale not the teller. Remember who I am."

~ ~ ~

The next morning at the pool, Consuela makes a silent decision. She has to tell him about Cecelia. He has to find out from her. Mercifully, he tends to keep to himself and Cecelia was not an everyday occurrence in his life. She has been struggling with how exactly to tell him. But he's got to know. "Look, there's something I have to tell you and there's no easy way."

"This sounds serious. Are you all right?"

Consuela takes a big breath. "Cecelia passed away, Columbus. I know you two were friends. I'm sorry."

He sits up on the edge of the pool, slips his feet into the water, keeps his back to Consuela. "When?"

"While you were lost inside yourself – about a month ago."

"Goddamnit."

"I'm really –"

"Goddamnit. I never . . . I never kissed them goodbye."

"Them?" she says. She wonders what in the hell he's talking about.

"Her. I mean her. I never said goodbye."

"Are you okay?"

"Not now." He slips into the water and starts a slow front crawl toward the far end of the pool, performs an efficient turnaround, and moves toward and past Consuela. He swims for another hour. Gets out of the water, exhausted and silent and dripping. Goes to his room, shuts the door to the world.

~ ~ ~

Columbus grieves Cecelia with an irrational intensity. There are no more stories. He'll chat briefly about the weather. He'll grumble about the food. He rejects Consuela's company and so she is relegated to watching him from a safe distance as he comes to terms with this death.

When he does let Consuela near, it doesn't go well.

"I was not there and then she died," he says. "I should have been there for her."

"You swam the Strait of Gibraltar and almost died –"

"I should have been there for her. Nobody should die alone. Nobody!"

Columbus picks up a chair and shatters the nearest window. The chair leg gets stuck in the wire mesh and is left hanging.

Columbus storms toward his room. Kicks over a wooden table with a half-finished puzzle of a running horse. Two indignant patients barely escape the table as it slams to the floor. They stand there with puzzle pieces in their hands watching Columbus disappear. He slams a door that is always left open and is off down the hallway.

"Let him go," Consuela says to the orderlies. "It's my fault. Just let him go."

~ ~ ~

Columbus sits in the corner of the dayroom, staring out the window, sunglasses on his face, rocking back and forth.

Consuela has had enough. She pulls a chair next to his and sits down. "It's not your fault," she says.

"I wasn't there for them," he says. "I left them alone and went off into the world chasing a dream."

"What?"

"A salmon moving upstream. There were poems. I was chasing poetry against the current."

"What are you –"

"People everywhere. And I am running away from them. I'm running hard and then there is thunder. A storm is coming. A big red storm." He does not stop rocking, nor does he acknowledge her. He mutters and rocks. Consuela pulls her chair away and attends to her other duties.

~ ~ ~

In the lineup for breakfast, Neil, who has some derivation of Tourette's syndrome, taps Columbus on the shoulder, asks him something or says something, and Columbus turns on him, pushes hard. Neil goes flying into the containers – rashers of bacon, and steel containers of scrambled eggs, and stacks of lightly buttered toast. Orderlies descend on Columbus and he's escorted back to his room.

"Buttfucker! Asswipe!" Neil shouts at the retreating figure of Columbus between two orderlies. "Fucking pig!"

~ ~ ~

He refuses Consuela's invitations to swim in the morning. He refuses to bathe. He makes a pass at Elena, who considers his proposition and agrees to meet him. One of the orderlies finds them in a closet, embracing, kissing. Columbus disengages, thanks her, and goes to his room.

~ ~ ~

"I have to tell you something. I know, I know you're sad right now and don't really want me around. I respect that. And you can have as much space as you need. It's just that . . ." She stops. She's not even sure he's awake.

Consuela is speaking through the little wire-mesh portal in his door. Columbus has his back to the door, is leaning against it, rocking slightly, staring straight ahead at the window. It's 5 A.M. The nightmare woke him and he had no idea what to do. Going back to sleep was not an option. Walking the hallways would require breaking out of his room. He knows how to do this. It's a matter of lining up the tumblers inside the lock with a straight pin, keeping tension with the tine of a fork. But he also knows that picking the lock again and walking around the institute freely is an activity that would certainly be frowned upon.

This dream is a swift horror. The first steps in a series of events he knows. He knows where this dream ends. The destination is a familiar terror. He's been avoiding direct acknowledgement of it for so long. In the darkness, he throws his legs over the edge of the bed, sits up, sighs. Walks over to the dresser and bends forward to see himself in the mirror. Dark shadows. Narrow face. Sunken eyes. He leans over the washbasin and pulls tepid water to his face, does it again, and again. He reaches for his towel but it's fallen to the floor. Once he finds the towel, he sniffs it for any hint of mildew, then dries his face and hands. After pacing for more than an hour, he's tired, ready for sleep, but not if that dream is waiting. And one can never be sure about dreams. So he hunches, leans back against the door, and rocks himself into a sort of meditative state. Her voice is a whisper inside his meditation. At first he's not sure it's real. He's not even sure it's a woman's voice.

"I have to tell you something. Are you there?"

"Yes." He whispers, a kind of mimicking echo.

"I think I need to let a different nurse take care of you. Maybe Nurse Emily. Or Frances. You always said you liked Nurse Frances."

"Why?" The thought of losing Consuela wakes him up fully – starts panic in him.

Yes, she thinks. Why would I think I could get away with not answering the why?

Columbus waits.

"Because I care for you in the wrong way."

"Is there a wrong way to care for someone?"

"Well, yes, when you are the patient and I am your nurse. There's a line. It's professional."

"And?"

"And I have feelings that go beyond professional."

"So it's okay for a patient to love a nurse, but not the other way around? That hardly seems fair."

"You love . . . ?"

"I have to get up. My knees are killing me."

"Columbus?" She's been whispering but now it's her full voice.

"You have seen me at my very worst, Consuela. You've seen me stripped bare of dignity, clothing, pride, and still . . . you found me. You found me and kept me safe." He stops. How could I *not* love this woman? he thinks.

~ ~ ~

They sit on the stiff wooden bench in silence for a long time, the television in the dayroom just loud enough to be heard but not loud enough to be deciphered. It's some show about oceans. There are colourful fish and coral reefs. Consuela is torn. She wants him to finish his tale, but she does not want to lose Columbus. She had no illusions about awkwardness.

She had confidence that there would be awkwardness between them. Just by telling him her feelings, no matter how oblique, she crossed a line.

She looks up at the television, then down at the floor. Columbus clears his throat and Consuela smiles.

"The Church of St. George in the town of Palos is a small stone structure with a modest bell tower. It was a mosque at some point in its history. Now a cross crowns its highest tower."

~ ~ ~

Inside, soft cathedral light fingers its way through fine dust. A cluster of candles illuminates one corner. The coolness of this sanctum conflicts with the pervading heat outside.

Tomorrow is the day, Columbus thinks as he enters the building. His captains will board their respective ships. They will all wait for him. They'll wait for him to board the *Santa Maria*. And then, with the blessing of the Church, they will set sail for the Canary Islands, and then they will push the edges of knowledge.

Columbus sits on one of the wooden pews and Father Antonio, who has come to bless the voyage in the morning, joins him. After a few minutes of silence, Columbus nods his head in some sort of inner understanding, as if he's made up his mind about something.

"Father forgive me, for I have sinned," he says. "And I am about to sin."

"Speak, my son," Father Antonio says. "My friend, what is on your mind? What weighs on you?"

"I have lied to all these men, Father. I've told them we can sail easily to Japan and to the Indies and the lands of Marco Polo. In truth, I have no idea how far it is across the ocean."

"You don't know? But all this time –"

"Just words. I lied to the king, to the queen, to the university commission. I know in my heart there is land out there but I don't know how far. The only way to find out is to sail and see for ourselves."

The father is silent, tuned inward. "You want my blessing?" he says finally.

"No, Father. I seek no blessing. I only need you to listen. I no longer have the heart to carry on. I no longer wish to continue on this journey. I have my ships. I have provisions and crewmen. But I no longer have my heart. Forgive me, Father."

Silence resorts to itself in the small church. Then the sound of a sparrow in one of the high windows. One problem at a time, Father Antonio is thinking. Columbus has no idea what he's doing. He has no idea how far he'll have to go to reach land. He's told all these men, kings and queens and God only knows who else, that he knows this can be done. And now he admits he does not really know. And God? Well, God had to know this. God knows all. And if God knows then God must want Columbus to do this thing. It is God's will. What is faith if it is not this journey into the unknown? The journey is a shining example of faith. They are truly in God's hands.

"Why?" Father Antonio whispers the word. The word

becomes more a long escaping stream of gas, a sorrowful sigh. "Why, after all you've suffered? After all your difficulties? After all your years of chasing this dream? Why? Why do you wish to give up?"

"I feel something horrible is about to happen. I know some tragedy is following me across the Western Sea."

"What could you possibly know? Only God knows the future."

"Juan once suggested that time is nothing but a fluid. The past, the present, the future, all mix together. Water is water is water."

"Only God sees all, Cristóbal. You are not God. You do not think you are God, do you?"

"No, Father, but my dreams. My nightmares. It's there! Some awful thing above me. It waits, Father. This journey is doomed to some catastrophe."

"Cristóbal –"

"So much death. So much death and destruction. And the thing is, I come through all right. Death is all around but it does not come for me."

"I do not know what to say to you. What do you want to do?"

"I want to defy my fate. I wish to disobey my destiny. I want forgiveness for what I'm about to do."

"God will forgive you. You have always been a good servant of God."

Columbus laughs. It's a sharp-edged, hollow sound that reverberates off the stone walls.

"Am I evil?"

"How can you say this, Cristóbal?"

"Where is evil if not inside of me? Does it exist there?" He points to the cross on the far wall. "Is it inside the men of the Inquisition who torture and kill in the name of God?"

"Not evil, good!"

"Both, Father. Both good and evil are here." Columbus pounds his chest. "Here . . . inside of me."

"What will you do?" Father Antonio has tears in his eyes. He has been a friend to Columbus for many years. He has seen his suffering. "Will you tell the men who believed you that they were wrong?"

"No. I will follow through with my deal. I have a deal with the king and queen and with the merchants who supplied the *Santa Maria*. And my men believe in this dream. I will find something out there. Something. And I will not mean to ruin it all, but I will."

"Cristóbal." Father Antonio doesn't know where to look – does not know what to say.

"If you truly wished to serve God, Father, you would take a sword and kill me. For everything I fear I am about to do."

"You do not know this, my friend. Nothing is written. The future is not written."

"And yet, I know." Columbus stands and he does not feel lighter. No weight has been lifted. Religion, faith, God – all these things fail again, he thinks. They offer nothing. No salvation. No relief. Nothing. "Come, Father, let's have wine together. We will make our own last supper, yes?"

"I cannot join you tonight, Cristóbal. I don't have the heart."

Columbus shrugs and sighs. He doesn't have the energy to

try and convince Father Antonio to come and have a drink with him. He just wants a drink. So Columbus leaves the disconsolate father sitting on the wooden pew in the church that was once a mosque and walks through the cool, triple-arched doorway into the dusty heat.

~ ~ ~

Consuela looks him up. She Googles Emile Germain, the Interpol investigator who thinks he knows the identity of her Columbus. She searches his name, along with the words *Interpol* and *missing*. She finds several stories attached to newspapers. She clicks on the link to the *International Herald Tribune* and starts to read.

"My God," she whispers. She reads about an Interpol investigator, an Agent Germain, who was involved in a gunfight with members of an alleged Al Qaeda cell in Paris. Bullets from the gunfight went through a wall and killed a young girl, who was in bed, asleep. The girl was a promising pianist, a prodigy. The investigator had been looking for a German woman, who'd been missing for almost a year. He'd tracked her to the address in the same building as the young prodigy. The men living on the main level had opened the door, seen the offered Interpol identification, and opened fire on the agent, hitting him twice. They left him in the hallway and fled into the street. The agent dragged himself to the doorway and fired at their car. They fired back. They shot badly, wildly. The sleeping girl was in her bedroom one floor up, in her bed, which was against the outside wall.

When the wine is gone, she opens another bottle and dials her sister's number. She'd like to call Dr. Balderas but she knows he's off for a week, skiing in Switzerland with his family.

"Hello, Sis. You're not going to believe what I just found out. There's this guy from Interpol . . ."

~ ~ ~

Consuela and Columbus are in the long hallway that leads to the pool. The stone walls make the hallway feel cold. The ubiquitous Moorish-style arches persist even in this small space. Columbus stops.

"What's wrong?" he says.

Consuela, three steps ahead, turns toward him. She's so tired. The man from Interpol weighs on her. She can't imagine living with the ramifications of inadvertently causing the death of an innocent.

"I couldn't sleep," she says.

"Why?"

"God, Columbus, why do you have to be so goddamned intense all the time! Let's just go swimming, all right?"

"Something has shifted in you. Your eyes have changed."

"Yes, I'm tired."

"It's more than fatigue."

"Trust me. It's lack of sleep. Why don't we switch today? I'll swim and you can watch. Or if you like, you can tell stories."

"Ah, you want a story. You want to know what happens don't you? Well, let me warn you, it's not the ending you might expect."

They arrive at the pool. Consuela slips out of her uniform. In her bra and panties, she slides into the water.

"Begin," she says, a little more demanding than she'd intended.

Columbus watches as she starts to quietly glide through the water. "Okay," he says. "Imagine two women squatting to relieve themselves in a forest, only a few feet apart. The air is as smooth as silk. The sky a pristine blue. These two women both love the same man."

~ ~ ~

"So, you are Beatriz," Isabella says.

"What?" Beatriz looks around and then finds a splash of colour through the leaves not ten feet away.

It's midday. It's stifling hot – more than a little uncomfortable, even to people who are used to such heat. They are peeing at the edge of a small orange grove near the town of Palos. It is the day before Columbus is to set off.

Isabella has minimal security. Nothing close. Her men watch from the perimeter. She's thinking she'd like to see Columbus one last time, but she knows a quick meeting, an official goodbye, is all she can probably safely arrange. Something, anything, would be better than smiling like an idiot and waving from some balcony with Ferdinand by her side.

"I said, you're Beatriz."

"Yes. Who wants to know?" Beatriz wipes herself with a handful of long grass and then drops it.

"Queen Isabella."

"Right. The queen."

"That's right."

"The queen, squatting in the woods to pee. Right."

"Could happen, couldn't it? Do you think the queen never pees?"

"Do I think the queen is human? Yes, of course. But you are not the queen. The queen would not squat in the woods. Isn't there some golden toilet somewhere?"

Isabella chuckles. "You're wrong about the queen. She would most certainly squat in the woods."

"Why would the queen be here, in Palos?"

"Do you not think the queen is interested in the voyage that will be embarking tomorrow?"

This gets Beatriz thinking. Of course, the queen will want to be here. Word on the street has it that she was instrumental in arranging for the ships. She and Columbus had a relationship of some kind. Why wouldn't she want to be here?

Isabella pulls her panties up and walks out from her station. She extends a thin hand with heavy rings adorning every finger, save one.

Beatriz looks at the rings. There's no guarantee these rings are real. How would she know? They could be fakes.

"Nice rings. I've got some nice rings, too." Beatriz holds out her hand, with only two modest rings, for this alleged queen to see.

"Guards!"

Four men with earplugs appear in less than five seconds. Three of them have handguns drawn and pointed at Beatriz. The fourth is planted firmly in front of Isabella. "It's fine,"

Isabella says. "Give us some room." One of the guards frisks Beatriz. Finds a small knife tucked between her breasts. They all pull back silently.

"Your Majesty," Beatriz says. "How could I have known?" She bows deeply.

"Oh get up. We're alone. I wanted to have a chat with you."

"Yes, Your Majesty."

How to begin? she thinks. "So, he's going. Columbus is off to prove he is right. How do you feel about that?"

"Well, I will miss him."

"Yes, our Columbus is a most amusing and entertaining man."

Beatriz speaks slowly, clearly. "We have children together. We all love him. He is my man. He is a father to his sons."

"You are not a wife, are you?"

"I wear this ring."

"But you are not his wife."

"We are bonded, committed, devoted, dedicated –"

"But not married."

"No," she says softly, slowly. "Not married."

"Well, we love Columbus, too," the queen says. "We love his enthusiasm, and drive, and pigheadedness. Let's walk, shall we?" She motions with her hand for Beatriz to precede her.

The two women begin to move through the grove. Sparse undergrowth makes the walking easy. And there is good shade.

"I am curious," Beatriz says.

"Yes, I bet you are."

"A couple of things, really. First, the ships. How did it happen that the ships appeared so suddenly? Everything was lost, hopeless. And then in a matter of days, it was done."

"And the second?"

"The second is difficult for me."

"Perhaps I can answer your second question before you pose it. I love your Columbus and I believe this love goes both ways. Unfortunately, I am queen. I have a husband and a country. If a liaison were discovered, it would not go well for me, nor would it be good for Columbus. It would be death all around I'm afraid."

Beatriz reaches down to her ankle and draws a knife – a squat stabbing blade.

Isabella looks at the knife and then at Beatriz. "Are you mad? They'll kill you. They don't take this security thing lightly." She nods almost imperceptibly toward the shadows of the forest.

"I could kill you first," Beatriz says. And in scant seconds, Beatriz is on the ground, her hand twisted up and across her face. The agent pulls the knife out of her hand and looks at her face. A deep gash from the corner of her mouth to just below her eye. The cut is deep and it bleeds instantly. Beatriz moves her hand across the side of her face. "Fuck," she grunts, her face in a mask of disbelief as she looks up at the guard.

Isabella, tackled by two guards for her safety, pulls herself up off the ground. She looks at her men, who have drawn their weapons. "Oh, put your guns away you idiots. Pick her up and see that her wound is attended to," she says. "Whoever it was that searched her did a piss-poor job by the way. Two knives. She had two knives. Now get her out of here and keep her out of the way until Columbus is gone." Isabella walks over and picks up Beatriz's knife, weighs it in her hand.

"Lose her in one of your institutions. Just keep her out of the way."

"You arranged the ships, didn't you?" Beatriz says.

When Isabella turns and faces Beatriz, her face is flat, devoid of emotion. Making herself appear to feel nothing is second nature to her. Her eyes, though, her eyes betray the anger rising in her. Her eyes become two sharp sticks.

"You did it because you love him!" Blood is seeping through Beatriz's fingers, dripping in rivulets down her neck and into the crevasse between her breasts.

Isabella thinks about her time with Columbus – a few meetings, a cup of coffee. Memories occur in spasmodic jerks. A yearning rises up in her and takes the place of her anger. "I need . . ." She breathes and then sighs. "I needed to put an ocean between this queen and that foolish navigator. I needed to stop this lust in me. It was the only way." She looks at Beatriz, who is held firmly by two guards. "It was the only way," Isabella whispers.

"So you do not believe he can do this?"

"Take her away," Isabella says.

"That's the difference between you and me. I believe in the man and his dreams. You believe in nothing! *Nothing!*"

"Stop! I'm the queen. I'm your queen. It would be best for you if you remembered that."

"Why don't you kill me, then? You have all the power. You are the queen but you'll never be my queen."

Isabella squeezes the knife in her hand. She notices her hand is sweating. She nods toward one of her guards and they continue to carry Beatriz, none too gently, through the woods.

You didn't want to kill me. You still don't, Isabella thinks. You and I love the same man. For whatever reason, we love Columbus. We share that.

Then there is only Isabella, and around her the orange trees rising up like the bars of a cage, and at the edge of the grove there are palm trees, and beyond that the ocean, and beyond that the sky. She can see one guard hovering at the periphery. Columbus can love Beatriz openly, Isabella thinks. Without constraint. No hiding. No lying. "He needs that," she says to the trees. "We all need that."

~ ~ ~

Consuela stops swimming. A sudden absence of water sound. Columbus stops walking. It's a cool day with clouds that seem thicker than the Basque sheep's wool at the market. Yesterday, Columbus moved the stones away from the pipe in front of the hot spring flow – to make it warmer for the coming days. The warm edge to the pool is welcomed today.

"Do you need that, Columbus?" she says.

"We all need love – to love and be loved."

"Not what I asked, Columbus."

"Do not fault the pious ones, because they also, like us, are seeking love and grace, in their own way, at their own pace."

"Hafiz?"

"Yes, Hafiz."

"You're not Hafiz."

"I am not a lot of things."

"You are certainly evasive, and vague."

He sighs. "Of course, I need love. To love and be loved."

"Who loves you?" She holds his eyes. Looks up into his face from the lip of the pool. She's not going to let go.

"I don't want to talk about this."

"You don't want to talk about it because Beatriz, Isabella, Selena, and even Juan are fictions. There is no love there, Columbus. They're not real like this water." She splashes water up onto the deck, and it fans into Columbus, smacks into him. "Even your kids are fictions. They don't exist. They don't love you."

His voice diminishes. "I . . . I love. There is love in my life. I love my girls." He gazes down the distance of the pool toward the far end, where the spring comes in. But there is no focus – his eyes are simply facing a direction.

Did he say girls? He looks utterly lost. Consuela stops pushing. She hadn't planned to confront him. Did she go too far? She remembers Dr. Balderas's assertion that Columbus must finish his story.

I love you, Columbus, she thinks. More than I should. More than you know. I want you well and out of here. I want you to be happy.

EIGHTEEN

IT TAKES THREE DAYS BEFORE he unlocks another chapter of his story. He arrives for breakfast in shorts and a grey T-shirt, sits down like nothing is amiss. Consuela does a double take.

"Is that –"

"Yes. It's Columbus," Benito says.

"He's wearing clothes."

"Yes."

"I'm not sure if it's a good thing or a bad thing," Consuela says.

~ ~ ~

"Well, of course, it's a good thing," Dr. Balderas says. "Mother of God! He's wearing clothes for the first time in months! He's going to come out of this, Consuela."

They're in his office, and Consuela has just lost a second game of chess. They have an agreement between them about talking shop. They don't – not for the first half-hour of their games anyway. They leave it alone, talk about life, their lives, anything. Dr. Balderas has been telling the story of how he met his wife. They'd been at a poetry reading in Madrid. And the poet, a woman whose name he used to know but has now forgotten, was terrible – dreadful.

"She read a long, long poem about some deceased pet. It went on and on and on. In the end, we started laughing. Rude, actually, but my God, it had to be done."

"A dead pet?"

"Yes, and a very long, sentimental poem. My wife and I were the only ones giggling. Everybody else either thought it was brilliant or they were too horrified to react. I don't see a way for you to avoid checkmate, by the way. Five moves, if you're careful."

She sighs. "Okay, enough chess. Let's talk about Columbus."

"Well, I recommend not making a fuss about his clothes. It's a good thing. Pretend this is how it's always been."

"That's it?"

"That, and he must finish. He has to finish the story."

~ ~ ~

They take their espressos out onto the upper deck. Columbus removes his shirt, a wild red Hawaiian-style massacre of flowers and swirls, but keeps on a ridiculous straw hat with a short, rolled-up rim. She rather enjoys this new, clothed Columbus. It's a welcome change. God only knows where he got the clothes, the hat.

"It all goes wrong at the end," Columbus says.

"What does?" She immediately knows what a stupid question this is and smiles at him knowingly.

"It's the night before they leave. Columbus and Juan are sitting in some café in Palos pounding the wine. Columbus gets a note. I get a note. I was always getting notes from women.

They just loved that lost navigator routine. The romance of a navigator without a ship. Worked like a charm."

~ ~ ~

The note reads only: "Meet me at Starbucks behind St. George Street at midnight."

It's unsigned. Columbus thinks he knows who it's from but he's not quite sure. He tips the messenger and then refills his glass with wine. It's likely Beatriz. They already said their good-byes weeks ago when he came here to start outfitting the ships, but it is like her to come to Palos for the final night. He can't even imagine how much he will miss her. She is his rock. The one steady, unflinching thing in his life. Beatriz and the ocean. Regardless of any of the other dalliances, he loves her.

"We're set," Juan says, sitting down. "We sail tomorrow morning."

"All my gear is aboard? You loaded the wine into my cabin?"

"Yes to both."

"Good. A toast, then." He pauses. "To whatever's out there." They raise their glasses and touch them together ever so lightly. Columbus looks at Juan and half smiles. "And may we, please God, not cause some sort of catastrophe, some sort of horrible disaster, some sort of hellish nightmare in which everything dies but I am unaffected –"

"Cristóbal. Breathe. Just take big breaths. It'll be all right. You'll be fine." Juan refills Columbus's glass.

"I just have this feeling" – Columbus interrupts himself to

gulp half the glass down – "that we are going to go against God's will. We are going to find something beautiful and utterly destroy it, not because we mean to but, rather, because we are just too bloody fucking stupid."

Juan refills his own glass.

"We are too stupid to understand beauty." Columbus is muttering now. "I do not understand beauty. I do not understand Beatriz. I did not understand my wife. I do not understand Isabella. Selena is a mystery. That pine tree over there. I do not understand that pine tree. This wine. I do not understand the colour of this wine –"

"Cristóbal," Juan says. "Big breaths and you'll be okay."

He's coming unglued, Juan thinks. On the night before he is to leave, his sanity has already set sail for parts unknown. I can only hope he'll be all right in the morning. This has got to be the wine speaking, muttering.

The waitress, whose name is Lucero, comes over and leans into Columbus, giving him a good long look. "The phone is for you," she says, smiling.

"What? Where?"

Lucero points at the bar. "You're the navigator who's going to sea aren't you? You're the one. You're the leader." She's flushed with excitement, fawning.

"Yes, yes, we set sail tomorrow."

"I just love sailors," she breathes.

Columbus closes his eyes. For Christ's sake. It's raining women.

"The phone?"

"Oh, yes. At the bar."

He leans on the bar, braces himself to hear her voice, and then picks up the phone.

"Chris, it's me, Isabella. I can't talk long because I don't trust the line. And too many people around. Meet me tonight –"

"Yes, I got your –" He stops.

"What? Listen, meet me tonight at the Plaza Hotel, at ten."

"Plaza Hotel, ten," he says. "I'll be there, my queen . . . Hello?" But she is gone. Columbus hangs up and gazes into space. The bartender brings him another glass of wine, and slides a note into place beside the glass. He softly taps the paper so Columbus is sure to notice it.

Oh, good God, he thinks. Now what? He opens the note and reads it. Then he reads it again and slides it into his pocket. Someone else wants to meet him at the Café Bordeaux at nine o'clock. Selena, he thinks. The Bordeaux is Selena's kind of café. Selena has come to say goodbye. Selena the safe and silent harbour, he thinks. She has always been like the moon, a distant and giving lover. He remembers feeling very safe with Selena. Always.

~ ~ ~

Consuela dreams about Beatriz. Beatriz is sitting across from her and they are sharing a bottle of wine as old friends would. The air is pristine. They're on a patio near the ocean. Consuela can hear seagulls. They're drinking chardonnay from fish-bowls. It's so pleasant Consuela starts to feel apprehensive; she starts to not be able to breathe. She looks across the table at this olive-skinned, voluptuous, dark-haired beauty. Her eyes are only kind, and there is gentleness in everything she does. Even the meticulous way she drinks wine is an exercise in gentleness. Her movements are so fluid – it seems she is almost dancing with her wine instead of just drinking it. Her face is soft and her eyes, understanding. She's telling Consuela about her love for Columbus. And once she begins to speak her love, Consuela can say nothing. She becomes paralyzed with fear. She's afraid she'll say something stupid, like: "I know." And then Beatriz would say, "What the fuck do you mean, you know?" Everything would be ruined. So Consuela is silent. She listens to Beatriz and the seagulls. She breathes the wonderful ocean air. She wakes up cold and shivering with her blankets on the floor.

Consuela grinds her coffee beans, boils her water, and gets ready for work. She needs Columbus to finish. She can't take much more of this. She wants to put him behind her, get on with her life, and live in the present.

It's drizzling. The light is sublime. Fog mixed with cloud swirls in the high branches of the trees, giving everything an even, kind light. They hustle across the dayroom courtyard. Just before they reach the arched entrance to the south wing and the forgotten swimming pool, she says, "And?"

"And what?" he says, stopping.

"And what happens next?"

"Of course, you want to know what happens next, but great stories should never be rushed. This is a story about obsession and love, and lust and imminent discovery. It is a story that marks a leap in knowledge and understanding for all of humanity. It changes the world into a far bigger entity."

"It *is* a good story. Do you think I'm rushing you?"

"I'm happy to keep going. Whenever you want, I am happy to tell you my story. Should we get out of the rain?"

But he doesn't continue. He swims and she waits and nothing comes. When he finishes his swim for the day, he looks at her with confusion in his eyes.

"I . . . I don't know what happened. I wanted to go on, to unravel more of this story. It just wouldn't come out. I couldn't find a way to begin."

"It's all right, Columbus. Stories can wait."

In fact, it's Consuela and Dr. Balderas, anxious in the wings, who wait. They wait for more than a week for him to continue.

"I know I started this," Columbus says at breakfast. "I know. But it's getting harder to keep going. I start to lose my breath when I think about coming to the end."

"All in good time, Columbus," Consuela says. "I'm not going anywhere."

~ ~ ~

He holds his fingertip on the top of his queen, but Dr. Balderas is suspended in something other than chess. His mind is not on the game. Even Consuela can see that any move involving the queen would be disastrous. But still, he holds his finger there, as if he is considering the possibilities of such a move. He is looking at the board but he does not see it. He moves his forefinger to his pursed lips.

"The women," he says, finally. "The women are his wife."

"The women are his wife?" Consuela is confused.

"Columbus. Columbus's women. Think about it. The queen, Isabella, represents strength, fortitude, and courage – and most important, she is sexual restraint. Selena is unconditional love. She asks no questions. She asks for nothing. Beatriz is the archetypal mother. Cassandra – was that her name? – she represents lust, desire, wild abandonment. All these women are representations of Columbus's wife. His real-life wife."

Consuela can feel the blood drain from her face.

"What?" she says halfheartedly.

"It's just one piece of the puzzle. I couldn't get my head around all these women Columbus sleeps with, or in the case of Isabella, doesn't sleep with. This parsing of personality traits makes sense. He's not a philanderer in his real life. He probably loves his wife very much. What I don't understand is why Columbus never beds Isabella. If I'm reading your reports correctly, they're crazy about each other." He's about to go on but glances up at Consuela and stops. "Are you all right, Consuela?"

"Bathroom," she says quickly. In a flash she's in the hallway. In scant seconds she's standing in the bathroom with the door locked. The lock click echoes in the small room. A strip of fluorescent lighting sparks to life, hesitant and yellow.

Breathe, Consuela, she tells herself. She slides down the wall so her buttocks rest on the floor, her feet still flat on the tile. Her forearms rest on her knees. *This can't be,* she thinks. *How could I be so stupid?* Even with the air conditioning and the cool tile on her back, Consuela is sweating. She can feel the wetness on her back, and under her arms.

Why hasn't Columbus slept with Isabella? It's a story. There must be a thousand ways to tell a story in which this lust is consummated. There was plenty of opportunity. Just make up some motel room in Barcelona, or Madrid, or Marbella. Find some clever way to shake off her bodyguards. Wear disguises. But Columbus has not told this story. Their relationship is taut with sexual tension. It's restrained, withheld, and ultimately forbidden. Just like . . .

It's me. I'm Isabella. Oh, fuck.

~ ~ ~

"Does he know who he is?" Emile sips his coffee. Dr. Balderas had been pleased to show off his new Italian espresso machine. When Emile had asked for a *café cortado*, the doctor jumped up and made one for himself, too.

"Not yet," Dr. Balderas says, "but we believe he's close."

"How close?"

Dr. Balderas hesitates.

"Look, it'll take us a few days, perhaps as long as a week, to confirm who he is. But if he is this missing Canadian, I'll have to let the Canadian embassy know we've found him. They'll want to notify his family. And eventually, sooner rather than later, they're going to want to take him home."

"How much can you delay that process?"

Emile smiles. "Depends on how convincing an argument you can make."

"Nurse Consuela is supposed to be here." He looks at his watch. It's not quite eight-thirty.

~ ~ ~

Consuela is guarded when she arrives at Dr. Balderas's office. She hesitates at the door. She does not know how to feel about this Interpol agent. It's possible he holds the key to Columbus, and she's not sure she wants the key.

Emile stands when she comes into the office.

Well, that's old-school Cary Grant, she thinks. Nice. So far, her mother would approve.

He reaches out his hand. "I'm Emile Germain. I'm with Interpol. I've been chasing your Columbus patient for a few months." He smiles. "I've had other cases along the way but he kept pulling me back to Spain."

His handshake is firm, not overpowering and not lame. His eyeglasses are folded flat in his shirt pocket – they look like they might be wire-rimmed reading glasses. Consuela looks at his shoes. Her father always harped about how you could tell a lot about a man by the way he took care of his shoes – or didn't. He's wearing stylish, brown dress shoes, slip-ons – more pointed than any pair of conservative wing-tipped oxfords. The shoes are not polished. But they're not in rough shape, either.

"Do you know what happened to him?" Consuela sits across the room from the two men – she wants space.

"My office identified four files out of our database – all of these men are possibilities. We need time to confirm his identity, but judging from these pictures, I'd say we've got a pretty good idea. We think he was in Madrid on March 11."

. Dr. Balderas breaks in. "Everything fits, Consuela. They think he might be a Canadian." He hands her four pictures inside a red-and-white Interpol folder, which she flips through quickly. The pictures are fairly conclusive, though not 100 per cent. The man in the pictures has short hair, or his hair is covered by various hats. He wears glasses in a couple of the photos. The eyes seem to be right. Consuela returns to the first one. Yes, this one certainly looks like him.

"I thought . . ." Consuela says. She inhales sharply. "He's not Spanish? He's Canadian?"

"Yes, and this creates a bit of a problem," Dr. Balderas says.

"You mean beyond the fact that he still believes he's Columbus," she says.

"Well, that and the fact Mr. Germain is going to have to report in. He'll have to let the Canadian embassy know we've got one of their people. I've let Mr. Germain –"

"Emile, please," Emile says.

"I've briefed Emile on our progress. I've given him my opinion. I've told him that based on your reports over the past couple of weeks, and the changes I've witnessed in Mr. Columbus, that he's close. And we'd like a little time."

"Nurse Consuela?" Emile says. "You seem to be crying."

"Oh shit," she says, wiping away her tears. "It's nothing. I've been weepy for days. I'm a little overwhelmed. This is great news."

Emile crosses the gulf between them and hands her a hand-kerchief. It seems to be an honest gesture, not ostentatious.

It's just something he does when women around him cry. Consuela looks at it, then up at him. He shrugs. "My mother insisted her boys always carry a handkerchief. Old habits, you know?"

Consuela takes the handkerchief and dabs the corners of her eyes. "Thanks."

"I'd be interested in your opinion, Nurse Consuela. How close do you think he is to coming out of this?"

She stands up and crosses the office, looks down into the courtyard. These windows need cleaning, she thinks. A fly skitters along the glass. I've no idea, she thinks. "I'm not a doctor," she says.

"You see him every day – have seen him almost every day. Right now, I'd value your opinion more than any doctor – no offence intended." He nods at Dr. Balderas.

"He's close to finishing his story. It's almost done. But I don't know if he's ready to face whatever it is that happened to him."

"I think," Dr. Balderas says, "what Consuela is worried about is the reality. We could pressure him to face his reality and push him even further away – lose him completely."

"How much time do you think you'll need? I can be exceedingly slow when it comes to my paperwork."

Consuela smiles.

"We need a week, maybe two," Dr. Balderas says.

"Okay. That's not a problem. I'll need at least that long to run the DNA. There are no fingerprints on file for this alleged Mr. Nusret. I'm having a file on him forwarded to your e-mail account, Dr. Balderas, but let me tell you what I know . . ."

NINETEEN

"WELL, YOU COULD TELL HIM it's a standard test – that the same test is being done on every patient in the institute."

Consuela smiles. "He's delusional, not stupid. What do I tell him when he asks what the test is for?"

"Tell him the test is looking for influenza antibodies," Emile says, "that this test will help with the development of a flu shot."

"Is this in any way close to ethical?"

"You're responsible for his well-being. This test will help us be sure that he is who we think he is." Emile is surprised to find himself feeling envy. He's envious of Columbus because he gets to be with Consuela every day – well, every day she works. He looks over at Consuela. Clearly she is weighing the ethics of this test. Emile finds himself liking her more for her hesitation.

"Okay," she says. "Okay. I'll get you a DNA sample."

"One more thing," Emile says. "What time does your shift end?"

"Are you asking me out on a date?" She shakes her head as if this would be entirely out of the question.

"Well, we could call it business, but it's been a long time since I've had a glass of wine with a woman who pushes me on the ethics of my job."

"No," Consuela says. "I couldn't possibly go out and talk about business. But I'd love to see what an ethical glass of wine looks like."

~ ~ ~

"I have a home in Paris," Emile says. He catches the waiter's eye and holds up his thumb and forefinger for two more glasses of wine.

Not a house, or a flat, or an apartment, Consuela thinks. "That sounds like code for 'A woman is waiting for me in Paris,'" Consuela says. She stops. "I'm sorry, that's none of my business."

"It's all right. It is actually a pretty homey apartment. There used to be a woman there, but she took her leave two years ago. And I'm outside the realm of relationship right now."

"That's a very odd way to say you're single, Mr. Germain."

"I'd be willing to step back into that realm for someone like you, Ms. Lopez. You did say Lopez?" Shut up, you idiot, Emile tells himself.

"I didn't say."

"Oh? I'm sure Dr. Balderas introduced you as Consuela Emma Lopez."

Consuela shakes her head.

"Well, it must have been on your name tag."

Consuela smiles and shakes her head again.

"Okay, I asked around. I dug around a bit," Emile says. "I know about that stop sign in Barcelona – the one you ran in 1997."

I looked you up, too, she thinks. Consuela can't help wondering where Emile was shot. She finds his eyes. Is there hurt there? Is he still damaged there? Grey eyes, with shards of hazel. The same confidence she sees in Columbus's eyes. An even self-knowledge. A groundedness. Yes, Columbus is deluded. But still, he has these same eyes. This Interpol man has not shaved in a while. She wonders if this is by choice. He has a strong, narrow nose. Brown hair with an undercurrent of grey. Even when he places the small wire-rimmed reading glasses on his face, he's attractive.

"I think I'm flattered," Consuela says.

"Well, I'd like to know about you, beyond your work, beyond Columbus. Where were you born? Have you lived in Sevilla all your life? I want to know your story."

Consuela sips her wine. "Well, I like to read."

~ ~ ~

In the dining hall, Consuela sits across from Columbus and looks into his eyes. She wants to tell him she's tired. Tired of the stories and tired of being in love with someone she can't touch, or hold, or simply take for dinner. He's a man without substance. She has been in love with a five-hundred-year-old ghost. She's afraid of the end.

"Beatriz winds up in a place much like this," Columbus says. "In a mental institution with wire screens over windows and locks on doors, security guards, orderlies, and drugs."

~ ~ ~

"She's sleeping soundly," someone says.

Beatriz hears this and does not move. She listens to the people moving around the room. She listens to their conversations and judges their numbers and where they are in the room.

"What happened to her? How did this happen?" A woman's voice.

"Some sort of knife fight." A man. It could be one of the security agents. One of the queen's men.

"It's going to leave a scar. It was a deep cut." The woman again.

"A shame. She's really quite pretty."

A gentle touch on her forehead.

"She'll be out for quite a while."

And then the sound of a door closing. The hinges creak. Two sets of creaking and then silence.

Is she alone? There's no window in the door. Beatriz knows this for a fact. She remembers checking it on the way in. But did they both leave? She waits. And waits. But how long to wait? If she waits too long there is a chance she could actually nod off. She managed to palm most of the pills they gave her but she could not avoid ingesting some pain medication.

Finally, she decides to risk one eye. Through a sliver she sees the lights have been dimmed. There are only three candles on a table across the room. Slowly, Beatriz moves her vision entirely around the small room. She realizes she's been holding her breath. Breathe, she thinks. Breathe.

She sits up and flips her legs to the floor. That motion doesn't feel quite right but it's not as bad as it could be. The door handle begins to turn. And the door is opening. The nurse comes in.

Beatriz is just as she left her. The hinges squeak again and Beatriz is up and out of bed in a flash. Her clothes are not in this room. She finds and dresses in a set of green cotton pants and a simple smock. She's a little wobbly on her feet but the wobbliness is not debilitating. She takes three bottles of pills. Then she's at the window, pulling the latch and swinging the windows outward into the night. The heat hits her like a small fist. She had taken the air-conditioned hospital for granted.

Eventually, after convincing herself that this was the only way, Beatriz jumps out the window into a hedge. It seems to her that she's flying, in slow motion, through the air. The drugs help her landing. She's still medicated enough to not really feel that her arm is broken.

Finding the harbour is not easy. She has no idea where she is, but once she gets beyond the grounds, there are prostitutes on every corner. She figures she's got to be close to the dock.

She has no idea what time it is. From the shadows she watches the yawning guard on the dock for half an hour. She's starting to feel her arm. Eventually, he steps out of the light and behind a few boxes to relieve himself, and Beatriz steals quietly up the plank. She cocoons herself in Columbus's cabin, under his bed.

She has no plan and she is equipped with only her love for Columbus. Her sons are in good hands at the monastery. They're safe and well cared for. She and Columbus will discover the new route together. Well, no, that won't work. Not with that ego of his. Even though he plays at being the selfless navigator without ships, Beatriz knows there's an ego in there. Now that he's got his ships and he's off, he'll need her to keep that swollen self-worth in check. It's a good thing she's there. Well, she's going to be there for everything.

The gash in her face was painful at first but the pills from the hospital, which she choked down dry, keep her mostly numb. There's a physician on board, she remembers. He'll take care of my arm in the morning, after they sail. Maybe he can look at this gash in my face, too. Her arm only feels a little funny as she slides under his bed and drifts into a dead sleep.

~ ~ ~

All the signs are there, but he denies them. Most of the time he stops his love and desire at the door. To love this woman is not a hard thing. He chooses to love Consuela. But these other emotions are tied to the idea of love. The symptoms of being in love, when she is around, are unmistakable. Sometimes he finds it difficult to breathe. His heartbeat quickens when she is around. He can't eat if he thinks about her, does not want to eat, does not care about food. He wants to make love with her – to be lost, as Columbus is lost with so many of his lovers. To drink wine with her. To drink her body with his fingertips, his lips . . . to kiss. Ah, to kiss Consuela would be to die sweetly. But he denies entrance to these emotions. He will not let them exist where he lives. They have to wait outside. Why? What is it in him that denies Consuela?

"You win again," he says. "That's checkmate. I'm never going to understand the nuances of this game."

"Columbus, you're not fucking with me, are you? You're not letting me win?"

"Why would I do that? I care about you."

"Well, you just avoided the question by asking a question, and I suspect you are so much more than you appear to be."

"This was a long game, and the lead vacillated between us the entire match. You won it by making better moves."

"Oh, Columbus, I'm not sure if that's an answer."

He looks at her as she sets the chessmen in their starting positions. Her astounding blue eyes – a cross between periwinkle and navy. Shoulder-length black hair and a smile that ruins him. It's as if her smiles do not come from a shallow place but, rather, come from the holy place in her, where prayers, and faith, and love exist. It is not that she rarely smiles. Consuela smiles often. It is just that he has noticed her smiles are not frivolous. They are, indeed, like prayers, like colourful flags with prayers printed on them.

"Columbus?"

I must be tired, he thinks. The in-love Columbus normally does not lean this far toward Consuela. And he's not done yet. He considers what it would be like making love with her. The sounds she might make. The feel of her skin. Her scents. The feel of the back of her leg, just beneath her buttocks. Her ankles. Her armpits. Her mouth on his. Her mouth kissing him. Surrender. Surrendered . . .

"Columbus!" Consuela is smiling. He's lost. He's off dreaming about himself, she thinks. Dreaming about sailing. "Hello, Columbus? This is Nurse Consuela to Columbus. Are you there?"

"Yes, I'm here. Where else would I be? A new game, then. A game in which I shall endeavour to humble you with my chess skills." He rubs his hands together and studies the board. Columbus stills his breathing. He stops thinking about Consuela. He looks at the board as if it is the first time he's ever played chess.

Consuela smiles. "That's what I want to hear." You are a liar, she thinks. But such a lovely liar.

Columbus looks at the board. It is not in his character to make sure all the pieces face the front, or even the same way for that matter. When it comes to chess, the symbol of the piece – even a haphazard representation – is enough. Once each piece is in place, he will pause and look over the terrain. He will think through every beginning sequence he can remember. He will try and match the beginning of a game to the time of day, the weather, or the colour of the sky. Sometimes he'll play something stupid just to see the result.

Consuela pushes a pawn two squares into the centre of the board. Columbus thinks about pawns – the quiet, underestimated foot soldiers – the soul of chess.

He smiles at Consuela, but she can see it is forced. "Selena," he says, "came to say goodbye. She came to Palos, to say goodbye."

~ ~ ~

Selena has never asked anything of Columbus. Not a promise. Not a conversation. Not even a word about when he might be back. Nothing. They communicated with loving gentleness and soft pleasure. She did not need words, or promises, or pronouncements of love or devotion. Their couplings became candlelit rituals. They moved toward holiness. This holiness was all Selena required of him. She took the sporadic love-making as a small gift to herself whenever he happened to visit the estate where she worked. She took the half-dozen or so postcoital conversations as glimpses – not as a summation of a man. Only the moments mattered. The moments were beautiful. Perhaps this is stupid, she thinks. But I just want to speak my love.

The night before Columbus sails, she waits. She arrives at 8 P.M. and waits. She waits at Starbucks, nursing a coffee for as long as it will go, and then ordering another. Part of her wants to run. Columbus intimidates her – his desire, this dream of his, consumes or pushes everything in its path out of the way. But she is also in awe of his drive and his intelligence. With each hour that passes, she faces her flight instinct. And each time, her need to communicate her feelings wins out. She just wants to ask this one thing of Columbus – she wants him to listen to her love. That's all. She does not need a return decla-ration. She only needs him to smile and nod his understand-ing. She tells herself that if this fails, she will have at least tried. She will at least have tried to tell him what she feels.

At 12:10 A.M., she considers the possibility that he didn't get her message. She thinks about the last time Columbus visited the estate outside Córdoba. They walked in the fields behind the barns, each step releasing swirls of heady, thick lavender scent around them. He'd passed her a bottle of wine with a cork pushed in just far enough for easy access. She drank and remembers the sweet hint of apple in the wine, the pervading scent of lavender, the clusters of stars and galaxies swirling in the sky, the small jangling sound of bells from a flock of sheep across the road. They sat for a long time in silence. It seemed something was on his mind and he'd turned inward – he seemed to be dancing with a problem or a decision, and Selena honoured his silence. She would not ask what was wrong, nor would she ask what he was thinking about.

Perhaps she has no right to ask more than a memory of moments.

~ ~ ~

In the morning, Consuela looks in the mirror and notices, for the first time, a series of subtle changes in her posture and in the way she looks. Her skin seems smoother than she remembers and her eyes sharper. She has to adjust the small makeup mirror in her bedroom. It's too low. Either it's been moved or she's sitting taller on the stool. But the mirror can't have been moved because she leans into it every morning without touching it. Something has changed in her.

In the car Consuela realizes she needs to know about Isabella. She has to know what, if anything, happens between Columbus and the queen. But she does not know how to move him in that direction. There are days when she wishes she could be blunt, or even violent. She'd like to shake him – get the remaining stories to fall onto the ground. Then they could stand around and look at the bones of his stories, all haphazard and abstruse on the pebbles. In the clear light of day, they could perhaps make sense of these bones, put them in order, find the end, and more important, find the beginning before the beginning.

At breakfast, Columbus is focused on the contents of his coffee mug and nodding to himself. He seems on the edge of something. Consuela knows better than to make small talk when he's like this. She's got a pile of paperwork. It's the end of the month. So she grabs a mug of coffee and retreats to her office. There is a small gaggle of puzzlers across the room, patiently placing puzzle pieces, rotating, trying again and again to make the picture complete. One patient is standing at the window staring out. Columbus approaches the two-way mirror, drags a chair over, and sits down. This movement in front of her desk catches her attention. He looks directly into the mirror and Consuela feels a prickle at the base of her neck. She inhales. Holds her breath. This was how it began.

Columbus leans forward, elbows on knees, hands clasped.

~ ~ ~

It's dangerous to walk on the docks after sundown, but that is what Isabella feels she must do. She closes her bedroom door – moves quickly and silently through the connected room, out the door, into the hallway, and down the back stairs. Her security team is diluted. Some are with Ferdinand and her most trusted security team is watching Columbus. Only a small detail is sitting outside her door, two men and a woman, having a late dinner. On the street, she wraps her cape tightly around her body, pulls the hood up, and heads for the dock.

Perhaps Columbus will never come back from this venture, and this worry motivated Isabella to travel to Palos. He should know that I care about him and wish him success and a safe return, she thinks. I have to try to let him know how I feel. Perhaps he could take this small love of mine with him. This love is nearly weightless, would fit in a pocket, could be carried in a breath. This love could rest, inaudible, on the surface of the skin until it was needed. How does she give him this small thing without saying it out loud? What can she say that he will understand as: *I love you!*

In the harbour are the three ships. She paces. She walks the dock until she begins to know the intimacies of it – the way it creaks, where it groans. At the far end of her route, she hears somebody coming and ducks out of sight behind a pallet of crates. A woman draws a man down the street away from a bar, toward the harbour. They stop perhaps ten metres from Isabella's hiding spot. The man leans back against the wall, and the woman kneels, moves forward toward his groin. Begins to move in a steady cadence. Isabella watches, fascinated. The man is moaning. This coupling goes on for ten minutes, and then fifteen, then twenty.

"It's no good," the man says finally, pulling away and starting to fasten up his pants. "I've had too much wine."

"This way, then," the woman says. She pulls up her skirts and backs into him – bends forward, hands flat on the wall. They begin to move again. This time the woman's moans are louder than the man's. Isabella wishes they'd just hurry up and finish. She is not disgusted but, rather, irritated. This takes her away from her watch. She's worried she might be at the wrong end of the dock. The woman grunts rhythmically, breathy sounds.

Christ, Isabella thinks. If this goes on much longer I'm going to go down there and help out. They need to be done. For God's sake!

After another ten minutes, the man again pulls away. "It's no good. It's terrific – you . . . you are terrific. But I've had too much wine . . . mush too mush wine. I have to sleep. I'm on the *Santa Marina*, I mean the *Santa Maria*, at dawn. I must sleep, woman."

She moves in close and whispers in his ear. The woman smiles. She hikes up her skirts, leans back with her shoulders touching the wall, hips and pubis thrust out. He kneels in front of her and begins to give her pleasure. The woman does not moan right away. She hums. She bites her lips and hums.

Isabella is stuck. She's embarrassed and doesn't want to see or hear any more. She does not want this public reminder of what she could have had with Columbus, of what she used to have with Ferdinand. She's claustrophobic in her tiny space beside the stacked crates. Regardless of the black, star-riddled sky above her, and the expanse of the harbour beyond, and the verisimilitude of wide-open ocean beyond the harbour, Isabella feels encased. She has no idea what time it is. The queen has no need of a watch. It's got to be getting close to ten o'clock.

I should just walk out into the street, excuse myself, and offer an apology, she thinks. Wish her luck with her orgasm, wish him luck with his voyage, and be on my way. But she's been here too long, watching. They'll think she's twisted. It's too late. She's committed for the whole show.

Then the woman begins to really moan and move. Like she's riding a wave.

"Oh, yes. Yes, yes . . . Ohhh, *estoy por acabar!*" And then there is the sound of water dripping. The man coughs. The woman slides down the wall to the ground and the man moves beside her, slips his arm around her.

Thank God. Isabella almost applauds. The woman helps the man to his feet and they briefly discuss her apartment, which is only a couple of blocks away. Then they trundle up the street. The queen is relieved. She can go back to the Plaza Hotel. If she's late, Columbus will wait. He'll be in the bar just off the lobby having one of his bloody Scottish beverages.

~ ~ ~

The phone is ringing. Consuela is in the bathtub. She doesn't care. This is the third call she's smiled at and then ignored. Of course, it's a cordless phone. She could have brought it with her to the bathroom. Her coffee mug is on the tub's edge and the press is sitting on the toilet seat. The water is steaming. It's mid-afternoon and raining. Sevillians always seemed shocked at the rain – like it's a freak of nature, not part of nature. She sinks into the water so her knees and breasts and nose become islands. She imagines she is Columbus floating naked in the Strait of Gibraltar, with sharks, whales, and jellyfish all around. It would be substantially cooler than this bath. Consuela has no inclination to re-enact Columbus's journey to that degree. She's happy in her hot water. She closes her eyes. Drifts, tries to float. Thinks about being naked and adrift in so much water. She imagines the night sky, the stars, the waves, and the ocean current pushing her toward the Mediterranean. The vulnerability of being naked in so much water is frightening. A shiver strikes up her spine – a shiver in a hot bath. Consuela sits up in the tub. The hollow water sound echoes around the tiled bathroom. "He's out of his fucking mind," she says.

She shakes away the Strait of Gibraltar and takes a sip of her coffee. Outside, a car honks. She can hear the *shhh* sound of tires on wet pavement. She wonders about the sex show Isabella witnessed and has a sudden craving for a cigarette. She is always surprised by these cravings. In order to quell this one she tiptoes out of the tub and makes footprints on the hardwood floor to the kitchen. She opens a bottle of wine, a German Goldtröpfchen, starts to look for a wineglass but quickly decides against it – the bottle is fine. Consuela slips back into the silky water. Her skin has cooled enough that there is pleasure in this re-entry. Consuela takes a mouthful of the wine, gulps it down. Its cold sweetness is a nice change. She places the bottle on the toilet seat beside the coffee press, then leans back.

It's not a bad thing to drink alone. Oh, Faith would disapprove. Rob would smile, pull her aside later, and ask if it's a regular thing or an exception. Her mother would pretend not to hear. Her father would raise his left eyebrow, a gesture Consuela has never been able to comprehend. And Columbus? He would approve wholeheartedly. He might say something stupid like: *In water one sees one's own face, but in wine one beholds the heart of another* or *With wine and hope, anything is possible.* Or he'll start to tell another story, another puzzle piece to the whole picture. Consuela fears the end. She fears that last piece. What if he stays Columbus? What if he goes deeper into himself? What if they lose him completely to this story? At the same time, Consuela does not want him to stop when he is so close to the end. But there is a date stamp on this man now.

She has been trying to be with Columbus as much as possible, and trying to make it appear as if she could care less. She has been lurking, hanging around at the periphery, waiting for the end.

Consuela wishes someone would slip in behind her and attempt to describe her beauty by reading Hafiz ghazals aloud. She drifts in this small fantasy for a while. The phone rings again, and for some reason, Consuela gets out of the tub, drips her way to the kitchen, and picks it up.

"Meet me for a glass of wine," Emile says. "I'd like to listen to you for a while."

"Okay," Consuela says. Christ, she thinks. I've had a snootful of wine already.

~ ~ ~

Two days later, Columbus again pulls a chair in front of the mirror, and trusting that Consuela is there, begins to spin out another piece of the puzzle.

~ ~ ~

After Columbus leaves for his appointments, Juan begins to doubt. He begins to ruminate and fret. The reality of what they're going to do begins to sink in. It's well after three in the morning when he boards the *Niña* and meets with the second-in-command, Niccolò de Strabo, for a drink. Juan produces a bottle of the Uisge Beatha Scottish drink. They sit together on deck in the dim light and share what they know of what they're about to do.

"Columbus, he's a bright man," Strabo says. "He knows things he has not shared with anyone."

"Like what?" Juan lights another beedi.

Strabo smiles like this is an incredibly stupid question. "Well, he has not shared it with anyone."

"So how do you know it exists?"

"Because it must. There must be evidence from beyond the limits of our travels across the Western Sea. He's not suicidal."

"Yes, but is he sane?"

"You think he's crazy?"

"I just asked the question."

"It is, I think, too late for such questions, my friend. You've signed up. We sail west in a few hours."

"To Columbus, then," Juan says, raising his cup.

"To us, my friend." And Strabo touches his cup to Juan's.

They continue to drink. They drink the Scottish beverage neat, and as the light offers long strands of orange and pink in the eastern sky, the bottle is nearly empty. Juan has smoked nearly a whole pack of his beedies. It is not a solid line of smoking but, rather, a dotted line through the night.

Juan is not sure why he joined the crew. Friendship? He doesn't wholly believe. He does not believe in what they're about to try to do, but for some reason, he feels obliged to take Columbus up on his offer. Perhaps it's as simple as having enough faith to do something he doesn't understand.

Juan hesitated over Columbus's offer, and then said yes to himself and got on board. What if this dreamer is right? He's not right, but what if he is? What if? What if they sail right into history by finding the Indies, China, Japan? The implications of being the first to discover such a route are beyond what he can imagine.

~ ~ ~

The garden is a fragrant treat – an olfactory gift. They walk along the stone pathway and cannot help but step on a variety of thyme, and the smell is delightful. It fills Consuela with hope. It feels to her as if she is breathing green sunlight.

"I'm sorry," she says. "Help me understand this. You put Juan on a ship? The guy knows nothing about sailing. Doesn't that seem a bit absurd?"

"Yes. It was a matter of friendship. And Juan is somebody who is not afraid to tell the truth, even if the truth is not what I want to hear."

"You invited a one-handed ex-soldier who likes to paint on a voyage that's going to require sailing expertise." She sits on a stone bench and Columbus sits next to her. He looks smaller today. His hair is pulled back as usual, but his face is narrower, his eyes sunken, his skin sallow. Has this been an evolution she didn't notice because she's too close, or is this sudden? Regardless, Columbus has become diminutive.

"He'll be fine. I trust he'll find a way to contribute." He sighs heavily. "Columbus needed someone who would see things with new eyes and speak the truth."

"By Columbus, you mean you."

"I mean Columbus. Something happens, Consuela. Something happened."

"What happened?"

"It goes bad. First, a woman is found floating in the harbour. The morning before the voyage. She's floating naked and dead. Only her face, torso, and legs are visible above water. People gathered in Palos for the launch looked down and saw this armless woman. The water is black and thick around her. It is as if her arms have been cut off. It was in the papers. They thought she was a prostitute."

"That's what happened?"

"No. It's one thing that happened. Not a good omen, this dead woman floating face up in the harbour. I should know who she is. I can see her face and I know it, but I cannot give her a name. Not a good sign for Columbus."

Consuela takes his hand in hers. She looks at him. He's unshaven, frail, lost. "Do you know who you are?" she says.

"Today, right now?"

"Yes, right now."

"I have no clue."

TWENTY

HE CLAMS UP. HE ASKS for and then demands sleeping pills. Consuela prompts him a couple of times. He deflects, feigns a cold, or a sore throat, or fatigue. He is amused at small things. He finds the sky – cloud formations – fascinating. Sparrows mesmerize. Flowers delight. All these things have become more important than stories.

"I want to give him a bottle of wine," she says. "I want to loosen him up and persuade him to finish."

"We have medications for that, Consuela." Dr. Balderas stands. Looks out the window.

"Check," Consuela says, sliding her bishop into position. "I'd rather not drug him up when he's so close."

Dr. Balderas smiles, sits down, looks at the board. He hadn't seen this coming. It's aggressive and risky, which is a style of play he's not witnessed in his favourite nurse.

"Okay. But it's got to be private. That's an interesting move."

"Columbus taught me. It's a derivation of something called a gambit."

~ ~ ~

On a day when the sky is ripped with grey and cool breezes arrive in blusters from the Atlantic, Consuela tells Columbus she's procured a bota of wine and asks if he'd like a drink.

"Ah, you are seducing me," he says. "This behaviour is not unappealing. It's about time you tried to take advantage of me."

"I am not seducing you," she whispers. "I just want to share a bottle of wine with my . . . friend." She almost said favourite patient but that would be too outlandish for her to handle. Feeding patients booze is forbidden. It's against the rules. Even though she has permission, this goes against everything she knows about being a nurse. "Not here, though. Meet me at the pool."

~ ~ ~

"It's been a while since I had a drink of wine with a beautiful woman," Columbus says. He's sitting on the edge of the pool, presiding over the pool, with his back to the doorway. She has grown to love the way he always knows when she is in the room. No matter how quiet she is or how careful she is about her scent, he knows.

"I saw this coming days ago," he says.

"What did you see?" Jesus, this isn't going to work, she thinks. She starts to panic.

"The weather. Cooler weather. I adjusted the temperature of the water."

Consuela dips her toes into the pool and she finds the water is hot. They decide to move their deck chairs so they can put their feet in the water. Consuela passes the bota to him and he sprays a long stream of wine into his mouth. They pass the bota back and forth. If this first bota doesn't do the trick, there's another just inside the pool-room archway, which she dropped off as she came in.

"So what's going on in that head of yours, Columbus? Do you know who you are today?"

"The ugly dreams are back. I can't seem to dream about anything pleasant." He stops. Takes a couple of barely controlled breaths. "Butterflies would be nice. Puppies. Kittens. Anything but what I find in my sleep . . ."

"Do you want to talk about your dreams?"

"We have talked about them. They're ugly things. Horrifying. And I am here with a beautiful woman, and the wine is good. So no, I don't want to talk about them."

"Thank you, by the way."

He looks at her, perplexed, then nods. "Well, you are a beautiful woman, regardless of what you may believe or think."

They finish the bota and Consuela stands.

"Where are you going?"

"Do you think I would bring just one bottle of wine?"

"Nurse Consuela, you little vixen. I'd offer to get up and help you find that bottle but I'm not entirely certain I can."

"We will taste the Pesquera now. I'm told it is an excellent Spanish wine. One of the best."

"And the first bottle?"

"A bordeaux," she says matter-of-factly.

That's enough to push him back into the story. His eyes become sad and dark, edged with pain. The creases on his forehead deepen. He clears his throat and sighs heavily, then leans back in his chair and begins. "Ah, yes, the Café Bordeaux. This is where things go terribly wrong . . ."

~ ~ ~

Columbus arrives at the Café Bordeaux a few minutes early. There's a lovely warmth to this place. Brownish, reddish, orange colours permeate the room and give it a comfort beyond its plush chairs and thick carpets. Selena wants to say goodbye, he thinks. This is her kind of café. It feels like Selena. It has the feel of privacy regardless of how public it may be.

He passes a table of four monks, hoods up, heads down, focused on the mastication of their food. He and Juan drank at least a bottle of wine each at the previous café, and upon sitting down, Columbus immediately orders another. The waiter is a small ferret of a man with a slender moustache. He is not friendly but his efficiency makes up for this. The wine is presented, uncorked, and poured with little fanfare. Columbus appreciates this man's sharp-edged professionalism. If he hadn't already filled his roster of sailors, he'd have invited this man along.

At the next table, separated from his by a dwarf palm tree, a mother and her two daughters, young girls about ten and twelve years old, are having dinner. The daughters have long dark hair, brushed and shining. They are so well behaved. Their mother, a woman who has a knowing smile, seems pleased, proud to be out with her daughters. Her smile makes Columbus feel she understands her daughters, that she listens with love. Columbus cannot help but overhear their conversation.

They are discussing what they will wear the next day to watch the ships set sail. This pleases him. The younger daughter talks excitedly about starting school in the fall. The older rolls her eyes.

Columbus takes another sip of wine. There's no stopping this now, he thinks. He will sail in the morning. They will discover whatever is there. He thinks of the falling rock – a five-metre-high rock he has been pushing for the past ten years. Finally, he has loosened it to the point where it is going to fall. The rock is in motion, it has momentum, and Columbus can't stop it.

He looks up in shock when she arrives, and he is stunned when she sits across from him, lets her hood fall to her shoulders, smiles. Her eyes have receded into her face, pupils dilated, and her complexion is sallow, pasty. Whatever drug she's on, it has not been kind to her looks.

"My love," Cassandra says inside a breathy whisper.

"Cassandra." Columbus is off-kilter. This is a surprise. "Cassandra?"

"No kiss, Columbus? Have you no kisses for me?"

Columbus leans across the table and kisses her cheek gently. There is a faint scar along her jawline. Her skin feels cool and moist. She seems altered, like life itself has withdrawn slightly from her body.

"Have I become your sister?"

"My sisters are all at home in Genoa."

"Genoa. Well, I did not know that. You have family out of this country. Keeping secrets are we, my love? I thought we had no secrets. I thought we shared everything."

"We shared one evening –"

"And a night and a morning and an early afternoon."

"Yes, of course, a beautiful time, but a short time."

"And now you are leaving me."

"Cassandra, I am leaving everything, everybody. Not just you. I have two sons. And I have a wife."

"You have a wife?"

"Well, it is fairly common knowledge."

"Not to me. You didn't think it important to share that piece of vital information with me?"

Columbus leans back in his chair. "There was not an appropriate time to share my life's history with you." It would not be wise to volunteer any information about Beatriz or Selena, he thinks. Not now. Not ever.

"We could make the time, if only you would not do this thing tomorrow."

"Cassandra, it is set. I sail tomorrow with the tide. There are three ships. And there are many men counting on me. The king and queen are counting on me."

"And what of me? Were you going to leave without saying goodbye?"

Columbus begins to feel very twitchy. He does not like the way this conversation is going. She seems to be calm but there is some sort of violence hidden under the skin. Perhaps her voice is too calm. "Well, I will remember you. I will take you with me wherever I wind up."

"And what about my love?"

"Your love?"

"Yes, I love you, Columbus. I love you like life itself. I have always loved you. I have always been waiting for you. All my life I have waited."

"But I have not seen you for seven years."

"And I have loved you all that time."

"It's been seven years!"

Her voice changes to something frozen and hard. "And during that time how many others have there been? A dozen? Two dozen, my love? A hundred, my love?" Her hands are in white-skinned fists on the table.

"But I must leave tomorrow, and I cannot take you with me. You understand that I have been waiting for this moment for all of my life? Would you deny me this voyage?"

Columbus stands up. He's through with this. This is ridiculous. He was hard pressed to even recall her name and now she is talking of love!

Then the waiter with the slender moustache is standing beside him, whispering in his ear. "You must sit down, Señor Columbus." Columbus looks at the waiter, measures the strained seriousness of his voice, and sits.

Cassandra looks across the table, speechless. Not only is she being shunned; she's being interrupted and ignored.

The waiter pulls up a chair beside Columbus. He has a small, white towel draped over his left shoulder.

"What's going on?" Cassandra says.

The waiter's voice is just loud enough. "If you want to stay alive, you'll shut up and drink your wine."

"What –"

"It's your faith, Columbus. The inquisitors. The university. Your obsession. Your belief that you can do this despite the known facts. The inquisitors are coming for you. They say you are possessed. They say your ideas about the size of the world are heretical. They may be here already."

"Who are you? How do you know –"

"I'm a friend who wants to see you set sail tomorrow."

"Okay," Columbus says. "You've managed to scare me. What do you want me to do?"

"When I leave your table, wait one minute and follow me behind the bar and out into the kitchen. Wait there. We'll get you to your ship." The waiter stands up, smiles, claps Columbus on the shoulder. "I'll bring you another bottle right away, sir," he says.

Cassandra watches the waiter's back as he moves toward the kitchen, and then she faces Columbus. "You've planned this to get away from me," she says. "I'm not going to let you run off. I love you. I shared my body with you, as if we were married!" Columbus is counting to sixty. He's only at thirty when it all changes.

"I have been completely true to you, my love . . . are you listening to me?"

He risks a look over his shoulder. Cassandra's voice slows down – he can't understand what she's saying. The waiter is moving in slow motion. He's behind the bar, but he has not gone into the kitchen. Instead, he flips the towel off his shoulder – in a suspended arc – and drops it on the floor, like he's starting a race or signalling for some event to begin. The towel seems to take forever to hit the floor. The waiter is off, almost running down the passageway toward the front of the restaurant. *Is that right?* Columbus is thinking. *Should I still go into the kitchen? What's going on?*

Two strands of fear pound through his body. He can't breathe. He fears the Inquisition – he has been pushing the edges of tolerance with his desire to redefine the map of the known world, and he has been vocal about his doubts in God, his growing disdain for the religion behind which the Inquisition hides. He also fears the waiter may have been lying. What if there's something else going on? What if? What's in the kitchen? Then the waiter, moving toward the front of the restaurant, turns toward Columbus's table – it's such a fleeting glance. In that micro-fraction of a second their eyes meet, and Columbus knows something is about to happen. One of the girls at the next table is eating ice cream – smiling, laughing. The waiter is going in the wrong direction, hell-bent on getting out of the room. Columbus pushes his chair back. It scrapes the tile floor – groans, tips over with a bang. He has to see who's in the kitchen. He has to see. He has to know. His legs are leaden. He can't move fast enough. He glances back. Cassandra is standing, her mouth open. The mother of the two girls is half standing, watching him. The waiter is almost at the front door. Columbus pushes through the kitchen door. It's empty. An acrid burning smell. Dull, stainless-steel appliances. Chopping blocks. Racks of knives. A cardboard box on the counter against the wall. Stacks of plates. A pot of something boiling on the stove. A broken plate in the middle of the floor. A frying pan on a gas burner with its contents burned – the smoke beginning to fill the top of the room. The kitchen is vacant. Nobody is there. "Shit." He turns around. Stands still for a second. There isn't a waiter in sight. *Come on,* Columbus tells himself. *Move!* Everything in him is screaming to get out of this restaurant, but he runs toward the table with the girls instead. He looks toward the front of the room. The waiter is near the door, pushing his way through four men putting on coats. He has to get to the girls and their mother. He's got to get in between the kitchen and their table. He's acting on instinct and adrenaline and fear doubled. Cassandra is nowhere in sight. The mother looks surprised to see him running directly toward her. She's gathered her girls in close, an arm around each daughter. She's leaning toward the door, like she's going to get out of the way of this madman. No, he thinks. Not them. Not these girls – not this woman. No! Columbus dives at them, pulls them to the floor, and the explosion pushes the bar, the wall, and most of the kitchen into the dining room. The air around him seems to be moving in both directions. Something jars his back, his spine. He feels the impact – a sharp pain and then nothing. A table smashes into his head as it flips across the room and through the window. The sound of breaking glass. Dishes smashing. Screaming. The café empties quickly, chaotically.

Gabriel is one of two agents whose assignment was to follow Columbus and keep him safe. He was on the street when the window blew out – a shower of shattered glass sprays across the road. Car alarms honking up and down the street. He's frozen for a split second as he figures it out. Then he's moving against the flow of people – moving through, toward Columbus. At the same time, he's screaming into a tiny microphone in his sleeve: "It's a bomb. He's down," he says. "Code red, goddamnit. The subject is down. We need backup." Gabriel moves past the mother and daughters. *They were behind Columbus,* he thinks. *Maybe Columbus is all right, too.* The woman who was at Columbus's table comes out of the washroom, looks around, and heads for the door. She slips and falls near the doorway, gets up, and disappears into the street.

Columbus opens his eyes. He can't see anything except the ceiling. He can't move his body. He can't move his arms or legs. He can't see the girls or their mother. He can't lift his hand to shield his face from the overhead sprinklers. He blinks the water away the best he can.

A sort of odd silence folds itself around the remaining disorder. Somewhere in the background he hears horns honking. Columbus's breathing is fast and threadbare. He notices this – wonders why he's breathing so quickly. *Are they okay?* he thinks. *Are the girls okay? The mother?* They're not in his peripheral view.

He smiles. Relaxes into his view of the ceiling and even the steady sprinkle of water on his face. There are rough wooden beams. He begins to count the beams in the room. He suddenly craves a cigar. Does he have any cigars? Is there a cigar in his pocket? Yes, a cigar would be nice right now. The queen will be most disappointed. I have made promises I will not be able to fulfill. Promises, promises, promises . . . and there will be no journey across the sea. All that fuss for nothing. Nothing! But I'm breathing. I'm breathing. There. That was a breath. That's good. As long as I am breathing . . . I . . .

Perhaps I'm not going to ruin everything. It's going to be all right, Beatriz. I'm not going to see what's out there. Not for me to do. Somebody else's problem. Blood. Blood. There won't be any blood now. It's all changed. All changed. No more blood.

But still, I'm breathing. There. There's another breath.

Gabriel holsters his gun. He's not sure why he drew his weapon. He leans over Columbus. Columbus sees that this is one of the queen's guards; they were all issued Walther PPKs.

"Don't move," Gabriel says.

"That won't be a problem," he whispers.

"What?" Gabriel leans closer.

"The girls, the mother – okay?"

"They're fine. They got away."

"Tell Beatriz. I'm sorry."

"Beatriz?"

"I'm breathing. I am . . . tell Beatriz . . ."

Gabriel pulls a tablecloth from a sideways table and makes a couple of sloppy folds, slides it gently under Columbus's head. "Hold on," he says. "Help is coming. You're going to be all right." He does not believe this man is going to be all right. He hopes this is not noticeable in his voice. He looks down at his hands – they're covered in blood. Under Columbus's head, the red expands into the white tablecloth.

Gabriel looks down at Columbus. Is he breathing? He seems to be smiling.

"Tell Beatriz I'm sorry . . ." Columbus thinks he says it. He's not sure. Doesn't matter.

Columbus tries again to smile. Thinks, *Isn't that odd?* Exhales.

TWENTY-ONE

SHE'S PACING BACK AND FORTH in front of his desk. It is the morning of the day of the feast of Our Lady of Lourdes. Dr. Balderas sits and watches while Consuela paces across his vision and rants. Her movements are frenetic, inconsistent, and at times spastic. She's been with this patient since he arrived. This morning, he's taken the storyline in a direction none of them had considered.

"He has no idea who he is! And he killed himself. He killed Columbus off in his story. Columbus doesn't survive. He dies. We have to put a suicide watch on him now, tonight, tomorrow – for a month. I don't care how long, but now . . ." Consuela wants a cigarette. She considers pushing the doctor aside and rifling through his desk drawers to find one.

"Done," Dr. Balderas says.

"You don't understand. He's dead. In his story, he died."

"I said you could have your suicide watch. I'll arrange it myself."

"Good. That's good. Thank you."

"What else did he tell you? Is there more?"

"There is no more. He's dead. The story's done. And I have to tell you, I did not see this coming. I thought he was going to get on his fucking ships and sail out of the damned harbour . . .

The end, and now it's time to be sane! Flick the goddamned sanity switch! It's time!"

Dr. Balderas quickly glances at his chessboard. He'd dearly love to play a game. Clear away the fluff. Refocus. But he knows Nurse Consuela would not respond favourably to an offer of a game right now.

Consuela knows she needs to calm down. She'd love a game of chess – to be lost inside that world of thinking ahead, speculating about what your opponent is thinking, and so on, and so on. But she knows Dr. Balderas would probably think she had lost her mind if she offered a game, so she is silent.

~ ~ ~

"It's just a matter of time now," Dr. Balderas says. "Columbus doesn't exist anymore. He's given himself nowhere to go."

"That's what worries me," Consuela says.

"That's why we've got a watch on him."

Dr. Balderas, Emile, and Consuela are in the small board-room connected to Dr. Balderas's office. From the window, they can see Columbus, sitting by himself in the far corner of the upper patio. Emile is leaning on the edge of the table.

"Have I missed something?" Emile says.

"His last story. Columbus dies in his last story. It's there in the report you're holding." Consuela turns away from the courtyard. "He's telling these stories about himself. So he basically killed himself off. There is no more Columbus. So who is he now? That's the question."

"What's the next step?" Emile leans forward.

"If we assume Columbus is Julian Nusret, we know a lot about him. We've got a good selection of buttons we can push. It's just a matter of pushing the right one."

"Buttons?"

"A daughter's name. His wife's name. A city. A gentle reminder of his life. Some snippet of information that will get him to move out of the fifteenth century."

Both Emile and Dr. Balderas turn and look at Consuela. Emile looks worried, concerned. The doctor, intense. She gets up and pushes her way through the door into the hallway. Around the corner, Consuela stops and leans against the wall, closes her eyes, and breathes.

~ ~ ~

Consuela is out for dinner with Faith and Rob. Emile finds them at Becerrita, one of Consuela's favourite restaurants. She loves the roast lamb, the pork in crab sauce. But her absolute favourite is the specialty: oxtail croquettes and baked white prawns from Isla Cristina. Consuela picks Becerrita because she knows Rob appreciates the wine cellar, which is outstanding, and there's actually a cigar menu. Rob smokes the occasional cigar. Faith disapproves.

Consuela drank almost an entire bottle of Cava before hopping in a taxi for the restaurant. This conspicuous consumption is a purposed buffer against her sister's good intentions. She's surprised when their dinner isn't a set-up. Faith and Rob arrive without a mystery date for Consuela. There is no tagalong friend. Instead, they have news. Faith is going to have another baby. Consuela is going to be an auntie, again. Faith's tone is subdued and delicate. She tiptoes toward the word *baby* – pads the word with cotton batting. Consuela takes her hesitation as an underscoring of the fact that Consuela has no man in her life, no immediate prospect of family. It's as if she has to be delicate about it because it might upset Consuela, the sister who is so far from having a baby of her own.

"Faith," she says, "that is the best news I've heard in months. Congratulations, you two." She glances toward the entrance and sees a face she knows – and he's coming her way. Consuela was about to stand and offer a toast to baby number three. Instead, she stands up to greet him. "Mr. Germain. Emile. What a nice surprise. This is my sister, Faith, and her husband, Rob."

"I'm so sorry to intrude. Dr. Balderas said I might find you here. Well, he suggested a few places. I left a message at the institute but I thought . . . well, I have some paperwork I need you to look at with regard to Mr. Columbus."

"Con? I thought you dropped the Columbus patient."

"Not now, Faith." Consuela sits down and picks up her wineglass, takes a big gulp.

"There's a spot at our table, Emile, is it? You're welcome to join us." Rob stands up, motions with his hand.

"I don't want to intrude."

"It's no trouble, no intrusion," Faith says. "We'd love it if you joined us."

Consuela looks at Faith, rolls her eyes, then looks up at Emile's face. "Sit," she says.

~ ~ ~

After their meal, Faith and Rob say their goodbyes. Faith gets one last embarrassing stab at the spinster Consuela by mentioning what a wonderful auntie Consuela is, and what a great mother she'll make someday.

"Oh God, that's embarrassing," Consuela says after they've disappeared into the throng of pedestrians walking past the restaurant. "I'm sorry."

"She means well. I can see she means well."

"Yes, what's that saying about the road to hell being paved with good intentions?"

Eventually they move to the bar section at the back of the restaurant, where they order another bottle of wine. They start to go over everything they know about Columbus and Julian Nusret. They share information back and forth over good thick wine. They talk about the fact he was found swimming in the Strait of Gibraltar. Consuela does a distilled retelling of the adventures of Columbus. She talks about his escape and his swim across the strait. Emile tells her everything he can remember about Julian Nusret.

"He was a professor who specialized in fourteenth- and fifteenth-century European history. Last spring, while on vacation in Spain with his family – he had a wife and two daughters – they wound up at the wrong place, at the wrong time. Madrid train station on the morning of the bombings. For some reason, he was separated from his family on a train platform the morning of March 11. His wife and two daughters were killed. There were reports of people seeing this Julian Nusret after the explosions but he disappeared . . . vanished."

He tells her about the eyewitnesses, about the chaos, the screaming and blood everywhere. Witnesses say they remember the strangest things. A bird singing. An airplane. The temperature of the pavement. The curve of a twisted bit of train track. A hovering silence. Then the sirens started. "One of my witnesses said the missing man was crying. One woman only noticed somebody holding a leather bag, looking through the rubble. Apparently he stopped to help several people get out of the wreckage."

Emile reaches across the table, gently slides his fingers inside hers. "My guys say just a few more days for the DNA results, but I'm convinced."

Consuela feels like she's going to cry and she doesn't want to do that. She's so tired.

~ ~ ~

Consuela joins Columbus on the upper dining-room patio where he is taking his coffee. She does not know how Columbus has managed to get Frederica to make him espresso every day. She's almost afraid to ask. It's mid-morning. He's got one of the sturdy wooden chairs from the dining room leaned back against the stucco wall. Thick clouds obscure the sun and extend to the horizon. The air is humid and sweet.

"I want to tell you a story," she says. "Now that you have delivered the ships to Columbus and he's out of the picture, I thought it might be a good time for me to tell you a story."

"How fortuitous," he says, smiling. "It seems I've temporarily run out, and here you are. Thank you."

"Oh, don't thank me yet. You might not like this one."

"I love all stories. Don't worry about me."

"Okay," she says slowly. "This story is about this professor. He worked in Canada, at McGill University, in Montreal. His wife and two daughters were killed –"

"I don't want to hear this story."

"Not all stories are happy," she says. "Not all stories can be happy."

Columbus stands up. His chair folds onto the ground with a bang. The espresso demitasse shatters. "Stories can be whatever you want them to be," he says.

Consuela fights the impulse to reach out and touch his hand. "Life is not a story, Columbus."

"Of course life is a story. Life is only a story."

"Sometimes bad things happen in our lives, and eventually we have to face them. We can't hide . . . not forever."

"This is not a good story," he says. "I don't like this. I can't . . ."

Columbus is rocking back and forth, stalled between sitting again and leaving. His back is to her – his gaze is across the courtyard, toward a gathering of orange trees. Consuela pulls the folding chair off the ground, sets it back up, sits back down in her chair, and waits. He keeps rocking.

"I want to go," he says, finally. He doesn't move.

"Go then," she says. "But can I say something before you go?"

Another long pause and then in a whisper: "Okay, but not that story."

"It's just . . . you were someone before you came here . . . I think you know this."

"I'm not that guy. That's not me."

"Look, if you ever want to tell me your story, I can listen with an open heart. Telling someone what happened is important. It's the same as you letting me know the story of how Columbus got his ships."

He starts to mutter. She can barely hear him. "There's no rule. There is no rule. There is no rule. There is no rule."

"No rule?"

"Grieving. No rules about grieving. No rules about how to be sad."

"I'm here when . . . if you're ready. You know I can listen, and –"

"I'm not that guy. I have to go." He starts off across the courtyard – small, quick steps. "That's not me."

TWENTY-TWO

FIVE DAYS LATER, CONSUELA gets a call from Emile, excited and babbling like an idiot. It's three in the morning. Consuela had just drifted off, after a night with the girls at a flamenco bar. She definitely had too much sangria, talked too much, had a puff of someone's cigarette, drank some more, and got up and danced. She doesn't dance. She most certainly does not dance flamenco. She did tonight.

She almost does not recognize his voice. He's shouting above loud music, calling from the bathroom of a bar – telling her to *Wake up. Wake up for Christ's sake.*

"Have you been drinking? Do you realize what time it is?"

"Those are excellent questions, Consuela. The answers are *yes*, and *it doesn't matter.* I talked to his brother. He called from Quebec City two days ago."

"Who? Whose brother?"

"Julian's – your Columbus – his brother. We talked for an hour. He told me Julian and his wife honeymooned in Tangier." The music gets louder for a few seconds, like someone just opened a door and then let it shut.

"Tangier, so?" Consuela is not following. Why is Emile so excited?

"Julian went on his honeymoon in Tangier. In Morocco. Across the Strait of Gibraltar. It's the piece of the puzzle I didn't have an answer for. I didn't understand how the Strait of Gibraltar fit until now."

"Okay, I'm wide awake."

"Look, I'll be back in Sevilla tomorrow night. I'll call you when I get in." He hangs up. Consuela sits and looks at the receiver in her hand until it beeps. She hangs it up and then sits in her bed until she has to pee. Sleep does not come easy. It is finally purchased with two glasses of warm milk and a shot of brandy. She does not work the next day, sleeps until 9 A.M., and goes to the gym. She calls Dr. Balderas, tells him what Emile told her. She meets Emile in the bar at Enrique Becerra. He kisses her gently on each cheek – then pulls back a bit, looks at her with pure joy. "I missed you, Consuela," he says.

Dr. Balderas weaves his way through the restaurant toward their table.

"He was trying to connect with his wife," Dr. Balderas says. Before he sits down, the owner, a man Consuela could easily imagine as Salvos from Columbus's story, comes over immediately and shakes the doctor's hand.

"Wine?" he says. "I have an extraordinary pinot I know you'd love. The blackberry flavours practically jump out and slap you in the face."

"That sounds fine, Ernesto."

Dr. Balderas sits down across from Consuela and Emile, who look amused and surprised. "I'm a regular," he says. "We play chess."

"What do you mean he was trying to connect with his wife?" Consuela says.

"Swimming the Strait of Gibraltar was a subconscious desire

to join his wife, the memory of his wife in Tangier. Something in Columbus was trying to connect with his wife."

They sit silently as the waiter appears at their table, opens the wine with a certain efficacy, and pours with elegance. Dr. Balderas tastes the wine – lets a sliver roll around his mouth, waits, then looks up at the waiter and gives an almost imperceptible nod.

"So," Consuela says. "What do we do now?"

~ ~ ~

The day is a gift. The morning air is fragrant with the heavenly scent of orange trees. But it's also humid and hot. The sky is already a striking, flawless blue. There is no wind. Not even a faint breeze. It's as if the day is holding its breath along with Consuela. She and Columbus are in the lower courtyard, moving toward the swimming pool. He is in front of her, in his robe, a towel draped around his neck. She stops walking, stands still, and watches as he moves away from her. Her heart is racing.

"Julian," she says.

Columbus stops. He does not turn around. His legs wobble; they buckle. He goes down hard, and then he is kneeling on the cement.

Consuela moves in front of him, crouches, then sits cross-legged on the ground.

His hands cover his face. "My daughters' names are Chloe and Jane. Jane is thirteen. Chloe is eleven. My wife, was lovely. I found them . . . I was chasing someone . . . and then I found them. I thought it was thunder. But the sky was blue. It was so blue. They were so beautiful."

He's having a hard time with his breathing. Can't seem to get a full breath.

"Chloe and her mother were together, peaceful, embraced. Jane was alone. I couldn't find her arms. I don't want this . . . I don't want to feel this. My little girl's arms were gone."

Consuela stops breathing. Not breathing is the only appropriate response she can muster. This catches her by surprise. She doesn't want this, either. She wants to be alone in her bed curled into a ball, headphones on, and drunk beyond compare. She does not want this picture. It's a picture that will never go away. She takes a breath.

"I know," she says. Consuela leans forward to embrace him and he collapses into her.

Julian arrives back at the station, winded and confused. Three thunderous bangs and a clear blue sky. There's so much smoke. People screaming. He's going down a flight of stairs toward the smoke – fighting against desperate people moving in the opposite direction. He's going the wrong way. *Bombs,* someone says. *Bombas.* He pushes through people. At the same time, he's looking at faces. What were they wearing? What were his girls wearing? He just needs a glimpse of a face or a garment. He begins to see bodies through the smoke, some still alive, some not moving. They won't be here, he tells himself. They're already out in the street looking for him. They won't be here. They're not here. A silence enfolds the scene.

Consuela is not sure she wants to hear any more. He's telling his own story now – a hesitant revelation in a hoarse whisper. There is no fifteenth-century façade. And just like that, she thinks, Columbus vanishes.

Julian helps a slender young woman with a head wound to the stairs – starts her on her way up and out. He keeps looking, but they're not here. Chunks of train everywhere. He pushes over a seat. Gets tripped up on some wire that grabs his pant leg and won't let go. He picks up somebody's running shoe – the laces are singed. Does he remember what Jane was wearing? Chloe? Jane, a grey hoodie. Chloe, a blue shirt with the name of some hip-hop guy on it. Rashmi . . . Rashmi is wearing. What the hell is Rashmi wearing? Doesn't matter – they're up on the street looking for him. He carries the shoe for a while. Somewhere among the wreckage and the bodies and the smoke, he drops Rashmi's bag, her poems. This bag has become irrelevant. It no longer matters. He has to find them. He does not remember hearing anything. At some point there were sirens but not for a long time. He stops, jumps to the tracks to help an elderly Japanese man to his feet. The man is holding his left forearm with his right hand. Lots of blood. He pushes the old man up onto the platform. The smoke is making him dizzy. He craves a breath of clear air. He's moving in slow motion through wreckage. Why did this happen? Who would do this? He's hazy, staggering. He trips over a dead dog, a German shepherd. He turns around and finds a single black pump and knows. This is one of Rashmi's pumps.

"They were so beautiful," he says to Consuela.

~ ~ ~

He does not retreat from reality but an overriding grief wraps itself tightly around Julian. His voice flattens. He becomes methodical and pragmatic. Some things need doing, others do not. Bits of the past year drift in and out of his consciousness. He remembers swimming. He remembers the strait. He remembers a small child named Aabida. And there was a story, a tale, an adventure. He remembers being Columbus as if Columbus were a beautiful dream. But none of this matters anymore. He's going home. Maybe there is a life there, in Montreal. There is a house. He remembers a house. There are the pieces of a life. There is a city he loves. He's going home.

The gears go into motion. A woman from the Canadian embassy arrives the next day and interviews Julian. She is efficient, well briefed, and extremely compassionate. Three days. He'll be on an airplane in three days. She's taken care of a replacement passport but a passport is hardly necessary. They're sending an airplane. This woman will be on the plane with him. She'll take him home. Julian declines an offer of putting him up in a hotel. He'll stay at the institute for three more days.

~ ~ ~

Dr. Balderas smiles into his office and barely recognizes his patient. Julian's hair is combed. He's fully dressed. Even his posture is more upright – he seems pulled up and taller. He seems more intense, more present, and very sad.

The cloudy light steals through the venetian blinds to give the room an even flush. It's a kind light. Not gloomy. Doves, Julian thinks. This sky is the colour of doves. There were doves on campus, outside his office window, in Montreal. Turtledoves or mourning doves – doves of some kind anyway. A combination of greys, with tinges of brown. That colour is this day. This day is grey and delicate and hollow.

"I have to ask," Dr. Balderas says.

"Julian. My name is Julian Mehmet Nusret, Doctor. I was named after a famous Turkish writer, who was an advocate for free speech, particularly the right to criticize fundamentalist Islam. I understand Al Qaeda has claimed responsibility for the bombings."

"Still to be determined, but yes."

"Irony."

"I am truly sorry for your losses, Julian." The doctor stops, picks up a small sculpture of a horse, examines it, measures its weight in his hand, then places it carefully back where it belongs. "Where is home, by the way?"

"You know very well where my home is, Doctor. Montreal. Do you want me to recite my address and postal code, too?"

Dr. Balderas smiles. "I've never been to Canada. I hear it's beautiful."

"Listen, I want to thank you for not giving up on me. I . . ." He shakes his head. "I'm at a loss."

"It's all right. I wouldn't know where to begin, either."

"I hope I wasn't too much trouble."

"It was an interesting journey, Julian."

They sit in silence. A squeaky metal cart moves by in the corridor outside the closed door. Julian can smell coffee. He turns toward the smell.

"Do you want a cup of coffee? I just made a press."

"I would. Black. Thank you. What is it the Turks say about coffee? That it should be black as hell, strong as death, and sweet as love? I'll forgo the sweetness today."

The doctor gets up and retreats to the small sitting area behind his desk. He comes back with two steaming mugs.

"I take mine black, too," he says.

Julian inhales the scent of the coffee like he's been away from it for years. He takes a sip. Closes his eyes. He places the mug carefully on a stone coaster on the side table. "What happens now?" he says. "My daughters, my wife, gone, and I should have been there, with them, to protect –"

"You would be dead, too."

"What kind of God would . . . I should have been there to protect them, to protect my girls."

"Not about God. It's not your fault. It was heartbreaking and awful, but it's not your fault you're alive."

Julian takes a sip of coffee and notices Dr. Balderas noticing his hand is shaking. He's angry and confused, outraged, and resigned. He doesn't know what to feel first. But somebody did this on purpose. Because of religion, or politics, fear, or oil, or any variation of fundamentalism. All the meaningless, stupid reasons.

"What happens now?" Julian whispers.

Dr. Balderas looks at his patient – tries to comprehend the pain he's had, is having, will have. "What happens now," he says, "is you face your pain and move on. You live through it. It's not something you have to do alone. I know a very fine therapist in Montreal."

~ ~ ~

Emile sticks out his hand and Julian takes it. Emile can see an open bag on the bed behind Julian.

"The embassy wanted to buy a whole new set of luggage. Our luggage in Madrid, after a while, was shipped back to Canada. But I have nothing to put into a set of luggage."

"I am sorry for your loss, Professor Nusret."

"I . . . I don't know who you are. I'm sorry. Are you from the embassy?"

"I'm Emile. Emile Germain. I'm with Interpol. I've been following you across southern Spain. I'm sorry it took me so long."

"Oh, so you're the Emile that Consuela talks about. She's told me a little about you. You've made an impression on her. Something about dedication and doggedness, and listening. You're a good listener." Consuela could do worse than this man, he thinks.

"Look, I know you're getting ready to go home, to go back to Canada. I wanted to meet you. I wanted to let you know that I've been lost. I've been at the bottom of sadness. And . . . and it's possible to find your way back."

"Something happened to you," Julian whispers. It's more a statement than a question.

"I got shot. And a girl was killed. They say it wasn't my fault." Emile stops. He can't seem to catch his breath, but he pushes through. "After, I couldn't find my way. I lost meaning, misplaced the purpose to any of this." He raises his hands, palms up, half pointing to anything and everything. He looks around the room, at Julian, past the window, into the oak tree, across the wall, and back to Julian.

Emile pulls his reading glasses out of his shirt pocket and loops the stems around his ears, pushes the bridge up on his nose. He does not know why he put his glasses on. He's not going to read anything. Christ, he thinks. This man lost his wife and daughters, his whole family. My problems are bits of fluff. "Nothing I say right now will be of any comfort. I know this. But I hope at the right time, you'll remember me – that I'm all right. I made it through."

Julian sits on the edge of his bed, looks out the window, lets silence move into the space between them.

Before the shooting Emile would have been uncomfortable with this sort of damaged lull. But not now.

Julian looks over at Emile. "Thank you," he says.

"God, I hope I didn't just sound like some sort of affirmative, positive-thinking, self-help asshole. I only wanted to let you know the pain doesn't have to be permanent."

"That's what I heard," Julian says, nodding. More silence interjects itself.

After a couple of minutes, Emile clears his throat. "Look, I have to go but I wanted to –"

"Thank you for not giving up on me," Julian says. "Without your determination I might still be five hundred years ago . . . It's better to know, to be now. To be *now* . . ." Julian drifts out of the room and into a replay of what he knows about his now.

Emile fades into the background. He does not hear Emile say, *Take care, my friend.* Nor does he notice Emile as he places the brown envelope containing Rashmi's notebook into the bag on the bed.

~ ~ ~

Consuela meets him in the dining room, where Julian sits staring at the lemon grove across the courtyard. Behind the lemon trees there are palm trees – green splashes in the sky like fireworks. He is sitting in his chair, the one in which he's spent many days and weeks – months, in fact. Now he seems lost in this chair. "Come with me," she says. "Let's get you out of here." She takes his hand.

Julian follows her down through the mezzanine, through the front garden area, and past the parking lot. He looks around like a newborn baby – as if everything he's seeing is new and fascinating. She nods to the guards and they walk together through the main gate. Julian stands at the edge of the street. The air is silky, the light diluted and kind. Across the narrow cobbled street is a small sidewalk café. There is a woman sitting, reading a newspaper, and taking her coffee. The balconies above the café all have cast-iron balustrades, most have plants. At the end of the street there is a pale-coloured building that looks like it may be a cathedral. A man on a moped putters by. A red Volvo is parked down the block.

"I'm still in Spain," he says, half surprised, but adds: "Of course, I'm in Spain." He takes a big breath.

"I'd love to buy you a drink," Consuela says. This idea, blurted out, makes her blush.

"That would give me much pleasure. But I insist that I pay. Dr. Balderas was kind enough to loan me his credit card. He expects me to use it. I don't want to disappoint him."

They walk across the street to the café and sit at one of the sidewalk tables. A waitress places menus on the table, announces she'll be right back to get their order. There are four blue cornflowers in a narrow vase in the middle of the table. A white tablecloth. The music is a single cello playing inside its own echo. There is no direct sunlight.

When Julian looks at her, Consuela knows. She sees the truth of him. This man is not Columbus. Each wrinkle and stray hair speaks of a different man. There's an efficacy in his movements that was not there three days ago. There is no omnipresent hope, no abstruse pigheadedness, and no hysterical obsession with sailing away. There is no passion for acquiring ships. And yet, he will fly away tomorrow to the continent Columbus never stepped upon but is credited with discovering. She gets it. She knows he has to grieve. He has to be alone. He needs time to gather what remains of his life into the present tense. Part of Consuela is screaming that she should cling to this man no matter what – that she ought to hold on to him for dear life. But not now. They cannot converse at length, not in the present. They met more than five hundred years ago, when Columbus was desperate and obsessed – when he would do almost anything to get his caravels and go to sea. When the Inquisition was running around poking its narrow bone of a finger at all that was different. When a powerful queen single-handedly ran the country. They met inside the Columbus story – factual or not. That's where Consuela is and, for now, that is where she must stay.

It was Columbus she fell in love with. She has no idea who Julian is, except a missing, presumed-dead Canadian professor who had a wife and daughters. Surely Columbus was a meshing of Julian and everything he knew or thought or understood about Columbus. But Columbus is not looking back at her.

"I –" He stops, looks away, then comes back to her face.

To Consuela, he looks torn in two, like a man with one foot in the present and one hesitant foot in the past. He's off balance, dizzy, muddled by reality. It's an appropriate disposition for a man who spent most of the last year insisting he was Columbus – a man with one foot in the Middle Ages and one foot firmly in the Renaissance.

"I know," she says. "It's all right."

He half smiles, an awkward, painful gesture, then finds almost firm ground. He shakes his head and looks down at the flowers on the table, then back up at Consuela. "No, you don't know, Consuela. The feelings . . . Columbus's feelings. They're *my* feelings. He's still here, in my heart."

Consuela can't remember the last time she cried. There's no stopping these tears and she doesn't care. She can barely breathe. "Mine, too," she says.

He takes a deep breath. It seems he's alone at the Cape Race lighthouse on the southeastern shore of Newfoundland. Alone with the dusk. Alone with the rain. Alone with the shushing sound of the ocean. In between the waves, he thinks he can hear his own heart beating.

~ ~ ~

Julian arrived in St. John's, Newfoundland, yesterday morning. By noon, he'd stowed his gear on board the tall ship the *Dolly Varden*, he'd met the captain, a few of his fellow crewmen, signed some papers, and now had a couple of days before the ship embarked.

He had persevered for two months in the house in Montreal. He'd tried. But he couldn't go into his daughters' rooms. He could not sleep in his own bed – instead, he slept on the couch in the den. He was eating every two days. He was drinking before noon every single day out of a green coffee mug. He hurt his back moving all three cases of the chardonnay, a gift from a co-worker, from the basement to the bottom half of the fridge. Julian added painkillers, for his back, to the mix. He ignored the telephone with a passion and was abruptly hostile when friends attempted to visit. There was no movement. No healing. He felt like a ghost, an apparition who imbibed – never quite drunk but never truly sober, never truly there. Julian felt like he was starting to disappear – soundless, swallowed. There was no evidence of a life. There was only scant evidence of consumption.

One night, at around 2:30 A.M., while he played Scrabble against the computer the word *thole* came up. He ignored it, trusted the computer, but then no, he opened his dictionary: *thole* 1: v. tr. to undergo or suffer (pain, grief, etc.). Oh, that's just perfect, he thought. He wouldn't know where to begin to use it in a sentence. But he tholed. He was tholing the weight of loss. At 6 A.M., surfing around the Net after losing eleven games to the computer, Julian stumbled across a reference to a tall ship sailing out of St. John's. On a whim, he'd picked up the telephone and let them know he was interested. They'd asked questions for thirty minutes. The next morning, Julian opened an e-mail telling him he'd been signed on as part of the crew.

In his last night in the Montreal house, he'd dreamt the girls were making him pinkie swear his love – "Pinkie swear that you love us" they giggled, holding their pinkie fingers in the air. "Do I have to?" he said, playing with them, teasing them. He turned away for a second, and when he turned back, they were gone. They'd vanished. There was nobody there to hear and he so ached to say he pinkie swears his love. He woke up empty and silent, in a cold sweat. He crawled into the shower without turning on the bathroom light, and cried until the water ran cold.

Twenty minutes before his taxi arrived to take him to the airport, Julian placed Rashmi's journal on the bed, their bed, and closed the door. He had not opened the book. He did not know how it got into his bag. He opened the doors to each of the girls' bedrooms – stood silently for a few minutes in each entranceway.

A friend from the university was coming the next week to pack up these rooms and put the house up for rent.

~ ~ ~

The road to the Cape Race lighthouse goes bad fairly quickly. It crosses twenty kilometres of barren land, virtually treeless and gloriously inhospitable. It feels windswept. It is desperately beautiful. Puddles dot the road like shallow bowls filled with silver.

At the lighthouse, he parks the car, pulls a sweater out of his bag in the trunk, and walks toward the ocean. He doesn't bother locking the car. He bypasses the lighthouse and moves toward the shoreline where huge slabs of scarred rock drop into the water – a grey, sharp-angled descent. It's not raining now but it must have been earlier – the ground is wet, the grass is wet.

Out to sea, clouds obscure the horizon into an estimation of where it might be. The sky is a grey-white sheet, unremarkable and dull, pathetically hung out to dry. There are no sandy beaches here. There is nothing soft about this meeting of land and water. These rocks razor into the ocean and the water looks frigid.

~ ~ ~

Julian lets down his walls. He finds a patch of grass, sits down, and lets his walls dissolve. It feels okay to be unguarded here. It does not take long for Rashmi to come and sit beside him on the grass. He keeps his eyes on the ocean, thinks he can smell vanilla.

He slips back in time twenty years. He had never expected to travel all the way to Pamplona. He was in Paris, on vacation before going back to university, and found himself with an extra week. He'd had to phone his parents to get them to deposit some money on his credit card – told them it was a good opportunity to practise his Spanish. Really, he wanted to go to the bullfights in Pamplona. He wasn't into the running-with-the-bulls macho thing – it was the bullfights that appealed to him.

He's in a bar near the Plaza de Toros, on his third bottle of beer, when she comes in. She stumbles in the doorway, and as she falls, hits her face on the edge of his table. This memory has always been slowed down. It takes an eternity for her to fall. Her expression is not so much shocked as bemused and surprised that she is, in fact, falling. She manages to get one arm out but only enough to partially break her fall. Her head glances off the edge of the table. Julian can't move. It's as if he is in some sort of nightmare in which he can't move his legs or his arms. Normal time comes back only after she hits the floor with a thump.

Julian helps her up. He offers his hand, and she takes it. Her eyes are sparkling, azure, and kind. They're the kindest eyes he's ever seen. There is a deep cut underneath her left eye. Blood drips onto her dress, the droplets disappearing into the black fabric. He gets a cloth from the bartender, folds it neatly, and puts it on her face – tells her to hold it there, put pressure on it.

He picks up her shoe and a book. He hadn't noticed she was carrying a book.

"I'm afraid the heel of your shoe is broken," he says. "Your book is fine, though. I'm Julian."

"I'm embarrassed," Rashmi says. "Embarrassed and clumsy. I'm pleased to meet you." She pulls the cloth away. The blood seems to have slowed but she places it back over her wound anyway. Then she smiles at Julian for the first time. Even as a young woman, lines formed at the edge of her mouth when she smiled – more pronounced on the left than the right. It made her smile a bit uneven, almost unsure. It was an old-soul smile in a young woman. Julian was young enough to be in love almost instantly. The next day he found a bookstore and bought everything by Hafiz. She was reading Hafiz, so he would read Hafiz. It was his first exposure to ghazals. He found these non-linear stepping-stone poems much to his liking. He and Rashmi, in the months and years that followed, explored Hafiz together. Hafiz was an inspiration for Rashmi's own poetry.

Julian used to tell the girls that their mother fell into his life. He would grin and lean back in his chair: She saw me and immediately felt woozy with love. Then she stole my heart with one smile – one beautifully awkward and crooked smile.

Rashmi would say her smile was crooked that day because she was applying pressure to the cut under her eye. She was following his instructions. She thought Julian knew what he was talking about. She put pressure. She probably should have had stitches.

Eventually Julian mentions he's going to the bullfights tomorrow and would she like to join him. It takes him a while to meander around to this. He wants to know about her first. Where does she work? Where does she live? Does she like the bullfights? Is it all right that he's asking so many questions? And what is her name – beyond embarrassed and clumsy?

She works in a café called Café Biscay, not far from where they are. She lives in Pamplona – she was born there. Her father took her to her first bullfight when she was six years old – to her mother's chagrin. She is an avid fan. Of course, any question is welcome, so long as she gets to ask some, too.

"My name is Rashmi."

"So will you be my guest at the bullfights tomorrow? The seats are perhaps not what you're used to, but –"

"I can't," she says. "I have to work tomorrow." She offers this statement of fact with one of her smiles. In Julian's mind, there is no way that smile could lie.

"The next day, then?"

"You'll pick me up at the café?"

Years later, the faint line of a scar that marked their meeting was still there. It was there when they honeymooned in Morocco – when Rashmi bought the candelabra at the market and the man kept trying to sell her a five-candle version of the one she wanted, but three is perfect, she'd said. Near this shop, Rashmi bought a pale green scarf the size of a sari. Rashmi was wearing that scarf on the way to the hospital for the birth of each of the girls. It became a sort of holy garment for her.

The night Chloe was born, they were halfway to the hospital and Rashmi made Julian turn the car around, to go back home and get the green scarf. It was her touchstone. "I wore it when Jane was born. I had it all through Morocco and in Paris on our honeymoon. We have to go home and get it."

"Do we have time?" He looked at his wife, who was breathing slowly through her mouth.

"Of course we have time," she said in a strained and borrowed voice that Julian barely recognized.

He remembers watching her contemplate a move, leaning forward over a chessboard. They were in a café in Montreal, a block off the Main. It was fall and she was wearing the green scarf. The girls were at a movie. Rashmi would tilt her head as she extrapolated the possible ramifications of a particular move. Sometimes when she tilted her head, the scar under her eye became a fine silver line.

The night before the train station in Madrid, the girls were finally asleep and he was opening a bottle of wine as Rashmi moved around their room in bra and panties – laying out clothes for the next day. He put the cork and the corkscrew on the side table, and leaned back against the pillows and the headboard. For Julian, this was one of the most profound benefits of being married. He got to watch the woman he loved move around the room in her bra and panties. She could be doing anything. Washing her face. Putting on her makeup. Finding a book. Ironing. It was the familiarity of it that made it so lovely for Julian. It was one common moment in a long line of similar cherished moments. It was both comfortable and erotic. Perhaps it was erotic because it was so nonchalant –

there was no pretense. It was what it was. Julian always felt lucky to be able to stop what he was doing and watch. They drank the wine, a very nice bordeaux, propped up in bed, watching an old movie on TV. They'd both seen *Casablanca* more than once, but the movie was still able to capture them. He remembers moving tight to her in bed, and at some point before sleep, whispering his finger along the scar under her eye.

~ ~ ~

Not your fault, Rashmi says. She looks across the table of the bar in Pamplona with her crooked smile and he inhales sharply. She looks across time at him with her sad blue eyes and her kind face. *It's not your fault,* she says.

I could have done something . . .

There is nothing you could have done. It's not your fault.

I left you alone.

You couldn't have known what was going to happen. It's not your fault.

I know, he whispers. *I know, but I carry this weight – this guilt.*

The sound of the ocean rises up – moves through him with surprising strength.

I miss you, he thinks. *I miss you so much. I don't know how to live without you and the girls. There is only this hole.*

Of course you know how to live, Jules. Don't be foolish. She reaches out her hand as if to smooth his face, but stops. Her eyes brim but she does not cry. She sits up straight, lifts her chin, and breathes deeply. *It's like this,* she says. *Life always goes away. Love doesn't. It's your job to carry on, to love.*

Julian sits for a long time, adrift in memory. It's begun to drizzle a bit – on and off. He pulls down the brim of his cap to shield his eyes. He has no more tears. His sorrow can go no deeper. It has no more words. He takes a big breath. There is only right now, and what's next. There is the deep, green-grey smell of ocean. The light is fading quickly and the approaching blackness is not some city darkness – there's a thickness to it. Julian does not mind the darkness. This is a nice tuft of grass. He hugs himself against the chill. He knows the ocean will soon be only the sound of the ocean. Very soon, the Cape Race lighthouse will burst to life and push a hole far out over the Atlantic. It will push through the darkness, clouds, and rain. Julian will not be able to look at this light as a warning. He will see it only as a beckoning. If Columbus is out there in the Atlantic and he needs a way in, this light will be a beacon. Somehow he'll make it through the killer reefs and jagged rocks along this shoreline. He'll avoid the icebergs. He'll find a beach and put in to shore. We all need Columbus, he thinks. Columbus does not turn away from adventure. He dreams big and then chases those dreams. He sails, fearless or fearfully, into the unknown. He looks toward the horizon with curiosity and wonder. And Columbus loves ferociously. Julian feels an illogical obligation to see what comes ashore. If it's Columbus at 4 A.M., well, he wants to welcome him with open arms and an open heart. Surely he can wait until then without freezing to death. And instead of driving the ugly Portugal Cove South road in darkness, he can sleep in the car tonight – use his raincoat as a blanket. He needs Columbus to come ashore, to walk up the beach, boots full of water, smiling with the innocence of a little kid. Together they can drive back to St. John's in the morning. Then the next day, he and Columbus can go the other way on board the *Dolly Varden* – they can start again on the Atlantic.

But first, this lighthouse has to do what it's been doing for more than a hundred years. A few steady drops pelt down with a promise of more to follow, but Julian ignores the rain. He waits. He sits at the edge of the ocean and waits.

ACKNOWLEDGEMENTS

Thanks to Hilary McMahon at Westwood Creative Artists, who was my first reader, and who responded to my semi-neurotic, exuberant e-mails with such kindness and compassion. Thanks also to Natasha Daneman and Chris Casuccio at Westwood, and to my editors, Lara Hinchberger at McClelland & Stewart, Alison Callahan at Doubleday, and Charlotte Greig at Picador, for understanding the book, loving the book, and helping to make it better.

Thank you to Dr. Anthony S. Joyce, director of the psychotherapy research and evaluation unit, Department of Psychiatry, University of Alberta, who with a couple of preliminary e-mails helped identify and solidify some of the psychiatric pathologies presented in this book.

Thanks to Dr. Leah Fowler (CF), who read an early draft of this book and whose comments reshaped its tone and texture; Elena Ray for her words on wounds; Cara Winsor Hehir for her consultation on Newfoundland; Wayne Silver for his advice and consultations, over much wine, on Arabic; Roberta for her help with the sweetness of Sevilla; Gail Sidonie Sobat and Geoff McMaster for their warm hospitality, sustaining laughter, and constant support; Dean Baltesson, my friend in life; Terence Harding for his steady encouragement; Laurie

Greenwood, who has been such a lovely, warm wind of support; and Mark Kozub, Randall Edwards, Michael Gravel, Gordon McRae, and all my Raving Poets comrades in verse.

Thanks to Donya Peroff, whom I have never met, but whose edits on a previous manuscript taught me so much about writing, and to Marc Côté, who made that happen.

Thanks also to John and Anna, at Miette Hot Springs Resort (Anna, for your exquisite Greek coffee). For me, there is no better place on this planet to write.

To Cindy-Lou, who holds the kite string while I flitter about the sky. In your most frail gestures are things which enclose me, still.

And to Marie Mackenzie for making me pinkie swear, a lot.

~ ~ ~

While this is not a historical novel, much of what goes on in this book is based on what we know, or what we think we know, about Christopher Columbus.

Books and academic papers on Christopher Columbus, or with references to Columbus, that I read over the past five years and that may have influenced this novel include *The Mysterious History of Columbus: An Exploration of the Man, the Myth, the Legacy,* by John Noble Wilford; *A World Lit Only by Fire: The Medieval Mind and the Renaissance: Portrait of an Age,* by William Manchester; and "The Hospital of Innocents: Humane Treatment of the Mentally Ill in Spain, 1409–1512," by Emilio J. Dominguez, in the *Bulletin of the Menninger Clinic.*

I also was probably influenced, to a small extent, by watching Ridley Scott's movie *1492: Conquest of Paradise*. References to saints all came from www.holyspiritinteractive.net.

I owe a debt of gratitude to *The Tao of Steve* for Father Paulo's rant on women.

Photo credit: Randall Edwards

THOMAS TROFIMUK's first novel, *The 52nd Poem*, won several awards, and his second, *Doubting Yourself to the Bone*, was a #1 bestseller (*Edmonton Journal*) and a *Globe and Mail* Best Book of 2006. *Waiting for Columbus* won the City of Edmonton Book Prize and was shortlisted for the Georges Bugnet Award for the Novel. Trofimuk lives in Edmonton with his wife and daughter. You can visit his website at www.thomastrofimuk.com.